STAR TREK®
MYRIAD UNIVERSES

ECHOES
AND REFRACTIONS

STAR TREK®
MYRIAD UNIVERSES
ECHOES
AND REFRACTIONS

Geoff Trowbridge
Keith R.A. DeCandido
Chris Roberson

Based upon *Star Trek* and *Star Trek: The Next Generation*®
created by Gene Roddenberry

Star Trek: Deep Space Nine®
created by Rick Berman and Michael Piller

POCKET BOOKS
New York London Toronto Sydney Turing

Pocket Books
A Division of Simon & Schuster, Inc.
1230 Avenue of the Americas
New York, NY 10020

This book is published by Pocket Books, a division of Simon & Schuster, Inc.,
under exclusive license from CBS Studios Inc.

This Pocket Books trade paperback edition August 2008

POCKET and colophon are registered trademarks of
Simon & Schuster, Inc.

For information regarding special discounts for bulk purchases,
please contact Simon & Schuster Special Sales at 1-800-456-6798
or business@simonandschuster.com.

Cover design by Alan Dingman
Cover art by John Picacio

Manufactured in the United States of America

10 9 8 7 6 5 4 3 2 1

ISBN-13: 978-1-4165-7181-0
ISBN-10:   1-4165-7181-7

The Chimes at Midnight

Geoff Trowbridge

Prologue

2274

"Ambassador Sarek, it is an honor to receive you," the Andorian said as he bowed his head and spread his arms in a gesture of respectful greeting, which the Vulcan diplomat returned in kind. "My name is Thelin th'Valrass. Welcome to the Andorian Science Institute."

Thelin had previously met Vulcans only in passing. Despite having served in Starfleet for many years, including a five-year stint as first officer of the *U.S.S. Enterprise* among its multispecies crew, never did he have the opportunity to work closely with any of Vulcan's stoic and reclusive citizens.

"The honor is mine, Thelin of Andoria," Sarek replied. "I have followed your work with great interest. As you are no doubt aware, the Vulcan Science Academy is awaiting my report on your new research in climate modification."

Atop his white-haired head, Thelin's two antennae began to twitch with subtle enthusiasm at the mention of his current project, now having been under way for nearly four years—ever since Thelin had retired his Starfleet commission and returned to his homeworld. Recent experiments had indeed produced some revolutionary results. "I look forward to presenting our findings, Ambassador, and to answer any questions you might pose. Please, if you will follow me." Thelin turned away from the entrance and strode purposefully toward the interior of the building.

At the rear of the decorative, homelike foyer area, the Andorian placed his palm upon a biometric scanning pad against the wall, and two large doors slid apart in response, revealing a long, sterile-looking corridor. "The environmental lab is, in fact, on the ground floor. But we will arrive much more quickly by using the turbolift."

"Very well," Sarek agreed. A quick turn to the right and the doors of the lift slid open before them. Upon entering, the doors resealed themselves and the car began its swift journey in a horizontal direction.

Thelin continued. "As you're no doubt aware, the gradual cooling of Andor's temperate climate zones has caused great hardship over the past few centuries for much of our population. While we have resolutely adjusted our habitat, the reduction in our agricultural output has seriously impacted our self-sufficiency."

"Indeed," Sarek said. "I am aware that the Andorian trade deficit is a growing concern."

The lift stopped and the doors opened, revealing a waiting Andorian student in a lab coat—a *chan* whose white hair was tied into several tight braids that swayed in front of his blue-skinned face. The youth nodded his acknowledgment, and Thelin bobbed his head in return before the two men passed him by and began walking down the hall. "So about fifty years ago, the Presider of the Council announced a plan to warm the planetary ecosystem, using crude greenhouse gases and reflective solar sails, similar to the techniques used on Weytahn centuries earlier."

"And this, of course, failed to take into account the effects upon the Aenar," Sarek said.

"You are correct," Thelin replied. The Aenar, a blind and telepathic subspecies of the Andorians, lived only in the extreme northern wastes of the planet . . . and as it happened, Thelin himself was of mixed Aenar parentage. "The government's efforts caused a uniform rise in temperatures across the globe. While this did help to extend the growing season in parts of the world, the effect upon the Aenar habitat was catastrophic. Settlements near geothermal reservoirs began to experience seasonal thaws. Ice canopies housing entire cities became unstable."

"Yes, I recall an Aenar contingent making a plea to the Federation when they could get no relief from the Andorian council," Sarek said. "The incident very nearly threatened Andorian membership in the Federation."

Thelin looked down at his feet and his antennae hung droopily, the conversation having triggered memories that he was not terribly eager to share. "And sadly, race relations with the Aenar have not yet fully recovered. Among members of a warrior race, such disagreements do not end lightly. Technically, an *ushaan* between the Aenar ruling family and the previous presider remains unfulfilled." He stopped before a door labeled *Climate Laboratory—East Wing* in flowing Andorian script. "Having a vested interest in returning harmony to the races of my world, my desire to find an amicable solution to the conflict was one of my reasons for leaving Starfleet to return to Andor."

Sarek nodded, his face revealing the wisdom of one forced to confront issues of bigotry and intolerance in his own life. "And the other reasons?"

Thelin wistfully stared off into nothingness and quietly sighed. "Family, of course." He pressed his palm against the pad on the wall, and the door slid aside and beckoned them forward.

A cacophony of voices greeted the two men as they stepped into the laboratory. About a dozen technicians, mostly Andorian, moved about between the various consoles lining the walls of the spacious room, engaged in various activities, either reading or recording data. At the far end of the lab, the walls sloped inward, tapering to a seam that neatly bisected the area, and large bay-style windows indented the veneer of the sweeping concave surfaces at regular intervals on each side of the room. To the left, the windows faced out upon an outdoor landscape darkened by thick storm clouds that threatened to unleash their torrential downpours at any moment; but to the right, the windows peered into the interior of the Institute's huge biosphere, populated by numerous species of lush vegetation in tightly controlled environmental conditions under artificial illumination.

Seated at one of the consoles farthest from the door, a young human woman turned her head toward Thelin, her shoulder-length blond hair fluttering down about her shoulders. Next to her sat a boy of about twelve, also blond but with curlier locks, his gaze fixed upon the screen in front of him with wide discerning eyes that seemed to suggest a level of knowledge that far surpassed his chronological age. The woman smiled, rose from her seat and blithely approached the two men.

Thelin bowed to the woman in greeting as she approached, then turned to his Vulcan guest. "Ambassador Sarek," he said, "allow me to introduce our new adjunct project leader, Doctor Carol Marcus."

The woman started to reach out her hand, but caught herself, apparently just then remembering that Vulcans generally eschewed casual physical contact. "Ambassador, this is a genuine honor," she said.

"Doctor Marcus," Sarek replied. "I have studied your recently published journals, and I have found much that is quite intriguing."

"Well, thank you; that's high praise indeed," Carol replied.

"Doctor Marcus joined our team about six months ago," Thelin explained. "Her theoretical work on the selective modification of ecosystems was of particular interest to us, and when the Institute heard of her availability, we actively recruited her to come to Andor."

"Thelin, you could hardly keep me away," Carol quipped. "This was such a tremendous opportunity, not just to develop theoretical science but to also actually apply it in ways that benefit the people of this world. . . . Anyway, it's been a great experience thus far."

Thelin smiled. "Well, Ambassador, allow me to introduce you to the rest of the team." They turned back toward the center of the lab and for the first time noticed a small flurry of excitement surrounding the young boy, still seated at the station where Carol had been supervising his work. Other researchers had gathered around the computer screen with obvious interest and were talking animatedly, though quietly, among themselves.

"David?" Carol called out. "Excuse me, Ambassador."

As Carol hurried back to the console, Sarek turned toward Thelin with an eyebrow raised in inquiry. "The boy, David Marcus, is Carol's son," Thelin explained, as the two of them advanced across the lab toward the commotion at the far end. "They are both native to Earth, but Carol has been attached to projects throughout the entire quadrant, and her boy is always with her. He's a bit of a genius, that one."

"Indeed?" Sarek said.

"Yes. He's an exemplary student, despite the lack of any formal classroom structure. I hear he has already passed several Federation universities' entrance exams." As they walked, Thelin glanced over at the ambassador's face, and couldn't help but notice that Sarek's eyes, intently focused upon the young boy, seemed to betray a sense of painful recollection, or perhaps forlorn longing—an oddly emotive expression for the usually stern Vulcan diplomat.

They approached the workstation, and over the shoulders of the assembled crowd they could see on the computer screen an image of a pulsating, spherical waveform. Thelin craned his neck as both his eyes focused upon the screen, straining to read the technical data that splashed down a column on one side of the display. His antennae stood erect, though they were of little help in interpreting the technical readouts. He perked up his ears.

Carol had fought her way through the crowd to join David, who was actively observing and modifying the properties of the simulated energy wave. "So you simply ran the same simulations of the bioelectrical energy matrix?" she asked her son.

"Right," David replied. "But for the first time, I tried to integrate the metastatic properties of the meta-genome that we studied a few years ago."

"And the reaction was self-sustaining?"

"Yep. . . . If the data is right, this wave can be used to convert any matter into other complex molecules, depending on how we configure the matrix. And the scale is unlimited."

"Unlimited?" Carol was incredulous. "As in, an entire planetary ecosystem?"

"Well, yeah, in theory . . . I guess," David replied.

The lab was shaken by the boom of a loud thunderclap. Looking out the windows to the outdoors, Thelin could see that the dark storm clouds that had gathered were finally unleashing their torrential downpour. He turned toward Sarek, who still watched the boy dolefully. While Thelin was certainly interested in the potential breakthrough that young David had apparently stumbled upon, he was more immediately concerned with the demeanor of his guest. "Mr. Ambassador, are you not feeling well? Can we provide you with anything?"

Sarek turned toward Thelin, then bowed his head as a look of shame emerged on his features. "Forgive me," he said. "It seems that my thoughts are focused elsewhere. May I be seated?"

"Of course." Thelin motioned him back toward the end of the lab nearer the entrance. The area was now cleared of any other technicians as they had all congregated down near Carol's console to observe the new discovery.

Sarek seated himself in front of an unused workstation and Thelin took the chair next to him. The Vulcan closed his eyes, allowing himself a brief moment of meditation. For the first time, Thelin truly noticed the physical effects that years of stressful duty had imprinted upon the ambassador. The man was only 110 years old—typically the prime of a Vulcan's middle-aged years—yet his face was etched with lines that suggested a lifetime's worth of grief.

Sarek opened his eyes a moment later and spoke. "Not long ago, I returned from a mission where we had rescued several . . . abandoned children from a deserted planet. More than this I cannot reveal. But suffice it to say that the mission had a profound impact upon me."

"I see," Thelin replied with understanding. "And seeing young David reminds you of these children."

"Partly," Sarek replied pensively. "But mostly his precocious intelligence reminds me of my youngest son."

"Ah," said Thelin, uncertain if he should press for further details. He was not aware that the ambassador had any young children. "What is his name?"

"His name was Spock . . . and he died at the age of seven, alone in the wilderness, during his *kahs-wan* ritual."

"Oh . . ." said Thelin, now wishing he had erred on the side of discretion. "Ambassador, I had no idea. I am truly sorry."

"Thank you for your condolences, but your sympathy is unnecessary." Sarek had regained tight control over his composure. "It is normal to carry grief for the dead, but this was thirty-seven years ago. It is illogical to react emotionally after the passage of so much time."

Thelin tried to compose a reply that would express his understanding of Sarek's sorrow while remaining respectful to Vulcan mores of logic and emotional restraint. But before he could solve the conundrum, the door slid open and a pretty, young Andorian girl—a *zhen*—entered, and immediately approached him.

"Hello, Thelin," she said quickly and with a bit of nervousness. "I'm very sorry . . . I know you're with the ambassador and all, but you have a call from Thali, and . . . well, she says it's really important."

Mortified, Thelin sheepishly looked over at Sarek before responding to the young girl. "Zheva, I'm terribly busy here. Was this some kind of emergency?"

Zheva's antennae turned inward, expressing her uncertainty, and she opened her mouth to reply, but Sarek silenced her with a wave of his hand before turning to Thelin. "It's all right. Go and attend to your affairs. I will remain here and try to learn more about your team's timely discovery."

Thelin remained unsure what to do. He had not heard from Thali in some time, which was unusual and had caused him some concern as of late. After all, they had been betrothed for a few years now. But they were not yet legally permitted to marry. Such decisions required the approval of the Eveste Elders—an enclave whose sole purpose was to determine which Andorian quads were most suitable for reproduction. Given the complexity of Andorian sexuality, requiring marriages in groups of four, public concern about the declining Andorian population had grown in recent years, and thus the Council had enacted a complex set of laws and regulations regarding the arrangement of the *shelthreth* marriage bonds.

Having known each other since early childhood, Thelin had followed the somewhat tragic circumstances that led to the dissolution of Thali's own marriage bond, involving the untimely death of one member and the emotional breakdown of another, before the *shelthreth* had produced any offspring. Which was why, following his five-year stint aboard the *Enterprise,* Thelin had been honored by Thali's request that he return to Andor to join her, and to petition the Elders to approve a new arrangement. Owing to the circumstances of his youth, he had never been bonded himself. Nevertheless, he felt rather strongly his social and familial responsibility to produce children . . . even though it had meant giving up an assured promotion to a captaincy. If Thali had to speak with him regarding a matter of some urgency, he felt obligated to listen. "Thank you for your understanding, Ambassador," he said with a slight bow to Sarek. "I shall try to rejoin you as quickly as possible."

Thelin turned and quickly exited the lab with Zheva closely following him. "Would you please send the transmission to my office, Zheva?" he said.

"Of course," Zheva replied. They both reached the T at the end of the corridor and went separate ways. Thelin passed a couple of offices before turning in to one that bore his name on a plaque, and the door promptly slid aside to permit his entry.

"Lights," he commanded, and the illumination flooded the small room, revealing the sparse décor of his office at the Institute. A few shelves hung from the far wall with odd knickknacks, a holo-image of his *zhavey,* and a few padds loaded with science manuals and research documents, hastily placed for future reference. But the rest of the walls were mostly barren.

Thelin promptly seated himself at his desk and pulled the display monitor close to him. "Computer, incoming transmissions," he said.

"One active communication," the computer responded. *"Thali sh'Dani currently on hold."*

"Answer," Thelin said, and the screen flickered to life, revealing a middle-aged Andorian *shen,* her deep-blue skin much darker than Thelin's own pale complexion, her thick white hair coiffed in a full-bodied style adorned with a few small braids hanging down the sides and across her face—a face which bore a deeply troubled expression.

"My *sh'za!*" Thelin said. "I wasn't expecting to hear from you this week. Is everything all right?"

Thali closed her eyes and breathed deeply, then reopened them, revealing a purplish tint in the whites, and Thelin realized that she had been crying recently. *"All right? No, Thelin, everything is not all right."*

A dozen terrible thoughts raced through Thelin's mind, and he felt his blood pumping, readying him to leap into action for whatever need his bondmate might have. "What? What has happened?"

Thali cocked her head to the side, her antennae hanging droopily, and a sad smirk crossed her face. *"Zhavey received a communication from the Elders this morning. They finally made their decision."*

Thelin's heart sank. For nearly three years the Eveste Elders had been dragging their feet concerning their petition to marry. Given the reproductive imperatives handed down by the Andorian leadership in recent years, this was highly unusual; but they were a highly unusual case. Very little scientific data yet existed regarding reproductive compatibility between the Andorians and the Aenar, and this had resulted in one delay after another as the Elders debated how to proceed. "What does it say?" Thelin asked, already dreading to hear the justification for the denial.

The woman picked up a padd from the desktop in front of her and read in a hollow, dispassionate tone. *"In the matter of petition for bonding in marriage: The Council of Eveste Elders recognizes and respects your desire to select a mate with whom you have an intimate familiarity. While such pairings are oft permitted, they remain bound by decree of the procreation imperative. The council finds that insufficient scientific data yet exists to ensure reproductive compatibility between the Aenar and the mainline Andorian race. Therefore, with regret and without prejudice, the council has no alternative but to deny your petition at this time."*

The padd clattered down onto the desk as both Thelin and Thali sat in silence. A single tear ran down Thali's cheek.

Without prejudice, Thelin thought. *What an ironic choice of words.* After taking a long moment to collect his thoughts, Thelin took a deep breath and spoke. "Thali . . . we've known all along that this would be a struggle. We've been dealing with it for years now."

"Yes, Thelin, that's right . . . for years." She closed her eyes for a moment, and when they reopened, it seemed as if her despair poured forth from them. Her voice was reduced to a faint squeak. *"How many more years shall we keep up the charade?"*

"Thali . . ." Thelin stammered. "It's not over yet. It's . . . it's just our first appeal. We'll try again when the next enclave convenes in a few months. I know geneticists who can testify on our behalf. After all, I'm living proof that the two races are entirely compatible. Not everyone will be so closed-minded."

"Thelin, do you really believe that will change anything? The decision is made. They want us to bond with our own kind. Our relationship is too reckless for them to abide it."

"This is preposterous," Thelin spat, his resentment for the aloofness of the Elders beginning to stir a passionate reaction from deep within him. "Three years we've waited, and when all is said and done, they simply announce that they can't stomach an interracial bonding."

"*Stop it,*" Thali said with enough emphasis that Thelin was taken aback. *"Don't turn this into a racial issue. You know the reasons for the genetic profiling. They have to be sure we're compatible. It's the law. There's nothing we can do about it."*

"Genetics?" Thelin gave out a laugh of indignation. "What do you think race is, other than a matter of genetics? They can't see anything beyond the shade of our skin and the social perceptions. Do you deny that our application would have been approved years ago if not for my Aenar blood?"

"Oh, Thelin, you're acting so callow! Of course there are social factors to consider." She slowly shook her head, giving him a look of sympathy. *"It's complicated, Thelin. You stay there, holed up with your climatologist friends, yet you have no idea what the climate is like out here in the real world. We aren't just bringing together four people for some cheap* tezha. *We're talking about the bonding together of four* families, *and earning the blessings of an older generation that is set in their ways, with no desire for reconciliation with the Aenar. Sometimes you just have to accept when a plan isn't going to come to fruition."*

Thelin was unyielding. "All right. Fine. Then it's time for us to pursue other avenues. We'll find an Aenar couple to bond with. We have discussed that possibility. The Aenar aren't subject to the decrees of the Council. We could arrange a bonding entirely on our own, without interference, and begin right away."

Thali snorted. *"Honestly, Thelin . . . would we really want our children to have a blind, helpless* zhavey *trying to raise them?"*

This, Thelin thought, was entirely uncalled for. He felt his frustration giving way to outright anger. "What are you saying? My *zhavey* was blind, and she raised me practically on her own!" His mother may have lacked sight, but like most Aenar she was also a telepath, enabling her to nurture him in ways that most other Andorians could never understand.

Thali sighed. *"It doesn't matter, Thelin. Don't you think that my* zhavey *and I have looked into every possible option? She contacted the Aenar Ministry of Health more than a year ago. She even posted inquiries, trying to gauge the reception of potential Aenar mates. It seems that your work is quite well known among them."*

Thelin had no idea that such an effort had already been under way. He suddenly found himself bewildered as to why no positive news had been relayed to him concerning this. "And . . . ?" he anxiously prompted her.

"The Aenar don't trust you, Thelin. They aren't convinced that your intentions at the Science Institute are in their best interests."

"What are you talking about?!" Thelin shouted, feeling his blood beginning to boil with stunned outrage. "I gave up everything to come back here and try to help them! *Everything!*"

"I know," Thali whispered, tears now streaming down her cheeks. *"Starfleet was always everything to you. You've always looked back. Never forward; never embracing our efforts to build a new life together."*

For a moment he had no reply. "That's not true," he eventually blurted out, not at all convincingly. "I've supported you every step of the way."

"Yes," she agreed. *"But it's not about me, Thelin. It's about* us. *I'm sorry, I just . . . I can't do this anymore. I have to move on while I still have time. Zhavey has already withdrawn her appeal to the Elders and released you from our bond. She will contact you later to finalize everything."*

"Thali!" Thelin shouted, reaching out to grip the screen with both hands. "We can still talk about this! Don't . . ."

"Good-bye, Thelin." The screen blinked off, and her face was replaced with the emblem of the Science Institute.

Thelin picked up the screen and violently flung it from the desktop, smashing the housing and spilling the various electronic components from within onto the floor. As he did so, another loud thunderclap shook the room as the storm front intensified outside the building. He fell back into his chair, breathing heavily, waiting for the spell of rage to pass.

His mind was racing, his thoughts a chaotic maelstrom as he attempted to process what had just transpired. Had the last three years of his life truly been spent in vain? His resignation from Starfleet, his efforts using science to try to reconcile his two parent races. . . . Had it all been for nothing?

Andorians were taught from birth that they could not subsist as mere individuals. They had to be made whole. The *shelthreth* would provide that. But how could one become a whole vessel when he was unable to reconcile the two halves of his own self?

Minutes went by, and as the intensity of his emotions gradually began to diminish, similarly the questions surrounding his future came slowly into focus. Thali was right. He had come back to Andor out of a sense of obligation, to make right the wrongs of his own *thavan,* to honor the commitment to family that society demanded. But he already had a family—the only family he had ever known.

It was then and there that he made the decision. There was no need to agonize over it, no need to weigh his options. He was returning to Starfleet.

1

Eleven Years Later

"Scotty!" Kirk called desperately into the ship's intercom. "I need warp speed in three minutes or we're all dead!"

At the science station, Captain Thelin felt the palpitations of his antennae as the adrenaline rushed through the veins beneath his pale blue skin. The *Enterprise* was in danger, and he was, after all, its captain, even though Admiral James T. Kirk was currently in command—a fact that the Andorian didn't begrudge him, for the admiral's experience had most assuredly saved their lives several times already this day.

But as Thelin looked down at the spherical waveform on his console, growing in intensity with each passing second toward a violent detonation that would surely ensnare them, it appeared that Kirk might have finally exhausted his seemingly endless supply of clever schemes.

"No response, Admiral," Uhura announced from the communications station.

"Scotty!" Kirk fruitlessly continued to shout into the intercom, even as the silence clearly suggested that Commander Scott in engineering was either too busy or, heaven forbid, too badly injured to reply. Kirk turned toward the helm. "Mister Sulu, get us out of here, best possible speed!"

"Aye, sir," Sulu replied. But Thelin knew that impulse drive would not provide them with the necessary speed to escape the blast range of the Genesis Device.

Next to Thelin at the adjacent science station stood Dr. David Marcus, the brilliant son of Carol Marcus and James Kirk—the man who, despite his youth, was credited with the invention of the Genesis Device. He stared at the readouts on the consoles, quietly wringing his hands, no doubt grappling with the knowledge that his own creation was to be their undoing.

With grim irony, Thelin recalled the scene as the young boy first discovered the wave in the lab on Andor eleven years earlier. He had always wondered why, following his departure from the Institute to return to Starfleet, the whole project had eventually been classified, with the Federation's tightest security protocols managing the flow of information in and out of the Marcus laboratory on space station Regula One. Little did he realize then that the Genesis team had discovered a power so revolutionary that it could transform the surface of an entire planet.

A power that, in the wrong hands, could be an unbelievably potent weapon.

Thelin watched the image of the U.S.S. *Reliant,* crippled in space, fading into the distance ever so slowly. Too slow, he knew, to save them. Aboard that ship was a madman, Khan Noonien Singh, who had stolen the Genesis Device and now had begun a buildup toward detonation. And the *Enterprise,* itself crippled and without warp drive as a means of escape, was counting down the minutes to its doom.

"Admiral," Uhura called out. "I have Doctor McCoy, down in engineering."

Standing next to the captain's chair, Kirk stabbed the intercom switch on the armrest. "Bones! What the hell is going on down there?"

"Jim," the doctor's voice was heard amid a cacophony of activity in the engine room. *"Scotty's suffering acute radiation sickness. I've given him shots of hyronalin and cordrazine, but he won't be conscious for a few minutes."*

"We don't have a few minutes!" Kirk shouted.

Finding himself unable to remain seated any longer, Thelin

stood and began walking toward the sound of McCoy's voice in the center of the bridge. "Doctor," he said. "Who is currently in charge of the engineering team? I must inform them what is at stake."

"Thelin, where's the sense in that?" the doctor responded with irritation. *"Use that thick white-haired head of yours. You trained these kids. They know what's at stake. Now let them do their damn jobs!"*

Thelin bit his lip almost hard enough to draw blood and turned back toward the science station. The doctor was right, of course, as he usually was when invoking logic to counteract Thelin's impulsiveness. Truth be told, most of the cadets down there knew their way around a warp coil better than their captain. Nevertheless, to sit idly by and wait to live or die ran contrary to every fiber in his being.

With a loud sigh he fell back into his chair. The image on the display before him cast an eerie glow about him as it grew in intensity. There was no stopping it, and the ship was completely vulnerable without any way to raise the shields. Unless . . .

"David," Thelin said. "The Genesis wave is primarily meson energy, is it not?"

"That's right," David replied, his tone a mix of puzzlement and curiosity, "at least initially. But once the wave contacts matter, the matrix breaks the covalent bonds between atoms, producing alpha particles that get reconstituted into—"

"Yes, so we must ensure that the wave doesn't contact the ship. The *Enterprise* shields could be reconfigured to disrupt meson waveforms at the proper frequency."

"But we're in the middle of the Mutara Nebula! I thought the shields were inoperative?"

Thelin struggled to remain patient, despite the situation. "The shields are unable to function in their *standard* configuration. The matter and energy of the nebula would overload them in seconds. But what if we altered the scheme to produce selective screening at the subatomic level?"

David considered this. "You mean . . . we could differentiate between fermions and composite bosons, and tell it to ignore all particulate matter . . ."

"Precisely. Then use the shield harmonics to cancel the frequency of the wave."

David turned toward Kirk, who was now approaching the two men, intrigued by what he had overheard. The young scientist's eyes darted back and forth, from his father, looming so near with his unspoken expectations, to the technical readouts that grew more alarming with each passing second, as he quickly contemplated the idea. "Well . . . yes, I suppose, as long as the initial waveform is disrupted, then the matrix can't initialize. But . . ." He helplessly shrugged his shoulders. "I've got no experience in deflector engineering."

"That's not a problem," Thelin assured him. "Just compute the harmonic values based upon our shield frequency and feed them to my screen. I'll begin reprogramming the emitters."

"Excellent thinking, gentlemen," Kirk said in earnest as David seated himself and frantically began to make calculations. Buoyed by renewed hope, the admiral whirled himself around, back toward the navigation console. "Time, from my mark."

Ensign Croy, the blond-haired male cadet at the navigation console, checked the chronometer. "Two minutes, fifteen seconds."

Kirk approached the young officer and placed his hand upon his shoulder, managing to force a smile through his anxiety. "Well, Ensign," he said. "You have my apologies. Most cadets don't have to face the no-win scenario twice in one week."

"Yes, Admiral," Croy replied, struggling to maintain his composure under the presently harrowing circumstances. "But you yourself said that how we face death is just as important as how we face life."

"Yes, I did," Kirk agreed. "And if we get through this, I'll make sure your record reflects your expertise on the subject."

"Thank you, sir." He paused as if considering whether to say anything further, then turned back toward his mentor. "Sir, do you really think we'll get through this?"

"I don't know, Ensign," Kirk answered with complete honesty. "But in the hands of my science officer and my son . . . well, I like our chances."

Back at the science stations, his fingers fluttering over the keypads, David entered his final set of equations into the console. "That'll have to do it," he said not altogether confidently.

"I have it," Thelin replied. "Compiling the final configuration now." It would *have* to do it. For the sake of Thelin's crew. For the sake of Thelin's superior officer—a man to whom he had repeatedly pledged his loyalty, and who over the years had earned his unwavering respect.

Additional seconds ticked by, though the passage of time had become impossibly difficult to gauge as the bridge had fallen into an uneasy silence. "Time to detonation," Kirk barked out.

"Thirty seconds," came Sulu's reply from the conn.

"Distance from *Reliant*?" Kirk asked.

Chekov looked up from the tactical console with resignation. "Four thousand kilometers," he meekly offered.

Not nearly enough, Thelin thought. *The shockwave alone might destroy us, even with the adjusted shielding.*

Kirk leaned forward in his seat, his exasperation beginning to shatter his mask of confidence. "Thelin? David? I think now might be a good time to try out that new shield configuration."

"Stand by, Admiral," Thelin replied. His hands shook. The console was responding so slowly; he wanted to scream, and to pound his fists into the keypads. *Save the new template, reinitialize the modulation sequence . . .*

"Fifteen seconds," Sulu announced.

David watched Thelin from a few feet away, silently urging him on.

"Thelin?" Kirk cried out.

The Andorian finished punching in the final code sequence.

"Shields going up now!" he yelled out triumphantly, releasing all his frustrations. He sat back in his chair and exhaled, and for a moment wondered if he had even remembered to breathe the last few minutes.

"Six . . . five . . . four . . ."

"All decks brace for impact!" Kirk shouted into the intercom.

Thelin looked over and met David's eyes. Had they done enough? Neither of them seemed to know the answer.

"One . . ."

A blinding white flash filled the viewscreen before them.

In roughly the same instant, the wave violently collided with the rear of the ship. The hull lurched forward, and the cadets unfortunate enough to be standing about the bridge instantly found themselves sprawled on the deck. Quickly they scrambled to their feet and stumbled back to their respective stations.

"Report!" Kirk shouted.

Chekov struggled to pull himself back up toward the console. "Structural integrity at fifty percent," he yelled over the din of alarms and voices that now surrounded them. "Inertial dampeners are restabilizing."

"Trying to regain attitude control," Sulu announced from the helm.

Thelin watched the viewscreen as the starfield tumbled about dizzyingly, punctuated by flashes of energy as the shields dispersed secondary waves from the explosion. Thankfully, the ship's dampening field had adjusted following the initial impact, sparing the crew from any additional ill effects as the vessel continued to tumble out of control through space. That they all had not been reduced to their component atoms meant that Thelin's shield modifications had worked. However, the information on his console wasn't all positive. "Aft shielding down to twenty percent," he called out. "Emitters have failed in proximity of decks seventeen and eighteen."

"Hull breaches reported near the landing bay," Uhura relayed from the communications station. "Emergency forcefields are in place. Reports of casualties coming in, Admiral. Medical teams have been dispatched."

"Thank you, Commander," Kirk said, his voice reflecting all too clearly the pain from knowing how many young officers and crewmen had already given their lives on this mission. "Navigator! Ship's status?"

"Yes, Admiral," Croy replied, cycling through the relevant readouts. "Distance from explosion, approximately ten thousand kilometers. Traveling at a rate of two hundred kilometers per second . . ."

"Attitude control is now restored," Sulu interjected. "Aft view on screen."

The bridge crew gasped at the sight displayed before them. Amid a fiery backdrop as the Genesis effect continued to produce subatomic reactions throughout the matter in the nebula, the boundaries of a great spherical planetoid had begun to take shape, growing in size as additional matter continued to accrete into the globular mass at the center. Already they could begin to make out a solid surface—primordial seas of magma and superheated elements, vomiting forth flaming geysers into the developing atmosphere of toxic gases.

At the sound of the rear bridge doors sliding open, Thelin turned to see Carol Marcus enter the bridge. Like the rest of the crew, she stood agape, staring at the screen in amazement.

Kirk turned to face her. "My God, Carol," he mumbled. "Look at it!"

Carol walked over to her son and clasped his hand. Their eyes remained riveted to the screen. "David," she whispered. "Did any of our simulations ever produce anything like this?"

"We never even considered the effect of the matrix in a nebula," David said.

Thelin felt a shudder vibrating through the deck, and for the first time he realized that he'd felt precisely the same sensation just a short time earlier—in fact, it seemed to be repeating at regular intervals.

"Admiral," Croy suddenly said with alarm, breaking the spell over the others. "Ship speed is down to one hundred fifty kilometers per second and slowing."

"Slowing?" Kirk said. "Sulu, go to full impulse."

"Sir, we're at full impulse power now," he replied.

Sensing the danger, Thelin quickly performed a scan of the surrounding space. "Gravimetric waves, sir," he said. "That would explain the sudden accretion of the nebula matter. The gravitational fields are too intense for the ship's weakened impulse engines."

"Sulu! If we get the mains back online, can we warp out?"

"No, sir," he replied. "We couldn't possibly engage warp fields in a gravity well this strong. It would tear the ship apart. I'm adjusting ship's attitude to apply tangential thrust. It's the most conservative way to counter the pull and break orbit."

Another shudder rippled through the hull. Warning lights illuminated on the conn and navigation consoles, and the voice of Ensign Croy rang out in panic. "We're still losing altitude!"

"Keep it together, Mister," Kirk scolded him. "Just keep us in orbit for now."

"But, sir!" Croy replied. "Every time another wave hits us, I need to recompute our parabolic trajectory."

Back at the science consoles, David shook his head in frustration and, seeing no other option, rushed up to the helm at the front of the bridge. "Guys," he said, "this is just simple physics. Keep applying the thrust at a tangent. I've computed the period of the gravimetric waves as well as the drag coefficient. All you have to do is program a delta-V using the . . . um . . ."

"The ventral thrusters?" Sulu offered.

"Right!" He paused, as if suddenly realizing where he was and what he was doing, and he turned around to face his father in the captain's chair. "I'm sorry . . . uh, sir. I just . . . I knew that I could—"

"No, David, that's . . . that's just fine." Kirk stood, and awkwardly placed a hand on his son's shoulder. "That's excellent work!"

David looked down with a sheepish grin. "Thank you," he said simply.

Kirk looked over David's shoulder. "Ensign Croy? Can you work with Doctor Marcus here to plot us an escape orbit?"

The young ensign made a futile effort to conceal his continuing nervousness. "Yes . . . Of course, sir."

"Have at it, then!" Kirk replied with encouragement.

Thelin smiled as the two young men quickly got to work. He would monitor the course calculations from his own station, but he had no doubt that his cadet and the admiral's son would have the ship safely out of danger in no time. Granted, he was still coming to terms with the shock of discovering that Admiral Kirk even *had* a son, but Thelin was happy for him, and touched by the moment they had just shared on the bridge.

"Course laid in," Croy said.

"Altering heading to new course," Sulu said, offering a quick smile to the lieutenant seated next to him.

The minutes passed without incident as the *Enterprise* gradually ascended into higher orbit, while the viewscreen displayed the amazing spectacle below them as the planet gradually cooled, producing life-giving oceans, clouds, and even the telltale greenish bands of primitive plant life. *The fires of creation,* Thelin thought, *given to mankind.* Thus spoke the ancient Andorian legends of Uzaveh the Infinite, who had banished Thirizaz, the original *thaan* of the First Kin, but sent the Fire Daemon to feed his insatiable passions—fires of desire that could serve to bring the kin together and to make them whole . . . or that could be used to destroy, and to recreate in service to arrogance and vanity.

Thelin had never been a particularly religious man, but at that moment he felt fairly certain that Uzaveh would not be pleased.

Thelin followed closely behind Kirk into the *Enterprise* sickbay. Immediately the combination of scents assailed his senses— sterile antiseptics amid the acrid odor of burned flesh. This was the part of a captaincy that Thelin abhorred. The notion that young men and women under his charge had paid such a price with their bodies, some with their lives, was a difficult concept to accept. But on this day, it was Admiral Kirk who was in command, and who was the first to stop at the end of each bed and look each patient in the eye, silently if not vocally thanking them for their sacrifice.

At the far end of the wing, next to the doors leading to other wards and offices, Doctor McCoy finished giving instructions to one of several nurses dealing with the influx of casualties, and after updating the chart of the patient nearest him, he approached the two men.

"Bones," Kirk said warmly but solemnly. "How are you holding up?"

McCoy sighed heavily. "Well, it could have been a lot worse, Jim. Mostly burns, a few broken bones . . . but fewer casualties than what we got when the *Reliant* attacked us. The kids who got the worst of it are back in the ICW. They're the ones who were in the shuttlebay when the blast from the Genesis wave compromised the hull."

Thelin knew enough about the Genesis wave and its effects to fear the worst. "How bad is it, Doctor?"

McCoy nodded his head in the direction of the hallway behind him. "Come see for yourself."

Kirk and Thelin followed the doctor's lead, but not before Kirk took a quick gander about the room. "I thought David had said he was coming down here."

"He's here," McCoy said, looking back over his shoulder. "He wanted to spend a few minutes alone in the morgue."

"The morgue?" Kirk said.

"Well, yeah, the scientists that Khan murdered at the Regula One spacelab are in there. They were David's colleagues and friends, you know. I'm sure he wanted to pay his respects."

"Of course," Kirk replied with embarrassment. "I'm sorry; I should have realized."

McCoy stopped before the door reading *Intensive Care Ward*.

"It's all right, Jim. We've all got a lot on our minds right now." The door slid open and he stepped through. Kirk and Thelin closely followed.

On the bed nearest the door laid a young man, the eyes on his cherubic face closed in quiet but uneasy slumber. The readouts on the monitor above him flashed routine status updates and echoed his heartbeat in a steady audible rhythm. McCoy approached his bedside and gripped the seam of the sheet that lay across the patient's bare torso. "We're keeping him sedated for now, partly due to the pain, but mostly because he's not quite prepared to deal with this yet." He drew down the sheets until the cadet's full frame lay uncovered.

"Oh my God," Kirk gasped.

The man's body appeared strong, chiseled and perfectly healthy from his head and torso down to the lower seams of his undergarments. But about halfway down his thighs, the skin became discolored and increasingly mottled. The muscular tone weakened considerably at about the area where his knees had once been, beyond which the bone structure disappeared, and each of his limbs tapered off into a tentacle-like appendage with a dark leathery surface, the ends gently quivering as they curled up into tight spirals.

"The explosion did this?" Kirk asked with astonishment.

"The wave did it," McCoy clarified. "It's like it fundamentally altered his molecular biology, right down to the DNA. His limbs were reconstituted into something much more genetically primitive."

"Could it be reversed?" Thelin asked.

McCoy blew out his breath and shrugged. "I dunno . . . Maybe, with genetic modification therapy. It won't be easy for him, in any event."

"Dammit, Bones," Kirk bitterly complained, "I need more than that. What am I supposed to tell this kid's parents?"

"Calm down, Jim," McCoy chided him. "I know what you're feeling, but use your head. It's not your place to plan out his rehabilitation. He'll get the best treatment Starfleet has to offer. Your job is to make sure his parents know that their son put his life on the line to save the Federation from a terrorist with a dooms-day weapon."

Kirk held up his hand in acquiescence. "You're right . . . as usual."

Thelin had always admired McCoy's pragmatic ability to rein in Kirk's headstrong nature—something Thelin himself, as a highly emotional first officer, had never quite been able to do. It seemed as though the doctor's medical instincts gave him insight into the psychological, as well as the physical, needs of the com-mand crew.

"We've got four more crewmen with similar injuries," McCoy went on. "If you want to see . . ." He cut himself short and tilted his head to look over the shoulders of Kirk and Thelin, nodding as the sound of footsteps approached from behind them.

"Thanks, Doctor," David was heard to say. "Like you asked, I engaged the security locks when I left the morgue, and I . . ." He stood looking over his father's shoulder at the unconscious pa-tient. Thelin turned toward David, only to see the young man's face turn as white as the Andorian's own hair. "Oh no . . ." David moaned, then turned and walked swiftly back out of the room.

"Excuse me, gentlemen," Kirk said, then hurried out the door after his son.

He found David back in the main corridor outside sickbay, lean-ing against the wall and breathing deeply, as if trying not to be-come violently ill. Kirk approached him slowly, not sure if he would be emotionally ready to discuss what he had just witnessed. "David? Are you all right?"

"No, apparently not," he softly replied, looking down at the deck. "It seems that I'm some sort of mad scientist bent upon creating Frankenstein's monster."

"David," Kirk said in a firm, fatherly voice as he placed his hand on his son's shoulder. "You didn't do this. What you saw in there was the work of a gang of madmen—outlaws—who corrupted your invention into something it was never meant to be."

David was trembling. "I should have known better. I should have been responsible enough to realize that the galaxy is full of evil psychopaths like that *Khan* . . ." He spat the name out angrily.

"David, we can't . . . *paralyze* ourselves out of fear of what others might do. We can't withhold our gifts from the universe because we don't trust that they'll be used wisely. We just need to have faith that the good out there will outweigh the bad. That's why we're out here, exploring, seeking new cultures, sharing our knowledge . . . because we believe that ultimately it can only make us stronger."

David raised his head high enough for his eyes to see out from beneath his knotted brow, and he met his father's gaze, and smiled gently. "Good words," he said. "You know, I was wrong about you . . . and I'm sorry."

"Well, we all need to forgive," Kirk said, "as much as it may wound our pride. If we were driven only by our anger and spite, we'd all end up like Khan."

David was now steady on his feet, and together they began walking back down the corridor toward the turbolift.

"I know you're angry," Kirk continued. "Angry about the deaths of your friends, the theft of your work, and . . . angry that I wasn't there to be your father when I should have been." They stopped, and Kirk turned to face David, gripping both of his arms. "But don't let that anger define who you are. You're so much more than that, David . . . and I'm proud of you."

"I know," David replied with complete honesty. "And I'm very proud to be your son."

The journey back to Earth aboard the *Yorktown* was rather uneventful for David Marcus and his mother, and the duration, though brief, provided David ample opportunity to reflect upon the sudden appearance of his father in his life.

Surprising to him, James Kirk was not at all what he had expected. Of course, David had never asked his mother much concerning the admiral, but reputation alone had led David to anticipate a brash, swaggering arrogance about the man . . . when in fact, Kirk's actions during the recent crisis reflected an intelligent, thoughtful leader who obviously cared deeply about those who served under him. The brief moment they had shared outside the *Enterprise* sickbay had swiftly torn down barriers that David had thought were impenetrable, and the young man now felt committed to further exploring the relationship.

But for now they were separated, as the *Enterprise* was left light-years behind, slowly limping back home behind an escort, barely able to sustain warp drive.

David shared a meal with his mother in their quarters that night, then retired for some well-earned rest. His dreams, however, were troubled. Throughout the night, visions of the tortured scientists on Regula One repeatedly tormented him, and the sounds of their screams continually echoed through his mind. He had left them there to die. He had run away and hid deep underground, ostensibly to save Genesis . . . but had he really only saved himself?

He awoke the next morning in a cold sweat just as the *Yorktown* was entering the Sol system. After he had showered and dressed, he and Carol devoured a quick breakfast just as the vessel began procedures to enter the spacedock in orbit around Earth—a planet where David had not lived on a permanent basis since he was very young; yet now, with nowhere else to go, he and his mother were faced with the unforeseen prospect of finding a home there. It was while the final docking routines were locked down that the message came through to David and Carol—an official government communiqué, requesting (or rather, politely demanding) their immediate presence at a formal debriefing.

As they disembarked the vessel along with numerous Starfleet cadets who had transferred from the *Enterprise* for the return voyage, they were greeted by a Starfleet admiral in full uniform, accompanied by a shorter, older man smartly dressed in typical business attire. "Doctors Carol and David Marcus?" he inquired.

"Yes, that's right," Carol replied.

"Good morning. I'm Admiral Harold Morrow, Starfleet Command. This is Mack Kane, Federation Secretary of Defense."

The elder gentleman nodded to them. "How do you do," Carol replied in an even tone, though David knew her well enough to realize that she was concealing a fair amount of nervous surprise. Neither he nor his mother had anticipated that this meeting would be with two of the top officials in the Federation's entire defense command structure.

"If you would please just follow me a short way," Morrow continued, gesturing further down the hall. "I apologize for the suddenness of this request, but it was necessary. Hopefully we can keep this brief. I know you are both anxious to return home."

"Actually, Admiral," Carol replied as they moved down the crowded corridor of the spacedock, "we had been stationed at the Regula spacelab for more than a year. Neither of us has a home on Earth."

Morrow seemed taken aback. "Oh, my apologies. Well, if neither of you is able to secure housing right away, you're welcome to stay tonight in guest quarters at Starfleet Command. Here we are," he said, entering the door to a small conference room. The four of them filed in and took seats around a display monitor at the end of a long table, though Morrow remained standing. "Can I get any of you something to drink?"

They all shook their heads. "We're fine, thank you," David spoke up.

"Very well," Morrow said, taking his seat, then grimly focusing his gaze upon Carol and David each in turn. "Doctors, we're in the midst of a crisis. Word has spread much faster than anticipated . . . though I suppose it would have been naïve to expect the creation of a new planet in the Beta Quadrant to go unnoticed by our adversaries. No doubt the explosion was picked up on long-range scans, probably by the Klingons, and by the next day the entire subspace net was buzzing with rumor and innuendo. Today, I don't think there's a spacefaring civilization this side of the galactic core that doesn't know about the Genesis planet."

"Have they learned anything about the technology behind it?" Carol asked.

"That's one of the things we wanted to ask you," Kane replied. "We've read Kirk's reports, but we need to be very clear. This Khan Noonien Singh . . . he compromised the Regula laboratory and retrieved the Genesis Device. Is there any possibility he gained access to your technical databases?"

"No," David replied. "We made certain of that. We . . . that is, several members of our staff sacrificed themselves to buy us time, so that we could get all the data secured in the underground cave."

"And such actions are indeed heroic, and will be recognized," Morrow said. "So aside from the device itself, which was detonated during the battle, all other confidential data was successfully secured? We need to be certain of this."

"Yes," Carol said confidently. "We're quite certain."

"Very well," Morrow said. "Doctors . . . I'm sure that, in the wake of the incident with Khan, it's clear to both of you the danger that Genesis represents, were it to fall into the wrong hands."

"Yes, crystal clear." Carol nodded.

"Then I trust that both of you will understand why, in the interest of Federation security, President Roth has no other option but to place control of the Genesis Project entirely under the oversight of Starfleet."

Carol sighed. Certainly this was not unexpected, but it carried such a sense of finality—an abrupt ending to years of intense work—that was difficult to acknowledge. She turned toward David, whom she expected would not be so agreeable.

But David, feeling defeated but cooperative, shrugged meekly. "I'm not surprised. A few days ago, I would have been infuriated, but now . . . I understand."

"Good!" Morrow smiled. "I'm glad we're all on the same page. Because the fact of the matter is, we still require your expertise."

"Oh?" Carol said.

Kane leaned forward. "Even though Starfleet will command the forthcoming operations," he said, "we still are going to require civilian involvement. Look, we've got ambassadors from every planet in both quadrants beating down the door wanting to know what this new technology is all about; they've got genuine concerns. But other than the limited data collected by the *Enterprise,* we still don't know enough to set any policy going forward."

He tapped a couple of controls upon the monitor in front of David and Carol. An image appeared of a smiling, dark-haired Starfleet captain. "This is John Esteban, captain of the science vessel *U.S.S. Grissom.* He's a good man . . . smart, creative, but knows to do things by the book. He's putting together a crew for the first fact-finding mission to Genesis. And Doctor," he said, indicating Carol, "we'd like you to be on board. They ship out tomorrow."

Carol looked down at her hands. "Sir, I'm honored by your request, but . . . is this an order?"

Kane shook his head. "You're a civilian, Doctor Marcus. I can't order you to do anything."

She raised her head and faced him humbly. "It's just that . . . an awful lot has happened these past few days. And while I fully understand and respect my civic duties, right now I think my first responsibility is to contact the families of Jedda, Zinaida, March, Madison—all our friends who were killed at Regula One—to express my condolences."

"I understand," Morrow said. "We can still find . . ."

"I'll go!" David interjected.

Morrow looked at him under a raised eyebrow. "Are you sure you're up to the task?"

Carol jumped to his defense. "Admiral, my son is more intimately knowledgeable of the Genesis technology than I am.

Although," she added, turning to David, "he'll have to promise me that he'll be careful."

David smiled sheepishly. "Mother, I think I can take care of myself."

"Very well, then," Morrow said. "Doctor David Marcus, you'll need to report to Captain Esteban aboard the *Grissom* at oh-eight-hundred tomorrow morning." He looked both of them over. "I'm sure I don't need to tell either of you that any unauthorized discussion of Genesis with *anyone* is prohibited. The existence of the planet may be common knowledge, but the secrets of the technology behind it must be contained at all costs."

"I understand, sir," David replied, "but I am curious. You mentioned the Klingons. What are we telling them about this?"

Morrow looked over to Kane, who gave a slight shrug before responding. "Right now, not much . . . except that a scientific experiment had some extraordinary unintended consequences."

"And they're buying that?" David asked.

"No, they're not," Kane replied, shaking his head. "Ambassador Kamarag of the Klingon Empire tells me that the High Council is demanding access to the planet. We've assured them that they will be allowed to send a representative, but not yet. Not until the *Grissom* returns and we know what we're dealing with."

David nodded. "What about the Romulans?"

"Ah. With them, at least we're making a token gesture." Kane tapped a few keys on the display, and an image of an attractive young Vulcan woman appeared. "Her name is Saavik. Ever heard of her?"

David and Carol shared a glance, and both shook their heads.

"She's become something of a young celebrity—a Vulcan national, but she's also half Romulan. I don't know her entire background, but she was raised as an orphan at the Gamma Eri science station, so her scientific knowledge is pretty formidable. But now she's become a diplomat." He pressed another key, bringing up a picture of her alongside a middle-aged human male. "Seems that

Ambassador Sarek of Vulcan pulled some strings and got her an internship as an aide to John Talbot, the Federation ambassador to Nimbus III. In her eighteen months there, she met the Romulan ambassador, Caithlin Dar, and apparently they became pretty close. Now that she's returned . . . hell, Saavik's practically the poster girl for Federation-Romulan relations."

He flipped off the monitor. "Anyway, she'll be joining you tomorrow, along with whatever team Esteban can recruit in the next twenty-four hours."

Morrow, sitting with his hands clasped together, nodded and turned back toward the doctors. "Any questions?"

They had none. Morrow and Kane extended their hands, and following a few firm shakes, the Marcuses were dismissed.

As they filed out the door, Carol held her son by the arm. "I mean it, David . . . please don't do anything foolish out there."

"I'll be fine, Mother," David said. "Maybe this 'Starfleet experience' will be good for me." And then he laughed. "Can you just imagine what my father will think?"

Carol kissed his cheek. "Call me before you ship out," she said.

"I will," he replied.

And Carol walked away, leaving David alone with his thoughts, contemplating what his own reaction would have been a few days ago had he known that he would be embarking on a Starfleet mission.

2

David Marcus still found the experience of traveling through the transporter a little unsettling. Unlike Starfleet, which used the devices regularly for moving personnel to and from orbiting ships while assuming the risks and the incredible energy costs, civilian use was much less common. Of course, with all his recent experiences on the Regula One lab and aboard the *Enterprise* and the *Yorktown,* culminating in his transfer to the *Grissom* for the return journey to the Mutara sector, David had been transported more times in the past few days than he cared to remember.

However, the disconcerting notion of having his own component atoms momentarily torn apart and reassembled was quickly forgotten as he and Saavik materialized on the surface of the newly created Genesis Planet. A pastoral scene emerged around them, with fields of prehistoric ferns extending for hundreds of meters in front of them to the base of a large plateau, atop which sat more varied forms of vegetation not easily identifiable from a distance. Behind them lay the edge of a great forest, with tall, majestic trees whose sweeping branches formed a vast enclosed canopy, providing shelter for the more exotic plant life that thrived within. To set foot upon this world for the first time—a world that he played an active role in creating—was an indescribable thrill.

Saavik, with her tricorder in hand, was already actively scanning the surroundings, frowning at the displayed results. They had just met the day before, but already David was rather intrigued with her striking beauty, and her complex and seemingly conflicted affect. In the short time they worked together at the science stations of the *Grissom,* Saavik had left no doubt about her intelligence; but both her enthusiasm for knowledge as well as her frustration with the unusual data they had collected were reflected in a muted but clearly apparent emotionalism. David wondered if the admixture of Romulan genes could really have such a pronounced effect, or if there might be some other explanation.

"The symptoms of geological aging are even more pronounced than what we were reading from orbit," Saavik said. "I'm reading some tremendous instability here."

"That's really odd," David said as he removed his heavy equipment pack from his back to retrieve his own tricorder.

"Is it any less odd than our detection from orbit of four different climate zones within the same sector?" Saavik inquired.

"The whole thing is odd," David said, powering up the device and beginning his own scan of the area. "I mean, sure, the matrix is designed to produce a varied climate. But it's like everything has been . . . I don't know, amplified . . . and accelerated somehow."

Saavik shouldered her own tricorder and reached into a pocket. "Any theories, Doctor?"

"I have a few," David said, allowing a touch of concern to creep into his voice. He looked up at her. "And please, call me David."

"As you wish," she replied, retrieving her communicator and flipping it open. "Saavik to *Grissom.*"

"*Esteban here,*" came the immediate reply. "*Saavik, what's your status?*"

"Orbital readings are confirmed. We have life-form indications approximately two point four kilometers southwest, at bearing zero-two-four. Radioactivity detected in the same vicinity, well within safe levels."

"*Very well. Proceed, Saavik, but exercise caution. This landing is at captain's discretion, and I'm the one who's out on a limb.*"

"I'll try to remember that . . . . Captain."

David smiled at Saavik's thinly veiled contempt. They both hoisted their gear and turned to their left, marching parallel to the forest's edge. Together they followed the tree line, stepping carefully through the knee-high vegetation. Even though he knew that the planet couldn't possibly harbor any advanced life-forms yet—the unknown readings notwithstanding—David still found himself feeling nervous about their inability to see what might be lurking beneath the greenery around their feet.

For the first kilometer or so, the vegetation slowly began to thin out, and the ground sloped upward. The distance from the forest edge on their left to the foot of the plateau on their right was gradually decreasing, and on the horizon they could see a point where the two would meet at the apex of the hill they presently ascended. The humid air, fresh with the scent of oxidized compounds emanating from the woods, was unexpectedly cut by the chill of a cool breeze in their faces.

David looked over at his hiking partner, and feeling that the silence was becoming awkward, decided to make a little small talk. "So . . . what about those Starfleet folks, huh? It was like pulling teeth to get them to let us beam down."

Saavik shrugged. "It is logical for them to take precautions when dealing with unknown phenomena."

"I guess so," David admitted. "But clearly there's something down here that wasn't part of the original matrix. Makes sense that you'd want the best scientific minds to investigate."

"I agree."

"Right. Well, luckily Captain Esteban agreed, too!" He laughed nervously. Saavik shot him an odd glance. David began to seriously regret all the years he'd spent holed up with older scientists, never having much opportunity to develop relationships with girls his own age.

He regrouped, opting for the more personal approach. "I, uh, understand you know Ambassador Sarek pretty well."

"Correct."

"Yeah . . . I met him once, on Andoria, back when I was . . . oh,

I dunno, about twelve or thirteen. How did you come to know him so well?"

A pause. Saavik flipped her hair back out of her face and stared off at the Regula sun, dipping down toward the horizon off to their right. "Sarek saved me from Hellguard when I was ten years old," she simply stated.

"Hellguard?" David asked. "I'm not sure I've heard of it. Is that a planet?"

"Yes, in the Romulan Neutral Zone. It's the planet where I was born."

"I see," David said, wanting to know more but being careful not to pry too deeply. "So then . . . your parents lived there?"

Saavik continued to look straight ahead, engaging in the conversation with all the emotionlessness of a biographer reciting someone else's profile. "I never knew my parents. My mother was a prisoner, most likely raped, and she died shortly after I was born. The Romulans later left the planet, and I was abandoned. I lived a feral existence with other orphaned children until we were found by the Vulcans, and taken to the Gamma Eri science station."

"Oh my God," David said with a mixture of both horror as well as newfound respect. "I'm sorry . . . I had no idea."

Saavik faced him with a look of mild confusion. "You need not apologize for something that was beyond your control."

"Well, no, I didn't mean . . ." His voice trailed off, and he sighed. He hadn't spent nearly enough time around Vulcans, and was beginning to realize that his comments would require a more logical foundation if this conversation was to go anywhere. "I meant to say, it is unfortunate that your childhood was so difficult. But I'm quite impressed at how, in spite of all that, you grew into such a successful young woman."

Saavik looked down, and feelings of dread crept into David's mind as he was certain that she would soon become annoyed with his clumsy attempts to compliment her. But those feelings melted away when a subtle smile softly creased her cheeks. "I am honored that you think so . . ." Her eyes met his. ". . . David. But what we make of our lives is based entirely upon the choices we make in the present, not upon events that occurred in the past."

"I agree," David replied. "Still, it's so incredible that you're helping to mend the fences with the Romulans. A lesser person might hate them for what they did to you."

Saavik cocked her head. "It would be illogical for me to hate who I am."

David had no response.

As they finally crested the hill, the sun disappeared behind gathering clouds, and the cool breeze gained intensity until it became a swirling wind. And when they gazed out beyond the top and over the other side, it appeared as if they had transported onto another world.

The forest ended abruptly at the top of the hill, and the landscape beyond was much more barren, dotted with hardier-looking plant formations, mostly cacti and tundra. And strangest of all, the ground, as far as they could see, was blanketed with a white sheet of freshly-fallen snow. The two scientists exchanged puzzled looks.

David lifted his tricorder from where it hung on the strap from his shoulder, and quickly scanned the area. "This doesn't make sense," he said. "The Genesis matrix is still actively modifying the meteorological properties of this area. It should be dormant by now."

"Is it safe for us to proceed?" Saavik asked.

David turned the tricorder toward her and swept it up and down. "As far as I can tell, yes. The matrix is no longer showing any metastatic effects."

The two of them struggled to keep their balance as a sudden tremor shook the ground beneath their feet, threatening to send them both tumbling back down the hill. David grabbed Saavik's arm, and she clasped his opposite hand in response, keeping their equilibrium steady until the rumbling ceased a few seconds later.

Their communicators both began chirping in unison. "*Grissom to landing party!*"

Saavik quickly retrieved hers and flipped it open. "Saavik here."

"Saavik, the geological instability we're reading is increasing throughout your sector," the concerned voice of Esteban rang out. *"And we just recorded a quake at your location. Are you both okay?"*

"We're fine, Captain," Saavik replied.

"Doctor Marcus?"

David flipped open his own communicator. "Marcus here."

"David, we're reading a severe and unnatural age curve on the planet. I'm getting nervous up here. Do you have an explanation?"

David paused before clicking the button to respond. "No, Captain. We're reading the same things, but I'm going to have to study the data in more depth before I can formulate a theory."

"Well, theory or no, if things get much worse, I'm pulling you both out of there. Understood?"

"Yes, sir," David replied. "We're less than a kilometer from the life-form readings. We'll have something for you shortly. Marcus out."

Saavik looked at him. "David," she said with concern. "You do have a theory, don't you?"

"Later," he said abruptly, trudging off across the snowy terrain. "Let's find what we came for."

Along the distant horizon, a line of mountains could be seen, and with a flash of bright flame, one of the peaks erupted with a massive fireball, shooting red-hot rock and ash high into the skies over the outlying lands. Several seconds later, the shock wave rattled their eardrums, and whittled away at what little fortitude they had remaining.

They hiked the last kilometer in silence, awed by the bizarre weather patterns, and growing increasingly troubled by the small tremors rumbling through the ground with increasing regularity. Their path took them down into a shallow valley flanked by rocky bluffs. As the readings from their intended target began to suggest a very close proximity, the vale abruptly opened out to their left and they rounded the corner of the cliff, where before them the object of their search sat on prominent display.

Like a great monolith left behind on this primitive world by some advanced civilization eons ago, then felled by the winds of time, they beheld a massive sheet of metal, perhaps thirty feet high, embedded in the snow-covered soil at a sharply diagonal angle, the top leaning against the nearby cliff face. The smooth surface, though seared by the heat of atmospheric friction, looked relatively undamaged and bore markings that were all too familiar to David. In fact, the only serious blemish marring the integrity of the object was down the right side, where it seemed as if the metal had simply been eaten away by some ravenous unknown force.

Saavik was already scanning the object with her tricorder. "Tritanium alloy," she read from the display, "with duranium outer plating."

"That's part of a registry number," David said, pointing to a set of figures displayed upside-down, about halfway up the length of the object. " 'Seven-oh-one.' When the Genesis Device exploded aboard the *Reliant,* the aft section of the *Enterprise* was compromised by the effects of the wave. I think this is a section of the shuttlebay door."

Saavik scanned the surrounding area. "Presumably it would have impacted nearby and rolled to this position. But there is no sign of an impact crater."

"Well, the graviton waves were still in flux," David said. "It could have soft-landed."

Saavik raised an eyebrow as she again retrieved her communicator. "Fascinating," she said, as she flipped it open. "Saavik to Grissom."

"Esteban here," came the reply. *"Have you found anything?"*

"Yes. It would seem that we have discovered a section of the *Enterprise* hull."

"Damn . . . Saavik, do you detect any proprietary Starfleet technology attached to the wreckage?"

She continued to scan the object as David approached it, ducking his head into the shadows cast upon the ground behind it.

"Negative. It appears to be nothing more than a section of the outer door to the shuttlebay."

"Well, we'll have to check it out anyway. I'm sending down a Starfleet landing party to document your findings. What about the life-form readings?"

"Saavik, look at this!" David shouted from his half-concealed position behind the door.

"Stand by," Saavik said, and she approached David, who had stepped back and was scanning the ground at the base of the wreckage.

In the soil directly behind the object, sheltered from the surrounding snowfall, dozens of small flat wormlike organisms, each about an inch long, slowly maneuvered their way along the ground. Though clearly primitive, their size was shocking to the sensibilities of the two scientists, who knew that nothing more advanced than embryophytic plant life should have been manufactured by the Genesis matrix. David completed his scan. "Apparently these were microbes on the inner surface of the door, probably left there by the bay crew on *Enterprise*."

Saavik studied them with puzzlement. "But how could they have evolved so quickly?"

Their communicators crackled to life. *"Marcus and Saavik, stand by to receive the landing p—"* The end of the transmission dissolved into incomprehensible static.

Saavik held her communicator close and spoke loudly. *"Grissom,* this is Saavik. You're breaking up. Are you receiving interference?"

Esteban's voice struggled to break through the noise. *"—reading an artificial disturbance—"*

"—energy surge from astern, sir!" came the voice of *Grissom*'s communications officer.

Additional static. *"—God! Red alert! Raise shields!"* Esteban's voice shouted out with marked panic.

David met Saavik's eyes and they shared a horrified look. "What's going on up there?" he asked rhetorically.

"Take evasive action! Stand by on—!"

Another burst of intense static, and then complete silence.

"Saavik to *Grissom!*" she implored. "Come in, Captain!"

No response.

"Oh my God!" David cried out. "What the hell just happened?"

Saavik's hand shook as she closed the communicator. She swallowed. "It would seem that the *Grissom* was just destroyed by an enemy attack."

"Wha—? Then how are we going to get off this planet? We've got to call for help!" He fumbled to find his own communicator in his jacket.

"David!" Saavik shouted. "Logically, the only people within range of our transmission would be the ones who just destroyed the ship."

David stared at her for several seconds, then removed his empty hand from his pocket. "You're right, of course." He took a couple of unsteady steps, then leaned back against the nearby rock and covered his face with his hands. "Oh, God . . ."

He pressed his fingers into his eyes, hoping to somehow blot out the truth of their circumstances—to expose all this as a surreal nightmare and end it swiftly and conclusively. He was brought back to reality by a hand on his shoulder. "David . . . this planet is destroying itself, isn't it?"

He dropped his hands from his face, wringing them firmly as he stared up at the sky. "Yeah, I think so."

"What went wrong?" she implored him.

He sighed. "I used protomatter in the Genesis matrix."

"Protomatter," she echoed. "An unstable substance that every ethical scientist in the galaxy has denounced as dangerously unpredictable."

"It was the only way to solve certain problems." His voice was racked with guilt. "My mother never even knew. That aspect of the project was entirely my responsibility."

"I understand your desire to demonstrate your worthiness to

your mentors," Saavik said. "But in this case, your impatience has placed us in an untenable situation."

David attempted to collect himself. "All right. So . . . these people who destroyed the *Grissom*. Are they more of Khan's men? They already killed all my friends at the Regula One spacelab— the ones who sacrificed themselves so that we could escape with Genesis. Naturally, they would be trying to track down the rest of us."

Saavik gave him a puzzled look. "That is highly unlikely. Khan was a first-generation augment from Earth's late twentieth century. His only surviving followers perished aboard the *Reliant.* Do you not know the history of your own world?"

"History was never my best subject."

"Indeed," she agreed. "But whomever they are, we must presume that they will come looking for us. Logically, our best course of action is to avoid capture until Starfleet sends another vessel to investigate."

"Right. Um . . ." He lifted his tricorder and turned around, sweeping it across the breadth of the rocky cliffs that loomed up behind them. "We can follow this ridge until it meets higher ground, a few kilometers away. Those hills contain some kelbonite ore, which should help to mask our life signs and block any transporter beams. Maybe we can find some shelter there."

"Excellent," Saavik said as another tremor shook the landscape, sending small boulders tumbling down from the nearby precipice. "Let's proceed."

The landscape grew much more difficult to navigate as they sought higher elevation, the ground becoming layered with uneven rocky soil. The snow had ceased, and the vegetation surrounding them reverted back to a more traditional arrangement of deciduous trees and bushes. The tremors continued to increase in both frequency and intensity, and the wind began to howl ever louder as it swirled about them. As the sun dipped below the horizon and the veil of dusk began to fall about them, they finally reached a plateau that jutted out from the face of a hill, where they discovered several small grottoes in the rock of the hillside that could offer protection from the elements and, hopefully, from their pursuers as well.

Within the confines of one of the tiny caverns they quickly set up a makeshift camp. The air was still reasonably warm, so no fire was necessary. They consumed a few rations as David's tricorder lay on the ground next to them, periodically flashing various warnings about the geological instability of the planet, as well as the presence of additional life-forms in the vicinity—presumably in the midst of an extensive search for the two members of the *Grissom* crew who were still unaccounted for.

David studied Saavik's dimly lit face as she sat staring off into the night sky, her half-Vulcan countenance only partly masking the apprehension she clearly felt. His own emotions were a jumble of remorse for his own negligence and dread from the hopelessness they now faced. In spite of this, he felt a strange compulsion to laugh, and did so, albeit halfheartedly. "How ironic is it that I took this assignment because I wanted to impress my father?"

"Starfleet Admiral James Kirk," Saavik said matter-of-factly. "I had surmised from your biographical profile in the mission briefing that the two of you were not particularly close."

David shrugged. "I barely know him at all," he admitted.

"Then why do you place such importance upon his acceptance of you?"

David considered this. "Good question. Growing up, it was just my mother and me. We had each other; I never thought we needed anyone else. And from what I knew of him, well . . ." He laughed. "I didn't think I even *wanted* to know him."

"Based upon reputation alone," Saavik interjected, "he does seem to possess the trait that I believe humans call 'cocky.' "

"Bingo," David said, smiling. "But that was before I saw him in command of his bridge . . . before we had our first real talk. And now I wonder what my 'cocky' father might have been able to teach me about leadership, had I ever made the effort to include him in my life."

Again Saavik looked pensively off into the distance. "I cannot compare your upbringing with my own. At Gamma Eri, I was mentored by a scientist named Salok. He did an acceptable job of raising us to learn and appreciate the Vulcan disciplines, but he was not . . . *nurturing* . . . and certainly not tolerant of my emotional instability. Only Sarek seemed to understand."

"You and the ambassador remained close?"

"He was able to come to the station only about once per year, but I awaited his visits with eager anticipation. He always took a special interest in my development. He . . . cared about me, I suppose in a way that a father would care for his own child."

David watched her as she spoke, sitting forlornly within their dark, barren surroundings. She had never known maternal affection; he had never experienced the benefit of his father's commanding presence. Each of them was somehow incomplete, and he felt that he wanted to hold her—that together, somehow, they could both become whole.

"So then, I assume that Sarek was never married?" David wondered aloud.

"He was, but that was many years ago," she explained wistfully. "He has not remarried since his wife died in a shuttle accident, two decades before you and I were born." She turned to face David with a mischievous expression. "Curiously enough, she was a human woman. I presume he found her emotionalism to be . . . enlightening."

"Well, geez, what a missed opportunity!" David joked. "You read my profile, you knew my mother was single . . . Why didn't we try to get the two of them together?"

A small smile crossed Saavik's face—an event so infrequent yet so charming in its exotic flair. "I confess that when I read your profile, I was . . . intrigued by you."

"Oh, really?" David said with interest.

"Certainly. You're young, intelligent, idealistic . . . and I've always enjoyed the company of humans. You're not weighted down by this pointless, constant repression of your feelings." She spat out the last sentence with subtle but palpable bitterness.

"And what are you feeling?"

She laughed nervously and looked down at her lap. Beside her, David's tricorder continued to flash its incessant warnings of their imminent doom. "Right now, I am . . . terrified. I feel like that damn ten-year-old girl back on Hellguard again . . . running . . . hiding . . ." She lifted her head to look at him, and a single glistening tear ran down her cheek. "I do not wish to die here."

David gingerly slid closer to her, until their knees were practically touching as they sat on the cold stone floor, and he took each of her hands in his own, clasping them gently but firmly. "We're not going to die," he confidently stated. "Not here. Not now."

"Is that your logic?" she asked, her voice steady but her eyes betraying her desperation. "Or just a feeling?"

"A feeling, I guess." He confidently raised his chin and nodded. "A human intuition."

"What else do your feelings tell you?"

He reached up and tenderly wiped the wet streak from her face. "That no woman so beautiful should ever be so troubled."

As David lowered his hand, Saavik raised her own hand to meet his, and they pressed their palms together. Their eyes remained locked as Saavik slowly slid her hand around to the opposite side and caressed his fingers with a slow downward motion. David sharply caught his breath as a warm, tingling sensation of pleasure flowed freely through the palmar nerves and upward through his arm. Their palms re-joined, and then David began the process anew, softly stroking Saavik's long, supple digits as she closed her eyes, her breathing slowly accelerating, her limbs trembling with excitement. As they clasped their hands together again, David could feel the intense heat from her body, while his own heart pounded fiercely, threatening to burst from his chest. Their lips met, and in perfect unison their bodies slowly sank down to the ground.

On the distant horizon, another volcanic mountaintop erupted, its hot magma shooting forth into the air. And the ground once again trembled, shaken by nature's primal throes.

The sharp concussion of an explosion rocked David from his slumber, and he shot up to a sitting position, squinting as his eyes adjusted to the morning light. Slowly, he shook off his dream-induced stupor and regained the memory of his present where-abouts. Saavik sat beside him, appearing fully awake and looking oddly neat and well groomed, as if every hair on her head just ef-fortlessly fell into place. The recent noise seemed to have had no effect upon her composure. "Hey," David called to her.

"I'm glad that you're awake," Saavik said. "I was going to have to rouse you myself."

Taking a deep breath, David's olfactory nerves were assaulted by a smell of sulphur hanging heavy in the air. He shook his head in an effort to clear his senses. "What was that noise?" he asked.

"Another eruption," she said, "but not a volcano. Fissures are opening in the continental crust. Readings suggest that it won't be long before the planet's tectonic plates begin collapsing into the mantle."

"My God," David said. He looked out across the landscape, observing the plumes of smoke billowing out from several newly created vents, the morning sky becoming painted with a hazy red glow.

"It's not safe here," Saavik announced.

"You can say that again."

"I'm not referring to the geological instability," she explained, picking up the tricorder and pointing to the display. "The search party is closing in on our position. And the life-form readings appear to be Klingon."

"Klingons? Can't say I've had the pleasure of meeting any, but it doesn't sound promising for two stranded and unarmed scientists, does it?"

"No, it does not," she agreed. "Come on. We must try to stay ahead of them and find new shelter."

Quickly they gathered their gear and moved to the mouth of the cave, then carefully began maneuvering their way down the rocky slope of the hillside toward the valley floor about fifty feet below. As he struggled to maintain his balance during the descent, David admired the lithe motion of Saavik as she appeared to navigate the terrain with little difficulty, even while continually observing the readings on her tricorder. The device began to beep its various warnings more rapidly as it tracked the motions of their adversaries.

"I have at least two readings off to the west," Saavik said, pointing to her left. "These two are sweeping the area but continue to approach our location. I also have a third, off to the northeast, somewhere beyond that ridge." She pointed right, toward the eastern edge of the raised plateau situated before them, the base of which was just a few hundred meters distant.

Behind her, David tried to focus on the tricorder's display as it bounced chaotically in her hand. "That's not good," David observed. "This means we have only one route of escape. Once we reach the base of this hill, we're essentially hemmed into the gorge between it and the ridge up ahead. Our only hope is to outrun them to the east, until the path opens into the clearing about a kilometer away."

"Then we must increase our pace," Saavik said, and did so. David struggled to match her speed, and despite a few tense moments when he feared losing his footing and tumbling headlong down the slope, they eventually finished scaling down the hillside and began a brisk run toward the eastern end of the gorge.

Minutes quickly passed in tense silence. Before them, the path briefly widened into a small clearing. The wind, increasing in intensity, swirled and howled throughout the open space. Above them, the sky was rapidly darkening, the sun blotted out by innumerable rising clouds of volcanic smoke and ash.

Saavik suddenly stopped, frowning down at the tricorder display. "Damn."

"What is it?" David asked, stepping up to look over her shoulder.

As outlined on the screen, the Klingon who was on his own had evidently rounded the adjacent ridge and entered the valley at the east end, and was now just a few hundred meters directly ahead. Saavik turned around and began scanning behind them, in the opposite direction. Two more life-sign readings flashed alarmingly. "It would appear that we are trapped," she said.

David immediately began glancing around at the high rock walls to either side of them, desperately looking for a place with a manageable slope or with easily accessible purchases that might allow them to climb out of the chasm, but even if both of them were skilled at rock climbing, there simply wasn't enough time to do so with any hope of a timely escape. "There's no easy way out of here," he conceded.

No response.

To his own surprise, David found himself in the unfamiliar position of envying the Starfleet officers who participated in planetary away missions on a regular basis. Surely they would have received training on how to deal with hostile situations such as this. They wouldn't be standing here like fools, wondering what their next move should be.

Not to mention they'd have those shiny Starfleet-issue phasers.

So be it. He'd think his way out of this like a scientist. He knew the problem; now what were the possible solutions? "Okay, so that lone Klingon to the east will be entering this clearing in a few minutes. We have two options. One is to give ourselves up and hope for the best."

"I would not recommend that option," Saavik replied. "Our welfare will be of little concern to them."

"I agree. The other option is to hide." He swiveled his head about, considering where they might find sufficient camouflage, and settled upon a thicket of dense brush at the base of the southern wall of the gorge. "Come on," he said, motioning her to follow.

"We cannot expect a member of the search party to simply pass us by," she protested as they maneuvered in behind the growth, still tracking the imminent approach of their adversaries with the now-silenced tricorders. "He will be tracking our life signs as well."

"Then we have to hope to take him by surprise," David said as he flung his pack to the ground, feigning confidence as he supposed a leader should. "It's all we've got."

"Your fortitude is admirable," Saavik replied, perhaps not entirely with sarcasm, before settling into a hushed silence as the Klingon entered the clearing.

Still exhausted from the run, David struggled to keep his labored breathing under control as he held his body as still as possible. Huddled close together as they were, he felt the warmth of Saavik's body next to his, and suddenly sensed a bit of awkwardness—they had shared something special the prior evening, and it seemed churlishly insensitive not to even have spoken of it the following morning. Granted, this was clearly not the most appropriate time to discuss the finer details of their personal relationship. Yet their untimely but propitious bond had deeply affected him, and as he gazed at her face peering out from their shelter, with her calm façade masking what he insightfully discerned to be tension and fear, he felt instinctively compelled to protect her.

From a distance, through the gaps in the tangle of branches and leaves, the Klingon didn't appear all that formidable—small of stature, his disruptor holstered, his attention focused upon his own tricorder in his hands. He had slowed his pace, sweeping the device from side to side as he attempted to narrow down the location of his quarry. The beeping sounds emanating from the tricorder increased to a furious rate, until finally the Klingon stopped and raised his head, staring directly at the foliage that concealed the sources of the two life signs he had sought. He turned off the device and pulled out his disruptor as he slowly advanced toward his hidden prize.

"You, in there!" he shouted. "Come out with your hands where I can see them."

David and Saavik remained silent and unmoving. The Klingon continued to approach.

"I said come out of there!"

David thought he could detect the slightest hesitancy—even apprehension—in the Klingon's gruff voice, and it emboldened him. His adversary now stood just a meter or so from the brush and was seconds away from pushing the branches aside to peer within. At his side, David gripped the strap of his own tricorder, allowing the device to swing loosely from the end, and waited. Just a bit closer . . .

In a single blurred motion, David sprung up from his crouched position and swung the tricorder in a wide arc, forcefully connecting with the side of his assailant's head.

Momentarily stunned, the Klingon stumbled backward with a muffled groan; David, his fear now conquered by the effects of adrenaline, sensed his opportunity and leaped forward, clearing the top of the bush and colliding with the Klingon, sending them both tumbling to the ground.

As he landed, straddled on the Klingon's chest, David immediately grabbed the disruptor with both hands and attempted to pry apart the fingers that tightly held it. The weapon shook as the Klingon struggled to maintain his hold, and both he and David began to grunt with exertion. Despite the Klingon's superior strength, David's two hands slowly began to twist the disruptor out of his foe's unyielding grip as if torquing a wrench on a stubborn bolt, until the Klingon suddenly thrust out his free left hand and grabbed David's throat.

As the fingers constricted his windpipe and choked off his air, David shifted his right hand to his throat in an attempt to interpose his own fingers far enough to relieve the pressure. With a firm pulling motion, he created enough separation to allow a lungful of air before the grip was tightened even further. His left hand remained on the disruptor, no longer with any reasonable chance to snatch it away. He now hoped merely to prevent his opponent from using it at this close range.

Beneath him, he felt the Klingon's chest expand with a deep breath, and then with an explosive burst of force, David was flung by the neck to his left. In the same instant the Klingon used the strength of his legs to thrust his torso upward, knocking David off balance and rolling them together over their outstretched arms, jarring the disruptor loose from their clutches. David came to rest on his back, still gripped by his throat, with the Klingon astride him. He was able to tilt his head to the left just enough to see the weapon, large as life, lying mere inches in front of his eyes, and tried twisting his left arm at an impossible angle to retrieve it, only to see the Klingon's free hand land upon it and raise it up. But it was held by the barrel, not the grip, and as the Klingon fumbled to turn it in his hand, David knocked it from his grasp, sending it flying some distance out of their reach.

Growling, the Klingon again tightened his fingers around David's throat, and this time the young scientist, now in an entirely defensive position, was forced to use both hands to try to prevent his windpipe from being crushed. The Klingon's free right hand casually reached down to his belt and unsheathed a cruel-looking dagger. The blade was raised high, and David's eyes widened, helplessly awaiting the deadly downward thrust as his vision began to darken from lack of oxygen.

And suddenly the Klingon stiffened. He loosened his grip on David's neck, the dagger dropped from his hand, and he fell away to one side, revealing the stooping frame of Saavik, who had just released her own grip upon the Klingon's shoulder.

David gratefully sucked in lungfuls of air as he stared in wonder at Saavik. He had heard about the power of the Vulcan neck pinch, but often wondered if it was merely a myth. He was only too happy to see his doubts proven wrong.

"Are you injured?" Saavik asked.

David quickly took inventory of his body's moving parts. "No," he said with a raspy voice as his larynx slowly recovered from the abuse it had taken. "I guess I'm okay."

"Very well," she said with urgency as she quickly scampered over to the disruptor lying a few meters away and bent to retrieve it. "We must keep moving."

David struggled to his feet. Together they turned to the east and took no more than a few quick steps when a voice rang out behind them.

"Halt! Drop your weapons. *Now!*"

They froze. Saavik let the pistol drop from her grasp, and they both raised their arms in surrender.

"Turn around."

They did so, and saw another Klingon guard, scowling viciously as he held his disruptor trained upon both of them. In front of him, marching toward them with cocksure determination, was the Klingon commander, looking over his new prisoners with glaring disapproval.

"I am Commander Kruge of the *I.K.S. Katai.*" He did not make eye contact as he addressed them, giving the haughty impression that to be his audience was considered a privilege. "Your ship in orbit has been destroyed. And my science officer tells me that this planet will soon destroy itself. How fortunate for you that I intend to safely remove you from this place. But you need not show me your gratitude just yet; in due time, you will happily repay me for my generosity."

David scowled at the insincerity of the Klingon's words. "This is Federation space!" he exclaimed. "You can't just come barging in here like this!"

"Yet nonetheless, here I am," Kruge said, turning toward David. The Klingon looked David up and down, then shook his head and rolled his eyes. "I have seen the reports of a Starfleet admiral, describing in lurid detail how this planet came to exist. So I come here seeking answers, which you will gladly provide."

On the ground directly in front of them, the other Klingon guard began to stir, moaning miserably. Kruge looked down upon him with disgust.

"No, Maltz, don't get up," he said with condescending pleasantness. "We have everything under control. I should have known better than to trust you to handle a weakling human . . ." He then turned toward Saavik, and looked her over disapprovingly. "And a Vulcan woman."

"*Half* Vulcan," Saavik sternly corrected him. "I am also half Romulan."

Kruge's eyes widened with sudden revelation. As he stepped toward Saavik, the increasingly turbulent winds blew his long hair outward in a halo about his head, giving him the unsettling appearance of some kind of messianic zealot. "Aaaaaah . . . So then, it is true. The Romulans have conspired with the Federation against us."

"I am here only as a neutral scientific observer," Saavik said.

"Yes, of course," Kruge's voice dripped with sarcasm. "You will stand by 'neutrally' while the Federation tests out its new ultimate weapon, and plots the destruction of the entire Klingon Empire!"

The rumble of another earthquake shook their feet, providing an ominous punctuation to Kruge's words. He backed away from the young woman and began to slowly pace the ground in front of her while his two subordinate officers looked on. "It wasn't long ago that Klingons and Romulans were openly sharing each other's technology. I knew a Romulan woman . . . Charvanek, I think was her name. She was instrumental in getting the first cloaking device installed in my vessel."

Saavik raised her voice against the howl of the storm. "I'm sure you were quite smitten with her."

Kruge spun around in response. "She was a crazy bitch!" He approached Saavik again, his gaze locked upon her face. "But she was honorable. I trust I can expect the same from you?"

She considered this. "Well, I'm not crazy," she said. "But two out of three are reasonably accurate."

The commander squinted for a moment as he worked out the comment in his mind, then broke into a wily grin. Behind him, the horizon was dotted with distant volcanoes belching forth clouds of ash and occasional explosive eruptions of bright lava, staining the sky in deepening shades of crimson, and casting the Klingon's face in a demonic glow. "This may yet turn out to be rather interesting," he said.

Another tremor reverberated through the ground, and the escarpments surrounding them began to shed huge boulders, tumbling down into the ravine where they stood and narrowly missing them as the rocks rolled past. Maltz, who had gotten to his feet and retrieved his weapon, looked about them with growing consternation.

Kruge produced his communicator and activated it. "Transporter room! Five to bring up. Activate beam."

As the five figures were dissolved by the particle beam, the ground they had been standing upon heaved forth, breaking apart and then collapsing into a gaping chasm, releasing flames that licked their way up the sides of the abyss—releasing the forces within that would slowly tear apart the planetary crust, destroying the newborn world.

The squalid interior of the transporter room on Kruge's vessel slowly materialized around David, and he was immediately assailed by the dank smells that could only be produced by a dozen Klingon officers in cramped quarters on a ship with clearly inadequate ventilation. Without a word, he and Saavik were forcefully shoved from behind off the transporter pad. The young scientist turned and scowled at the Klingon entourage assembled on the pads behind him, but they simply laughed derisively while pushing their prisoners inexorably forward.

Upon reaching the open central corridor that spanned the length of the ship, Kruge shouted a command in Klingon, bringing his men to a halt. David felt a hand on his shoulder and the point of a disruptor lodged in his back. Kruge circled around to the front of the group and leveled his gaze at his two captive Federation scientists.

"The two of you," he said in English, "have been captured as enemies of galactic peace. If you choose to cooperate, I will reciprocate by sparing your lives. If you choose otherwise, the consequences will be most unpleasant. So, to begin, you will tell me the secrets of the Federation's new Genesis super-weapon."

David averted his gaze, nervously looking over at Saavik. Though maintaining her composure, the half Vulcan had set her jaw, and her sweeping eyebrows drew together sternly—clearly she was expending tremendous effort to hold her temper in check.

"We were sent merely to investigate the planet, and to report our findings," Saavik replied evenly and with amazing calm. "But we are not enlisted in Starfleet. Of the technology behind Genesis itself, we have no knowledge."

Kruge stepped up to Saavik until his face hovered just inches from hers, and stared into her unblinking eyes. Despite being a few feet away, David thought he could feel the hot draft from the Klingon's breath. "Then I hope that pain," Kruge growled, "is something you enjoy."

Saavik's only reaction to the taunt was to raise an eyebrow in mock allurement. "That," she said, "would depend upon the circumstances."

Kruge continued to stare her down for a few moments, but this time did not appear to find amusement in her impudence. David suffered a few tense seconds in fear of Kruge's response before the Klingon finally backed away and turned to the officer who held Saavik in his grip. "Maltz, take them both down to the lower deck." He continued to speak in English, obviously wanting his captives to understand every word. "Escort the woman to the brig. Torg, take the human to interrogation and . . ." He looked squarely at David. "*Prepare* him." With that, he spun on his heels to the right and, several steps later, vanished through the door to the bridge.

"Move," Torg commanded, pushing David and Saavik down the long corridor in the opposite direction. As they crossed from the forward hull into the main wing hull, they passed several doors to crew quarters and an open entrance into what appeared to be a rather primitive sickbay. The steady hum of the impulse engines grew louder as they approached the engineering section at the aft end of the ship.

David felt his heartbeat racing as his imagination conjured up a hundred potential techniques of Klingon torture, each passing through his mind in alarmingly vivid detail. He tried to calm himself by concentrating on the benign ones—perhaps they would have nothing more than a small wooden stool in a barren room with a single antique incandescent light bulb suspended overhead. He forced out a quiet laugh. "What do you think, Saavik? Will these guys do the old good cop, bad cop routine?"

Saavik looked at him with an expression of pained confusion.

"Never mind," David said. "But don't worry." He held up his chin, feigning confidence as best he could. "After all, we don't know anything, right?"

The young woman's tone was of sad resignation. "Of course not," she lied, glancing at their wardens. "But I somehow doubt they will accept that."

"Enough talking!" Torg shouted as he directed them to a stairwell on their right, descending down to the lower deck, appearing even more dimly lit than the one above. At the bottom of the stair they were made to stop, each of them still held at gunpoint. Maltz directed Saavik to the right while Torg forcefully shoved David toward the left.

"Hey! Take it easy!" David shouted. "Why do you have to separate us anyway?"

"You don't want her to watch this, human," Torg sneered.

"David!" Saavik called out as the distance between them grew. "Remember your friends on Regula One!" And then she disappeared around the corner into the brig.

Less than a minute later, David had been flung into a plain metal chair adorned with restraints in the center of a small, sterile-looking room. Torg had holstered his disruptor, and presently

was pinning David's right arm down to the long, flat armrest of
the chair while he worked to secure the large metal clasps to his
forearm. For an instant David considered making a lunge for
Torg's weapon while both of the Klingon's hands were occupied,
but even if he were successful, David doubted that one man could
get very far attempting to overpower a crew of a dozen armed
Klingon officers.

He winced as the restraint tightened and bit into his skin, then
Torg mercilessly began work on the other arm. David gazed
around the room, noting the lack of any décor whatsoever, and in
fact becoming amazed at the cleanliness compared with the rest
of the ship, leading him to believe that the room had not previously been used—at least not for its intended purpose. Perhaps,
he hoped, these Klingons weren't that skilled in the finer arts of
interrogation after all.

Once Torg had finished securing his prisoner's ankles to the
chair, the door slid open, and he stood at attention as Kruge slowly
entered, followed by Maltz and flanked by a leashed animal that
appeared to be a monstrous cross between a wolf and a giant liz-
ard, with matted hair, long sharp teeth, and an immediately noticeable foul odor. In the opposite hand from the leash, Kruge
held a large crescent-shaped sword with cruelly sharpened points
at each end. Whether this grand entrance had been masterfully
planned to produce a terrifying effect, from David's perspective it
most certainly had achieved that result.

Kruge took his position directly in front of the chair, with Maltz
and Torg standing idly along the wall behind him. But Kruge did
not even look at David yet; instead, he faced the side walls and
began casually performing some form of martial arts exercises
with his weapon, while leaving his formidable animal sitting at
the foot of David's chair to snarl menacingly at him.

With his eyes anxiously trained upon the beast, David decided
to go ahead and open up the negotiations. "Uh, have you informed the Federation that you're holding one of their citizens?

There's not much I can do to help you, but I'm sure they'd be willing to negotiate. I mean, you don't want to start an interstellar incident, right?"

Kruge halted and slowly turned his head to the young man. "An incident?" he said incredulously. "You have the audacity to suggest that I may begin an *incident?* The Federation creates a technology capable of incalculable destruction, they even allow a Romulan woman access to its secrets, while at the same time insulting the High Council on Qo'noS, and yet with typical Federation bravado and insolence, you claim to be the injured party."

He stepped up to the chair and leaned forward menacingly until he hovered just inches from David's face. "Then injured you shall be," he snarled, as droplets of spittle shot out from between his teeth, "unless you tell me what I wish to know."

David gulped. He was going to have to try awfully hard to make this sound believable. "Look, I'll be glad to share whatever information I have," he said, grinning in what he hoped was a cooperative-looking expression. "But I didn't even know anything about Genesis until I received the assignment to investigate the planet. When I . . ."

The back of Kruge's hand made a violent impact against David's nose.

The young scientist's vision exploded with a white flash as the pain shot up through his sinus cavities, and moments later the blood began to gush forth from his ruptured mucous membranes.

"Don't toy with me, human," Kruge said calmly. He motioned for Torg to join him in front of their bound captive, and the subordinate obliged all too eagerly.

David lay back as the searing pain continued to pound throughout his nose, up into his forehead and back to his temples. He opened his mouth to let out an agonized groan and tasted the saltiness of his own blood dripping down past his lips.

Kruge had nonchalantly resumed his swordplay routines. "Let me keep this simple for you, human," he said amid a phantom parry and a lunge. "If you are telling the truth, then you are of no use to me. I would advise against any further attempts to convince me of your ignorance."

The possibilities raced through David's mind, and he struggled to evaluate his options despite the pain. Perhaps he should tell Kruge *something* . . . A few base principles about metastatic waveform matrices, or the propagation of protomatter . . . Surely that wouldn't be enough for these adversaries to actually build a weapon, would it?

"Perhaps a simple question will spark your memory," Kruge said. "Where is the base of operations for the Genesis research team?"

No, that would be too much information. Granted, the Regula One spacelab was now deserted, but unless Starfleet had retrieved them, the databanks were still hidden away in the Genesis Cave beneath the surface of the planet. "They never told us that," David lied. He sniffed and briefly gagged as the blood continued to flow freely down the back of his throat. "They just sent us directly to the planet."

"Torg," Kruge commanded. "See if you can jog his memory."

Torg balled up his fist and swung in a wide arc, viciously connecting with the left side of David's face.

His vision flashed again and he cried out, and for the moment the pain was replaced by a thundering dull ache that permeated his entire skull. His vision slowly returned but was altered and unfocused as the room swam dizzyingly around him, punctuated by tiny flashes of colored light. With each beat of his heart the pain became more pronounced until the pounding throb felt as if his head might suddenly explode. He heard the fevered snarlings of the foul animal at his feet, expressing its approval of the proceedings.

"It is pointless to prolong the inevitable," Kruge pronounced, now parading back and forth in front of his prisoner like a crazed martinet at a military tribunal. "One way or another you will tell me what I want to know."

"Commander," Maltz called out from the back of the room. "We could simply use the mind-sifter to retrieve all his knowledge."

Kruge swung around to face him. "I am not interested in your infernal gadgetry!" he shouted. "You'll leave me with a prisoner who is a drooling vegetable without control of his own bowels. I may still need him for leverage." He turned back toward the chair and held up the end of his weapon, prodding David's chest with one of the sharply pointed tips. "And that fact may keep you alive, though you'll wish you were dead. Torg, break his finger."

Grinning wickedly, Torg reached down and curled his fingers around the pinky of David's left hand. David's eyes widened with horror. For an instant he was willing to blurt out anything at all to prevent the forthcoming infliction—he wanted to yell out an impassioned plea to stop the torture, and to pledge his cooperation, but some part of his mind refused to offer up the words . . . refused to surrender while he still drew breath . . .

With a yank of Torg's grip the bones of David's finger emitted a gruesome cracking sound.

Like a jolt of electricity driven by a force of thousands of volts, the excruciating sensation shot through the nerves of his hand and arm. From deep within David's chest an agonizing wail burst forth, nearly powerful enough to shake the bulkheads loose from the ship's inner hull.

Kruge waited for the scream to abate, but still had to raise his voice over the din of David's labored breathing. "You have the power to make it stop, human," the Klingon commander hollered. "It's time to cooperate. Now, tell me where the Genesis Project is headquartered."

Regula, David thought, envisioning the planet as his eyes remained tightly squeezed shut. *Just say the word. The Regula One science station. Say it and the pain will stop . . .*

And the voice of Saavik echoed in his memory. *Remember your friends on Regula One.* His friends—those who gave their own lives to protect their secrets from those with evil intent.

"Shall I try another finger, sir?" Torg asked impatiently.

Kruge considered this. "No," he decided. "Let Maltz do it."

Standing several feet away, wide-eyed, the Klingon demurred. "Thank you, sir, but that is not necessary."

"Necessity is irrelevant," Kruge barked back. "I'm giving you an order."

Maltz stepped forward but did not yet make a move toward their wounded hostage. "Commander, where is the honor in torturing a frail human who perhaps has no information to give?"

"Do not lecture me with platitudes about honor!" Kruge bellowed. "You have been a constant thorn in my side with your spineless compunction! Why don't you show your honor by protecting the entire Klingon race from this scheming human *petaQ?*"

Maltz sighed with contrition. "Yes, sir," he said, and stepped up to the interrogation chair.

David lifted his head from the back of the chair where it had lain, having focused on a single spot on the ceiling during the recent discussion to try to regain his composure, despite the fiery anguish that burned throughout his body. He looked down at his left hand and for the first time saw his pinky finger pointed upward at a grisly unnatural angle, until the view was obscured by Maltz as he reached down to grip the next finger from the same hand.

Regula, David thought. *Just say the word and the pain will stop.* In his mind he could see the lab, the computer banks, the Genesis torpedo in its storage ark as they fled the onslaught of Khan; and he could hear the screams of those they left behind, who bought time for their escape with their own lives, the screams that continued to echo through his mind . . .

His own scream rang out in sympathy as another finger was brutally snapped. No longer could he distinguish the pain of one injury from another; the pain surrounded him—enveloped his entire being. He was submerged in its cold fluidity. He struggled against his restraints, frantically trying to kick his legs, as a drowning man attempts to claw his way through the oppressive medium without purchase or foothold, desperate for one last lungful of air . . .

Kruge resumed his exercises with renewed vigor, seeming to draw energy from the suffering of his prisoner. "It is time to end this now," Kruge said stridently. His movements with the sword grew more frenzied. "Give me a name. Where can I find the secrets of Genesis?"

Visions flashed through David's mind: Doctor Delwin March on a slab in the *Enterprise* sickbay, his throat slit from ear to ear . . . the pale visage of Doctor Vance Madison, who had exsanguinated while strung upside-down in the slaughterhouse of Khan's creation . . . the shrill screams of Zinaida as Khan repeatedly slashed her flesh into ribbons, demanding to know the escape route of David and his mother . . .

The weapon spun around furiously in Kruge's nimble hands. "Tell me what I want to know!"

So many lives lost . . . lives that must not have been given in vain . . .

The sword now rose up high above Kruge's head, still spinning with uncontrolled hysteria. "Give . . . me . . . Genesis!!!" he shouted.

David achieved a moment of calm confidence, and met Kruge's eyes, burning his gaze deep into the Klingon's pupils. "You can all rot in hell," he hissed.

"*Aaaaaaaaaaaaahhh!!!*" Kruge screamed, his banshee wail slowly building until with a blur of motion the sword descended onto David's exposed wrist, instantly slicing through flesh and bone and impacting the hard steel of the underlying armrest with a cold, metallic *thunk*.

His eyes wide as saucers, his mouth gaping in a silent scream, David watched as his left hand rolled away and fell to the ground with a pitiful thud, leaving behind a severed stump spraying forth his blood in steady, rapid pulses. The pain was gone as he quickly succumbed to shock. The periphery of his vision began to shrink into darkness.

"Maltz, take him to sickbay," the voice of Kruge commanded. "Cauterize his wound. Then leave him in the brig while you prepare your mind scanner."

The sound of the words and the lights of the room faded into oblivion as David sank into unconsciousness.

"Ah, here we go!" Kirk finally reached into one of his kitchen cabinets, having already opened three of them in quick succession while trying to remember where he'd stashed the recent gift. "I really need to get myself a wine rack."

Carrying a bottle in one hand and two glasses in the other, he returned to the sitting room of his San Francisco apartment, where Thelin was seated comfortably and watching him with interest.

"Romulan ale?" Thelin said, his eyebrows raised. "Jim, you know this stuff is illegal?"

"Transporting it is illegal," Kirk clarified. "You'll have to speak to the good Doctor McCoy about that. But as long as it's here . . . Cheers."

"Cheers," Thelin responded in kind, holding up the glass of bluish liquid in keeping with the human tradition before taking a sip, and feeling the caustic liquid assail his palate, some of it wasting no time and being absorbed directly through the soft tissue of his mouth into his bloodstream. Romulan ale was one of those rare spirits that seemed to affect all species equally, whether their blood was based on iron or copper.

Kirk smacked his lips, and then peered into his glass for a moment as if pondering the motion of the sloshing fluid within, before setting it down on the small table that stood between them. He looked up at Thelin. "Thank you for coming," Kirk said. "I wasn't sure if we were still on good speaking terms."

"What?" Thelin said incredulously, his eyebrows raised and his antennae turned inward. "For what possible reason would that be so?"

"I took command of your ship," Kirk replied. "I took your cadets out on an assignment that they weren't prepared for. A lot of good young officers died." He picked up his glass again, paused for a moment in thought, then tipped it upright and downed the rest of the drink in a single swallow. "And then . . ." he said, his voice slightly hoarse from the irritation of the ale, "I gave your ship back to you as a banged-up hunk of wreckage. Both you and the *Enterprise* deserved better."

"Jim," Thelin said, setting his own glass on the table. "First of all, those cadets knew their responsibilities when they took their oaths. Don't trivialize their sacrifices by blaming their unpreparedness."

Kirk stared off at the opposite wall. "You're right, of course. Again, I owe you an apology."

"Second," Thelin continued, brushing aside Kirk's contrition. "You did what was necessary to save the galaxy from the machinations of a madman intent upon getting his hands on a weapon of practically limitless power."

"You were the one who saved the ship," Kirk said, pointing at the Andorian.

"Jim, all I did was use the knowledge I had acquired purely by good fortune. You were the one forced to make the difficult decisions. It's what you've always done. I don't have your gift to always recognize what must be sacrificed to accomplish the ultimate goal."

"Sacrifice . . ." Kirk mumbled. He stood, and began slowly pacing the floor. "That's what the no-win scenario is all about, isn't it? Knowing when to make the ultimate sacrifice?" He stopped, and his shoulders drooped in dismay. "And in my own vanity, that's something I was never willing to do. None of us sacrificed anything to stop Khan—not me, not you . . . only a bunch of wide-eyed kids blindly following orders like good little soldiers. I don't know if I want to make those . . . 'difficult' decisions anymore."

Kirk turned toward the window and looked out at the skyline. The sun had begun to sink below the horizon, its reflected rays shimmering in the waves of the nearby waters and casting an auburn glow over the distant span of the Bay Bridge. "Seeing my son on the *Enterprise* bridge with us made me realize a lot of things . . . like the fact that these kids aren't giving their lives for my personal glory. They're the future of Starfleet, and David is my own future." He turned back toward Thelin. "I thought that my life seemed so empty and meaningless because I wanted back my command. Only now do I realize that all my life's accomplishments mean nothing unless I can pass on a legacy to my son."

Thelin considered the middle-aged human and the pain of his sudden epiphany regarding the responsibilities of fatherhood. Human society, he knew, was quite varied in its approach to marriage and child-rearing. Unlike Andor, Earth did not provide the same level of education, the same culture of preparation for the duties of parenting. But even on his own homeworld, some had begun to reject the honored traditions of family loyalty—the First Truths—as quaint and archaic. He didn't entirely understand how a man could choose not to play a role in the life of his son, though he had gained painful firsthand knowledge of just such a tragedy from his own childhood. But neither was he prepared to judge the human for it.

"The child is flesh of your flesh, blood of your blood," Thelin said to the admiral. "David is your continuation. You are wise to recognize this."

Kirk softly laughed. "I can't say that I feel very wise right now. I feel like I'm plotting a course into uncharted territory. And it's damned frightening."

Thelin picked up the empty glass from the table next to him. "If I may be so bold, perhaps it is time to refill the drinks."

Kirk smiled, seated himself back in his chair and began to pour more ale from the bottle. Thelin watched him as he set down the bottle and stood up to hand over the glass. Even as Kirk felt these moments of uncertainty, he still carried himself in the manner of a person who would show no vulnerability—the manner of a leader.

"You'll do fine as a father, Jim. In fact, I daresay you're the closest thing to a father I've ever had."

With the glass at his lips, Kirk nearly choked on a mouthful of the blue liquid. "Thelin, we're practically the same age!" He wiped off his mouth with his sleeve.

"Age is irrelevant," Thelin replied. "You've been a mentor; you've provided authority and discipline. We've known each other for twenty years, and in that time, I've grown more under your guidance than in all my years spent from birth to adulthood."

Kirk waved him off. "That's the alcohol talking."

"Perhaps. But even if so, it nonetheless speaks the truth."

Kirk shifted in his seat, his nonplussed expression shifting through several distinct phases as he attempted to reprocess the nature of the relationship they had shared all these years. "Well, Thelin, I'm . . . touched," he finally said. "But . . . what about your own father? I don't recall you ever sharing much about him. Is he still alive?"

Thelin stared into his drink. He considered trying to change the subject, but as the ale had somewhat dulled his inhibitions, he instead chose to relent and respond with frankness. "My *charan* yet lives, but traditionally he would not be actively involved in child-rearing. My *thavan,* however . . . I do not know. I've had no contact with him since I was very young."

"I'm sorry," Kirk said. "I hadn't known."

"Of course not. We would not normally speak of such things. Our privacy is sacrosanct." He finished his drink, set down the empty glass, and continued. "My *zhavey,* I believe you know, is an Aenar from the northern provinces of Andor. My father met her while vacationing in the Weyzhiss Mountains, and she returned with him to Laibok. The sanctioning of marriage was less restrictive at that time, and interracial unions were never arranged at all. So, they found suitable partners on their own and bonded.

"They were something of a novelty at the time, with so few having intermarried with the Aenar. But then it was during my youth that the race riots began."

Kirk nodded. "Yes, I remember hearing about the uprisings while I was living on Tarsus."

"The government's climate-change project had been a veritable disaster for the northern regions, and violent responses were met with more violence. My mother became a target of public scorn, and the rest of her bondmates lacked the courage to defend her. So the bonding was dissolved, and my *zhavey* was left to raise me on her own." He sighed with resignation. "I wish I could report that things have markedly improved, but I do not believe it to be so."

Kirk set down his own empty glass. "These racial problems," he said. "Is that the reason you haven't begun a family yourself?"

"Partly," Thelin replied, trying to stem the flood of memories of Thali flowing into his mind. "Suffice it to say that Andorian courting and bonding rituals are . . . complicated."

Kirk grinned and gave a friendly roll of his eyes as he stood and gathered the glasses from the table. "Why does that not surprise me?"

"It doesn't really matter anymore," Thelin said, forcing an air of confidence. "Starfleet has provided me with all the family I need."

Kirk moved toward his kitchenette area, calling back over his shoulder to Thelin. "We've polished off the ale, I'm afraid. But the food synthesizer was just restocked. Anything you want, it's on me." Having quickly washed his hands, he turned back around. "The perks of being an admiral include delicacies, you know," he said, winking. "Fresh Andorian redbat with tuber roots?"

Thelin opened his mouth to politely decline the offer when the doorbell suddenly chimed. Puzzled, Kirk looked at his current guest and gave a slight shrug. "Hold that thought," he said, and started toward the entrance to his apartment.

"You weren't expecting anyone else?" Thelin asked.

"Not tonight, no." Kirk reached the door and pressed the control near the frame to slide it open.

At the door stood Carol Marcus. Though she was smartly dressed in an attractive blouse and slacks, her clothes appeared unkempt, and her hair was similarly disheveled. Her swollen eyes were red with irritation and dried tears left streaks down her unblemished complexion. "Oh, Jim, I came as quickly as I could," she said in a shaky voice, then stepped through the doorway and threw her arms around him, burying her face in his shoulder.

Though Thelin could not see his face, the bewilderment in Kirk's voice was apparent as he tried to calm the distraught woman. "Carol? What's wrong? Tell me what happened!"

She lifted her head and sniffed, looking into his eyes with her own confused expression. "You haven't heard? You're not monitoring the subspace feeds?"

"Well, I . . . No, I'm not. I mean, I saw that I had a message to contact Morrow, but I hadn't . . ."

"Jim!" Carol cried out, pounding her fists into his chest. "We lost David!"

Kirk stiffened and dropped his arms. He quickly swung his head round to look at Thelin, who still sat observing, mirroring his own dumbfounded expression, then turned back to the mother of his son. "Lost? What . . . Carol, what are you saying?"

Carol pushed past him into the apartment. She sniffed again, wiping her nose with her hand, and then letting out a quiet wail as she threw her arms back down to her sides. "The *Grissom* was destroyed," she said.

"Destroyed?" Kirk said incredulously, walking up from behind to stand next to her. "How?"

"I don't know," Carol replied. "Attacked maybe . . . the last transmission said something about an artificial disturbance and an energy surge."

"Artificial? What does that mean?"

"Goddammit, Jim, I don't know!"

Kirk grabbed her arm, spinning her around, away from Thelin. "Carol," he implored her, "they were on a mission to explore the Genesis Planet. It's possible that they weren't aboard the ship."

Carol's voice dropped to a dull monotone as she had now drained her last reserves of emotion. "There is no more Genesis Planet. It's gone."

Kirk opened his mouth, agape, then shook his head before speaking. "I don't understand."

"Destroyed itself," she deadpanned. "Blew up. It's gone. It's all gone."

Her knees buckled and she fell into Kirk, this time planting her face into his chest, while her own chest heaved with pained moans of despair. Kirk wrapped his arms around her, and his eyes peered out over the top of her hair. And as Thelin looked into those eyes, he saw only an emptiness as vast as the deepest reaches of space.

3

The hard metal floor of the brig rushed up to meet David with all the gentleness of a shuttle accident. He heard the buzz and faint crackle as the forcefield was reengaged at the entrance to his cell. The impact caused blood to start dripping again from his nose, which was almost assuredly broken.

For the time being, he lacked the will, and most likely the strength, to move from his prone position. The harsh coldness of the ground was actually refreshing as the sweat continued to roll from his overheated brow. He found comfort in the sound of his own breathing, and in the sensation of his own pulse throbbing throughout his body, reminding him that he remained alive, at least for now.

The feel of a touch upon his shoulder pierced his trancelike state, and suddenly he found the strength to shriek and pull away. But then a soothing voice brought forth a sense of peace, and gently pulled him back from the brink of panic. "David, it's me. It's Saavik. Try to relax. You're having an acute stress reaction."

He turned his head toward the sound and struggled to bring the image into focus. The sight of her face and the firm gaze beneath her arched eyebrows instantly calmed him, and he reached out with his right hand to touch her cheek. "Saavik?" he said, and suddenly burst into uncontrolled sobbing. She reached her arm around to embrace him, slightly lifting his head and shoulders from the deck, and David buried his head into her lap, letting the cleansing tears flow freely.

He wasn't sure how many minutes passed before his breathing

began to steady and his fragile composure returned, but eventually he looked back up into her eyes. As he gazed into them, he suddenly became aware of a sensation—a tranquil warmth that seemed to emanate from her, the piercing gaze soothing his mind, and the caress of her hands calming his frayed nerves. "Saavik," he repeated. "I didn't tell them anything."

"Just relax," she instructed him. "Can you sit up?"

"I . . . I think so," David said, and he turned his body, attempting to prop himself up with his left arm, forgetting that his limb now ended at a cauterized stump, hastily wrapped in dirty cloth. The pressure of the wound against the deck sent a searing jolt of pain throughout his body, and he cried out as he rolled over onto his back, cradling the limb over his stomach with his good hand. The agony of phantom fingers burned mercilessly at the end of his arm.

Saavik allowed a moment for the initial wave of pain to pass, then once again cradled his shoulders. "Your injuries are not life-threatening," she said, unwrapping enough of the dressing to get a view of the amputation site. "They managed to stop the bleeding, despite the crudeness of the ligature. Allow me to help you up."

With a forceful assist from Saavik, David managed to rise to a sitting position. For the first time, he looked down upon the mangled remains of his left wrist. The skin was charred and encrusted with dried blood. A whiff of seared flesh entered his nostrils, and he gagged, feeling the bitter sting of bile rising up through his throat. He closed his eyes and turned his head, desperately hoping for the spell to pass without soiling the floor of their cell.

When he finally managed to let his eyelids flutter open again, he saw that Saavik's demeanor appeared more uneasy. She glanced out of the cell's entryway, to ensure that the nearest guard was safely out of earshot. "David," she said. "We may not have much time. Did they tell you what they plan to do next?"

"I didn't tell them anything," David mumbled, slowly shaking his head. "I didn't tell them anything."

"David!" she said with sudden firmness, gripping him by the shoulders. "Listen to me. Did they tell you whàt they plan to do next?"

He stared back at her. The memories of his recent interrogation remained fresh in his mind, but the thought of replaying them in search of clues was untenable. He began to shake. "I don't . . . I don't know . . . I think so, but I . . ."

"I can help you, David," Saavik assured him. "But you must help us first. Did they say anything before they returned you to the brig?"

David closed his eyes. His breathing grew more rapid, and his pulse quickened. He remembered the pain, the flash of light . . . the sight of his own blood spraying forth . . . the voices. Kruge's voice.

"Aaahh," David wailed, trying to form some coherence out of the jumble of impulses shuffling through his memory. He licked his lips. "Um, he said, a . . . a mind . . . mind-sifter."

"Indeed," Saavik said with resignation. "As I had feared."

David noticed the obvious change in her demeanor. "What?" he inquired. "I'm not going to tell them anything. I won't let them have Genesis. So many people . . ."

"David, you can't . . ."

"So many people have died!" he cried out. "And it's my fault. They're going to have to kill me, too."

"You *can't* resist the mind-sifter!" Saavik admonished him. "You don't understand. I would have the mental discipline to resist it, but you cannot. They will empty your mind, David."

He stared at her, horrified by her sense of certainty. "Oh, God," he muttered, looking about the cell in desperation. "Then we can't let them take me again. Oh, my God!" He struggled to his feet, agitated, and began pacing the length of his cell. Suddenly he turned, and pointed down at her with a trembling finger as she remained seated in the center of the floor, his sanity now pushed to the brink. "You . . . you have to kill me. You've got some . . . some sort of Vulcan death grip thing, right?"

Saavik rose and walked over to one of the slabs protruding from the walls that served as the only places to sleep in the cell. "David, come and sit down," she calmly said.

Drained of all emotion, as well as any remaining motivation for action, David simply did as he was told, robotically crossing the room and seating himself beside her. He envied her stoic Vulcan calmness as Saavik locked her gaze upon him.

"We are in agreement that they cannot be allowed to acquire the secrets of the Genesis technology," Saavik said. "And as long as we live, they will seek to retrieve it from our minds. Logically, we must convince them that we do not have the knowledge they seek."

David nodded. "Okay," he said.

"I will have to join with your mind to prepare you for your next interrogation," Saavik continued. "I admit that I never received much training in the esoteric mental disciplines, and certainly I have never melded with a human before. But the fact that we have been intimate together should facilitate the process."

David let out a snort, spraying specks of blood from his nose onto his tunic. "Gosh, you make it sound so sexy when you say that."

"David, please try to concentrate," Saavik reprimanded him. "We may not have much time. Look at me."

David looked at her. Although she had the benefit of not yet having been subjected to Klingon interrogation, she still looked amazingly composed, and strikingly beautiful. The only real evidence of their harrowing captivity was the bloodstains down the front of her tunic, deposited there by David amid his tears just minutes earlier. David considered the traumatic events of Saavik's childhood, and how she had seemingly drawn strength from them, and now her impressive demeanor provided just enough inspiration to make him believe that, just perhaps, they could survive this. Saavik reached out with both hands and touched his face, her fingertips gently prodding the area around his temples, slowly moving to find an optimal position.

"My mind to your mind," she said.

David felt a brief moment of disorientation. He could still see Saavik seated before him, but suddenly his mind seemed unable to reconcile that visual data with the sense of her presence—both next to him and within him. Yet he wasn't alarmed; rather, his trust in her made the sensation oddly comforting.

"My thoughts to your thoughts."

David closed his eyes, and the conflicting visual sensations became clearer. In fact, he now realized that he was seeing his own face through Saavik's eyes, and it wasn't a pretty sight—his visage was blemished with welts and bruises, his left eye was a purplish mass beginning to swell shut, and his nose and mouth were caked with dried blood. Perhaps sensing the discomforting effect of the view, Saavik closed her own eyes, and without the visual distractions, David found himself awash in a sea of thoughts, memories, ideas . . . and he wasn't even sure which ones were his.

David, he heard Saavik's voice, though he realized she wasn't actually speaking—instead, he seemed to somehow feel the words within his mind. *Concentrate. . . . Your knowledge of the Genesis technology is found within your memories. We must visualize a system of organization.*

The words were cryptic, and yet David understood precisely her meaning. The maelstrom of images surrounding him began to coalesce—to arrange themselves into recognizable patterns, individual bound codices, sorting themselves methodically . . . categorically.

Surrounding him, an image began to come into focus of four walls . . . a comforting room, rustic and antiquated in its design, with chairs and a sofa, lit by the blaze of a fireplace, with hardwood floors and shelves . . . lots and lots of shelves. And onto the shelves, archaic bound paper books representing all the accumulated knowledge of his life fell into place. He stood enclosed within a quaint but familiar library—the official archive of his mind.

Next to him in the room stood Saavik, looking about with approval. *Excellent,* Saavik commented. *Now you know what we must do.*

Indeed, he did know. In the center of the room lay a large, colorful throw rug. David grabbed the edge and threw it aside, revealing the floor's wooden slats beneath. Saavik kneeled, setting her palms upon the floor, and found a hidden latch. She turned it, and a hidden trap door was revealed. The aperture swung open with a creak, exposing a dark shaft that fell away into nothingness.

Together they approached the long shelves and began to selectively remove volumes from the stacks. David held a book in each hand: *Biochemical Modification of Ecological Systems,* and *Principles of the Meta-Genome.* He tossed both into the hole in the floor. Saavik removed *Molecular Waveform Reorganization* and *Propagated Metastasis* from the shelf, and they followed the others into the darkness beneath their feet. As a well-coordinated team, they pored over the contents of the library and, one by one, removed anything that might reveal David's intimate knowledge of the secret Genesis technology, and concealed it within the hidden vault.

Once they were satisfied, they closed and sealed the trap door, the seams around the opening disappearing into the gaps between the floorboards, and Saavik pulled the rug back into place.

As they stood in the center of the room, David looked around, assessing what they had accomplished. The shelves about him were by no means bare—in fact, they'd worked to eliminate any large gaps that might arouse suspicion. But now for the first time, David became aware that something significant had been changed within his memory. The science, his research, the myriad experiments that made up the Genesis Project . . . all that knowledge was gone from his mind. He could hardly remember what the project even entailed, except for what he had discovered during their recent investigation of the Genesis Planet.

Saavik, he said, though at some level he realized that he wasn't actually speaking the words. *It's all gone! It's . . . it's my whole life's work, and I can't remember any of it!*

Relax, Saavik assured him. *The knowledge is still buried deep within your subconscious. It can be retrieved. But now it is important that you assume the role . . .*

"Hey! None of that in the brig! Keep your hands to yourselves!"

David spun around to see Torg standing at the entrance to the library with two guards close behind him. As the Klingons approached, the tranquil image of the room around him began to shift, losing focus and cohesion, until the illusion completely faded away. David was still seated in their cell aboard the *Katai,* and Saavik was still gently holding his head between her fingertips. Torg forcefully placed his arm between them and shoved Saavik aside, and she fell backward onto the hard surface of the metal bench. Infuriated, David lunged at Torg, but the other two guards each grabbed an arm and easily restrained him.

"Don't try to be a hero, human," Torg admonished him. "If you cooperate, there's a slim chance that you may get out of here alive."

"You'll have to forgive me if I have trouble believing you," David shot back.

"David!" Saavik said, having pulled herself back up to a sitting position. "You need to cooperate. Just do what they ask. After all, we have nothing to hide."

He stared at her, and realized that she was right. His mind felt as barren as an empty house, once lived in as a home, but now bereft of all furnishings except for bare hooks on the walls and stained carpets on the floor. There was nothing left to be hidden.

David Marcus made no effort to resist as Torg strapped restraints onto his arms and legs as he lay face-up on the cold steel table in the *Katai* sickbay. He felt mildly nauseous as the odor of charred flesh and ozone still hung in the air from the earlier "treatment" of his amputated limb, and the pain still left him in a terribly weakened state. But even if he still had the strength left to fight, this was the fate to which he had resigned himself. This was the risk that Saavik had asked him to take, and he was willing to gamble his safety for her, not to mention for the sake of the entire Federation.

He did briefly test the strength of the bindings, more out of curiosity and instinct than any real expression of protest. This, he thought, was how they used to bind prisoners on Earth hundreds of years ago, before executing them by injecting them with lethal doses of chemicals, and they too rarely fought against the inevitable. The difference was that David, at least, held on to the hope that he might survive with his faculties intact.

Maltz approached the table holding a thin tricorder with a large display. He punched the buttons and adjusted the dials with a certain disturbing eagerness, then attached a few wires and cables to it before handing the entire contraption to Kruge, who came up behind him, looking on with mild interest. To the other ends of the wires he attached a large metallic halo, which he fitted over David's temples. One additional wire fed into a crude control panel of sorts mounted upon a nearby pedestal.

David remembered hearing stories about the Klingons and their ability to wipe the memories of their adversaries. He had no idea what a "mind-sifter" looked like, or if the device they were currently employing was in any way typical. He could only hope that Maltz knew what he was doing, and that he would show some level of restraint before permanently emptying his mind.

"My lord," Maltz said, "you will see the bipolar montage on the readout, filtered into alpha and beta waveforms. Once we scan to a depth where visual data can be resolved, it will appear on the screen."

"Yes, yes, just get to it!" Kruge spat impatiently.

"Of course, sir." He flipped a switch on the control panel, and in that instant, David lost control of his mind.

That is not to say that he had lost his sanity; but rather, all of the conscious functions of his brain—things that he had spent a lifetime assuming were in his own complete control—were suddenly at the whim of a mechanical device. Images from his past were forcibly and chaotically dredged out of his deepest memories and played out before him. Unlike the mind-meld he had experienced earlier with Saavik, this was not a warm, shared experience. This was rape.

David focused his concentration despite the unpleasantness, making use of his own limited mental discipline, aided by the energy he had wisely conserved by not resisting until now. He had to bring order to the turmoil cascading through his memories. Knowing exactly what they were looking for, he simply had to provide a frame of reference, and to lead them precisely where they wanted to go.

Like pieces of a puzzle, the random flurry of memories and bits of knowledge began settling into an orderly mosaic. . . . He had returned to the library. The same images of antique books, representing all of his codified memories, still lined the shelves. The fire still burned in the fireplace, the pictures still hung upon the walls, and the rug still concealed the secret vault of his deep subconscious.

No sooner did the placid image appear than it was disturbed by a fierce commotion. The walls of the room shook and the sounds of repeated battering against the entrance reverberated through the hardwood floor until the door violently crashed inward. Dark figures swarmed in between the jagged edges of the ruined framework and descended like vultures upon the neatly arranged stacks surrounding the room. Though humanoid in shape, they had no obvious features, existing more as vague shadows. Individually but with breathtaking swiftness they rifled through the books, checking each title before unceremoniously throwing them aside.

Additional figures shuffled throughout the room, opening drawers on endtables, knocking items off shelves, and even peering intently into the burning logs in the fire. In a short time, the room was completely ransacked—the shelves emptied and the contents of David's mind haphazardly scattered in random piles all over the floor. On some barely conscious level, David was aware of the jumbled mess the mind-sifter had made of his memories. But at least they were still intact.

Having failed to find the information they were seeking, the ghostly shapes began to circle the room aimlessly, until they stopped all at once, as if receiving new instructions. One by one, the beings turned and headed toward the exit.

The last remaining figure had stood alone in the farthest corner of the room, awaiting its turn to depart following all of the others. Finally it took a step forward only to stop short at the sound of a loud *crunch*. The scene around it appeared to freeze in time. The shadowy specter slowly kneeled and retrieved an item from the floor.

It was a picture frame. Though the glass was shattered, the vibrant colors of the frame seemed to emit a soothing, radiant glow. The static photograph set within, while undamaged, had a peculiar quality about it—the image was not only soft, seeming to phase in and out of focus, but also appeared almost surreal, as if the product of some unrealized fantasy.

The photograph was of James Kirk and Carol Marcus. And a small brass plaque at the bottom of the frame read, "Mom and Dad."

The surrounding surfaces in the room began to shimmer and slowly dissolve away, revealing the colorless, sterile walls of the Klingon sickbay. The black, featureless figure still gripping the picture began to morph into a more rigidly defined shape, developing unpleasantly familiar features, until David saw Commander Kruge standing before him, staring down at the tricorder in his hand.

"What is it, my lord?" Maltz said from somewhere behind David's head.

Kruge's eyes had widened to a point where it appeared his eyeballs were at risk of popping from their sockets. He slowly exhaled, then asked, "The device is off? These images are saved and filed?"

"Yes, m'lord," Maltz replied, craning his neck to get a glance at the screen.

David found that he was panting with exhaustion. The mind-sifter had drained both his mind and his body of energy in ways that he had never known were possible. He felt confused and disoriented, and certainly lacked the stamina or the will to endure another session, should it come to that.

Torg looked over Kruge's shoulder at the tricorder display. "It's the Starfleet admiral!" he exclaimed, pointing to the image of Kirk. "The one from the recording you obtained!"

"Yes, I know," Kruge replied. "The Genesis commander himself. Maltz! You're sure the boy knows nothing of value?"

"We could try a higher setting, and wipe his mind completely," Maltz said. "But it appears unlikely that he would have any useful knowledge."

"Then put him back in the brig," Kruge replied, his face revealing the cunning machinations already at work within his own mind. "Don't damage him any further. We've just found ourselves quite a valuable hostage."

In the eighty-three years since the Rigel colonies had achieved Federation membership, Rigel X remained the one world where U.F.P. governance still seemed to have little appreciable impact. True to its roots as a trading outpost established hundreds of years earlier, the planet had no native inhabitants and relatively few permanent residents, save for the owners of several hundred merchant shops and service industries, passed down through families over many generations. Given the overwhelming majority of visiting traders and patrons who were not Federation citizens, precious metals and crystals were still the preferred units of currency, food was bartered as often as parts and supplies, and law enforcement was lackadaisical when it was available at all.

Thelin had arrived on the nighttime side of Rigel X with some trepidation, having never visited the colony before, and with discretion requiring that no one in Starfleet be aware of his presence there. Prior to his departure, he had chosen to confide in Kirk only as to his travel plans, but did not share his reasons, much to the confused chagrin of the admiral. Far too many unanswered questions yet existed to justify getting Kirk involved in a potentially explosive, emotional situation just two months after the death of his son.

The Andorian entered a dark, dreary-looking tavern—the name of which, he noted, with irony, read "The Clandestine Rendezvous" in the Orion language—at precisely five minutes prior to the designated time given in the mysterious communiqué he had received. Predictably murky and crowded, the room was filled to capacity with patrons from dozens of different worlds—some humanoid, some not; some citizens of the Federation, some of various species that Thelin didn't even recognize—all in various stages of intoxication. A green-skinned Orion woman served up drinks from behind the bar, and an odd musical motif played in the background—twelve-toned, from the sound of it.

Moving toward the rear of the room, he climbed a few short steps to an upper platform set off from the rest of the establishment by a long, sweeping railing. By some miracle he located an empty table near a back corner, secluded enough to remain inconspicuous yet positioned so that he could observe the entire bar. Within moments an Orion waitress approached him.

"Hi, hon," she said with forced brightness. "Are you waiting for someone?"

"I hope so," Thelin replied. "Or else I've made this trip for nothing."

"Well, can I get you something?"

"Just Altair water."

"Got it," she said, and disappeared back into the crowd.

Minutes passed. A human-looking man approached his table, diminutive in stature, with long, dark wavy hair, holding a multi-colored, sparkling drink in his hand. "Why, Thelin of Andoria!" he exclaimed. "Is this seat taken?"

Thelin scrutinized the man's face. Something about him

seemed awfully familiar, but the memory was fleeting, and he couldn't nail it down. "I trust it shall be, if indeed you are the one who brought me here."

The man smiled, setting down his glass, then seating himself in the chair opposite Thelin. "Well, of course. I have some very important information to pass along from some very important people."

"You mean some very important criminals," Thelin construed. "Otherwise we wouldn't be going through all this subterfuge."

The man laughed heartily, and shrugged in acknowledgment. "You always were the clever one, weren't you? My . . . it's been a while since we met on Deep Space K-7, hasn't it?"

A light of recognition flashed on in Thelin's mind. "Arne Darvin!" he exclaimed with more than a hint of revulsion, recalling the man's role some seventeen years earlier as a surgically altered Klingon spy.

Darvin nodded noncommittally as he sipped his drink. "Well, I go by many names, and I must say I've rather grown to detest that one in particular . . . but if it helps to breed some familiarity between us, so be it."

"I thought you were in prison," the Andorian said.

"I was in prison," he said scornfully, "for several months before I was returned to the Empire in a prisoner exchange."

"They released you? Pfft," Thelin spat. "I'd have thrown away the key." The Orion waitress returned and set down a glass of clear liquid in front of the Andorian.

"Oh, come now, Thelin," Darvin said. "No one died except a few thousand of those miserable furry little beasts. If anything, I did the people on that station a favor."

"You're very lucky that I discovered the tribbles had been poisoned," Thelin said. "If that grain had reached Sherman's Planet and been fed to the colonists, thousands of *people* could have died."

"Oh, yes, of course, I'm *very* lucky," Darvin said as he raised his glass to his lips again while rolling his eyes. "Please, keep reminding me to express my eternal gratitude. I tend to forget such things."

Thelin shook his head. "And now here you are . . . an errand boy for intragalactic outlaws."

"What would you have me do?" Darvin's affable façade had begun to crumble away. "Did you think I could return to Qo'noS? I am without a house, without honor . . . a pariah within the Klingon Empire. *Where would you have me go, Thelin of Andoria???*"

Thelin had no answer. He casually looked about, but Darvin's fit of pique didn't seem to be attracting any unwelcome attention.

"That's what I thought," Darvin continued. "You pampered Federation types are so accustomed to your lives of ease, everything provided for you. I'm just looking to secure my next meal. So spare me your platitudes."

Thelin sighed, and took a long sip of his drink. He wasn't particularly interested in debating the wisdom of Arne Darvin's career choices. "So . . . would you mind explaining why we are here?"

Darvin's face visibly brightened. "Surely you learned all the pertinent details from my message?"

"If they were so pertinent," Thelin replied, "perhaps you should have been less cryptic. *'Prometheus in bindings for the sins of the father. A new Genesis must dawn. Tell no one.'* Along with the current stardate and coordinates of this place."

"I know!" Darvin grinned. "Clever, isn't it?"

"Many things seem clever to an imbecile."

"Oh, come now, Thelin, it's ancient Earth mythology! I thought someone with your gifts would at least have a clue." He leaned in closer, and raised his eyebrows inscrutably. "It's David Marcus, Kirk's son. He's alive."

Thelin's antennae quivered, then lay back nearly prone against his skull. His eyes widened, and his hand gripped his glass tightly enough that it was on the verge of shattering. "What are you talking about?" he hissed.

"It's true," Darvin said, leaning back and smiling smugly. "He and some half-breed Vulcan girl are in the care of a Klingon commander by the name of Kruge. Oh, don't try to contact him through any diplomatic channels. He's a rogue; the Klingon High Council would surely deny knowing anything."

"I'm sure they would," Thelin said through clenched teeth. "What does he want?"

"Ah! See, that's the best part," he said, maintaining his friendly pretense. "It's really not much at all . . . Not for the life of a Starfleet admiral's son, anyway . . ."

Thelin angrily pounded the tabletop with both fists. *"What does he want?!"*

"He just wants *Genesis,* my friend!" Darvin said brightly, spreading his palms outward. "That's all. Just a little friendly sharing of technology. After all, I hear it's just used for harmless terraforming . . . that's the story, anyway. I'm sure it couldn't possibly be just a front for a secret new Starfleet defense program."

Thelin looked away, fearing that the mere sight of the weasel seated before him would soon lead to an explosive loss of self-control. "What makes you think that either Kirk or I have any access to the project?"

"Don't play games with me, Thelin," Darvin said, a bit of seriousness creeping into his voice. "Kirk has been close to the project ever since the incident in the Mutara Nebula. That much we know. It won't be difficult for a Starfleet admiral to assemble and deliver all of the scientific data regarding the Genesis program."

"Is that all?" Thelin asked glibly.

"Just that," Darvin replied, "plus a working prototype of the Genesis Device."

The Andorian snarled with rage. "Are you kidding? You want us to just hand over a weapon like that to the Klingons?!"

"A *weapon?* I never said anything about a weapon!" He let out a gasp, feigning shock with ridiculous insincerity. "Are *you* saying that Genesis is a weapon?"

In a blur of motion Thelin jumped to his feet and lunged across the table, knocking both glasses to the floor. In an instant he held Darvin by the throat. At the surrounding tables, a few heads turned in mild interest, but no one seemed to find the outburst at all remarkable. "I should snap your neck right now, you miserable *shax,*" Thelin growled.

Darvin smiled widely, showing off his perfect surgically altered human teeth. "I know you should, Thelin." Then the corners of his mouth began to curl upward in a confrontational sneer, his eyes narrowed, and he whispered, "What you don't know is that I would *love* to see you try."

"I am a Starfleet captain," Thelin whispered back. "If I say that I killed you in self-defense, no one will question it."

"Yes, of course," Darvin replied, returning to his maddening congenial tone. "But unfortunately, Kruge is expecting my call within the next two hours. If he doesn't hear back with your acceptance of his terms, I'm afraid that poor David won't be coming home . . . *alive.*"

Thelin felt his pulse pounding through all of his limbs. He vividly imagined Darvin's self-satisfied face with an *ushaan-tor* blade embedded in his forehead. But clearly the exiled Klingon was holding all the cards. If David's life was truly at stake, there was no choice but to accept these terms. Thelin unclasped his hands and sat back in his chair as Darvin calmly worked to straighten his collar. "When do we make the exchange?" Thelin asked resignedly.

"Ah! I knew you'd listen to reason." Darvin jumped to his feet and pushed in his chair. "I'll be in touch. Expect a message with the stardate and coordinates to rendezvous with Kruge's ship. If we all just cooperate, this can be nice and painless, right? Anyway, I truly enjoyed seeing you again."

With a wave, he turned and began maneuvering his way back through the crowd.

Thelin remained seated at the table for a very long time. He knew that Kirk had barely been able to cope with the knowledge that his son was dead. He wondered how Kirk would possibly cope now with the knowledge that he was alive.

4

One by one, the images were downloaded via subspace transmission and appeared on Kirk's screen: blueprints, specifications, and technical documentation on the Klingon *B'rel*-class bird-of-prey. As he browsed through them, his demeanor visibly brightened. The last few days had been a nightmarish emotional roller coaster, driving Kirk into headstrong action without any second thought. His focus was solely upon David's welfare; the manner of the young man's liberation was an afterthought. But this new information would certainly put them in a much stronger position to accomplish that goal.

He reached out and pressed a few keys on his desktop terminal, bringing the video communication back onto the main screen. The face of a young Romulan woman reappeared, smiling, her long dark hair wrapped tightly into a tall pillar. *"I hope you will find the information useful, Admiral,"* she said.

"Ambassador Dar," Kirk said. "I cannot begin to express my deepest gratitude. Hopefully this will help us to resolve the matter without creating an intragalactic incident."

"No gratitude is necessary, Admiral," Caithlin Dar said from her office on Nimbus III. *"When you informed me of Saavik's capture, my responsibility was clear. Please bring her and your son back safely."*

"From your lips, Ambassador."

"Jolan'tru."

The image was replaced by the Federation emblem, and Kirk quickly tapped a few additional buttons, then waited for his new transmission to work its way through the subspace communications network. He sat back in his chair and slowly glanced around at the barren walls of his quarters aboard the *Enterprise*. He had cleared out all his personal possessions weeks ago, when the official announcement was made about the ship's decommissioning. Granted, he hadn't officially had quarters on the ship for years, ever since Thelin took over the captaincy. But he still felt at home there—a reflection of the fact that, in his heart, he had never truly given her up.

But now, his only personal effect in the room was a photograph of David.

After a few moments, the graceful features of Nyota Uhura's face appeared on the terminal viewscreen. "Commander!" Kirk warmly acknowledged her. "Is this channel secure?"

"*Yes, Admiral,*" Uhura responded. "*In fact, I'm piggybacking onto the control signals from several sensor buoys in your area. Starfleet won't be able to trace it; don't worry. What's your status?*"

Kirk smiled. Uhura's communications skills were still held in high esteem, and he was lucky to have served with her so many years. "Steady as she goes, I guess. We should be nearing the DMZ around Klingon space in a few hours. Are you going to be able to lie low until this blows over?"

"*As a matter of fact, I'm now officially taking my leave, and unless they're on their way to arrest me, I plan to head out of San Francisco within the hour.*"

Kirk hoped she was joking. "I can't imagine they've discovered your involvement already. But . . . how is the buzz back at headquarters?"

"*Rather interesting! After all, it's not every day that a decorated Starfleet admiral steals a starship.*" Then her brow furrowed slightly. "*But as it happens, they seem to have their hands full with some other crisis right now . . . Some sort of unidentified probe slowly approaching the Sol sector, and it's been disabling all outposts and starships in its path.*"

Kirk wondered at this odd news, but under the circumstances he had more pressing matters at hand. "Well, we'll keep this channel open. Please keep me informed. I . . ." He paused. His fragile emotional state was strained to the point of breaking; he merely wanted to express his gratitude, but felt he could lose his composure at any moment. "I wanted to thank you again for your assistance. I wish there had been another way, but we couldn't bring Starfleet into this. The danger was too great."

"Admiral, your family is our family. I wouldn't have it any other way. The consequences are the least of my concerns."

Kirk averted his gaze. "Well . . . nonetheless, I'm grateful. And . . . very lucky to have such friends."

"Godspeed, Jim. Uhura out."

"We are approaching the designated coordinates," Thelin announced from the science station. "Scans reveal no ships in the vicinity."

Kirk fidgeted nervously in the captain's chair, and the rest of the skeleton crew on the *Enterprise* bridge seemed unusually apprehensive as well. This was no ordinary mission. Each of them had made a decision to risk his career in Starfleet so that Kirk's son might be saved—Thelin at the science station, Sulu and Chekov at the helm, and Scotty running a makeshift automation center from the operations consoles—and failure was not an option with so much at stake.

"No, they won't show up on scans," Kirk said. "Even the Klingons can't detect their own cloaked ships. See if you can discover an ion plasma trail. If they're in the vicinity, the impulse engines will leave a signature."

"A needle in a haystack," grumbled Doctor McCoy, the final member of the tiny crew, seated at one of the rear tactical stations with a characteristically dour expression. Normally he would be in the sickbay, preparing for the worst possible consequences, but given that the rest of the ship was deserted, it was only natural that he would choose to remain on the bridge. "Coming out here to meet a ship we can't even see? We might as well have painted a bull's-eye on the hull."

"We know they can't fire on us while cloaked," Kirk assured him. "If we stay vigilant, we can still have a tactical advantage."

Thelin silently agreed, but acknowledged to himself the caveat that a starship with just a fraction of its intended crew complement was in no condition to engage in battle. He reinitiated his scan with the new parameters. The data they had received on the new Klingon birds-of-prey had already proven useful. He only hoped it would be sufficient.

"We've reached the rendezvous point, Admiral," Chekov declared from the navigation station.

"Full stop, Mister Sulu," Kirk said.

"Aye, sir," Sulu replied. The hum of the impulse engines died away to a barely audible whirr.

A flashing indicator on Thelin's console grabbed his attention. "I've got something," he announced. "It might just be some ionized gas, but it's at bearing twenty-four mark two-oh-one."

"On screen," Kirk said.

The starfield adjusted its position on the viewscreen. At the center of the image, a rippling distortion effect was visible among the solid points of light. Kirk stood up and walked toward the helm, pointing at the display. "There!" he said. "That shimmering area. Do you see it?"

"Yes, sir," Sulu responded. "I think it's an energy form."

"Enough energy to hide a ship, perhaps?" Kirk asked.

"The cloaking device!" Sulu answered.

"Shields up," Kirk commanded. "If nothing else, they aren't going to have the element of surprise."

The distortion upon the viewscreen grew more pronounced until, within moments, it resolved into the image of a Klingon bird-of-prey. Thelin moved over to the communications console and read from the flashing indicators on the display. "We are being hailed," he called out. "Audio only."

"Put it on speakers," Kirk said.

The ship's intercom crackled to life. "*Starship* Enterprise," a voice, presumably that of Commander Kruge, rang out across the bridge. *"How kind of you to drop by. I trust that we have a business transaction to conduct."*

"Open a channel," Kirk coldly growled.

"Channel open," Thelin replied.

"Klingon commander!" Kirk shouted. "This is Admiral James Kirk of the Federation Starship *Enterprise.* We are here to retrieve two Federation citizens who you have illegally kidnapped, and are holding in violation of the terms of the Organian Peace Treaty."

"Do not speak to me of treaty violations, Kirk!" Kruge shouted back. *"The Federation showed its willingness to compromise the terms of the treaty when you created the Genesis weapon. We act only to protect our race."*

"You are mistaken," Kirk replied. "The Genesis technology is entirely peaceful. Its sole purpose is for climate modification and to prepare uninhabitable planets for colonization."

"Excellent," Kruge said. *"In that case, you should have no problem sharing this technology as a token of intragalactic goodwill. You know my terms. You will turn over all data on Genesis, and you will supply a working prototype of the Genesis torpedo. When we are convinced that you have acted in good faith to preserve galactic peace, we will release the prisoners to you."*

"I want to speak to them," Kirk said firmly. "I want assurances that they're all right."

"Stand by," Kruge said with annoyance. *"Brig! Patch your communicators into subspace channel one. Let the prisoners speak."*

They waited a few anxious moments while treated to the sounds of forcefields being released and bodies being shuffled about. Finally a Klingon voice, presumably one of the guards, was heard. *"Speak!"*

A pause. Then a voice was heard—shaking, hollow, sounding as if any pretense of hope had long since been abandoned. *"Uh . . . this is Doctor David Marcus of the Federation."*

Kirk slowly stood. He stared ahead at nothing, as if trying to envision the face of his son. "David? It's Jim Kirk."

"Oh, hey," David replied. *"So they sent out the top brass, huh?"*

"David . . . I would never leave you behind. I came as soon as I knew. Have they . . . have they treated you well?"

"*I'm okay . . . We've spent most of the last two months on Praxis, the Klingon moon. Not really my first choice for a vacation . . . The food kinda sucks.*"

Kirk grinned weakly. Further sounds of movement were heard over the speakers, and then the guard spoke again. "*Speak!*"

"*Admiral, this is Saavik of Vulcan.*"

"Saavik," Kirk said. "How are you holding up?"

"*I am fine, sir. And David's injuries are healing, though some post-traumatic stress remains in evidence.*"

"Injuries?!" Kirk exclaimed. "What injuries? What did they do?"

"*Enough talking,*" Kruge interrupted. "*If you want the hostages released, you will agree to my terms.*"

"What the hell did you do to my son, you bastard?!" Kirk shouted.

"*You will transmit your files on Genesis within the next thirty seconds. If you do not comply, I will kill one of the hostages.*"

"All right, dammit, just hold on." Kirk made a cutting motion across his neck with his hand, and Thelin, understanding the signal, interrupted the communication. "Thelin, you know what to do. Begin transmitting."

"Aye, sir," the Andorian responded. He flipped a switch, and the file transfer began. At the same time, interleaved on the same frequency, he initiated a bio-scan for life signs on the Klingon vessel. The surreptitious nature of the scan meant that it would not be detected unless their adversaries were specifically monitoring for such a ploy.

Within seconds he had his results. "I have them, Admiral. Two life signs in the brig on the lower deck—one human, one Vulcan. I'm feeding the precise coordinates to Mister Scott's screen. As soon as the Klingons drop their shields for us to transport the torpedo, he can transport the hostages out of there."

"Good work, Thelin," Kirk said excitedly.

But no sooner did the words leave his lips than the voice of

Kruge once again rang out across the bridge. *"That won't work, Kirk! We've detected your scan. Did you think I wouldn't be looking out for your duplicity?"*

"Reopen the channel," Kirk said. "Commander," he appealed to Kruge, trying to sound apologetic. "We just wanted confirmation that the two hostages are on board. After all, you could have been falsifying their voices."

"Listen very carefully, Kirk. The entire brig is magnetically shielded. Any attempt to beam out the hostages will get you a jumble of grotesque dead flesh."

Kirk whirled around to face Thelin's station, where the Andorian was already running scans to verify Kruge's claim. The results were distressing. "Confirmed, sir," Thelin said. "Beaming in or out of the brig won't be possible."

The computer console chirped. *"Transmission complete,"* it announced.

It didn't take long for the Klingons to examine the cache of electronic data files they had just received. The voice of Kruge was heard over the open channel, arguing with his bridge crew. *"What are you saying, Maltz? Why can't you read the data?"*

"It appears to be encrypted, sir," the voice of Maltz replied.

"Kirk!" Kruge angrily shouted. *"You're trying my patience!"*

"You have the data," Kirk explained. "Now it's your turn. Release the hostages, and I'll provide the decryption key and the Genesis torpedo."

"What kind of idiot do you take me for?" Kruge hissed. *"You expect me to give up my only leverage, so that you can beam over a torpedo already armed for detonation?"*

A silent pause, then Kruge continued. *"I will release one of the prisoners as a token of my . . . goodwill."* He spat out the last word as if it made him violently ill to say it. *"You will agree to simultaneous exchange and send over the Genesis device. This is not subject to negotiation."*

Kirk took a moment to consider. "All right," he said. "Your terms are understood. Stand by for transport."

The admiral turned to face his small crew—his friends, who

had put their entire careers on the line to accompany him on this mission. "Well, gentlemen . . . It looks like our hand is pretty weak, and we only have one card left to play."

"We vill support your decision, Admiral," Chekov said.

"Just give the word, Admiral," Sulu agreed.

"Aye, let's git on with it!" Scotty added.

Kirk looked over at Thelin, who merely bowed his head in approval.

"Thank you, my friends," Kirk humbly acknowledged. "To the transporter room."

Aboard the *Katai,* the Klingon transporter operator stood at attention as the doors opened and Torg entered, escorting the Vulcan prisoner. Visibly agitated as the young woman bantered with him, Torg growled at her, "You're being released! Now shut up and get on the platform before I disobey orders and disintegrate that pretty little mouth of yours."

Not willing to chance the possibility that Torg was serious in his threat, Saavik pressed her lips tightly together and stepped onto the nearest transporter pad. At the transporter console, Kruge's voice called out from the intercom. *"Transporter room! Prepare for simultaneous transport with* Enterprise. *Engage!"*

"Yes, sir," the operator responded. He moved the sliders on the control panel, and Saavik's form on the platform began to dematerialize, accompanied by the telltale whine and the sparkling energy from the containment beam. In the same instant, on the pad next to hers, a twinkling form gradually coalesced into the shape of a tall storage ark—a metallic obelisk about two meters tall with no readily discernible markings.

The operator punched the intercom on the console. "My lord, we have the Genesis device."

"Inspect the cargo," Kruge commanded. *"Report immediately when you have verified its authenticity."*

Torg approached the platform, and turned two metallic latches along the vertical seam at the front of the container. Slowly he pushed apart the two halves of the ark.

A phaser beam lanced outward from the interior of the ark and struck Torg squarely in the chest. With a muffled, nasal groan, he tumbled to the deck.

The officer behind the transporter console immediately stepped backward, fumbling about his holster for his weapon. But by the time he was able to successfully retrieve it, the two halves of the ark had splayed open, and there stood Chekov, his own phaser trained directly between the Klingon's astonished eyes. "Drop your weapon, *now,*" the Russian officer commanded.

The Klingon did so, his mouth standing agape at what was transpiring.

"What?" Chekov said. "You never heard the ancient Russian legend of the Trojan Horse?"

The Klingon shook his head.

"Ah, vell . . . Forgive me, but I need to stun you now."

And he did.

On the bridge of the *Katai,* Kruge impatiently drummed his fingers on the armrests of his chair. "What the *khest* is taking so long?" He punched the control to activate the intercom. "Transporter room! What is your status?"

No response.

"My lord!" Maltz shouted from the operations station. "Our transporter was just activated!"

"What?!" Kruge shouted, jumping down from his seat. "How is that possible? I ordered the shields raised!"

"They are, sir! No one can beam here from the outside," Maltz explained. "But our own transporter can still beam things onto the ship through the modulations in our shield frequency."

"Sir!" another officer interrupted. "I'm reading three . . . no, *four* intruders on board!"

"*Ghuy'cha'!!!!*" Kruge bellowed. "Remodulate the shields! I don't want anything else beamed onto this ship! You three!" He indicated the guards nearest the bridge entrance. "Intercept the intruders. The rest of you, secure the bridge!" He slammed his fist onto the intercom panel. "And brig! Kill the remaining hostage! *NOW!!!*"

The three guards quickly drew their disruptors and exited through the rear doors of the bridge, which opened into the long access corridor spanning the entire length of the hull.

"Down there!" the lead Kingon shouted, pointing ahead toward the aft end of the vessel. One of the intruders—a middle-aged human, by the looks of him—had just rounded the corner to the right at the far end and descended down the stairwell to the lower deck. The three guards rushed past the transporter room on the starboard side in hurried pursuit of their target. As they crossed the threshold into the main hull, shots rang out behind them, and two of the guards crumpled onto the walkway. The third guard turned just in time to see an Andorian and a darker-haired human, having just emerged from the transporter room into the corridor, fire the shots that sent his vision plummeting into darkness.

"Kill the remaining hostage! NOW!"

Kruge's words sent chills through Kirk's spine as they echoed through the hull of the *Katai.* The Starfleet admiral was now a desperate father, and he was wasting no time. From the instant he materialized on the Klingon transporter pad alongside Thelin and Sulu, he made a mad dash down the corridor to the stairway at the aft end of the ship.

Kirk flew down the steps to the lower level, his phaser in his right hand, his left hand steadying his descent. Upon reaching the floor of the lower deck, he gripped the end of the rail and spun himself around, using his momentum to propel himself down the short corridor to the brig. Without warning, the heat of a disruptor blast singed the hair above his ear and impacted the staircase behind him with a crack and the hiss of superheated metal. He dropped to one knee and rolled over, coming up to a sitting position with his phaser at the ready, firing. The guard at the door to the brig toppled forward.

With a nimbleness he didn't know he still possessed, he leaped over the guard's prone form and into the brig. The forcefield at the entrance to the cell was disarmed, and inside the cell stood the lone remaining guard—his left arm wrapped around David's neck, his right hand holding a disruptor against David's temple.

Kirk froze, horrified at the sight of his son. His face still showed signs of bruising from the torture inflicted upon him weeks earlier. His clothes were still stained and matted with dried blood. And his left arm still ended at the wrist in a grisly cauterized stump.

"Drop your weapon or he dies," the Klingon ordered.

Staring helplessly at the weapon aimed at his son's head, he did as he was told.

"Kick it over here."

The phaser spun to a stop at the Klingon's feet in the center of the cell. He shoved David away, over to Kirk's side just within the entrance of the cell, keeping his own weapon trained on both of them, then stooped to pick up the phaser. Pocketing the extra weapon, he then retrieved his communicator from another pocket. "Brig to Kruge!" he called into the device. "I have the Starfleet admiral! What are your orders, my lord?"

As the doors to the *Katai* bridge slid shut behind the three guards delegated to delay the intruders, the three officers remaining on the bridge with Kruge sprang into action. "Bridge doors are sealed," one of the men spoke from the security console.

"Shield modulations are complete," Maltz called out. "Nothing further can be beamed on or off the ship."

"Very good, Maltz," Kruge said. "Now go to the weapons console and target the *Enterprise* warp core. If they lower their shields for an instant, you're to blow them to *Gre'thor*."

Maltz moved to the console at the aft end of the port side of the bridge. "Target locked, my lord."

"Assume defensive positions," Kruge ordered, and the other two men scrambled to stand in between Kruge and the rear entrance to the bridge, disruptors at the ready. Maltz rose from his station and stood facing the doors with his weapon drawn as well. Within moments, they were aware of a commotion out in the corridor—banging noises as the Starfleet boarding party attempted to force their way through the doors, punctuated by occasional phaser blasts impacting against the metal. The racket increased in intensity, finally culminating in the sound of a shrill whine.

Kruge looked to his left, to his right, and above his head. "What's that noise?" he demanded.

Suddenly all fell silent. Then from behind them, at the fore of the bridge, a clear, commanding voice rang out. "Don't turn around. It would be so dishonorable to have to shoot you all in the back. Now, all of you, drop your weapons."

They did so. Seconds later, the bridge doors finally opened and Sulu entered, Chekov rushing in just behind him. The two men gathered up the assortment of dropped weapons, then ordered the four Klingon officers to place their hands upon their heads and to move toward the row of consoles on the port side of the bridge.

As Kruge turned, accompanied by his defeated men, he saw Thelin standing alone in front of the viewscreen. "You transported in here!" he grumbled, then stared coldly at Maltz. "I thought no one else could transport through the shields!"

Thelin looked at him with amusement. "No one else transported through the shields, you fool," he said. "I transported onto the bridge from your own transporter room."

The bridge intercom chirped, and the voice of a guard was heard from the lower deck. *"Brig to Kruge! I have the Starfleet admiral! What are your orders, my lord?"*

The three Starfleet officers exchanged hurried glances. "I'm on it," Sulu said, and he dashed through the doors and down the corridor.

The Klingon guard in the brig was growing visibly agitated as he shouted into his communicator. "Commander Kruge, come in! I have two prisoners on the lower deck! Requesting instructions!"

"Sounds like he's indisposed right now," Kirk observed. "Perhaps you should leave a message, and he can get back to you later."

"Shut up, human!" the Klingon spat, raising his weapon. "My last orders were to kill the prisoner. Perhaps I should carry out that order."

Kirk and David each took a step back, stumbling slightly as they crossed the threshold at the entrance to the cell. The exit into the outer corridor beckoned about ten feet away, but they couldn't possibly outrun a disruptor blast to reach it. "There's no need to kill anyone," Kirk argued. "We're your hostages. You can use us as leverage; take back the ship."

With a flurry of footsteps, Sulu rushed through the entryway.

"Stop!" the Klingon shouted. "Drop your weapon or these two men are dead."

Sulu raised his hands, his own weapon pointed benignly at the ceiling as he looked about the outer area of the brig, assessing the situation. "All right," he said calmly. "Don't do anything hasty. I'll toss you my phaser, okay?" He kept his left hand held high as he let the phaser hang loosely in his right, holding the grip by his fingertips. Slowly he stepped up to the entrance of the cell, leaning down to the ground, prepared to slide the weapon toward the Klingon guard.

And as he knelt, his left hand touched the control panel at the side of the cell entrance, engaging the forcefield.

The Klingon looked about as the shimmering bands of energy left him trapped within the cell. "Hey!" he shouted angrily. He fired his phaser into the forcefield, only to watch the bolt harmlessly dissipate throughout the barrier.

"Well, that was easy," Sulu said. "Admiral, the bridge has been secured."

"Good work, Mister Sulu. We need to go back to the main deck and see if a Klingon officer is still aft, in engineering."

"Oh, him? I intercepted him on the way down here. He was led by some large smelly animal. I had to stun that thing twice."

"Excellent," Kirk said, smiling. "Get back up there and get the rest of the crew secured."

"Aye, sir. And it's good to have you back, Doctor Marcus." Sulu turned and dashed back up the stairs.

Kirk and David remained in the brig, along with the Klingon guard who now sat morosely upon the bench in the cell. Kirk stared at David with contrition. "I'm sorry I couldn't get here sooner."

"You came," David replied. "That's all that matters."

And they warmly embraced, poignantly aware for the first time of the unbreakable bond between father and son.

The mood was jovial as Kirk and David entered the bridge of the *Katai,* and the *Enterprise* officers each in turn expressed their elation at David's safe rescue, his terrible injuries notwithstanding. Kruge and his three officers remained under guard on the port side of the bridge, scowling with disgust as they overlooked the proceedings. The image of the nearby *Enterprise* shone proudly upon the viewscreen.

Before long, the unconscious members of Kruge's crew had been safely secured in the brig. The two small cells were not terribly accommodating, especially when most of the occupants were lying prostrate upon the floor; Kirk suggested that the remaining four officers be housed in the *Enterprise* brig, where Kirk would have ample opportunity on the trip home to question Kruge about just how widespread support was among the Klingon High Council for his operation.

"Gentlemen," Kirk said, "Sulu and Chekov will stay behind to pilot the bird-of-prey. Thelin, I'll beam over first with David and prepare the *Enterprise* to receive the prisoners."

The rest of the crew nodded their assent. Kirk looked at David, a young man troubled and traumatized, but presently at peace, knowing that he was returning home. Kirk's son was safe, and all was right with the cosmos.

"I want to thank you all again," Kirk quietly offered to his crewmates. "You've all risked your lives and careers, and I will never forget it."

Chekov motioned toward the exit. "Admiral, may I have the honor of transporting you back to your wessel?"

"As you wish, Commander," Kirk replied. He flipped open his communicator as he and David followed Chekov through the doors. "Scotty, lower the *Enterprise* shields and prepare for transport."

"*Aye, sir,*" came the reply, and then the bridge doors closed behind them.

Doctor McCoy had just completed his final diagnostic procedures upon the calmly seated Saavik as the silence on the *Enterprise* bridge was pierced by the sound of two transporter beams penetrating the open area between the helm and the viewscreen. James Kirk, once fully materialized, stepped forward and looked about the bridge of his ship with satisfaction. Beside him, David spied Saavik among the rear consoles, and gingerly but rapidly rushed back to meet her. She stood, and they threw their arms around each other, sharing the joy and relief at their newfound freedom.

Smiling, Kirk followed his son, pausing to pat Scotty on the back as the engineer sat at an operations console monitoring the automation systems that continued to run the ship in the absence of a crew. Finally Kirk stopped in front of McCoy, who was still busily checking the readouts on his medical tricorder. "Well, Doctor," the admiral said. "Is our first patient doing well?"

"Surprisingly well," McCoy said. "No sign of any physical trauma. She's a little weak; probably hasn't eaten much during her captivity. But she'll be fine." He turned to face David, who had released Saavik from his embrace and had dropped into the chair next to hers, allowing himself to rest for the first time that day, if not in months. "Oh my God," McCoy said, noticing for the first time the severed limb. He adjusted the tricorder for the relevant diagnostic and began waving the scanner over the amputation site. He then readjusted the settings, and proceeded to scan David's entire relaxed form.

Kirk looked on anxiously. "How is he, Bones?"

McCoy gave a slight shrug. "Physically, his wounds have all healed. Not surprisingly, he's suffering some long-term effects of stress, but those will subside in time. But Jim . . . Lord only knows what they've been through psychologically. They're going to need more help than what I can offer."

"We're fine," David said. He looked over to Saavik, who smiled back at him meekly, but her uncertain expression suggested that she likely did not share his sunny self-diagnosis. "What?" David responded with indignity. "We were pretty much left alone the whole time we were held on Praxis. We never even saw Kruge while we were there."

Saavik turned to Kirk. "We were placed with the general population at a detention facility in one of the smaller mining towns on the surface of the Klingon moon, presumably so that Kruge could conceal his plans from the authorities on Qo'noS," she explained. "The inmates were mostly petty criminals. There was little significant danger."

"The Klingons were just normal people," David said. "I got to know a few of them. Just people—who had families, and their own hopes and dreams. Nothing like that Kruge," he said with a scowl. "That man is insane with paranoia."

"I'm not surprised," Kirk said. "You know, he's afraid of you."

"Huh?" David said incredulously. "Afraid of me? Why?"

"They fear the power you hold over them."

David shook his head. "I certainly never meant for anyone to fear me or my work."

"Best laid plans of mice and men," McCoy said.

David struggled to remember the significance of the phrase. "I don't understand. That's from a book, isn't it?"

"That's right," Kirk replied. "A poem, actually. It means that despite our best intentions, things often don't turn out like we'd planned."

David considered this. "Yeah, I guess. So now that my life's work is destroyed, what do I do now?"

"You figure out where you belong, David," Kirk assured him. "Where you can make a difference. And whatever you decide to do, I'll be behind you."

Back aboard the *Katai,* Sulu settled into the pilot's chair at the helm. "Did anyone think to bring a translator for written Klingon?" he chuckled.

"Take your time, Sulu," Thelin responded. "We're in no huge hurry to get back. For all we know, Federation police will be waiting to arrest us the moment we enter Earth orbit." He turned toward the line of prisoners standing in front of the navigation and weapons stations and gestured toward the doors with his phaser. "All right, all of you. To the transporter room. Let's go."

The Klingons moved in single file toward the exit. Kruge brought up the rear, following Maltz, with Thelin next to him, keeping him under guard. As they passed the final console closest to the doors—the weapons console—Kruge suddenly barked out, "Maltz! *DaH!!!*" And Kruge spun around, lunged, and grabbed Thelin by the throat.

Taken completely by surprise, the Andorian stumbled backward several steps and wheezed as the fingers of Kruge slowly constricted his windpipe, while the Klingon's hot breath beat down upon him.

In the same instant, Maltz whirled to face the weapons console directly behind him. Several feet away at the helm, Sulu leaped from his chair.

Thelin, still gripping his phaser firmly in his right hand, pressed it into the center of Kruge's chest and pulled the trigger. The Klingon's grinning face winced in pain.

In the fleeting moment before Sulu tackled him, Maltz pounded his fist down upon the firing control. The two of them tumbled in a heap of arms and legs onto the deck. The percussive sound of a torpedo launch echoed through the hull.

Thelin felt the grip of Kruge's fingers upon his neck slowly relax, and the dishonored commander sank to the floor and onto his back, his face still frozen in a twisted smile, his chest bearing the mark of an intense burn from Thelin's weapon. The phaser had merely been set to stun, but at point-blank range, the force of such a shot was almost certainly lethal.

A blinding flash emanated from the viewscreen behind them as the torpedo explosively impacted the secondary hull of the *Enterprise.* Her shields having been lowered for transport, there was nothing to mitigate the force of the blast.

The frantic voice of Scotty sounded over the intercom. *"This is* Enterprise! *What the bloody hell are ye doin'?!"*

Thelin rushed over to the communications console. Punching a control, he opened the two-way channel and put the Scotsman's stunned face upon the viewscreen. "Scotty! Are you all right? Did Kirk and David make it on board?"

"Aye, they're here, but ye made a direct hit on the warp core! All the main power systems are damaged; I canna even get a readin' on the anti-matter containment! What happened?"

"We had some trouble with our prisoners. Stand by," Thelin said anxiously. He rushed by Sulu, who had regained control over the three remaining captives, and thrust himself into the seat at the science station at the aft end of the bridge. Tapping the controls, he performed a quick scan and produced a display of the *Enterprise*'s status. The results were chilling.

Sulu peered over the Andorian's shoulder. "Hull breach on deck fourteen," he said ominously. "That's the upper level of the engineering section."

"Scotty," Thelin called out. "Can you shut down the anti-matter intermix?"

"Aye," he replied. *"But the automation system is down. I'll have to get down ta engineering."*

"You'd better hurry, Scotty. I'm reading a runaway reaction in the intermix chamber . . . probably caused by a coolant leak. If it isn't stopped, it could build up to a core breach in less than five minutes."

Kirk quickly moved into the frame next to Scott on the viewer. "*Chekov! Are you still in the* Katai *transporter room?*"

"*Yes, sir!*" the voice of Chekov replied.

"*Stand by,*" Kirk said.

The *Enterprise* bridge was illuminated by the eerie red glow of emergency lighting as Admiral Kirk moved from station to station, growing increasingly frustrated at the lack of useful information being provided on the readouts.

"Scotty," Kirk said urgently. "Is there any chance of restoring auxiliary power?"

"Perhaps," he replied. "But I canna do it from here. Nae without a crew down there." He rose from his seat and began to head for the bridge exit. "Don't worry. I've got a few more miracles left."

"Scotty, wait!" Kirk ran up to intercept him before he reached the door. "Engineering is fourteen decks down, and we're without turbolifts or transporters." He put a hand on Scotty's shoulder. "Not to put too fine a point on it, but you're not as spry as you once were."

Scott's eyes widened with indignation. "Well, I ne'er . . . !"

"We're completely blind over here. I need you on the other ship to monitor our status, and to guide me if I get into trouble. There's no time to debate. That's an order."

Scott sighed. "Aye," he said resignedly. "But when I get back, we're gonna have a wee little conversation about respect for your elders."

"Fair enough," Kirk said as he flipped open his communicator. "Kirk to Chekov. Beam the other four over to the *Katai,* and keep this channel open. I'm on my way to engineering." Scott, McCoy, David, and Saavik disappeared into the twinkle of the transporter beam; and Kirk was alone. He clipped the communicator to his belt and headed through the port side exit.

Kirk emerged from the Jefferies tube onto deck seven and rushed down the main corridor to the access door for turboshaft three.

The door opened onto a short platform protruding into the wide cylindrical area of the shaft where the turbolifts traversed the span between the decks of the secondary hull. Stepping onto the platform and turning to his left, he gripped the rungs of the vertical access ladder running alongside, and began a quick descent to the engineering section seven decks below.

Knowing he was in a race against time, he skipped over every other rung, and his hands simply slid along the outer frame of the ladder. He was forced to count the decks as he passed them, for they were not labeled on the interior of the shaft, although he noted with annoyance that the designers had elected to number the numerous individual turbolift landing decks—each level having several turbolift stops along its breadth—as he passed a sign misleadingly indicating "Deck 52."

Thelin's voice rang out from the communicator, still active, hanging on Kirk's belt. *"Jim . . . We estimate less than one minute before antimatter containment becomes critical. After that, the only option is to eject the pods from the warp core."*

"Acknowledged, Captain," Kirk replied. "I've reached the upper engineering level. Stand by." He swung from the ladder onto the platform and forced his way through the access door.

Instantly his senses were assailed by the lingering effects of an electrical firestorm. Clouds of smoke bellowed forth, and his lungs protested as he waved his hands in front of his face, waiting for the polluted air to vent into the turboshaft behind him. His eyes burned, and he blinked rapidly in an attempt to focus on the scene laid out before him.

To his left, a gaping hole in the hull provided an accidental window to the starfield outside, with emergency forcefields in place to hold in the pressurized atmosphere. To his right, he looked down on the lower deck of main engineering, where every console was little more than a burned-out shell—some smoking, some still shooting forth electrical sparks. The torpedo's explosion had triggered a raging inferno throughout the engineering section, and without any damage-control teams on board, no one was available to put out the blaze.

The warp core itself, while blackened from the effects of the fire, appeared to be uncompromised. However, the characteristic hum of the warp drive seemed much louder and more high-pitched than what would be expected from a ship at full stop. Without sufficient coolant to stem the reaction, a failure of the antimatter containment could be imminent.

"Scotty, are you reading me?"

"Aye," came the response from the communicator still strapped to Kirk's belt.

"The engineering section is gutted . . . it's a total loss. We have no computer control over anything."

"You'll have ta manually close the valves on the vertical intermix chamber," Scotty said. *"On the lower level, there's an access panel in the floor on the aft side of the warp core, beneath the horizontal chamber. Right in front o' the junction."*

"I read you, Scotty. Stand by." Kirk swiftly shimmied down the ladder to the lower level. Aided by the ever-increasing light from the warp plasma in the core directly before him, he threw aside the floor panel and gripped the spokes of the wheel for the cut-off valve. He twisted it rapidly, despite a new awareness that he was growing quite fatigued.

"Jim," Thelin broke onto the comm channel. *"We're reading an awful lot of radiation leakage throughout that section. It's approaching dangerous levels."*

"Acknowledged," Kirk replied as the wheel came to a halt in the closed position. "Intermix valves are closed." He stood up, but perhaps too abruptly—his vision suddenly clouded, and his knees buckled. He dropped back to one knee. He found himself longing for some fresh air, as it seemed that he could not catch his breath.

The sounds of random chatter began to stream forth from the

communicator. *"No effect,"* the voice of Thelin said. *"The magnetic bottles are too far weakened. Containment is still failing."*

"Aye," Scotty acknowledged. *"The coolant leak must be more widespread than we thought."*

Kirk took a deep breath. "Status, gentlemen?" he asked with frustration.

"Admiral," Scotty replied. *"It's no use. We've got ta eject the antimatter pods within the next two minutes or the explosion will destroy the whole ship. Without computer control, you'll have to manually detonate the explosive bolts. It's five decks below."*

Kirk considered this. His strength was failing him as the effects of the radiation sapped the energy reserves from his body; he didn't know if he could reach his target in the allotted time. But was such an effort really justified? The ship had been racked with horrific damage from the assaults of Khan, and now from the Klingons. She was now just a shell of a once mighty vessel, but she had served her purpose this day: David was alive and well. So why was Kirk still clinging to the past when he should be looking to the future?

"Chekov," he said. "Beam me out of here."

"Aye, Admiral," the commander responded. *"Prepare for transport."*

The reddish hue of the Klingon transporter effect enveloped his body, and he waited for his surroundings to morph into the less familiar environs of the Klingon transporter room. Several seconds passed. The process seemed to be taking far too much time.

Eventually the effect dissipated, but Kirk remained among the charred consoles of the *Enterprise* engine room. Still kneeling, he removed the communicator from his belt and brought it up to his face, hoping that the urgency in his voice might carry more effectively. "Chekov? What's wrong?"

"Stand by, sir," came the anxious response.

Frantic shuffling sounds streamed forth, which Kirk soon interpreted to be Scotty entering the *Katai* transporter room to assist Chekov. *"Just as I thought,"* the Scotsman said. *"Admiral, the breach is causin' too much gamma radiation leakage in your vicinity. It's inter-ferin' wit the transporter beam. If ye can move toward the aft end of the deck, we might get a clearer signal."*

Kirk struggled to his feet and broke into a run alongside the lengthy horizontal intermix chamber that extended many meters back toward the rear of the ship. The muscles in his legs burned with exhaustion, and a wave of nausea flooded over him. His vision again began to leave him, and his balance soon followed, sending him toppling onto the deck. His breath came in quick gasps as he fought to remain conscious. "Scotty," he gasped. "I think you'd better try again."

The transporter beam enveloped him once again, but this time, the duration was much shorter and ended more abruptly. The cold steel of the engineering deck remained solidly beneath him.

"Ach!" Scotty shouted. *"It's these infernal Klingon transporters. The coils are overheatin'. We can try again in about forty-five seconds."*

Kirk fought the urge to close his eyes and succumb to beckon-ing sleep. "Thelin . . . estimated time until the core breaches?"

A pause. *"About . . . thirty seconds, Jim."*

Kirk was able to do the math. "Raise your shields, Thelin."

Clearly mortified, knowing that transport was not possible through raised deflector screens, the Andorian stammered his re-ply. *"Sir, we . . . we can still try to beam you out before—"*

"The explosion could destroy your ship, too!" Kirk shouted with a final burst of strength. "Now, raise the shields!"

Another pause, and Thelin's reply came, sounding as if no words in his lifetime had ever been more painful. *"Aye, sir."*

Kirk's field of vision began to dissolve into thousands of twin-kling points of light as he began to succumb to the effects of the radiation. And yet he was content. Alone, he and his lady would meet their final fate together—while his legacy would live on in his progeny.

"So here it is . . . the no-win scenario," he mumbled with a smile. "How did I do?"

And consciousness left him for the last time.

• • •

In the instant before the transmission went dead, the speakers aboard the *Katai* roared with a fearsome din as a shock wave shattered the hull surrounding Kirk's communicator, and a moment later a raging fireball consumed every cubic inch of the artificial atmosphere within the body of the doomed vessel.

The viewscreen displayed the exterior view of the *Enterprise* as her graceful curves were fractured, torn asunder by the forces of the hellish inferno. The doors to the bridge opened, allowing Scotty and Chekov to rush in, only to witness the horror playing out before them. Together with the rest of the crew, they beheld the destruction of what had been a home for long years, and the death of a man who, if not literally their father, had provided the wisdom of a father in so many ways.

As the sad wreckage slowly drifted out of view, Thelin marched back over to the three remaining members of the *Katai* crew. He grabbed Maltz roughly by his garments and pulled the Klingon's face close to his own. "If you so much as twitch a muscle without my command," the livid Andorian snarled, "I will kill you where you stand."

Maltz smiled contentedly, appearing relaxed and at peace with himself and with his sense of fulfilled honor. "It is a good day to die," he said.

"Have it your way," Thelin hissed, and he flung Maltz to the deck. He pulled out his phaser and, in a merciless instant, blasted the Klingon's supine form into its component atoms.

The journey back to Earth was a solemn one. Sulu and Chekov quietly set about piloting the ship. Scott threw himself into the work of familiarizing himself with Klingon engineering. David secluded himself in his quarters, and Saavik expressed to McCoy her fears that the young scientist might be on the verge of a complete psychological breakdown. And Thelin mostly sat alone, in a hell of his own making, torturing himself with second guesses about the mission.

The bridge doors opened and Leonard McCoy entered, having just completed a cursory inventory of the Klingon sickbay—and based upon his mood, it seemed clear that he wasn't exactly pleased with what he had discovered. He approached the tactical station, where Thelin sat silently staring at a technical display. "How you holding up, old friend?"

The Andorian didn't turn his head. "I suppose you mean to tell me that I need to be rational and control my emotions."

"Not at all," McCoy said, easing into the chair next to him. "Grief is an emotion that we all need to work through. But if I know you . . . and I think I do . . . you're beating yourself up over this."

"Kirk is dead because I couldn't secure a damn prisoner."

"No, your prisoner destroyed the *Enterprise*," McCoy corrected him. "Kirk died because he's a gambler, and after beating the odds to save David—which, I might add, wouldn't have been possible without you—he decided to double down on the only other thing he's ever loved, which was that ship."

Thelin recalled the years spent at Kirk's side as his first officer—the numerous times that they had faced death together, and came through unscathed. "You're right, of course . . . but as gamblers go, he was never reckless. With Jim, life was always a series of risks calculated to increase the odds of a better future . . . for everyone."

McCoy smiled. "So we shouldn't question the choices he made today. This is an opportunity for us to celebrate everything he accomplished in life. I think you'll find that each one of us will look back on this day and remember the lessons he wanted us to learn . . . even now."

They continued to maintain radio silence for the duration of the trip. Thelin knew that the time would come when they all must answer to Starfleet for their actions, but for now, headquarters knew only of the improper "borrowing" of the *Enterprise* by a rogue group of officers. Thelin was not yet prepared to explain the loss of said ship and the death of a respected Starfleet admiral—Kirk's latest and final indiscretion notwithstanding—even though their arrival in a captured Klingon bird-of-prey would certainly prompt those questions and more.

As they entered the Sol sector and Chekov plotted their approach to the Terran system, their impending return forced Thelin and his crew at least to begin monitoring the subspace transmissions to gauge what kind of a welcome—or lack thereof—they might anticipate. No sooner had they activated the receiver and put the audio on the ship's speakers than they heard the terse response from the Klingon High Council to the capture of their ship.

"—capture of the I.K.S. Katai by the aggressive and unprovoked actions of Starfleet! To the men responsible: You are in illegal possession of property of the Klingon Defense Force, and you are holding the crew of the Katai without cause. We demand the immediate return of the vessel and its crew and redress for the injurious nature of these actions! Furthermore, unless Starfleet wishes to declare this incident as an act of war, the men responsible are to be turned over to the Klingon Empire forthwith to face immediate trial for their actions. Message will repeat. This is Brigadier Kerla of the—"

Thelin switched off the speakers in disgust. He looked over at Sulu and Chekov at the helm.

"Well," Sulu said. "At least Starfleet has plausible deniability."

"Perhaps, but . . ." Thelin shook his head. "Little good that will do them if we start a war."

"Bah," Chekov spat. "With what they did to Kirk's son? Then to blow up the Enterprise with the admiral aboard? We didn't start a thing. But we might finish it!"

Thelin held up his hand, stopping Chekov's rant. His other hand was held over the earpiece as he monitored the subspace transmissions broadcast from Earth. His face grew more troubled as he continued to listen. "It's President Roth!" he said softly. "Listen . . ." He flipped on the ship's speakers.

"—of the United Federation of Planets. Do not approach Earth. The transmissions of an orbiting probe are causing critical damage to this planet.

It has almost totally ionized our atmosphere. All power sources have failed. All Earth-orbiting starships are powerless. The probe is vaporizing our oceans. We cannot survive unless a way can be found to respond to the probe. Further communications may not be possible. Save your energy. Save yourselves. Avoid the planet Earth at all costs. Farewell . . ."

Thelin dropped the earpiece, and the three men on the bridge sat staring at one another in bewildered silence.

"Ladies and gentlemen of the Federation Council, and honored guests . . . With heavy hearts we assemble today for this, the first meeting of the Federation Council since the inexplicable attack by an unknown probe nearly one month ago."

Federation President Hiram Roth delivered his opening remarks from the podium at the head of the council chambers, on the first floor of the Palais de la Concorde in Paris, France. Outside the recently reinforced windows along the length of the side walls, behind the rows of council members and other dignitaries in attendance, the gale-force winds and driving rain continued to beat interminably against the glass, testing the resolve of the men and women within, who defied the wrath of nature as it struck out at them like a wounded animal.

The president had been quite adamant that, despite the wanton destruction leveled upon Earth by the probe a month earlier and the dangerous weather patterns that had persisted in the time since, the council would nonetheless meet on Earth as a symbol of their perseverance and fortitude. Being an Earth native, Roth had received a fair amount of resistance to the idea, many believing that his judgment was compromised by his grief over his homeworld, and indeed the pain in his normally staid bearded face was apparent as he addressed the assembly. But no one could doubt his inspiring determination to overcome this tragedy.

"Before we begin," Roth continued, "I should like us all to observe a moment of silence for those who lost their lives in the devastation wrought that fateful day, as well as for those enduring souls who remain, many of whom still await assistance, suffering and starving without any access to the basic services needed for survival. I should like us to remember all of the fine men and women in San Francisco, who perished in the destruction of Starfleet Headquarters, including many of our most respected leaders: Admiral Lance Cartwright, Admiral William Smillie, and the Vulcan representative to the Federation, Ambassador Sarek."

Seated near the farthest end of the uppermost row on the right side of the hall, Thelin bowed his head with reverence. He knew these men well—even a dignitary like Sarek, whose untimely death seemed a tragically fitting conclusion to a lifetime filled with private sorrow. At the same time, Thelin noted with chagrin that the loss of Admiral Kirk had been overlooked in the aftermath of the larger catastrophe.

The upside—if one could, in good conscience, view it as such—was that the insubordinate and possibly criminal acts of the *Enterprise* crew had been all but forgotten, at least pending the outcome of the current crisis. A perfunctory hearing had been held, primarily for the purpose of formally charging them with violations of Starfleet regulations, but for now they each retained their full rank and commission. The Judge Advocate General had most certainly taken under consideration the fact that they had captured a Klingon bird-of-prey with a fully functional cloaking device, which was now being examined in earnest by a science team on Vulcan.

Having allowed sufficient time for the attendees to silently pay their respects, President Roth raised his head. "Thank you. I should explain, for those who are unaware, that Admiral Morrow is not with us here today. He remains on Vulcan, working to establish a temporary base of operations for Starfleet Command, and he shall be in our thoughts during this very difficult time. Many ships of the fleet have been dispatched to Vulcan, while others, specifically the *Saratoga,* the *Shepard,* and the *Yorktown,* remain in Earth spacedock until the full effects of the damage from the probe's electromagnetic energy have been resolved."

For the first time, Thelin became keenly aware of just how dim the lights were being kept in the chamber for these proceedings. The probe's energy had damaged power sources around the planet, and given the inability to use solar power under the impenetrable global cloud cover, much of the planet remained in complete darkness during the night.

"We may never understand the reasons behind the probe's attack. Our own automated probes, launched from Alpha Centauri, have trailed the alien device these last few weeks, and it shows no sign of returning or deviating from its new course out of the Alpha Quadrant. Some of our greatest minds have even speculated that this was little more than a dreadfully misguided attempt at communication from an unknown but overwhelmingly powerful distant race. But we cannot dwell upon our past failures, or upon our fears of a future attack. Instead we must look to the future, beyond this tragedy, toward rebuilding and healing, and becoming stronger as a result."

The chamber responded with a smattering of polite applause.

"So without further ado," Roth continued, "I would like to yield the floor to Doctor Carol Marcus, scientist and environmental engineer, who has done extraordinary work over the past month, evaluating the damage to Earth's ecosystem and our plan for corrective action. Doctor Marcus."

A more enthusiastic response rippled through the chamber as Carol rose from one of the seats on the stage and approached the podium.

"Thank you," she began. "Ladies and gentlemen of the council, I cannot begin to express in words the magnitude of the losses that we have suffered. Most of the finer details regarding the destruction will be found in the report on your screens, and the file is freely downloadable into your personal databases. Suffice it to say that the coastal regions across the planet have been irrevocably altered by the actions of the probe, and while a complete assessment of the damage is still ongoing, the total number of casualties in these areas is in excess of thirteen million."

The figures came as a surprise to no one; nonetheless, simply hearing the statement aloud triggered a murmur of dismay throughout the assembly.

"The canopy of water vapor that still shrouds the planet will remain in place as long as the atmosphere remains so heavily ionized. Unfortunately, water vapor is a rather effective greenhouse gas, and as a result, global temperatures will continue to increase dramatically. Coastal areas that survived the initial devastation from the tidal storms will soon be inundated by rising sea levels.

"Additionally, the ability of the Earth's agricultural operations to produce a crop yield is practically nonexistent. Even once the storms subside, climate zones will be irrevocably altered, and the lack of direct sunlight will make farming impossible. Global famine is inevitable.

"The global health crisis is exacerbated by the lack of usable power sources in many communities, either due to electromagnetic damage or the lack of solar energy. Furthermore, the saline content of the saturated atmosphere has nearly destroyed the ozone layer; therefore, in a tragic irony, the only energy we are receiving from the sun is in the form of ultraviolet radiation that is harmful to biological life."

Another round of muffled and whispered voices spread through the chamber, as the delegates wondered just how much worse the news could become. Indeed, Thelin himself would have been utterly demoralized had he not been aware of what Carol Marcus had planned.

Carol's serious expression brightened with anticipation of what she would next be sharing. "As hopeless as things may seem, rest assured that we believe we have the technology to reverse much, if not all, of the damage to Earth's ecosystem."

She hesitated. Her eyes drifted over the crowd assembled before her and settled upon the Klingon ambassador, standing at the rear of the room beneath the windows of the spectator gallery with his arms folded. Nearly everyone in the room knew the reason for his appearance, and the subject at hand would not do much to make him more agreeable.

"By this time," she continued, "you all are well aware of the controversial research project formerly known as 'Genesis.' This was the culmination of more than eleven years of research in climate modification. Unfortunately, the project's ultimate goal—the terraforming of lifeless worlds for potential colonization—has experienced some . . . setbacks."

Thelin silently laughed at the understatement. He was amazed that Carol was able to discuss the matter with such composure, given the events that had transpired between her son and the Klingons as a direct result of the unscheduled detonation of the prototype in the Mutara sector.

"However, those failures notwithstanding, we still believe that on a smaller scale the technology is still viable. Our plan is to deploy a low-power Genesis wave with a modified matrix into the upper atmosphere to reduce the ionization and restore the proper balance to the atmospheric layers. The risks are minimal, and with the council's permission, and assistance from Starfleet, we can begin immediately."

Carol yielded the podium to Roth but remained standing beside him. The president maintained the optimistic tone of the discussion as he asked the council whether they had any questions. An elderly human man with olive skin held up his hand, and Roth pointed to him. "Yes, the representative from Earth's Indian subcontinent, er . . . Doctor Patel, is it?"

"Thank you, Mr. President," the man responded. "Doctor Marcus, what risks to the Earth's population are posed by this deployment of the Genesis effect?"

Roth retreated and Carol confidently stepped back up to the podium. "An excellent question, Doctor. Our modified Genesis matrix will contain no metastatic effects—nothing that will alter biological life-forms, and most important, no protomatter. Furthermore, the range of the effect will not extend beyond the upper atmosphere. The risk to the ground-based population is negligible."

Her questioner seemingly satisfied, Carol once again yielded to Roth. When no further questions were forthcoming, the president immediately asked for a motion to take a verbal vote. The motion was made and seconded, and when the hall erupted in calls of "aye" the resolution was passed without debate.

"And now, the discussion of Genesis brings us to the second order of business," President Roth said. "The honorable Ambassador Kamarag of the Klingon Empire has asked for permission to address the council today. I yield the floor."

Kamarag slowly marched out onto the speaker's floor in the center of the hall, his confident stride exuding conviction and purpose. He stopped directly in front of the raised platform at the front of the hall and raised his head high, his eyes drifting over the rows of delegates on each side of the chamber.

"Members of the Federation," he began, "on behalf of the High Council, and the citizens of the Klingon Empire, we should like to express our deepest sympathies for the tragedy that has befallen the Federation and Starfleet, and give our assurances that we are willing to assist in any way possible."

He paused as some muted clapping was heard from the delegates, but the light applause was nearly drowned out by a wave of skeptical grumbling.

"However," he continued, his tone becoming a bit firmer and less sympathetic, "the High Council remains quite concerned about the development of this new 'Genesis' super-weapon, which initial tests have shown is capable of destroying an entire planet in just a few days' time."

The grumbling grew louder. President Roth rose from his seat and hastened back to the podium, where he firmly pounded a gavel to restore order. "Please be silent," he admonished the chamber before returning to his seat.

"Thus far, the Federation's new policy of unwarranted aggression has gone unchallenged," Kamarag continued, "but we can no longer remain silent. As you are aware, just one month ago a Klingon commander, who earlier had chosen to independently investigate this threat in the interest of our imperial defense, found himself under attack in neutral territory by a Federation starship. He and at least one of his officers were murdered, his ship captured, and now we understand that both our vessel and its surviving crewmen are being held on Vulcan. Under the terms of the Organian Peace Treaty, which expressly forbids these acts, we demand the return of our ship and crew, and in lieu of a formal apology, we request the sharing of the Genesis technology, so that we might formulate a defense for the preservation of our race."

Throughout Kamarag's speech, the chamber slowly became more unsettled, and the sounds of angry disagreement and outrage gradually crossed the threshold from a subtle background noise to an all-out revolt. Roth once again approached the podium and banged its top with the gavel.

"Please come to order," Roth politely demanded, the lines of stress creasing his face more deeply with each passing second. "Ambassador, your demands are heard and will be considered in due time, for our investigation is ongoing. As I'm sure you are aware, Commander Kruge and his crew have been implicated in the destruction of two Federation starships and the deaths of many Starfleet officers. The grievances indeed cut both ways. Your request is tabled until the next meeting of the council, but as long as the Klingon government continues to cooperate, I am confident that the return of your vessel can be arranged."

The ambassador approached the edge of the stage and stared up at the Federation president, challenging him despite the difference in elevation, and he spoke evenly and resolutely. "And what about your secrets of the Genesis torpedo?"

Roth returned the firm stare, refusing to back down. "I give you my word, as the leader of the United Federation of Planets, that the Genesis technology is peaceful and benign. But it is also a highly classified technology and a matter of Federation security and intelligence. This is not subject to debate."

The staredown continued for several seconds until finally Kamarag forced a polite grin. "Very well," he said. "The Chancellor shall be in touch. I look forward to our next meeting." And he turned and marched quickly out of the chamber.

Thelin watched as Kamarag passed him by and disappeared through the doors at the far end of the chamber. "That seemed easy," the Andorian said out loud.

A Tellarite seated next to him turned and snorted loudly. "*Too* easy," he said dubiously, then returned his attention to Roth and the next matter at hand.

David opened his eyes, and the graceful features of Saavik's serene face slowly came into focus, even as, paradoxically, the most intense sensations of her presence gradually faded into oblivion.

She gently removed her fingers from David's temple and cheek while he looked around, reacquainting himself with his surroundings. The bed upon which he lay was warm and comfortable, and the room, while somewhat plain and sterile, was reasonably cozy by hospital standards. A hot reddish glow from the Vulcan sun helped to illuminate the room through the nearby window.

David took a moment to assess the status of his memory, and was overjoyed to discover that all of his repressed knowledge, safely hidden away in his subconscious during their Klingon captivity, had now, with Saavik's help, been restored to him. "Oh, gosh!" he exclaimed. "Saavik, I can't tell you how comforting that feels. I was afraid I'd never be able to do any scientific work again . . . not without starting my university studies over from scratch, anyway."

Sitting next to him on the edge of the bed, Saavik smiled. "It's just one more step toward making you whole again," she said. "How are you adjusting to your hand?"

He held up his left hand. The newly attached prosthetic was nearly indistinguishable from his lost extremity, except that the movement was a little erratic while he continued adapting to the artificially induced sensations. He tested his grip a couple of times. "It's impressive," he said. "And strong, too. I'll never have trouble with stuck bottle tops again."

Saavik raised an eyebrow. "That was a joke, correct?"

"Yeah," David laughed, "though not a very good one, I'm afraid."

Still smiling, Saavik acknowledged the humor with a nod. But then she looked down, appearing slightly anxious, and placed her hand upon David's natural one. "David, I . . ." She stopped herself, her expression a mix of embarrassment and concern.

David cocked his head. "What is it?"

She sighed. "It is wrong of me to intrude upon your private thoughts. But David . . . when I was just now joined to your mind, I was overwhelmed by the level of guilt that you are enduring."

David turned his head and gazed out the window at the skyline of the Vulcan city of ShiKahr. "Why shouldn't I feel guilty?" he quietly mused. "My father died while trying to save my life."

"And that was his choice, not yours," Saavik replied. "But it runs much deeper than that. Everything that has happened . . . the massacre at Regula One, our capture, and the torture you endured . . . You're unfairly bearing the weight of responsibility for all these events."

"Because it's mostly my fault!" David cried out, rising to a sitting position. "My mother gave me the responsibility of developing the matrix. She *trusted* me to use good judgment, and I was so smitten with the power of the technology, I never stopped to consider the consequences." He sank back onto the bed. "I don't even blame the Klingons for what they did to me. I deserved it."

"You believe that you deserved to be tortured and to have your father murdered?"

David sighed. "The point is, by creating what they perceived as a threat, I provoked them. I should have known better. Why should I hate them for doing what they always do? Would I blame a rabid animal if it attacked me after I poked it with a stick?" He took a breath to continue, but held it, and finally blew out the air and threw up his hands. "I mean, what about *you?*" he challenged her. "You told me what the Romulans did to your mother, and then they abandoned you as a child . . . yet you don't hate them!"

"I *forgave* them because I refused to let my circumstances define who I would become," Saavik said firmly, beginning to show a hint of anger. "I did not blame myself for actions freely chosen by other individuals. I did not wallow in self-loathing over a history that I could not change."

David turned away. He was lashing out blindly—he knew this. But he didn't know how else to cope with the pain. "I'm sorry," he said with chagrin. "Of course this isn't about you. It was wrong for me to bring up your past."

"Indeed, your logic was flawed," Saavik agreed. "David . . . This hospital offers excellent outpatient counseling. Your physical wounds have been cured, yes. But the full healing process will take much more time."

David nodded in agreement. He wasn't sure how the grief would ever subside, but he was willing to try to overcome it. Saavik touched his hand again and they sat together in silence for a while.

"So . . ." David said, looking to change the subject. "How goes the plan to fix Earth?"

"The plan goes well," she replied. "Your mother sends her regards, and promises that she will visit you again as soon as the mission is complete. I understand that Starfleet is granting her request to let Captain Thelin lead the mission."

"That's terrific," he said, but his dispirited voice still betrayed his regrets. He stared up at the ceiling. "You know . . . the whole time we were held by the Klingons, I kept thinking about what they might do to the Earth if they ever got their hands on Genesis. And yet after all that, after everything I did to resist, some unknown force comes along and destroys the damn planet anyway." He looked into Saavik's eyes, pleading for some kind of explanation—something that would make sense in his life. "What kind of twisted universe allows that to happen?"

Saavik had no reply.

Three hundred kilometers beneath the orbiting *U.S.S. Copernicus,* the wounded Earth writhed in throes of misery. The sparkling blue oceans, the fruitful multicolored landmasses, and the twinkling lights of civilization on the night side—all were enshrouded by the swirling, stormy masses of cloud cover that enveloped the planet, ensnaring the world within a trap of its own making.

Aboard the vessel, which had just departed the orbiting spacedock under the command of Captain Thelin, Carol Marcus stood on the bridge, staring at the violence of the planet's ruined atmosphere on the viewscreen; despite her lack of credentials as a medical doctor, today billions had placed their faith in her power to heal a world.

Thelin looked about at the hastily assembled crew. Some of the men and women he knew by reputation as respected science officers, but only Lieutenant Croy at the operations console—recently granted a full commission in the wake of the destruction of Starfleet Academy—had served under him previously. All of them were human, he couldn't help but notice . . . but that made sense. As Earth natives, they would have a vested interest in the mission's success.

"Well, Doctor Marcus," Thelin said. "The patient is waiting. Are you prepared to administer the remedy?"

Carol walked back around the captain's chair to the science consoles at the rear of the bridge, smiling at the Andorian's clumsy metaphor. "Yes, Captain, the trajectory is laid in. We can deploy the first torpedo at your command."

"Lieutenant Croy, fire at your leisure."

"Yes, sir!" said the young officer. He eagerly pressed the firing control on his console, and the concussive discharge of a torpedo vibrated through the deck. A moment later, the object came into view on the screen, streaking down toward the planet's upper atmosphere at a very slight angle of descent.

"Tracking . . ." Croy called out as the data began rolling onto his display. "Device is on projected course, descending at five kilometers per second."

"Telemetry confirmed," Carol reported from her station. "Device is online, status ready."

"Crossing the Karman line," Croy said. "On track for detonation at the stratopause boundary. Discharge in five seconds . . . three, two, one . . ."

A flash erupted near the horizon, producing a ripple that diffused throughout the upper atmosphere. Many kilometers below the point of the explosion, a clearing opened up in the cloud cover and pushed back the storm systems in a radial pattern. The effect decreased as it propagated farther outward, and gradually wispy cirrus clouds spread back over the hole in the canopy as the effect dispersed. But the net result seemed to suggest an overall decrease in the density of the clouds and in the severity of the winds.

Thelin turned in his chair to face Carol. "Report, Doctor?"

"Atmospheric scans commencing, Captain," she replied. The results slowly began to populate her screen, and with each new reading her smile grew more broad and her eyes more bright, until her entire face threatened to burst with enthusiasm. "Initial results show the saturation vapor pressure point is falling . . . The matrix is breaking down molecular oxygen and re-bonding into ozone . . . And the atmospheric ionization is being neutralized. Everything seems to be happening precisely according to the simulations. It's just . . . perfect!"

"Excellent news, Carol," Thelin said, and turned back to face the front of the bridge. "Prepare for second deployment," he announced to the crew.

"Torpedo room is standing by, sir," Croy said.

Carol softly mumbled a few words that Thelin, even with his sensitive hearing, was barely able to make out. "Hmmm . . . This is strange."

The captain turned his chair again. "What is it, Doctor?"

"Huh? Oh, sorry . . ." she said, apparently not realizing she had spoken aloud. "It's just that I'm detecting some ion readings here . . . they don't make any sense."

"What sort of readings?" Thelin asked. "Are some parts of the atmosphere not being de-ionized?"

"No, no," she replied. "It's up here, in the thermosphere."

"I don't understand," the Andorian said, his face masked by confusion. "Up here the thermosphere is *always* ionized."

"But it's concentrated," Carol said. "If I didn't know better, I'd say it looks like a plasma trail."

"From a ship?" Thelin wondered. "That isn't possible. All transports have been grounded for the duration of this mission. The starships are all in spacedock."

"Well then, what else could it be?"

"That's what I'm telling you, Carol . . . a ship is the only thing it *could* be. But if a ship were out there, we'd have visual confirmation . . . unless they had some sort of cloak—" He stopped short. His face suddenly grew even paler than usual.

The members of the bridge crew all stared at him. "Captain?" Croy asked with concern.

"Lieutenant," Thelin said slowly and deliberately. "Display the coordinates of Carol's ion readings on the viewer, wide angle."

"Aye, sir," Croy said, and the image on the screen changed to a wide view of the starfield, with the shining blue arc of the Earth along the bottom perimeter. Not far off in the distance, the massive structure of the orbiting Starfleet spacedock could be seen, where the few starships left in Earth orbit were safely housed while the deployment of the Genesis matrix was under way.

Thelin rose from his seat and stepped toward the viewscreen, stopping between the two separate consoles for ops and the conn. Studying the display, he pointed to a specific region on the right side. "Magnify that region."

The area of small, tightly crowded star patterns zoomed in to fill the screen, and in its midst, two areas clearly betrayed visible distortion effects—the starfield gently rippling and pulsing in contrast with the static surroundings. As they watched, a third area slowly moved into the frame alongside the others. Aboard the *Copernicus,* the bridge was deathly silent save for the sound of a few muffled gasps.

"Tactical officer," Thelin grimly addressed one of the young women stationed behind him, next to Carol. "Any indication that we've been scanned?"

"No sir," she replied nervously.

"All stations go to yellow alert," he commanded. "Ensign Lee, open a secured channel to Spacedock Command."

The communications officer quickly relayed the observations made by Thelin and his crew, and the command center of the spacedock sprang into action. Immediate communiqués were dispatched to Starfleet Command as well as the Earth defense forces, and whatever active crews were present on the docked starships were mobilized. *"Starship* Excelsior, *orders confirmed to intercept and investigate orbiting phenomena reported by* Copernicus. *Patching through* Excelsior *communications onto this channel."*

An audible blip, and the internal comm traffic from the *Excelsior* was piped through the speakers on the *Copernicus* bridge. *"—alert! Captain Styles to the bridge! Yellow alert!"*

A pause. *"Bridge, this is the captain. How can you have a yellow alert in spacedock?"*

Thelin shook his head in amazement. "That man is a danger to himself and to those around him," he muttered, sitting back down in his chair.

The entire bridge crew murmured in agreement. The rest of the *Excelsior* transmissions were mostly ignored.

Carol stood up from her station, gazing at the viewscreen, her sense of alarm momentarily giving way to curiosity. "So, if there are three cloaked ships out there . . . are they Romulan, or Klingon?"

"Or someone else?" Thelin suggested. "Seems like before long, everyone will have the technology."

"Sir," the tactical officer interjected. "I've just cross-referenced the readings with our database. The observed effect is consistent with a cloaked *B'rel*-class Klingon bird-of-prey."

Thelin's antennae bowed inward in consternation. "This doesn't make sense," he said. "If they wanted to spy on us, they'd only need one cloaked ship. Why send three?"

Croy shrugged. "Maybe they wanted to intimidate us?"

"I don't think so," Thelin replied. "They're much more cunning than that."

"Well, the cavalry is about to arrive," Croy said. "The spacedock doors are opening!"

"Full range on viewer," Thelin ordered.

In the distance, the huge doors on the topmost dome of the spacedock began to slowly slide apart, revealing the gleaming hull of the *Excelsior* as it waited patiently to emerge. Around the bridge of the *Copernicus,* the anxious crew grew restless, knowing that they were at best an even match against one bird-of-prey, let alone three.

The moment the forward hull of *Excelsior* began to poke through the aperture, one of the areas of distortion on the screen shifted, and began to move swiftly across the field of vision toward the spacedock.

"I've seen enough," the Andorian captain said. "Go to red alert. Ensign Lee, report to *Excelsior* that the bogey appears to be moving to intercept."

"Shields are up, weapons systems are charging," the tactical officer said.

"*Excelsior* acknowledges," Lee said. "Going to red alert status."

"Captain!" Croy shouted. "All three ships are decloaking!"

Sure enough, the three vessels simultaneously emerged from their shrouds. One bird-of-prey sat perched directly in front of the spacedock doors, engaging the *Excelsior* in a tactical staredown. But the much larger Starfleet ship appeared to blink first; as soon as it cleared the dock, it veered off before turning and settling into a central position amid the three Klingon ships.

The two Klingon ships that had sat unmoving throughout the previous maneuvers now split apart, aggressively taking flanking positions on either side of the *Excelsior*.

"Captain," Lee said. "Word from spacedock is that they have now mobilized the *Yorktown*. They'll be coming out to join us shortly."

"Acknowledge that," Thelin replied with some relief. The three small Klingon fighters would be no match for two massive Starfleet cruisers, and Thelin, while certainly not one to back away from a fight, knew that the tiny science vessel he commanded would be of little use were this standoff to destabilize into any sort of battle. "Helm," he said, hating the words he was about to say but fully appreciating the facts of the situation, "as soon as the *Yorktown* is free and clear of the dock, prepare to withdraw."

"Aye, sir," the helmsman said.

Inside the dock, the *Constitution*-class *Yorktown* could now be seen preparing to maneuver its way through the doors while a Klingon bird-of-prey still guarded the exit like a sentry. But before any part of the ship could emerge, as Thelin's crew looked on in horror, the Klingon ship's disruptor cannons unleashed a barrage of firepower directly upon the Starfleet vessel.

Immediately the scene around them dissolved into utter chaos. In response, the *Excelsior* fired upon the attacking Klingon ship, only to be hit with disruptor fire on both sides from the two flanking vessels.

Thelin leaped from his seat. "Helm! Run evasive maneuvers around the starboard-side hostile; tactical, lay down strafing fire as we pass. Force that vessel to disengage from the *Excelsior*."

Wasting no time, the *Copernicus* swept past the Klingon ship while repeatedly firing phasers upon it before quickly withdrawing to prepare for another pass. But their efforts seemed to have little effect. The shields on the bird-of-prey held, and it continued to pummel the *Excelsior* mercilessly.

"Sir," Ensign Lee shouted, holding his hand to his ear as he attempted to make sense of the subspace chatter the engagement had produced. "The *Excelsior*'s a sitting duck. She has to disengage."

Thelin reassessed the situation. While the bird-of-prey remained staked out before the dock doors, the *Yorktown* would be unable to get clear. "All right," he said. "Then it's up to us to eliminate that bird in front of the spacedock."

"Negative, sir," Lee responded. "*Yorktown* is a no-go. They're closing the dock doors."

"*What?*" Thelin shouted back. "Would you mind asking Starfleet Command just what exactly we're supposed to do out here?"

"Sir, Starfleet Command reports three available starships in the system at the Utopia Planitia shipyards. They've just warped out from Mars. They'll be here in five minutes."

"We could be *dead* in five minutes," the captain fired back. Such an amount of time, Thelin knew, was practically an eternity during this type of engagement, and his crew of science specialists had certainly not been prepared to go into battle. Had Federation Intelligence been caught totally unaware that the Klingons were planning to disrupt their mission? The devastation wreaked upon Earth had apparently crippled the government more seriously than anyone was willing to admit.

But, curiously, the Klingon ships now seemed content to sit and wait. The *Excelsior* had circled around and come to a more defensive position, but the birds showed no signs of taking further aggressive action. Despite the lull, Thelin knew better than to relax for even a moment.

"Captain!" Lee suddenly shouted. "I'm receiving additional transmissions from Utopia Planitia. They're reporting three more Klingon *B'rel*-class birds-of-prey now in orbit around Mars."

"Over the shipyards?!" Thelin exclaimed.

"Yes, sir!"

"Put it on speakers."

Lee flipped the necessary controls, and the confused, slightly panicked voices sounded out, overlapping one another with increasing intensity.

"—*have decloaked directly above the Odyssey Depots, coordinates twenty-seven point five degrees latitude*—"

"*—negative communications. Klingon hostiles are not responding to hails. No heavy cruisers are in range to intercept; we are mobilizing all light cruisers and scoutships—repeat, all light cruisers—*"

"*Oh my God . . . Platform fifteen, do you have visual at coordinates one-two-seven mark fifty-five?*"

"*Stand by . . . Confirmed, we have visual evidence of multiple energy surges, bearing—*"

"*They're decloaking! Red alert! Priority Starfleet Command, we count approximately sixteen . . . correction, approximately twenty D7- and K'tinga-class Klingon cruisers in attack formation! Incoming, bearing three—*"

"*Firing! Repeat, we are taking heavy fire! Starfleet Command, the shipyards are under attack! All vessels, engage at will, priority—*"

"*It's a goddamn armada . . .*"

Thelin looked about the bridge at his crew—all of them motionless, stunned, gazing straight ahead with open mouths. Carol Marcus, about whom he had nearly forgotten in the midst of the crisis, looked as if she wanted to curl up into a ball and hide.

"Planetwide broadcast to Earth from Starfleet Command," Ensign Lee said, his voice quivering ever so slightly. "Orders are for all Federation government personnel to evacuate the system."

"What?" Croy exclaimed. "They're abandoning the planet?"

"Pull it together, Lieutenant," Thelin admonished him. "It's just a precaution."

A drastic precaution, Thelin thought to himself. *An acknowledgment of the worst-case scenario.*

The Andorian gazed at the *Copernicus* viewscreen as desperate transmissions from the carnage at the shipyards on Mars continued to play over the bridge speakers. The three Klingon ships, so aggressive just moments ago, had returned to their passive, noncombatant postures. *Why are they still here?* Thelin silently wondered.

As if on cue, the bird-of-prey that had successfully neutralized the spacedock suddenly powered its engines and shot past the

Copernicus—not leaving orbit, but heading instead toward the horizon, seeking another target somewhere above the planet. The remaining two Klingon ships veered about to the front of the *Excelsior,* blocking any attempt to follow.

"Where does he think he's going?" Thelin asked aloud. "Helm, follow that vessel!"

The *Copernicus* turned hard about and set off in pursuit of the rogue Klingon ship, leaving *Excelsior* and the other birds-of-prey in their wake. The tactical officer spoke up. "Sir, I'm tracking another ship from Earth's surface," she said. "It's a Type-3 shuttlecraft, and it appears that the Klingons are on course to intercept. Its call sign is . . ." She gasped. "Captain, it's *Starfleet One*! It's the president's shuttle!"

Suddenly, the tremendous tension that had built up within the Andorian had a focus—a clear duty to perform—and he felt substantially better. "All right, people," he said with enthusiasm. "Our first priority is to make sure that shuttle gets clear. Power up weapons and fire on those *karskat* Klingons as soon as they're in range. Where's *Excelsior*?"

"Sir," Lee said, "*Excelsior* reports that the two other birds have reengaged them. They can't assist us in the pursuit."

"Klingon vessel in range," came the word from tactical. "Firing phasers."

The *Copernicus* phasers struck their target, but the Klingons' shields fully absorbed the energy of the blasts.

"Their shields are holding. No damage."

"Klingon vessel will intercept *Starfleet One* in thirty seconds," Croy called out.

"What's the word on the reinforcements?" Thelin shouted.

"The starships have been recalled to Mars, sir," Lee said with exasperation. "We're on our own."

Damn! Thelin thought. *Our weapons aren't powerful enough to penetrate Klingon shielding.* "Keep firing," he commanded anyway.

Unless we can penetrate their shields some other way . . .

"Carol!" he said, spinning around to face the scientist. "We still have a Genesis torpedo in the launching bay. Can you reprogram it from here?"

Carol shook herself out of her nearly trancelike state. "What? I mean, yes . . . I can make minor modifications to the matrix."

"My only concern is point of impact," Thelin explained. "I want the whole Genesis effect focused upon the deflector energy particles. Can you do that?"

"Yes, I think so," Carol replied, and swung around in her chair to face the console.

"Ten seconds," Croy announced.

Carol chewed on her lip as her fingers flew over the console, calling up screen after screen with lightning speed as she modified the parameters for the interaction of the Genesis effect. She was making progress, but it was taking time—too much time.

"The president's shuttle is now in range of the Klingon vessel," Croy said. "*Starfleet One* is taking enemy fire!"

"Concentrate all of our firepower on the Klingon weapons systems," Thelin commanded. "Try to poke a hole in those shields. Tactical, lock on target for the torpedo launch."

"Programming the Genesis device now," Carol said.

"Target locked," came the announcement from tactical. "*Starfleet One* aft shields down to fifty percent."

"Download complete," Carol finally shouted with relief. "Ready to deploy!"

"Fire!" said Thelin.

The torpedo shot out from the launcher and guided itself with precision toward the bird-of-prey, where it struck the deflector field in the aft section, briefly producing a shimmering fireball as the effect spread throughout the vessel's shields. The effect dissipated within seconds.

"Klingon shields are down!" Croy said excitedly.

"Fire phasers at will," the captain commanded.

The *Copernicus*'s weapons pounded the aft section of the ves-

sel with multiple phaser blasts until the ship erupted in a bright
fireball.

Ensign Lee spun around from the communications station.
"*Starfleet One* reports that they are free and clear!"

The crew erupted into applause, the tension of the officers being audibly released in the form of various shouts, whoops, and
cries of relief. Thelin smiled and sank back into his chair. "Good
work, everyone. Ensign Lee, any word from the conflict at Utopia
Planetia?"

"There's a ton of traffic, sir, but I can't make much sense of it.
But wait . . ." His face visibly brightened. "We're being hailed by
the *Excelsior*!"

"On screen," Thelin said.

The image of Lawrence Styles filled the viewscreen—seated
in the captain's chair, looking amazingly calm and collected,
surrounded by the members of his crew, to whom it seemed
composure had perhaps just now returned. "*Captain th'Valrass!*"
he said, using Thelin's formal name. "*We were just on our way to assist you. I trust you were able to dispense with your uninvited guest?*"

"Indeed, we were," Thelin said with a hint of bravado.
"And you?"

"*Oh, it took us a minute or two, but we were able to outmaneuver and
outgun those Klingon buzzards,*" Styles proudly bragged. "*I tell you,
Thelin, for a ship this size, she handles like a well-bred Chilean steed.
We're coming up on your position. Be there in a sec.*"

"Acknowledged," Thelin said. "End transmission. External
view." He turned and glibly rolled his eyes at the officers seated
behind him. A couple of the officers laughed heartily at his subtle
derision. But at least one officer at the engineering station stared
over Thelin's shoulder with a blank expression, focusing upon
something behind him. Thelin observed him for a moment.
"What?" he asked.

The officer pointed past the Andorian toward the viewscreen.
Thelin turned around.

On the screen the *Excelsior* was seen as it approached over the vast bluish arc of Earth below, set amid the familiar starfield with a million shining points of light. And many of those points of light weren't just shining. They were *shimmering*. Lots of them. Enough, in fact, to fill half of the sky with an eerie distortion effect.

"Thori help us," Thelin whispered.

"Sir," Lee said. "Receiving a transmission . . . A convoy of Federation shuttles and diplomatic vessels is leaving Earth."

"They'd better hurry," Thelin remarked. "Send to *Excelsior,* fall into formation and escort these ships out before that second invading fleet starts firing."

The convoy seemed to extend forever, as one small craft after another ferried out the Federation's top officials and ambassadors. As the last few ships cleared Earth's atmosphere, the Klingon cruisers began to drop their cloaks and descend en masse onto the planet. But none of them seemed interested in pursuing the escaping vessels. These ships seemed to have one mission and one alone: to subdue and control one of the greatest natural resources of the Federation—the planet Earth.

Lieutenant Croy put up the reverse angle on the viewscreen, and Thelin watched as the lonely circle of Earth began to fade into the distance. He could still see the tiny dots of the invading Klingon fleet as the sunlight glinted off the hulls—a swarm of tiny gnats descending upon a ripe fruit.

"We have to go back," Thelin said. "Coordinate with *Excelsior,* and raise Starfleet Command. Ask them how soon we can expect some damn reinforcements."

"Er, Captain . . ." Lee meekly spoke. "We've already received priority orders from Starfleet Command. We're to rendezvous at Vulcan. There will be no reinforcements."

Incredulous, Thelin gaped at him, then looked about at the faces of his crew, most displaying some blend of shock and grief. That was it? After all they had done, the system was to be considered a total loss? *There were still ten billion people on Earth!* "So . . . we're supposed to just leave them to the Klingons?" he muttered.

No one answered his retort, but it didn't matter. As far as he was concerned, the answer was "no." He wasn't giving up that easily. "Hail *Starfleet One.* I want to talk to the president."

The response didn't take long. "On screen," Lee said.

A middle-aged woman with deep brown skin appeared on the viewscreen, her eyes clearly showing the pain of the stress she had endured. "This is Penda Ubuntu, chief of staff to the president. On behalf of all of us, I want to express our thanks for your assistance with our escape."

"Thank you, Ms. Ubuntu," Thelin acknowledged. "If you would, please, I really must speak to President Roth immediately."

"I'm sorry, Captain . . . but that isn't possible."

Thelin briefly closed his eyes and took a deep breath in an effort to relax his frayed nerves. "Ms. Ubuntu, we've risked a great deal here today. I merely ask this one small courtesy. Please."

The woman looked down and sobbed mournfully before responding. "Captain . . . President Roth experienced a massive coronary attack during the escape. You can't speak to him. He's dead."

6

Five Years Later

Saavik rose from the bed she had shared with David the night before as the Vulcan sun pounded its hot morning rays through the window. Tossing her long hair away from the front of her face, she looked about the room for her clothing and personal effects and gathered them together, taking them with her as she walked toward the door to the adjacent bathroom.

From under heavy eyelids that struggled to remain open, David watched her from the bed, admiring as always her shapely curves and graceful movements. Her visits had grown more infrequent—in fact, this was only the third time they had spent the night together since her appointment as the Federation ambassador to Romulus about a year earlier, and, sadly, this particular liaison would be all too brief. She was due to return to the embassy on Romulus later that day.

After a few minutes she emerged, fully dressed and smartly primped. In the past, David had often wondered why, given the absence of any logical explanation, Vulcan women always seemed to invest a lot of time and energy into their physical appearance. But now knowing Saavik so intimately, he was beginning to believe that beauty just came very naturally to them, without their having to expend much effort.

"Good morning," he said with a smile, his voice deep and throaty from the effects of sleep.

"Good morning," she replied warmly. She had long since

learned to embrace human greeting customs and to stop questioning the logic of them. "Did you sleep well?"

"Not nearly enough," he said, rubbing his eyes. He looked over at the chronometer on the stand next to the bed. "Geez, is it really that early?"

"My shuttle is due to depart in the early afternoon." She sat down next to him on his side of the bed and they clasped their hands together. By now, David was accustomed enough to his artificial hand that he didn't have to worry about accidentally crushing hers.

David looked deep into her eyes. "Don't go," he said.

Saavik raised an eyebrow. "I have my responsibilities, David. But I'm not leaving just yet. I thought we might share breakfast together."

"I'd like that," he replied. "We haven't had much time to talk."

Saavik gave him a sidelong glance with a mischievous grin as she stood up. "You didn't seem to be in the mood to talk last night."

"Yeah, I know," David said as he tossed aside the bedsheets and swung his legs over the edge. "Sorry, that was my human lack of emotional control."

"Indeed," she agreed, as she picked up a tote bag from the floor and set it upon a small table near the door.

David dressed while Saavik packed a few scattered items in the bag. "So tell me," he inquired, "what inside information have you heard about the war effort lately?"

She briefly gave him a puzzled look. "Why do you presume I would know anything more than you?"

"Oh, c'mon!" David laughed. "You're in the employ of the Federation diplomatic service. I'm just a disgraced scientist turned social worker."

"You underrate your value to the cause, especially given your level of dedication." She zipped the bag shut and turned to face him, leaning against the table. "I do know that Admiral th'Valrass has just returned from a very successful series of campaigns in the

Archanis sector. Several Klingon military bases were completely destroyed."

"Well, good for him. Thelin and I go way back, you know. Nice to see that he's becoming quite a leader out there."

"Agreed," she said, though she was unable to conceal her lack of enthusiasm about the news.

David cocked his head. "Are the other efforts not going so well?"

She sighed. "That is difficult to assess. Most fronts in the war are effectively stalemated at this point. The Romulan Empire, though sympathetic to our cause, is still officially neutral in the conflict. And though I cannot give any specific evidence, there seems to be a level of . . . *desperation* in the Federation's attempts to court Romulan support as of late, particularly by the Vulcan High Command. Some have even broached the subject of re-unification."

David's still-tired eyes flew wide open. "Really? I had no idea that was even plausible."

Saavik shrugged. "Then you will be surprised to know that the V'Shar has discovered significant support for such an idea among the Romulan underground."

"The Vulcan intelligence agency? Wow . . . I guess they must be serious, then." David stepped forward and put his arms around Saavik's waist. "Wouldn't that be something . . . if the two worlds you've claimed could actually become one . . . and make you whole?"

Saavik smiled and bowed her head. "Romulus is truly a remarkable world. You should visit sometime."

"You're right," he said. "I should. After living here on Vulcan for the last five years, anything would be better than this infernal heat and high gravity."

"You would like it there. Four distinct seasons through multiple climate zones, lush vegetation, and awe-inspiring landscapes. It reminds me of . . ."

She paused and dropped her gaze, and David patiently waited for her to finish her thought. "Reminds you of what?"

She looked up again and met his eyes. "It reminds me of Earth."

David had no reply, so he did not attempt to craft one. Instead, he reached up and cradled the back of her neck, gently pulling her toward him while embracing her with his other arm, and tenderly pressed his lips against hers. David closed his eyes and allowed the warm intimacy of Saavik's telepathic consciousness to wash over him.

He wasn't certain how many minutes had passed when they each finally opened their eyes and gazed lovingly at each other.

"Shall we go eat?" Saavik asked.

"I'm famished," David replied.

The last in a long line of families finally stepped off the exit ramp of the transport into the warm Vulcan breeze. A single woman, her pretty face marred by the cumulative effects of grief and stress, led the way with her two preteen children in tow. The young ones, less conscious of the circumstances that had brought them from a besieged colony world to a Federation refugee camp, looked about with innocent wonder at the strange alien landscape, dotted by hastily assembled compact shelters, one of which would become their temporary home.

In the midst of the outdoor setting, David sat behind a portable computer on a table near the landing pad, assisted by a middle-aged Vulcan man with piercing eyes and an unusual amount of facial hair. The family ambled slowly up to the table.

"Hello," David said, making eye contact with each of them in turn. "Could I have your names, please?"

"I'm Jennifer Kilmer," the woman said. "These are my children, Daniel and Sarah."

David quickly entered the names into his database on the computer screen while his Vulcan assistant handed each of the new arrivals a blanket and a package of various human toiletries and other necessities.

"Welcome to the Le'Tenya Camp. I know that this is a very difficult and trying time for you and your family, but we will work very hard to keep you safe and comfortable while arrangements are made for more permanent housing. Does anyone in your party require medical attention?"

"No." The woman shook her head.

"Well, should you need anything, the advocate in the nearby watch station can assist you. Meals are served three times daily at the mess hall, and communications are available at the administration center about a kilometer up the road. You'll be staying in . . . shelter 67G." David handed her a small data padd. "You'll find all of the information here."

"Thank you," she said numbly, then gathered her children and slowly walked toward her new home. David watched her go, wondering as he often did what the future would hold for her and her family.

"It never gets easier, does it?" asked the Vulcan next to him.

"No, it sure doesn't," David replied, "Mister, um . . . I'm sorry, what was your name?" David was fairly certain he hadn't worked with this particular individual before—the man had enough unique qualities about him that he would have left a definite impression.

"My name is Sybok," the Vulcan said, smiling broadly.

"Right," David said. For the first time, he had begun to notice how oddly emotive this particular Vulcan was. Perhaps, given all the time he had spent around Saavik, David didn't find the man's quirks nearly as jarring as others might have. "Well, at least things aren't as bad as they were this time last year. Back then we'd get four of these refugee transports every day."

"Yes, I remember," the Vulcan somberly recalled. "It seemed for a while that the Klingons were determined to strike every colony world in the quadrant."

"Yeah . . . the bad news is, there probably aren't many left for them to attack." He paused, then tried to brighten his affect a little. "But the *good* news is, we're seeing more shuttles full of families who have escaped the tyranny of Klingon rule over the Earth."

The Vulcan nodded. "I hear the underground railroad is doing a tremendous job there." Then the conversation lapsed into an uncomfortable silence.

"Well," David said, looking about, "it looks like that's all of them for now." He ejected the data card from the terminal he had been using to record the names of the refugees and stood up from the table. "I'd better get this to the office."

Sybok rose to his feet with him. "I'll walk with you, if you don't mind."

"Sure," David agreed, and together they made their way along the service road that ran alongside the camp from the landing pad to the administration center, where the permanent employees of the operation were stationed.

They walked in silence for a minute or so, surrounded by the sounds of the displaced escapees as they struggled to settle into their new surroundings. Most of the voices were calm, but the relative peace was often punctuated with shouts of frustration or the troubled cries of children. David did not react to the distressing sounds of grief, but not because he had become desensitized to the suffering; his mind was simply focused elsewhere.

Sybok watched the young human with interest. "Forgive me," he eventually said, his face marked with a mixture of compassion and concern. "I couldn't help but notice your pain."

David looked at him with bewilderment. "My pain? What are you talking about?"

"The pain of loss," Sybok replied. "It haunts you."

"Of course I've suffered loss," David said with mild annoyance. He swept his arm across the sea of makeshift housing spread out before them. "Look around you. If you haven't noticed, there's a war going on."

"Yes, I know," the Vulcan affirmed, nodding. "But for you, it's something more personal—a sacrifice, made by someone close to you."

David's eyebrows drew close together. "Do you do this with *everyone* you meet for the first time?"

Sybok shrugged. "Some would call it a gift."

David rolled his eyes with a laugh, then threw up his right hand with exasperation. "All right, what the hell . . . It was my father, James Kirk. He was a Starfleet admiral. Five years ago he sacrificed his life saving me from Klingon captivity. Now I suppose you're gonna tell me that you can talk to his spirit, right?"

"Ah!" the Vulcan replied, raising his index finger. "I know who you are! You're David Marcus. It all makes sense now. You've actually done quite well for yourself—recovered from your trauma, assuaged your guilt, conquered your fear . . . *very* good! All that remains is the pain."

David stared at him and slowly shook his head. "Who *are* you???"

"Interesting you should ask. We have much in common, you and I. We each lost our fathers five years ago. My father was Sarek, the Federation ambassador."

A light of recognition went on in David's eyes. "You're Sarek's eldest son?" He suddenly felt embarrassed by the lack of respect he had shown. "Gosh, I'm sorry, you're just . . . well, you're not exactly like I'd envisioned."

"I get that a lot," Sybok said with a gentle smile. "Truth be told, I was never what you'd call a model citizen. Since I was very young, I've possessed certain empathic abilities that were, shall we say, incompatible with Vulcan customs regarding emotion."

David immediately thought of Saavik, and her struggles to maintain emotional control. "Yes . . . I'm sure I know exactly what you mean."

"But even though my father and I had been estranged, one day, about sixteen years ago—just following a visit to Andoria, as I recall—he sought me out, wanting to repair our relationship. And he truly helped to straighten things out for me. Got my life back on track."

"You're lucky you had a few years to get to know him," David mused.

"Lucky?" Sybok said with surprise. "Oh, at the time, perhaps. But now *you're* the lucky one, my friend."

"Oh?" David replied. "How so?"

"Because, Doctor Marcus, you can let go of your pain at any time. Your father's death had meaning and purpose. You know this. And the perpetrators . . . well, of course they're dead, but nonetheless you worked to understand their motivations and to forgive them. You don't even need my help, friend . . . You're free!"

David continued to walk for a few moments, staring ahead in pensive silence. "I guess I hadn't really thought about it that way." He turned his head toward Sybok. "And what about you?"

"Me?" Sybok smiled, but it was a cheerless, wistful smile. "My father was taken from me by an incomprehensible, faceless enemy. His death was senseless . . . empty." He stopped, facing David with a solemn expression. "Even with all my gifts . . . that, my friend, is a pain that never entirely goes away."

David had no reply.

"I must leave you now, but I am very glad that we met today." He held up his hand in the Vulcan salute. "Live long, and prosper."

David returned the gesture. "Peace, and long life," he replied.

As Sybok walked away, weaving a path through the crowd, a courier approached David with a padd in his hand. "Oh, hi, Robert," David said. "I was just on my way to drop this off," and handed him the data card.

"Thank you, Doctor Marcus," the man said. "This priority transmission just came in from the office of the president."

David gave him a puzzled look as he took the device from him. "You mean the president of the refugee commission?"

"No, Doctor," Robert said, shaking his head. "The president of the Federation."

The starfield that spread out before them shimmered and shifted in and out of focus, displaying all of the familiar visual distortions one saw when gazing through the interior of a Klingon cloaking field.

Admiral Thelin stood quietly before the viewscreen at the front of the bridge, his hands clasped behind his back, forming an austere silhouette for the officers seated at their various stations behind him. In recent years, these stars had become oddly familiar to him—perhaps too familiar, as these were constellations never seen from the skies of any Federation world. These were the skies behind enemy lines.

The Andorian turned to face his crew on the bridge of the *Katai*. The sight of so many familiar faces was comforting: Sulu, sporting his captain's insignia but ready and willing to sign on for such a critical mission, sat at the helm next to Chekov. Uhura sat at the communications station on the starboard side of the bridge, actively monitoring the subspace channels for any warning that their presence here might be suspected by the Klingons.

In fact, the only thing oddly disquieting about the scene was the empty captain's chair in the center of the bridge. Certainly the seat belonged to Thelin; after all, this mission had been planned and carried out almost entirely under his direction. Never in his career had Thelin shied away from the pressures and responsibilities of command. Nonetheless, despite the passage of years, the loss of James Tiberius Kirk was perhaps never more poignantly felt than at this moment—possibly the most critical juncture in the history of the Federation.

The Andorian walked back to the platform in the center of the bridge and, stepping up to the chair, paused, perhaps as a subconscious act of deference to Kirk's memory. Then he turned and seated himself. "Status report?" he inquired, pensively studying the viewscreen.

"We are now fifteen point two parsecs inside the borders of Klingon space," Chekov announced from the navigator station. "Arrival at the Qo'noS system in twenty-two minutes, current speed."

"All readings nominal at the helm, Admiral," announced Sulu.

"Communication channels are quiet, Admiral," Uhura said. "No indications that our presence is known."

"Mr. Scott?" Thelin called into the ship's intercom.

"Aye, sir," Scott's voice was heard over the speakers. *"Cloaking device is operatin' within normal parameters. Warp engines are at optimal efficiency . . . at least, optimal fer this Klingon junk heap."*

Thelin smiled at the observation. Indeed, the environment was cramped, dimly lit, and certainly showed little concern for aesthetics or ergonomics, but the crew had adapted well, especially since it was less than two weeks ago that they had received their orders to take the captured bird-of-prey into Klingon space.

The meeting itself had been something of a surprise. Certainly Starfleet's top brass had been gathering more often as a major incursion into Klingon space was being planned, but that operation was still months away . . . and most unexpectedly, this particular meeting had been called by Federation President Ra-ghoratreii himself.

Thelin had arrived on Vulcan just as the sun had reached its noon zenith, and although Andorians didn't mind the heat, and in fact preferred a warmer climate than that on their mostly icy homeworld, he nonetheless felt as if he had stepped off the transporter pad into a blast furnace. Luckily, it was a short walk from the outdoor transport station to the security checkpoint at the front entrance to the ShiKahr High Council Chambers, where the Federation president had temporarily established the seat of the government.

As the guards pored over his credentials, Thelin stared up at the palatial, ancient stone architecture of the Vulcan Council building, with its smoothly rounded abutments, sweeping skyward to meet at the tops of gently pointed towers. Nothing similar existed on Andor; but then, Andorian architecture tended to be more practical, built in piecemeal fashion as needs demanded.

The Federation Council was not currently in session, so the corridors of the building were relatively deserted as Thelin made his way to the designated council chamber. Within minutes he stepped off the lift and through an ornate set of doors into a spacious room, where two uniformed Starfleet admirals were already seated around a symmetrical but irregularly shaped conference table. At the head of the table sat Federation President Ra-ghoratreii, a look of severe consternation not quite hidden behind the Efrosian's long white facial hair.

The president rose from his seat and bowed from the shoulders to Thelin. "Admiral th'Valrass, thank you for arriving on such short notice."

"I am here to serve at your pleasure, Mr. President," Thelin replied, returning the bow.

The Efrosian gestured to the left side of the table. "I believe you know the Starfleet commander in chief, Admiral West."

The well-groomed middle-aged man, a human, stood and held out his hand. "Of course he does," he said. "It's good to see you again, Thelin."

Thelin took the proffered hand and gripped it tightly. "Admiral," he said. "So you have finally decided to retire the title of 'Colonel'?"

"Hell, it's been forever and a day since I served in the special forces," West replied. "But now that we've lost Morrow, and they asked me to run this dog-and-pony show, I figured it's best to keep things simple in the chain of command." A smile spread out beneath his mustache. "But for you, 'Patrick' will do just fine." He gestured to the Vulcan woman seated across the table. "And I believe you know Admiral T'Pragh?"

The short-haired woman nodded her acknowledgment. "Admiral," she said.

"Admiral," Thelin replied with a smile. "You're looking well. Have you lost weight?"

The woman raised an eyebrow but appeared at a loss for a reply.

As the men took their seats, the doors slid open again, and David Marcus quietly stepped into the room, timidly looking around at the pastel colors of the walls and floors, and at the artistic depictions of Mount Seleya that hung between the various viewscreens.

Thelin practically jumped from his chair. "Doctor Marcus!" he said, extending his arm to shake the young man's hand, in accordance with human custom. David smiled, showing some relief at the sight of a familiar face, but was still clearly puzzled to find himself at such a prestigious meeting. Thelin continued, "How is your mother, David?"

"Oh, she's, uh . . . fine, I guess," David stammered. "Retired now, of course. The situation on Earth really hit her pretty hard. She'd spent a lot more time there in her childhood than I had."

"I can only imagine," Thelin replied with genuine sympathy. "I hear she's living on Pacifica now?"

"That's right. I just don't think the Vulcan deserts were really her thing."

"Well, she should have come back to Andor. We have retirement homes on the shores of the Khyzhon Sea that are absolutely stunning." The Andorian bowed his head in respect, his antennae nearly lying prostrate against his white hair. "We worked together for years, and she is a truly brilliant mind. I know that the president would have liked her to join us today, but there was no time."

"Thank you, Thelin," David replied, "but it's just as well. I'm sure she wants to get away from all of this . . . politics and such."

"I have no doubt." Thelin smiled warmly, then gestured to the other representatives at the table. Following a second round of introductions, David took his seat next to T'Pragh.

President Ra-ghoratreii wasted no time in calling the meeting to order. "Lady, and gentlemen," he began. "I understand that this meeting is a little unexpected, but circumstances as they are, the potential exists for a fundamental shift in the war strategy." He focused his gaze squarely upon David. "Doctor Marcus, your presence here was requested for the purpose of a qualified scientific consultation. I must make it absolutely clear that any and all information disclosed here today is given in complete confidence, and that your divulgence of any such information without authorization is punishable as an act of treason against the Federation. Do I make myself clear?"

David looked as if he wanted to crawl under the table, or perhaps simply bolt for the door. But he swallowed and nodded his head. "Yes," he said in a near-whisper. "Crystal clear."

"Very well," the Efrosian said, apparently satisfied. "Admiral th'Valrass, would you please open with your report on the overall status of the conflict."

"Certainly, Mr. President," Thelin replied, and briefly looked to each of the other attendees in turn, hoping to convey the gravity of the information he was about to impart. "As we enter the fifth year of the conflict, the consensus among field commanders is that we have effectively reached an impasse. On one hand, our campaigns in the Archanis sector were quite successful, and have provided us with valuable positions from which to launch additional offensives into Klingon territory."

"You bet," West interjected. "In fact, we now have opportunities for strategic advances into the Klinzhai sector that we could only have dreamed about months ago."

"On the other hand," Thelin continued, "Klingon advances on two fronts are now beginning to seriously threaten the Alpha Centauri system, and with the Sol sector under Klingon control, we don't have the strategic presence from which to mount an effective defense." He looked over at David. "Despite the high costs the Klingons have incurred in holding the system, we . . . we still have made effectively zero progress toward reclaiming Earth.

"Most recently, Captain Sulu, in command of the *Excelsior,* returned from a mission to Organia. Unfortunately, the Organians have refused our appeals for them to intervene in the conflict. It would seem that, although they will energetically maintain the peace in their own territory, ultimately they believe the costs of war should compel the Klingons and us to abide by the terms of the treaty in our respective domains."

T'Pragh spoke up. "All our projections consistently show a protracted conflict with no means of imminent resolution. Unless the variables are altered with a radical change in tactics, the number of casualties will only increase over the next decade, with less than twenty-eight percent chance of victory."

"So then," West said. "A radical change it shall be, indeed. The plans for Operation Olympius are nearly finalized. I have no doubt this will be the turning point we're all waiting for."

David, looking as lost and confused as ever, finally gathered the courage to raise his hand and pose a question. "I'm sorry, please forgive me, but . . . what's Operation Olympius?"

Admiral West faced him with a self-assured cock of his head. "Son, it's going to be an all-out invasion. We're going to do precisely what those Klingon sons o' bitches least expect. We're going to take Qo'noS."

David sat back, wide-eyed, and whistled softly. "Wow," he said.

"This cannot be a decision made lightly," Thelin counseled. "On Earth, they had an expression about 'putting all of one's eggs into one basket.' Should we proceed with this mission, the expected casualties would almost certainly be in the millions—both Federation and Klingon ground forces, as well as Klingon civilians. Dozens of Starfleet ships could be lost. And there is no guarantee that the Klingons will surrender. If they do not, retreat is not an option. We cannot recover militarily should we fail."

"And that's why we won't fail, my friend," West replied. "It's a blitzkrieg strategy. They're going down, and that's all there is to it."

"I don't know," David said. "It sounds like an awful lot of destruction just to claim one planet."

West focused upon him with a glare that might possibly have had a stun setting. "Excuse me, son, but in case you hadn't no-

ticed, there's a war going on here. And there's no prize more sym-
bolic than the Klingon homeworld. You want to end this thing,
this is our only option."

"Not our *only* option, Admiral," Ra-ghoratreii said. The president sighed softly, and folded his hands before him. "Patrick . . . Thelin . . . I apologize for not seeking your involvement
with this prior to today, but several months ago, the Regula One
spacelab was appropriated for military use, under the direction of
Admiral T'Pragh."

All eyes turned toward the Vulcan woman. "Indeed," she said.
"After months of careful deliberation, we believe that the Genesis technology, originally developed in part by Doctor Marcus,
may be of strategic value." She turned toward David. "Your function here, Doctor, is to assist us with any matters of a technical
nature."

David's face reflected a mixture of both puzzlement and anxiety. "Well . . . thank you, I mean . . . I'm happy to help in any way
I can, but . . . are you proposing to deploy the Genesis effect on a
planetary scale?"

"Correct," she replied.

"Then I'm a little confused," David said. "I mean, we tested
that technology five years ago, and it failed miserably. The protomatter in the matrix caused the Genesis planet to destroy itself."

"No, Doctor," T'Pragh corrected him. "In fact, the first test of
the Genesis effect on a true planetoid was carried out just over a
month ago, in the Terra Nova sector. The protomatter effectively
decayed into standard elements, and the planetoid is now entirely
stable and quite fertile."

"But then, what . . . ?"

"The detonation in the Mutara sector five years ago simply
formed a planetoid from the gases and particles in the nebula.
Our analysis of the data following the planet's self-destruction
has led us to conclude that the matter in the nebula was of insufficient mass to form a stable planetary core."

A light of understanding suddenly flickered on within David's eyes. "So . . . then the matrix attempted to compensate for the lack of mass by increasing the intensity of the graviton waves?"

"Correct," T'Pragh replied. "And we have determined that, below a certain critical mass, the graviton waves will eventually tear apart any unstable planetary form. Furthermore, in lieu of a stable balance between mass and energy, the matrix remains active, driving the extreme biological evolution that you had witnessed."

A moment passed while David internalized this surprising new information, then his face broke into a beaming smile, and he was jubilant. "That's fantastic!" he exclaimed. "If the Genesis effect really is viable for terraforming, then . . . well, we can create new refugee camps, with everything they would need to start their lives over! And you . . . you can create new ground-based installations in that Klingon territory, to help with the war effort. Right?"

The Vulcan cleared her throat. "Doctor Marcus, please try to keep your emotions under control. We have many questions for you."

David quickly composed himself. "Right. I'm sorry, it's just . . . well, that's the best news I've heard in years. So, go ahead, I'm listening."

T'Pragh took a deep breath. "Doctor," she began. "Our simulations regarding surface deployment of the Genesis device have produced conflicting results. How far beneath the surface will the Genesis wave extend its field for molecular reorganization?"

"Er, well, that depends," David replied. "Lots of factors are involved, including the mineral content of the planetary crust, and the planet's magnetic field. But the field strength would decay exponentially the further underground you measured."

The woman set her jaw, beginning to show the Vulcan equivalent of extreme impatience. "What would be the level of biological metastasis at subterranean distances of ten, fifteen, and twenty kilometers?"

"Biological?" David said, his brow wrinkling with confusion. "What, you mean if life already existed there?"

"Correct."

"But why would you . . . Oh my God." David straightened his back, leaning ever so slightly away from the table, a wave of alarm washing over him. "Just what the hell are you proposing here?"

Sensing David's quickly fraying emotional state, Thelin raised his palm in an attempt to calm him. "David, please try to relax. This is just a discussion here. We're trying to assess all of the facts."

"No," he said, firmly shaking his head. "No, if we're going to talk facts, I demand to know what exactly is being planned."

"Doctor Marcus," T'Pragh said with a tone that could only be described as aggravation. "Any such information is given on a need-to-know basis."

"It's all right, T'Pragh," Ra-ghoratreii quickly interjected in a firm but calming voice. The four faces around the table turned to the president, who sighed heavily. "What we are proposing, Doctor Marcus, is a show of strength that the Klingon High Council cannot ignore. Plans are under development to deploy the Genesis device against the Klingon moon Praxis."

David's eyes widened with horror. "Praxis?" he whispered. "I know about Praxis. There are a half million people living there!"

"You're damn right there are!" West shouted. "A half million people in the employ of the Klingon military, running mining operations to produce energy for the weapons that are killing our people!"

"That's not true," David countered. "When I was a prisoner there for two months, there was no military presence at all. That's why Kruge kept us there—to keep us outside of the High Council's area of concern. It's nothing but civilian families living there. Good lord, there are thousands of people living underground— whole subterranean mining towns, kilometers beneath the surface! We can't possibly know what this will do to them!"

"David," Thelin said. "You don't understand the Klingon culture. Years of accumulated intelligence have taught us that you cannot make an arbitrary distinction between a civilian and a military target. The two are fully integrated into every aspect of their society."

"Intelligence? That's a misnomer if you truly believe things are so black and white." The young scientist shook his head, quietly laughing. "Unbelievable. This is *exactly* what they accused us of wanting to do. It's the reason they conquered Earth. It's the reason Kruge killed my father, and tried to kill me." He pushed back his chair and stood up from the table. "And I won't be a party to it."

Across the table, Admiral West stiffened sharply, and his voice thundered out. "Son, you can't just up and leave here. Not now."

David laughed in defiance. "Why not? Am I your prisoner here?"

West tapped the intercom panel on the table before him. "Security to council chamber four-two-seven. We have a young man who needs to be taken into temporary custody."

Back at his home, hundreds of miles from ShiKahr, David Marcus lay awake on his bed, staring up at the ceiling, which was dimly illuminated by the glow of street lamps that pierced the warm midnight air outside his window. Nearly two weeks had passed since he was summoned to that fateful meeting in the capital, yet the pain and bitterness would not subside—not while he waited for the other shoe to drop, not while he awaited the news that the attack had been carried out, using his own invention as a weapon of cataclysmic destruction.

He had fought himself these past two weeks, trying to keep five years of carefully woven emotional security from unraveling. Healing from his trauma at the hands of Kruge had been a struggle, but nothing had ever threatened to upend the very foundations upon which his recovery had been built.

For the first few weeks following his rescue from Klingon imprisonment, he had struggled through the stages of recoil—the

anger and confusion as he attempted to make sense of the violence inflicted upon him, and the impulsive act of defiance that
took his father's life. Thankfully, despite being stranded in the
unfamiliar environs of Vulcan, he had received excellent care. A
young male counselor from Betazed—a world of telepaths newly
admitted to the Federation—had taken special interest in his case,
and expertly guided him on his way to recovery, confronting the
demons that filled each fallow moment of his life with fear.

Understanding the nature of fear was the key. As David fought
a victim's natural tendencies to blame himself for the wrongs he
had suffered, he came to understand the motivations of Kruge
and the Klingons under his command—actions motivated by irrational fears that the Federation would seek to exterminate their
race. And with that understanding came freedom from David's
own fears of retribution for the creation of Genesis, and the ability to forgive the offenses against him.

Only now, five years later, after all of the healing was done, did
he see the truth. The fears of his Klingon captors weren't irrational at all. They had been right all along. David had spawned a
doomsday weapon, and his captors had acted justly to protect
themselves. David's whole system of values, of good and evil, so
painstakingly reconstructed in the wake of his trauma, had come
crashing down around him. And the faces of his dead tormentors,
newly empowered, threatened to plague his dreams once again.

So be it. If he wasn't going to be able to sleep, he would find his
peace another way. He would find absolution. He rose from his
bed and headed out the door. At least he was still a free man. He
likely had Thelin to thank for that. The meeting they'd attended
two weeks ago could have ended quite badly . . .

"Security, stand by!" Thelin shouted into the intercom before the
security channel closed. He rose to his feet, and faced Admiral
West. "Patrick, please. Tensions are obviously rather high. I have
known David Marcus since he was a child, and I will personally

vouch for his integrity. Before we venture down this path, I believe we owe it to ourselves to listen to what he has to say."

Frowning, the commander in chief considered Thelin carefully for several seconds, then spoke into the intercom. "Security, stand down. Close channel." With resignation, he turned to Ra-ghoratreii. "Mr. President, I will defer to your judgment on this matter."

The president glanced around the table, pausing at each person in turn. "Be seated, everyone. Perhaps we have been a little too insular as we stay holed up in meetings, deciding who lives and who dies. Perhaps we might benefit from the wisdom of a civilian scientist."

David sat down, exhaling with some relief and chagrin, but certainly not willing to let the matter rest. "Thank you, Mr. President," he said softly. "I apologize for my outburst. But I strongly object to the notion that wiping out a half million people in a military campaign is morally sound."

Thelin considered him with a solemn expression, almost signifying pity. "David . . . war by its nature is inherently immoral. But consider this. If we should instead proceed with the planned invasion of Qo'noS, the number of expected casualties is just as high, if not higher. Would you rather half of that number be Starfleet's finest men and women?"

"I refuse to accept that these are the only options!" David exclaimed. "It's a false dichotomy. We could . . . we could *bargain* with the Genesis technology. You said yourself that the Klingons are spending way too many resources defending their gains. They might be willing to surrender Earth voluntarily."

"This is about more than just Earth, David," Thelin replied. "Besides, if there is one thing we do understand about the Klingon culture, it's that they will not surrender unless it would be more honorable than continuing to fight . . . and only the threat of complete annihilation would make it so. That is the reason for *this* show of force, to crush their spirit, to make their efforts seem hopeless . . . this may be the only way. Yes, we may kill a half million people now, but a swift end to the war could save *billions* of lives in the long run."

"They won't surrender," David said. "They'll call your bluff. They'll know that you would never use this weapon against Qo'noS."

He paused. The awkward silence that David received in response to his argument hit him like a phaser blast to the chest. He suddenly felt dizzy. "Oh, no . . ." he mumbled. "You couldn't. You wouldn't commit an act of genocide against an entire race of people. You couldn't . . ."

"Doctor," Ra-ghoratreii said gently. "We're talking about the survival of the Federation."

David turned to T'Pragh. "You! You can't possibly agree with this. Where's the Vulcan logic in this course of action?"

T'Pragh raised an eyebrow. "The Vulcan High Command has debated this very issue at great length. And should such a decision come to pass, while regrettable, it is logical that extreme sacrifices must be made if it will serve the greater good."

"The greater good?" David replied, incredulous. "The greater good? I don't understand any of you. Where is the good in a future where the Genesis technology is an established facet of warfare? Where is the good in a universe that for all eternity will be teetering on the brink of Armageddon?"

"The universe will adjust," Thelin said. "Throughout the history of warfare, it always has. The question is where the good would be found in a universe without the Federation."

David felt a tightness in his chest, feelings of panic and hopelessness invading his mind. His breath caught in his throat and he choked back a sob. He could no longer raise his head to look Thelin in the eye.

"David," Thelin continued. "Your father spent his life protecting the Federation. He knew that sacrifices in the present are often necessary if we are ever to see any future reward."

Anger suddenly welled up in David's chest. "Don't you do

that," he said through clenched teeth. "Don't you *dare* use my father's name to say that the ends justify your means. You have no right."

"I have every right, Doctor," Thelin said with mild indignation. "I knew your father better than you can possibly imagine."

"My father believed in justice and forgiveness!" David spat back. "Not in condemning an entire race to die. He would never have . . . he would never . . ." And the words left him. He collapsed back into his chair, a defeated man.

At the head of the table, President Ra-ghoratreii rose to his feet. "Gentlemen," he said. "Both of your passions are admirable. And perhaps, years from now, these remonstrations will be studied with due reverence by the galaxy's wisest men, benefitting from the gift of hindsight." He pushed his chair under the table, and turned away, walking toward the large bay window that overlooked the skyline of ShiKahr. "However, on this day, we have only providence to guide us. And as the leader of the United Federation of Planets, my responsibility is to act decisively in the best interests of our peoples."

He slowly turned around. "Admirals, as of this moment, your sole responsibility is the planning and execution of deployment of the Genesis device against the moon Praxis. Thelin, you will take the lead, and conduct the mission aboard the *Katai*. The three of you will report to me again here, in one week, to discuss the final timetable."

He focused his gaze upon David. "Doctor Marcus, you are free to go. Please be aware that Starfleet Intelligence will monitor your movements and communications for the duration of this operation. That's all, everyone. We are adjourned." And with that, he slowly marched through the doors of the chamber.

Without a word, West and T'Pragh rose from their seats and followed the president out the door. Thelin remained seated, looking down at his hands.

Minutes passed as the two remaining men sat in silence. Motionless, David stared at the mosaic patterns on the surface of the conference table. He wanted to run . . . to get away from this place, to take a shower, to wash away any memory of what he had witnessed here this day. But he didn't even know where to go. Back to a home that was just a glorified refugee shelter? He didn't feel like he had a home. He didn't feel like anything really mattered any longer.

In time, David managed to muster the spirit to make one final plea. "Thelin . . . You still have time. You can still talk them out of this."

Thelin shook his head gently. "David . . ."

"Once you do this thing, the galaxy will never be the same. You're opening Pandora's box. You're unleashing a power that can never be reined back in."

Thelin continued to look down, unwilling to make eye contact. "I'm sorry, David. I truly am, but I have no choice. My only loyalty is to the Federation. I am Starfleet. It is . . . my family." He stood, and finally looked over to David, but the human was staring down again, lost in his misery. "*Thiptho lapth,* my friend," Thelin whispered.

And he departed, leaving David Marcus alone to contemplate his legacy.

The image of Praxis on the viewscreen grew steadily larger as the *Katai,* having finished scouting the area to Thelin's satisfaction, began its final approach. At first glance, the moon was unremarkable—a fairly typical large rocky satellite, its surface pockmarked with evidence of ancient impacts. But the moon had been colonized for many generations, with surface settlements too small to be seen from orbit without strong magnification. And deep within the planet resided some of the galaxy's most complex energy-mining operations, as the molten core at the center of the moon was tapped as a virtually inexhaustible source of power.

"Uhura," Thelin said. "Are the comm channels quiet?"

"Yes, sir," Uhura replied. "Just the normal interplanetary chatter."

"Well, be thankful these Klingon cloaks are good enough to fool their own defense networks." He turned his head down toward the helm. "Captain Sulu, put us into geosynchronous orbit around the moon, twenty thousand kilometers, equidistant from the two nearest sensor buoys."

"Aye, sir." The image of Praxis on the viewer shifted as Sulu turned the ship and settled into an orbital route. As it happened, they were positioned almost directly over the moon's terminator, and with each passing minute the surface of the world beneath them slipped slightly further into darkness. And whereas the lighted portion of the surface appeared to be barren and lifeless, marked with craters and the remnants of long-dormant volcanic peaks, the expanding shroud of night revealed the twinkle of artificial lights spread out over the surface of the sphere, condensing into the bright hubs of small colonies constructed within the safe confines of vast environmental domes.

All eyes on the bridge focused upon the tranquil scene laid out before them. Time itself seemed to slow, until Thelin broke the silence.

"Mister Chekov," Thelin said. "Program the trajectory for deployment of the Genesis torpedo near the equator, on the illuminated side of the moon."

"Aye, sir," he replied, intently setting himself to the task at hand, as if afraid that any hesitation might draw his attention back to the viewscreen.

"Captain Sulu," Thelin continued. "Prepare to drop the cloak and power the weapons systems, on my mark."

"Standing by, Admiral," Sulu responded.

Thelin climbed down from the captain's chair and stood behind the helm, still looking at the image of Praxis rotating slowly against a backdrop of alien stars shimmering through the cloaking field, providing a surreal, dreamlike view of the landscape before him . . . which, were they to be successful, would shortly be changed forever.

"Programming complete, Admiral," Chekov announced.

It was time. "All right, everyone," Thelin said in a firm but reassuring tone. "You all know your jobs. Let's do this thing and go home." He looked down at Sulu. "Now, Captain."

Sulu punched two keys on the console and moved a slider to its opposite position. As Thelin watched, the moon on the viewer before him suddenly focused into sharp relief. The lights dotting the breadth of the night side, providing illumination for the hundreds of thousands of settlements on the surface, beamed out at him in vivid clarity.

Half a million people—some living underground, or within protective forcefields that could minimize the Genesis effect. *We can't possibly know what this will do to them,* David had said.

"Awaiting orders to deploy, sir," Chekov said.

Once you do this thing, the galaxy will never be the same. You're opening Pandora's box. You're unleashing a power that can never be reined back in.

"Admiral?" Sulu inquired with a hint of alarm.

Thelin swallowed. His antennae stood firmly at attention. "Fire," he calmly commanded.

With a brief flash upon the viewscreen, the projectile launched from the torpedo bay and traced a long streak across the face of the moon as the rockets in its self-contained propulsion units guided it toward the horizon as it slowly descended to the surface.

"Re-engage the cloaking device," Thelin ordered.

"Activating now," Sulu replied. The telltale shimmer returned to the viewscreen's display.

"Admiral," Uhura called out from her station. "I have confirmation that our presence in orbit has been discovered. The Qo'noS defense network is going to high alert. Stand by . . ." She stared off, nodding slightly as she assimilated additional incoming information. "Ground-based defenses on Praxis are tracking the torpedo, but they're having trouble locking onto it."

Chekov nodded. "Then the targeting scramblers we installed on the device are working!"

"Captain Sulu," Thelin said. "Break orbit. Follow evasive pattern delta in retreat formation; we have to assume they'll be trying to track us visually. Let's get out of here."

"Aye, sir," he said. "Aft view on screen."

The *Katai* began to veer away on a course perpendicular to the moon's terminator, away from the system's sun, and the visible half of Praxis began to shrink away into a thin, bright crescent.

"Five seconds to device detonation," Chekov announced.

The seconds ticked away. The image of Praxis slowly reduced in size as the *Katai* continued on impulse power, clearing the gravity well of both the moon and the nearby planet. Somewhere on the opposite side, invisible to them, the Genesis device reached its target.

A few more seconds passed in silence, until Uhura spoke up. "Ground-based observers on Qo'noS are reporting an explosion on the surface of Praxis."

On the screen, the dim outline of Praxis was now barely visible as the sunlit surface had waned into darkness in the wake of the *Katai*'s hasty retreat. Suddenly, a fiery corona erupted over the horizon of the entire sphere, outlining its circumference with a hellish glow. In moments, the effect crept over the edge of the disc and began to wash over the surface of the moon, swallowing up the full breadth of the cratered surface in a spreading inferno.

"Admiral," Uhura said. "I'm monitoring communications . . . from Praxis."

Still standing directly behind the helm, Thelin spun round to face Uhura. "Communications . . . from the surface?"

"Stand by," she replied, squinting and looking down as she struggled to make sense of what she was hearing. "There's a lot of overlap, sir, and it's breaking up . . . the translator isn't able to do much with it. But I believe most of these are distress calls originating from subterranean sources."

"Underground mining settlements?" Thelin asked.

"I think so, sir," Uhura replied. She looked away, and Thelin noticed her eyes beginning to widen with shock.

Thelin turned back toward the viewer. The initial effect of the wave had passed, though the landscape of Praxis had become a maelstrom of both geological and biological activity. No surface settlements could possibly have survived the ravages of the wave, but there was no way to know what sort of changes the Genesis matrix could be working beneath the ground, where mining operations delved deep toward the moon's core. "Commander Uhura," Thelin said tentatively. "Speakers on."

The ship's intercom flared to life with a burst of white noise, which quickly died away, revealing the frenzied voices beneath the interference.

"Perimeter . . . forcefields holding . . . baQa' . . . ! . . . kind of energy wave . . . no response from the surface . . . read us? Qo'noS command . . ."

Intense static momentarily overwhelmed the transmission. At the helm, Sulu and Chekov exchanged glances, seeming not to know how to react.

". . . believed to be dead! Is anyone listening? Secondary wave impact . . ." Then shouts, followed by shrieks of alarm, or possibly pain.

". . . families are trapped! We cannot . . ." A female voice interjected. *"Molgoth? Come in . . . east barriers have been compromised! Can we still beam out the children? Molgoth . . . ? qeylIS . . . Qoy wIj tlhobtaHghach!"*

Additional shrieks were heard, and screams . . .

Then the speakers throughout the bridge produced nothing but a cold, empty hiss.

"Speakers off," Thelin whispered.

The noise ceased, and a stifling silence enveloped the bridge, punctuated only by the beeps and whirrs of the computer consoles that busily charted courses and analyzed data, morally oblivious to the event that had just occurred.

Thelin stepped back onto the platform at the center of the bridge and walked to the chair, but did not sit, instead facing the chair and gripping the armrests, leaning on it for support. "My God . . . What have we done?"

A beat passed. At the communication station, Uhura removed her earpiece, rose from her chair, and stood at attention. "We followed our orders, sir. . . . We did what was necessary for the sake of the Federation." And although her composure was unflappable, a single tear ran down the length of her left cheek.

Thelin did not move, even to turn his head in acknowledgment. "Yes, for the Federation . . ." he whispered. "But have we destroyed it in order to save it?"

The rest of the bridge crew stared ahead in silence. On the screen before them, retreating into the distance, shone a shining sphere of blue-green paradise, spawned in the depths of Hell.

7

Praetor Aratenik stood up from his chair at the head of the Romulan Senate, his ceremonial robes billowing about his tall, lanky form. His troubled expression foreshadowed the acrimony that would undoubtedly plague this session. The events of the past week were unprecedented on a galactic scale, and what happened today could chart a course for generations to come.

"The Senate calls to the floor Saavik of Vulcan," Aratenik announced, "the honorable ambassador from the United Federation of Planets."

Saavik rose from her seat in the front row of the gallery and stepped forward into the large round area in the center of the chamber. Beams of sunlight pierced through the high, arched windows of the domed ceiling, reaching the cartographic design splayed across the speaker's floor. Each of the eight members of the Continuing Committee, seated to either side of the praetor, focused their stern gaze on her.

"Ambassador Saavik," Aratenik continued, "do you wish to make an opening statement?"

"I do, sir," Saavik replied.

"You have five minutes," he said, returning to his seat. "Proceed."

"Thank you, sir, but I shall be brief," Saavik said, bowing her head in respect. She turned around to acknowledge the representatives seated in the rows behind her. "Honored Senators," she began, and then completed the turn to refocus her attention upon the praetor. "I am of course well aware that the subspace channels have been abuzz with rumor for the better part of a day. So allow me to confirm what will soon be publicly announced: Approximately twenty-one hours ago, Chancellor Gorkon of the Klingon High Council on Qo'noS extended to the Federation an offer to suspend hostilities indefinitely. Plans are under way to convene at a neutral location and negotiate terms for the surrender of the Klingon Empire."

Whispered voices began to stream forth from the gallery like water from a slowly opening spigot. While no one could rationally express regret at such news, the nervous tension underlying the reaction in the chamber was unmistakable. Saavik waited for the background noise to subside before continuing.

"The Federation acknowledges with regret the catastrophic loss of life in the military operations leading up to the present armistice. But we also celebrate the lives that will be saved by the cessation of further warfare and conquest. Federation relief efforts are already under way, and thousands of medical personnel and social workers have been dispatched to Qo'noS to provide aid in this difficult but hopeful time.

"The Federation once again extends its gratitude to Empress Ael and the Romulan Star Empire for their impartial support during this protracted conflict, and trust that a more peaceful galaxy will produce further cooperation among all the powers of the region, and the flourishing of diplomatic relations. On behalf of the United Federation of Planets, I thank you for your time and attention."

Saavik remained standing at attention as further mumbled voices rumbled throughout the chamber. Praetor Aratenik stood and raised his hand. "Thank you, Saavik of Vulcan. Now, if you will indulge the lines of inquiry from the seated representatives. We will begin with Proconsul Dralath. You have fifteen minutes."

Dralath rose from his seat at the praetor's right hand and fixed his steely gaze upon Saavik. Though appearing absolutely calm, the intensity in his eyes seemed to suggest a volatile zeal bubbling just beneath the surface. A guileful grin broke out upon his face.

"Ambassador Saavik," he began. "Among the members of this Senate, you of all visiting diplomats are held in the highest esteem, for you are indeed a lost child of Romulus, and your blood no doubt burns with the same passions as our own. It is because of this that your testimony on this day has left me in utter dismay. You were brought here today to explain the Federation's use of a weapon of seemingly limitless destruction, and yet you hide behind diplomatic bromides, dancing around the issue like a human ballerina."

Saavik took a deep breath. "Forgive me, Proconsul. I thought my meaning was clear. The Federation's actions with respect to the re-formation of Praxis served one purpose and one only: to bring about an immediate end to the otherwise interminable pain and suffering caused by this continuing conflict."

"The *re-formation* of Praxis?" Dralath exclaimed. "Is this the cloyingly benign term the Federation will use henceforth while it traverses the galaxy annihilating entire planetary civilizations?"

Saavik closed her eyes. How could Aratenik be so spineless as to allow a reactionary like Dralath to begin the questioning? "Sir," she began, before reopening her eyes and attempting to convey an expression of honesty and trustworthiness, "neither the members of this senate nor any other sentient beings in the galaxy need fear the motives of the Federation. We desire peace and stability, not conquest."

"Then tell me, Ambassador Saavik . . . Once the Federation has subjugated the Klingon Empire, what then? What will be the role of the Romulan Empire in this grand new order? From where shall we receive our assurances of peace and stability when facing a Federation more powerful than this galaxy has ever seen, with weapons capable of destroying entire planets on a whim?"

Saavik took yet another deep breath, struggling to keep her emotions in check. As long as Dralath—and those who deferred to his opinions—distrusted the most basic motivations of the Federation, this wasn't an argument she could possibly win. "Proconsul Dralath . . . and Praetor Aratenik," she said, turning back toward the leader's center seat. "Might I please suggest that you withhold judgment of our intentions until after the new treaty is signed. The Federation will extend an invitation to Ambassador Nanclus to attend the negotiations and to represent the interests of the Romulan people."

"I'm not certain that will be possible," Dralath said. "Empress Ael has already recalled Ambassador Nanclus to Romulus while the future of our diplomatic relations remains in doubt."

The future of our diplomatic relations? Saavik thought. *What the hell is that supposed to mean?*

"Clearly, Ambassador, you and the Federation have failed to grasp the severity of the Empress's concerns. For years, the Federation has given us assurances that they did not and would not produce or deploy weapons capable of destruction on this scale. In fact, I believe you will find that more than a few members of this governing body believe the Federation now to be in violation of treaty. We are faced with no alternative, Ambassador. Our only protection against a weapon of this magnitude is a policy of mutual assured destruction."

Saavik felt a lump in her throat and swallowed hard. "What are you saying, sir?"

Dralath stepped out from around his table and took several menacing steps toward Saavik's position on the speaker's floor. "What I am saying, Ambassador, is that the best scientific minds within our borders are already at work developing our own arsenal of Genesis weapons. We have already successfully produced the effect on a small scale."

By damnation of Shariel, Saavik thought. *At what cost did we stop this war?*

"I am truly sorry, Saavik," Dralath said, his tone suggesting perhaps a hint of genuine regret. "But you of all people should understand the need to ensure the survival of our race." He turned and marched back toward his seat at the committee table. "I have no further questions for the ambassador from the Federation," he said with cold finality.

"Very well," Aratenik said. "Next on the docket is Senator Pardek. You have fifteen minutes."

Saavik spent the remainder of the session listening absently to the questions asked of her and responding robotically with her prepared answers. She felt drained of all emotion, aggrieved over the damage to the fledgling detente with the Romulans, and in many ways betrayed by the people whom she represented. This was not a simple miscalculation. The galaxy had changed irrevocably, and the future was now more uncertain than ever.

The reports from the Federation News Service maintained an even and somewhat somber tone in the wake of the Praxis mission. Despite the unqualified success of the Federation attack, the deaths of nearly a half million souls in a single nightmarish event was difficult for any objective correspondent to convey in a dispassionate manner. Of course, as always, pundits from all along the political spectrum cast subtlety aside and weighed in for whomever was willing to listen—some claiming that no Klingon lives had value and that Qo'noS should be wiped from the map, others claiming that the Federation's own unconditional surrender would be preferable to the loss of even one more life.

But when word of the cease-fire came through just days later, the celebratory reaction that immediately spread through all the worlds of the Federation seemed entirely appropriate. Field reporters, no longer in danger from being stationed in a combat zone, freely captured these historic moments for posterity . . . and with those reports came images of the wounded civilians on both sides of the conflict—the men, women, and children who had paid a dear price for the enmity of their leaders. Among the survivors were about two thousand Klingons who had called Praxis their home, who had escaped the effects of the Genesis wave due, in whole or in part, to their deep underground habitation or the protection of various dampening forcefields.

Many of the survivors had already been rescued and relocated to Qo'noS for medical attention, with further rescue operations still under way. The instant that the Klingon High Council gave its authorization, Federation relief efforts mobilized, and within hours the first teams of doctors, nurses, social workers, and other disaster recovery personnel descended en masse onto the Klingon homeworld.

David Marcus walked down the ramp of his transport along with several dozen other relief workers—one of several teams sent to supplement the medical units that had landed the day before. As he set foot upon the landing pad, he mentally added Qo'noS to the growing list of alien worlds he had visited in his young life. The sun had just begun to set, and the buildings around him cast long shadows, made more ominous by the severe angles and embellishments of the imposing Klingon architecture. The air was still warm, and carried with it an unusual musky scent that David couldn't quite identify but found strangely appealing.

He followed the rest of the personnel as they crossed a wide street and poured through the doors of a large coliseum where evacuees were temporarily housed. As he entered, his senses were assaulted by a cacophony of bustling activity amid the sterile smells of medical supplies and the wails of the suffering patients.

Beds were laid out as far as he could see, filling the large lobby area and extending down long curved corridors on either side. Most of the patients were covered with sheets, but a few of their unnaturally horrific injuries could be seen here and there as the medical staff attended to specific cases. David's memory harkened back to the incident aboard the *Enterprise* five years earlier—an event he had never wished to relive, though now he had little choice.

His mood instantly improved when he glimpsed a familiar face. He rushed up to an elderly doctor attending to a young Klingon boy. "Doctor McCoy!" he said.

The doctor looked up and broke into a wide grin. "Doctor David Marcus! How in God's name did you get mixed up in all this?" He reached out his hand and David gripped it firmly.

"What can I say," David replied. "I guess I'm just idealistic enough to believe I can make a difference here."

"Well, your beliefs are spot-on. It's good to have you here, David."

"Thanks," he replied, hoping that McCoy spoke the truth. "So how are things going?"

"Oh, I dunno," the doctor said, casually looking about the area. "I guess when you consider that they've converted a sports arena into a triage center, things are going pretty well. Admittedly, I had to take a crash course in Klingon anatomy prior to my arrival— and it shows," he winced with chagrin. "But the good news is that I've spent the past five years figuring out how to reverse the effects of the genetic damage caused by the matrix. Even though a lot of these injuries are pretty horrific, most of the patients will eventually recover."

"I suppose that's good news," David said, trying unsuccessfully to match McCoy's level of optimism. He looked down at the boy on the cot in front of the doctor. The young Klingon was fully conscious, but seemed to be experiencing a great deal of discomfort. His torso was fully exposed, and the skin on the left side of his body was altered, growing darker and coarser the closer it was to his extremities. The effect continued along his left arm until it became sheathed in a scaly outer carapace; at the end of his arm, his hand had morphed into a primitive-looking talon.

David became aware that the boy was watching him, and shifted his attention away from the gruesome injury. "Hello! How are you feeling?" David asked him.

"What do you mean?" the boy responded with confusion. "I'm lying in bed. Why would I be feeling anything?"

"I mean, are you in any pain?"

Oddly, the boy's spirit seemed to brighten at the question. "Yes, my arm hurts a lot. But that's the will of Kahless. He put an angry spirit in there, so that it would help to claw the eyes out of my enemies!" He took a few playful swipes at David with his altered limb. "My father taught me all about Kahless. And now he's gone to be with him."

David's heart sank. "Your father was killed on Praxis?"

"He was working in the mines," the boy said. "But he was serving the Empire! Mother said he died honorably, and he would still go to *Sto-vo-kor*. Do you think he has met Kahless yet?"

McCoy held up his hand. "I'm sure your mother knows all about it. She'll be back in a few minutes, okay, son?"

"Okay," the boy replied, and resumed swiping the air with his novel appendage. McCoy motioned to David to follow, and together they made their way down the promenade around the perimeter of the stadium, which was lined with endless rows of cots and gurneys.

David raised up his prosthetic hand and examined the fingers as he flexed them repeatedly. He looked over at McCoy. "Doctor, do you believe in karma?"

McCoy offered back a perplexed expression. "First of all, we're both doctors here, so call me Leonard. Second of all . . . what the hell are you talking about?"

David shook his head. "Think about it. The Klingons killed my father. Now, a weapon that *I* created is killing the fathers of Klingon children." His eyes focused on the patterns in the stone floor under his feet. He felt too ashamed to raise them. "I just want it to stop. I want this all to be over."

"It is over, David," McCoy assured him. "You couldn't have stopped this, you know. Every weapon that's ever been fired in a war has relied upon technology that usually had benign origins. We always strive to better ourselves with invention and ingenuity, but someone else will always come along and try to use that same technology to create death and destruction. But we can't let those forces stop the advance of science. We just have to trust that, eventually, enough good people will do the right thing."

"I know you're right," David said, "but it doesn't make me feel much better." He stopped walking. Rows upon rows of injured Klingon civilians still lay sprawled out before him. The sounds of pain and suffering still filled the air. He looked up at the ceiling, sucked in his breath, and wept.

McCoy approached him and placed his arm over his shoulders. "It's all right, David," he assured him. "You're gonna be okay."

David sniffed, and reached up to wipe the moisture from his face. "It's just that . . . every day when I think I'm going to be okay, something new happens . . . some new unexpected crisis swoops down like a vulture and rips my heart out."

"Yep," McCoy said. "But the good news is that every day, it grows right back. The only time you should start to worry is if one day, it doesn't." McCoy gave him a pat. "You want to get to work?"

David smiled weakly. His heart remained in its proper place. As long as he still had the capacity to feel, he would be okay. "Yeah, I think I really do."

"Let's get to it," McCoy said, and together they approached a nearby bed where an elderly woman lay. McCoy picked up the chart. "Now, what can we do to fix you, young lady?"

". . . and it is the most sincere hope of every citizen of the Federation that, by establishing a peaceful and mutually beneficial coexistence, never again will any world under any banner suffer the tragic loss of life that befell all of us during this terrible period of strife and conflict.".

The words of President Ra-ghoratreii echoed through the conference hall at Camp Khitomer, a newly established settlement on a planet in neutral, unclaimed territory. Banners depicting the colors and symbols of each Federation world hung proudly around the outer walls of the great room, but among them, displayed in a prominent location, was the emblem of the Klingon Empire—undoubtedly an effort on the part of the Federation negotiators to appear conciliatory toward their defeated adversaries as they continued to arbitrate the terms of their surrender.

Upon the stage, beside the podium where the president was making his introductory speech to open the session, a conference table had been set. To one side, next to the president's empty chair sat the Vulcan vice president, Sentek, alongside Starfleet Admirals West and Thelin. At the other end of the table, Chancellor Gorkon of the Klingon Empire was seated with his daughter Azetbur, who, as senior councillor, assumed most of the roles of second in command; his chief of staff, General Chang; and his military adviser, Brigadier Kerla. Throughout the hall, rows upon rows of spectator seating remained unoccupied save for a court reporter and two security officers. Barring a massive failure of the treaty negotiations, those seats would soon be filled with diplomats, dignitaries, and press, poised to hear the announcement of peaceable accords between the two galactic superpowers. But for now, the session was closed, for without mutually acceptable terms, the cessation of hostilities remained tenuous and unsettled.

"Relief efforts are ongoing," the president continued, "and the unprecedented cooperation between Federation and Klingon organizations and agencies committed to the welfare of all our civilian populations bodes quite well for the future of our relations as we press forward into this new and undiscovered realm."

Thelin gazed across the table at the leaders of the Klingon people, who gave the outward appearance of being defeated in every sense of the word. Despite Ra-ghoratreii's earnest attempts to keep the tone of the occasion positive and uplifting, Gorkon let his head hang low, his eyes staring down at the table, his ears barely catching a word spoken thus far in the proceedings.

"Yet in the shadow of death, new life is brought forth: Our best scientific research teams have concluded that Praxis is now stable and fertile, and in due time will be quite well suited for resettlement. In fact, it would seem that providence has brought about a most ironic twist, as our data suggests that the planetary core had in fact been growing quite unstable, and that in lieu of radical intervention such as that brought about by the Genesis effect,

Praxis might have suffered a cataclysmic geological event within a year's time."

General Chang pounded his fist on the table. Though the chancellor seemed humbled, Chang and his one good eye—the one not covered by a dark, crudely attached patch—still retained a glimmer of spirited defiance. "*Ghay'cha'!!!*" he growled. "How much longer must we subject ourselves to this infernal Federation propaganda?"

The president paused his address. "Forgive me, General," he said, bowing his head with genuine sincerity. "It was not my intent to be patronizing."

"Patronizing?" Chang laughed softly, and his speech became soft and measured, almost rehearsed. "What other purpose can our presence here possibly serve but to be patronized? Our time is over; our age of glory has passed, carried on the winds of time. Have we not heard the chimes at midnight? Let us finish it. Let us sit upon the ground, and tell sad stories of the death of kings."

Ra-ghoratreii stepped out from behind the podium and slowly walked back to the conference table. "Perhaps it is better that we dispense with the formalities. Clearly we still have much work to do if we are to find common ground." He took his seat, and folded his hands atop the table.

Chancellor Gorkon lifted his head and momentarily shrugged off his trancelike malaise. "I fear, Mr. President, that the common ground may be so elusive as to be unobtainable. We sit here this day only because the High Council will not abide the genocidal elimination of our people."

The president's eyes widened with alarm at the suggestion. "Chancellor," he assured him. "I cannot stress enough our unilateral opposition to any policy that seeks the annihilation of another race."

"Is that so?" Gorkon replied cynically. "Where, then, would you draw the line if every Klingon who yet draws breath were willing to defend his honor to the death? When would you concede defeat while you still retain the power to wipe out billions in a single strike?" A simpering look crossed his sharp Klingon visage as he slowly shook his head. "Your challenge, sir, is not to compel us to sign whatever treaty you find acceptable. Your challenge is to convince billions of Klingon men and women to set aside their innate desires to seek honor in retribution, and to accept your vision of a brave new world."

Thelin spoke up. "Chancellor, I know that I speak for most Andorians when I say that our volatile passions drove us headlong into this conflict, with no thoughts of a peaceful resolution. But I have seen firsthand how the rules of war have changed. I have seen what it means to possess the power, not only to exterminate our enemies, but also to destroy ourselves in the process. We have reached a threshold, beyond which only through peace can either of our civilizations survive."

Chang stood up, his frustration bursting forth from every pore. "And what, pray tell, is so honorable about 'survival'? Thus conscience does make cowards of us all. You speak of peace; I ask, what use is peace when our generation will be remembered with dishonor for all eternity?"

Thelin kept his response calm and measured. "I would suggest, General, that future generations may judge you much less harshly than you anticipate," he said. "A great man once taught me that one's legacy is never measured by what one accomplishes in life, but rather by the hope one leaves behind when one is gone."

Chang stared at him for several long seconds before sitting back down. "Empty platitudes," he muttered. "Hypocritical moralizing from the greatest war criminal that the universe has ever known."

The room fell silent. Seated next to the president, Sentek raised an eyebrow.

War criminal? Thelin pondered. The words struck like a blade through his chest. Was this the reputation he had garnered for his actions during the conflict? Was that to be his legacy in the annals of the Klingon Empire?

"Now just a minute," Admiral West said firmly, extending a

scolding finger in the direction of the visiting entourage. "You're talking to a decorated Starfleet admiral. His actions have always been guided by the rules of war."

"Rules of war?" Brigadier Kerla interjected with a nonplussed inflection. "What an interesting choice of words. Here is what we know from our own intelligence reports: that Thelin of Andoria was directly responsible for the murder of at least two senior officers aboard the *Katai,* that he directed and carried out a series of civilian massacres against the Archanis colonies, and that he led the mission to deploy the Federation's new weapon, exterminating the population of Praxis as if they were bothersome insects." He turned toward the president. "What, precisely then, is *disallowed* under your 'rules of war'?"

"This is ridiculous," West said, leaning back in his chair. He gestured broadly with his right hand. "Shall we run down the litany of acts committed by the Klingon overseers against the population of Earth these last five years?"

"Stop it!" Azetbur shouted. All the delegates at the table turned toward the chancellor's daughter—her eyes narrowed, her teeth grinding with aggravation. "Have you all forgotten why we are here?" she asked softly. "What's done is done. The past is gone. We are not fit to judge our own prior actions. That right is left to Kahless, or whatever deity you choose to serve. What is at stake here today is the future of both our races. What we must decide is whether or not our children will be given a chance to grow up, and find their honor in their own way."

Thelin looked down. How would Uzaveh the Infinite, the Andorian creator, judge him? He had created nothing—he had no progeny, and he had left Andor at a critical time, when he might have helped to solve the crises plaguing the world. From his legacy, nothing was made whole. Instead, his path was marred by swaths of destruction.

Ra-ghoratreii nodded toward Azetbur. "Honorable councillor, at least on that point, we are in agreement. So I beg you, tell me . . . what must be done to preserve both of our people's futures?"

Chang shook his head. "How naïve have we all become? Can you not see the hopelessness of these desires? We are wasting our time here. I have lent my ear to the people of Qo'noS. They do not desire peace. They wish to die on their feet, *fighting* to the last. Hath not a Klingon passions? Prick us, do we not bleed? Wrong us . . . shall we not *revenge?*" He clenched his fist, and it shook with the repressed anger of a billion dishonored souls.

Thelin's heart sank as he assessed his role in the events that had brought them to this juncture. *You're opening Pandora's box.* David's words, now seeming so poignantly true, echoed through the Andorian's mind. As it happened, Thelin had known little of Earth mythology until his visit with Arne Darvin five years before had motivated him to do some research. But it was all too clear now. Starfleet was his beloved—his *Pandora*—and like a cursed son of Iapetus he had allowed her to release such enduring evils into the universe. Only one thing remained . . . and that was hope.

A hope that could be realized only through sacrifice.

Thelin rose to his feet. "The solution seems clear to me." All those present turned their attention toward the Andorian and his suddenly confident demeanor.

Thelin looked to each member of the Klingon delegation in turn. "Unquestionably, the Klingon people will not accept a peaceable accord unless honor can be satisfied. What you require is a pariah—a man who will accept full responsibility for the dishonorable acts against the Klingon Empire, and who will face the consequences."

Ra-ghoratreii raised a hand to silence him. "Thelin! Sit down. You don't realize what you're saying."

The Andorian looked down at the president, his antennae standing rigidly at attention. "On the contrary, Mr. President, I realize exactly what I am saying." And his voice firmly conveyed that realization—the wisdom of a man who, for the first time, fully comprehended his purpose in life. "Tell me, Chancellor Gorkon, would my extradition provide sufficient reconciliation to appease your people, so that they might accept a peaceful resolution?"

Gorkon blinked at him, pausing to consider in-depth the ramifications of this proposal. He looked over at his daughter, who raised her eyebrows with intrigue, and he nodded slowly. "I think, were we to properly frame this act as reparation for an honor debt, it might." He looked over to Chang, who remained silent but appeared mollified. "Indeed, it might. But you must be aware," he continued, returning his focus to Thelin, "your extradition presupposes your guilt. Of course, you have the right to a trial, where you will be found guilty and summarily executed."

"I understand," Thelin said. "But if this is the only way to stop an imminent apocalypse, is it not a small price to pay?"

Ra-ghoratreii held up his hand, becoming exasperated that this matter was proceeding so rapidly beyond his control. "Thelin . . . the Federation does not simply turn over Starfleet admirals for trial in foreign courts, especially in the wake of a military victory. If you do this, we will disavow any support for your actions."

Thelin faced him with immutable confidence. "What I do here today, I do of my own free will as an individual." *And for the first time,* he thought, *I will know my purpose. I will be the catalyst for reconciliation. I will become whole.*

The president stood and faced the Andorian, stepping in close to him and lowering his voice to a whisper. "Thelin . . . we don't yet know what other options may reveal themselves. If you do this, there's no turning back."

Thelin smiled. "Mr. President, we both know that there are no other options. Let me do my part. The rest is up to you."

The Efrosian bowed his head in a measure of respect that he afforded only the truly deserving few. "I—I'm not sure what to say, except that your sacrifice here on this day will not soon be forgotten." He placed his hand upon Thelin's shoulder. "Do you require time to put your affairs in order?"

"Sir, my affairs are in order. I have no family; yet I count among my children all the young men and women throughout the Federation who will gain hope for the future. For them, I regret having only one life to give."

Gorkon stood, and his daughter immediately did so as well. He pounded his fist against his chest, and then extended his arm in the manner of the Klingon salute. "Thelin of Andoria," he said. "For these last days of your life, you will be the bane of the Klingon Empire—an object of hatred, the lightning rod for the fury of a scorned and defeated race. You are the ransom for the sins of your people. But one day," he said, extending his arms and bowing from the shoulders, "I believe you will be remembered among the honored figures of our history. *Qapla'!*"

Epilogue

"Thank you!" David shouted behind him as he stepped quickly down the boarding ramp of the commercial shuttlecraft *Ladyhawke.* "You'll be back at this time tomorrow, then?"

"Unless you call to tell me otherwise," his hired pilot called back down to him. "You can raise me at the orbital spacedock."

The words began to fade, for David had already made his way down off the landing pad and onto the walkway that snaked its way through colorful gardens to the front entrance of the embassy. He turned and gave the pilot a thumbs-up signal, and the shuttle engines roared to life as the craft ascended through the twilight sky.

Romulus, David thought, as he added it to his ever-increasing list of visited worlds. The evening air was warm, but much more humid than the dry, desert environment he had grown accustomed to, and it tantalized the senses with smells of innumerable types of flora and other living things.

As he approached the large brass gates, they suddenly swung outward with surprising force, and there stood Saavik, stunning in a flowing gown as the lights of the mansion behind her cast a radiant halo about her silhouetted form. She rushed forward to where David stood and threw her arms around him, holding him so tightly that David wondered if she might be terrified to let go.

"I'm so pleased that you were able to come," she spoke softly into his ear.

"I'm really glad to be here," he replied. "I've wanted to visit ever since you took this assignment." They loosened their embrace, and David held her at arm's length, looking into her eyes, and finding within them an unmistakable glimmer of apprehension. "Saavik, what's wrong?"

She winced, and choked back a sob. "*Everything* is wrong, David. It's all falling apart." She took a deep breath, and looked up at the sky as starlight began to emerge from under the veil of dusk. . "The diplomatic crisis with the Federation is escalating. They're recalling ambassadors from planets throughout both quadrants. They've even pulled Caithlin Dar out of Nimbus III."

"My God," David said with shock. "I had no idea things had gotten so far out of hand."

Saavik nodded. "There's no assurance that the embassy here will remain much longer. The bureaucrats are more interested in winning an arms race than maintaining goodwill with the other galactic powers." She looked back into David's eyes and sighed deeply. "I'm sorry to burden you with this."

"No, don't be!" David assured her. "Your burdens are mine, too."

She smiled. "Have you had an evening meal?"

"Oh, I'm fine. I grabbed a bite on the shuttle."

"Then walk with me," she said, offering her arm to him.

As they strolled through the courtyard inside the embassy gates, David couldn't recall a time in recent memory when he had felt so much at peace. Quaint lanterns illuminated their path as they passed by ornately sculpted fountains, the sound of their trickling water blending beautifully with the rustle of the balmy breeze through the surrounding foliage.

Saavik was calmer now; David's presence seemed to soothe her volatile affect and to allow her Vulcan upbringing to manifest itself. They walked without speaking, but the silence was relaxed and comforting, as it could be only between two people who shared a genuine intimacy. Only when it felt appropriate did she finally break the stillness.

"As it happens," she said, "I am eligible to petition for Romulan citizenship. It is my birthright."

"But . . ." David responded with confusion. "Wouldn't you have to renounce your Federation citizenship? Sever your ties to Vulcan?"

"I don't know. Perhaps . . ." she said, sounding detached and indifferent. "But I don't know who to believe in anymore. All I know is that if I am to be recalled, and this embassy is to close its doors, I would rather stay here than return to Vulcan."

"You can believe in me," David assured her. "If there is no one else you can count on—no one you can trust—you can have faith that I will stand by you."

"Thank you, David," she said. "But I'm afraid we will be worlds apart." Her voice dwindled away to a weak whisper. "Don't worry about me. I've spent most of my life alone."

"Not anymore," he whispered back. He removed his communicator from his vest pocket with his left hand and flipped it open. "David Marcus to *Ladyhawke*. Captain Dillon, come in."

"Dillon here," the response came back.

"Change of plans, Captain," David said. "Go on and head for home. Looks like I'll be staying here longer than planned." He looked at Saavik and smiled. "Maybe a *lot* longer," he said softly.

"Roger that," Dillon replied. *"Good luck to ya."*

Saavik grasped David's right hand and caressed it. "You will do this for me?" she asked. "But . . . Earth has been liberated. What about your home? What about the Federation?"

David laughed sweetly. "Saavik . . . I've spent more years of my life with you than I've spent living on Earth. That's not my home. *Your* home is my home, whatever your decision may be. And besides . . ." He flipped his communicator closed and tossed it aside, then wrapped his arm around her and drew her close. "I think the Federation will be just fine without us."

A Gutted World

Keith R.A. DeCandido

Historian's Note

This novel takes place in the year 2373 on the Old Earth calendar, the equivalent of the fifth season of *Star Trek: Deep Space Nine* and the third season of *Star Trek: Voyager,* and in the vicinity of the events of *Star Trek: First Contact.*

A dirty house in a gutted world,

A tatter of shadows peaked to white,

Smeared with the gold of the opulent sun.

—Wallace Stevens

"A Postcard from the Volcano"

1

"I can assure you, Dalin, that I am but a plain, simple clothier. I've no idea where the shapeshifter might be."

Corat Damar—who still wasn't used to being referred to by his newly acquired rank of dalin—glared at the placid face and beatific smile of the man in the guest chair of his office. Behind him was a large glass door, currently closed against the noise and bustle of the Terok Nor Promenade. *This whole thing is a waste of time.* But Damar was a soldier, and his commanding officer had given him an order, so he followed it, and interrogated Elim Garak.

For all the good it will do.

"According to one of my sources," Damar said, "you were friends with the shapeshifter before he disappeared."

"I was hardly that, Dalin," Garak said. "In fact, Odo and I only spoke a few times. As a shapeshifter, he had no use for my services, and as a clothier, I have very little use for the ins and outs of station security." Holding up a hand, he added, "Present company excepted, of course, Dalin. And may I say, congratulations on your well-deserved promotion. I'm sure the Promenade will be far safer under your tutelage."

"Thank you." Damar said the words as insincerely as he could, which took little effort. He wanted nothing from the tailor save information that he knew he'd never get. The security file on Garak was huge and yet said absolutely nothing. He *might* have been Obsidian Order. He *might* have been a target of the Order's recently retired head, Enabran Tain. He *might* have been protected by Tain.

Damar hated the Order, and hated dealing with people who were even suspected to be agents.

But he had one more spin of the dabo wheel to make before he let Garak go. Holding up a padd, he tossed it onto the table in front of Garak, where it landed with a metallic clack. "And then there are the purchases."

"I make *many* purchases in my line of work, Dalin."

"Yes—textiles, sewing machinery, display units. And yet, the parts on this list don't conform to any piece of equipment that's registered for your shop. However, my colleagues on the station's engineering staff have informed me that these parts *are* essential to creating a containment unit."

"Really? How fascinating."

"Do you deny that you are creating a containment unit, Mister Garak?"

"Please, Dalin, it's just Garak—plain, simple—"

Damar rose to his feet. "There is nothing plain or simple about you, tailor!" Immediately, he brought his temper under control. "What is it that you intend to do with this equipment?"

"Simply a tinkering project I'm working on in my spare time. Business has been slow of late. Fewer Cardassians have come to my shop, and most Bajorans cannot afford my wares. If not for the Ferengi, I fear I would go out of business entirely. While the walk-in business is always appreciated from ships passing through, it's regular customers who keep the modern business alive, and those—"

Feeling the interrogation slip through his fingers again, Damar sat back down. "I don't care about the ins and outs of shop management, Garak. Just answer the question."

Garak shifted in his chair. "Yes, well, I'm afraid I'm not very . . . comfortable with telling the specifics to such a man as you, Dalin. You see—the device in question is . . ."

When Garak's hesitation threatened to go on for ten seconds, Damar repeated, "Answer the question!"

"It's a gift for a friend. A fairly salacious one, if you must know. You see, it enables the two users—or more, if they're so inclined—to—"

The sexual practices of Garak's friends were even lower on the list of things Damar wished to be informed of than the economics of Garak's business. "I want you to produce the device you're creating for your friend."

"Dalin, I *really* don't think this is the kind of thing that an officer of your standing should be exposed to. Really, it's quite crude."

Getting to his feet once again, Damar walked around to the other side of the desk. "I believe I'll be able to tolerate it." He grabbed Garak by the arm and hoisted the tailor to his feet with one hand. With the other, he picked up the padd with the equipment list. "Come on."

In truth, Damar knew this was a waste of time. Garak wouldn't have told the lie if he didn't have physical proof to back it up. If he was creating a containment unit—of the type, say, to hold the liquid contents of a shapechanger, similar to that used by Doctor Mora Pol on Bajor shortly after discovering Odo—he wouldn't make it obvious, and would have in fact disguised it as something else, such as a sex toy.

If he was telling the truth, then Damar was wasting his time and would look like an idiot.

Damar had never understood why Dukat had put the shapechanger in charge of security after Thrax's departure in the first place. True, he'd gained a reputation for mediating disputes on Bajor, and in the seven years he'd served at the post, he'd proven to be an able investigator, but to put him in charge of security on the Promenade? That was simply asking for trouble. No one knew what his species was, and he was cared for by a Bajoran scientist—yes, one who'd proven loyal to Cardassia, but still . . .

Odo's recent disappearance was welcome to Damar, and not just because Damar got his job—along with the promotion from glinn to dalin, which meant a significant pay increase as well as more prestige in Central Command. No, the shapechanger was trouble, and always had been. He was always fair to the damned terrorists down on Bajor. Dukat had said that made him an asset; Damar never subscribed to that notion.

He kept his iron grip on Garak's arm—and ignored the clothier's protests about it—all the way down the Promenade to the shop. Some garresh or other—Damar had yet to learn the names of all those under his command—stood at the door, which had been security-sealed for the duration of Garak's interrogation.

"Remove the seal," Damar told the garresh.

As the young soldier did so, Garak said, "I must once again protest the need for such a seal, Dalin. It creates the impression that my shop is a den of iniquity. That's all well and good for Rom's Bar—the Ferengi thrives on that sort of thing—but I run a *legitimate* business, one that suffers if it becomes a focus of attention from security personnel."

"That isn't my concern," Damar said. "Besides, it's standard procedure." He didn't bother to add that it only became standard procedure when Damar took over security.

"If you say so," Garak said with a shrug. "As I said before, my knowledge of security is limited."

Damar didn't believe that for a second. Once the seal was broken and the doors to the shop parted, Damar all but threw Garak over the threshold, then held up the padd. "You will produce every piece of equipment on this list and place it on your counter."

Straightening his outfit and making a small bow, Garak said, "Of course."

Someone on the engineering staff had shown Damar what the containment unit would probably look like. What Garak produced looked nothing like that. It didn't look like much of anything, in fact. But Damar did his duty and looked it over, and saw that all the parts were accounted for, and that it looked nothing like a containment unit. Damar could, if he squinted, see how it might be used as a sex aid. Frankly, Damar preferred Rom's holosuites—they offered a more complete package, and he didn't feel like he was cheating on his wife—but to each his own.

"Is there anything else, Dalin, or may I put this . . . rather distasteful object out of the way?"

"If it's so distasteful," Damar asked, "then why create it in the first place?"

"Friendship sometimes demands that one put aside one's own aesthetic sense."

Damar rolled his eyes. "Rationalize your perversions however you want." With that, he turned and left the clothier's, signaling for the garresh to follow. Once they were out of the shop, he said, "Keep an eye on him. I want someone on the Promenade patrol to be watching his store at all times."

As he spoke, he saw that Gul Dukat was walking into Rom's. "If anyone needs me, I'll be in Rom's," he said.

"Yes, sir!" the garresh said.

Quickly, Damar strode across the Promande, heading for the bar. Damar was grateful for the destination, as he'd found the Ferengi establishment to be the only place he felt comfortable on the entire station.

In truth, Damar hadn't wanted the position on Terok Nor. It was too far from home and family, and it was, he had thought at the time, a backwater assignment.

Legate Parn had assured him otherwise. Damar had been hearing rumors that Cardassia would pull out of Bajor, that what resources the world had left were not worth putting up with their tiresome resistance. Certainly the time Damar hadn't spent in his ever more fruitless search for his predecessor had been spent cleaning up messes made by the damned resistance.

But Parn had said repeatedly that Terok Nor was a critical station to Cardassia's future, and that there was no danger of Cardassia leaving Bajor any time soon.

Damar had, of course, heard other rumors, but he dismissed those. His stock in trade was evidence—following rumors just led you to a dead end.

Glancing back at Garak's shop, he added dolefully to himself, *And sometimes even the evidence takes you there.*

The Promenade was filled with people, but was not very noisy. The Bajorans knew to keep quiet, and everyone else was usually on their way somewhere else. Once he walked through the doors to Rom's, though, the ambient noise level went up considerably—especially since this was the "somewhere else" that many were on their way to. Both dabo tables were fully occupied, with winners screaming with joy and losers cursing. The *dom-jot* table had a wait, and most of the seats were occupied.

There was, however, a clear path from the door to the bar, because at the end of that path was Skrain Dukat. Everyone on the station knew to stay out of the gul's way.

As Damar approached the bar, the proprietor placed a large glass of *kanar* in front of the station prefect. "Uh, here you go, Gul Dukat. It's at the temperature you like—and it's, uh, on the house, of course."

Inclining his head, Dukat grabbed the glass. "Thank you, Rom. How is business?"

"Oh, it's fine. Although—" The Ferengi hesitated. "—one of the holosuites is down. I've tried to perform maintenance, but—"

"Say no more," Dukat said with a smile after swallowing some of his drink. "I'll have Karris take a look at it before she goes off duty."

Rom gave a wide, snaggletoothed smile. "Thank you, Gul! That's very nice of you."

"Nonsense. Your holosuites are one of the station's main attractions. I'm simply looking out for the station's well-being." He took another sip of *kanar.*

Damar remained standing behind Dukat. He knew that the gul had registered Damar's presence, and he'd been serving on Terok Nor just long enough to know better than to interrupt. Dukat would speak to him when he was ready, not a moment before.

"How fares your brother?"

Rom sounded almost petulant. "How should *I* know? Quark

hasn't spoken a word to me since he sold me this place and bought his moon! It's like I don't even *have* a brother!" Rom blinked a few times. "Actually, that's kinda nice, now that I think about it."

Dukat chuckled and gulped down more of his drink, before finally turning to look at his security chief. "Ah, Damar. Please tell me that you've made progress in your search for our elusive shapeshifter."

"I'm afraid I can't, Gul. I questioned Garak, but he claimed to know nothing."

Frowning, Dukat said, "I thought you said he'd obtained the pieces for a containment unit that could hold one of his kind."

"Yes—he showed me what he was building with those parts. Trust me, it wouldn't hold Odo, or much of anything else."

"You believe Garak to be a false lead?"

Damar hesitated. "I can't tell if he *is* a false lead, or if he is sufficiently good at covering his tracks. There's circumstantial evidence to support the notion that he's hiding something, and you've seen the same anomalies in his records I have—it practically screams the Order. But, as usual for the Order, there's no evidence. And he could simply be who he says he is—a plain, simple, *very* annoying clothier."

Laughing, Dukat put what he probably thought was a reassuring hand on Damar's shoulder. "I understand your frustration, Damar, believe me. I have my own—shall we call them issues?— with Garak. I believe you should search his shop—top to bottom. Leave no dress unturned. Anything that cannot be accounted for as belonging in a clothier's is to be confiscated."

This struck Damar to be as big a waste of time as questioning Garak—if he really *was* Order, he wouldn't be that sloppy—but he knew many of the people under his command didn't like Garak, and would take joy in ripping apart his store. If nothing else, it'd be good for morale. "It'll be done tomorrow morning, right when he opens."

"Good. Now, then—"

Whatever else Dukat was going to say was interrupted by an

explosion, followed by the sound of an alarm. Before he even fully registered the alarm, Damar's feet were moving, running to the exit and toward the ore processors.

His people were already evacuating personnel. The acrid stench of burning conduits filled his nostrils, and the air was thick with smoke. There was evidence of a fire, but the internal fire-suppression systems appeared to have done their work.

Activating his communicator with one hand while clearing smoke from his face with the other, he said, "Damar to infirmary, medical emergency in Ore Processing, Section 9."

"*On my way,*" said the voice of the doctor on duty.

Seeing one of his officers, Glinn Comra, Damar asked, "What happened?"

Comra handed him a data clip. "An explosion. Looks like pretty typical resistance stuff—and this proves it."

Damar glared at Comra, then took the data clip and activated it, at which point it played an audio file.

"*This is the Kohn-Ma. We have destroyed this ore processor to remind the Cardassians that we will not stand for their remaining on our world. We—*"

Angrily, Damar turned off the clip. He'd heard this tired rhetoric before.

Dukat approached the scene. "The resistance, I assume?"

"Yes." Damar handed the clip to Comra and said, "Continue rescue operations, then get a forensic team in here. It's past time the Kohn-Ma was ended."

Nodding to both Damar and Dukat, Comra took his leave.

Staring at Dukat, Damar said, "Why do we continue to remain on this useless rock? Even without incidents like this, ore production has gone down every year for the past five years. Meanwhile, rebel attacks have grown worse, especially after you had their religious leader killed."

Dukat let out a sigh. "Yes, killing Opaka Sulan did serve only to make her a martyr to their cause, didn't it? Still, nothing to be done. This station is far too important to abandon now, Damar."

With that, the prefect left the scene, leaving Damar to oversee rescue operations. A medical team had arrived, and started treating the wounded—the Cardassians first, obviously. The Bajorans could wait. As likely as not, the injured Bajorans were the ones who set off the explosion—or they knew who did. He made a mental note to interrogate them before they were treated—to use the promise of treatment as leverage for getting answers.

It probably wouldn't work—it almost never did—but it was worth trying on the off chance that he'd find one person who couldn't stand the pain. A chain needed only one weak link to break, after all.

2

No'Var Outpost
Near the Romulan Border
Klingon Empire

Lieutenant Krivaq, son of Gorv, simply could not win.
He had thought the posting to the No'Var Outpost would
be the relief he'd been desperate for. The third son of Gorv, he had
been spending far too much of his life of late mediating disputes
between the first and second sons. His older brothers were constantly going to Krivaq whenever they argued about something, and
they were *always* arguing about something. The disposition of the
House of Gorv's meager holdings. The proper way to prepare *rokeg*
blood pie. Who would retain possession of their mother's *bat'leth*.
The right price to pay for fresh *gagh*. The proper way to install a new
door on the front of the house. And on and on and *on*.

Then, at last, Krivaq was assigned to No'Var. It was on the
Romulan border, too far for real-time communication from Qo'noS,
which Krivaq had thought would be the end of his torment.

And it was. But a fresh torment had begun.

"There were three members of our House on Narendra III that
fateful day," Commander J'rak was saying as he paced the outpost's nerve center. He and Krivaq were the only ones on duty, and
Krivaq had only one more hour before he was off duty and could go
to the mess hall. There was supposed to be fresh *racht* today. Krivaq
loved *racht*.

But first he had to endure J'rak telling the Narendra III story.
Again. Krivaq had been serving on No'Var for five months now,

and he'd lost track of the number of times J'rak had felt the need to tell this damned tale.

"There was my grandfather, Kamril, after whom my House is still named. There was his cousin, Morgar, a doughty warrior who had won many battles against the Kreel. And of course, there was Morgar's mate, Vaga, who could shoot a *glob* fly from half a *qell'qam* away. They were assigned to Narendra III to defend the base and maintain its security."

And yet, they couldn't have been very good at it, since the base was destroyed. Krivaq was not suicidal enough to say that out loud, but he often thought it when J'rak started on the Narendra III story.

"Of course, they thought the base safe from the Romulans. After all, we'd heard nothing from them since the *Tomed* incident with the Federation."

J'rak laughed heartily, and Krivaq—whose back was to his commander—imagined he could see J'rak's corpulent form vibrate with the action. His armor was a feat of engineering; Krivaq could not believe that the Defense Force mass-produced uniforms for anyone that fat. It simply *had* to be custom made.

"If only that had remained so. The galaxy is a better place without those pointy-eared *petaQpu'* in it."

On that, Krivaq could agree. Romulans were cowardly and dishonorable—all the more so because they claimed to *have* honor.

"But suddenly, without warning, they attacked, unveiling those *khest'n* warbirds. Damn things plowed right through our defenses like *nothing*."

Krivaq was always amused when J'rak started referring to "our" defenses, as if he were there when it happened, not an infant back on Qo'noS.

Suddenly, J'rak put a hand on Krivaq's shoulder, almost causing Krivaq to jump out of his chair. He managed to suppress the shocked reaction—a warrior should never be shocked, after all—but it was a near thing, for his instincts had dulled horribly in this place.

"That's why this outpost is so important, Lieutenant," the commander said. "They did it at Narendra III, and two years later they did it again at Khitomer. You never know when those *toD-SaHpu'* will try to sneak across the border again. They were behind the House of Duras's coup, you know."

Of course I know that. Everyone *knows that.* Krivaq checked his chronometer, but it was still most of an hour before he went off shift. His stomachs started rumbling in anticipation of the *racht* that was still so far away.

The proximity alarm blared, blowing past his warrior's instincts and making him jump in his seat. In the five months that he'd been assigned here, that proximity alarm had only gone off when the supply ship came, and it wasn't due for another week.

Then he checked the readout and the rumble in his stomachs shifted from hunger to nausea. The alarm was coming from the other side of the Romulan border.

"We're picking up a ship on the Rom side—it just decloaked."

"What?" J'rak bellowed loud enough that it actually hurt Krivaq's ears. "Confirm!"

Krivaq re-took the sensor readings. "It's a warbird, bearing directly on this outpost, weapons hot."

J'rak spit on the deck. "Filthy *petaQpu'*. Go to battle alert! Arm disruptors and open fire!"

Touching a control, Krivaq put the outpost on battle alert. The lights changed to a dull red color, and the outpost's shields snapped into place.

The No'var Outpost had a full array of disruptor blasters and a quantum torpedo cannon, neither of which had been fired in the five months Krivaq had served there. He feared the disruptors would fail—but no, his status board indicated that the weapons fired as they were supposed to. They struck the Romulan ship head on.

"Rom shields holding."

"Continuous fire," J'rak said as other officers entered the nerve center. "Load torpedo cannon!"

"Yes, sir. Warbird firing."

Then the lights dimmed further, and Krivaq's console went dark. After a moment, it came back online—and his eyes widened at what it told him. "Shields *down!* We are defenseless!"

"Keep firing!" J'rak cried. "Hit them with a torpedo spread! And get those *khest'n* shields back up!"

Kivik sat at the console across from Krivaq and sneezed. He was allergic to *something* on the outpost, but nobody'd been able to figure out what. Krivaq usually liked it when he was on duty with Kivik because his sneezing always interrupted J'rak's storytelling.

"Shields won't reconstitute!"

Krivaq looked at his status board after the torpedo cannon was emptied. "Rom shields down to twenty percent." He gave the order to reload the cannon, while the disruptors continued to fire.

J'rak turned to B'Orl. "Get a distress call out! The *Mevak* should still be in range!"

When the torpedoes reloaded, Krivaq fired another volley, just as the Romulan disruptors struck the underside of the outpost.

Oh, this isn't good, he thought, even though the status board told him that the third torpedo had taken down the Romulans' shields and that the fourth and fifth destroyed the ship. "Rom vessel destroyed," Krivaq said, then waited for the cheers to die down before continuing: "But our reactor's about to go critical!"

"Reactor control to J'rak, we can't eject the reactor. It's going to blow!"

J'rak pounded the bulkhead. "*Quvatlh!* All hands—"

Krivaq's last thought before the explosion that destroyed the outpost cut off J'rak's instruction was, *Who will mediate the disputes between my brothers now?*

3

Praetor Narviat's Home
Ki Baratan, Romulus
Romulan Star Empire

Narviat, the Praetor of the Romulan Star Empire, sat in his favorite chair and pulled the blanket tighter around his shoulders, trying desperately to stave off the chill. The servants had already raised the temperature in his anteroom by four degrees, but it didn't help. With a shivering hand, he reached for the remedy the imperial physician had prescribed—a tea made from a special blend of herbs that the doctor was sure would ease his suffering.

But ultimately, there was nothing to do but wait for the chills to pass, for his ears to unclog, and for his nose to stop running. He tried to inhale, to smell the tea, and sniffed instead, smelling nothing but his own mucus—hardly a palliative.

The side door opened to reveal Charvanek, Narviat's consort and also his head of security. Worry lined her lovely face, and softened her hard eyes. It was a side of her few saw, and Narviat appreciated it.

"The representatives from the Tal Shiar are here," she said without preamble. She'd already expressed concern over his sickness, and she was not one to repeat herself, especially since Narviat was already doing all he could. "Shall I send them away?" Her tone implied that she thought his answer to the question should be yes.

"Who is here?"

"Colonels Lovok and Koval."

Narviat sighed. Or, rather, he tried to, but his congestion transformed it into a ragged cough that made his throat feel as if it were filled with loose gravel, and that almost caused him to lose his grip on the tea mug. After clearing his throat, he said, "No, I will see them."

"Narviat—"

"Lovok and Koval wouldn't be here if it wasn't important, my consort. Allow them an audience."

Now Charvanek's eyes burned, but she only said, "As you wish," and departed through the same door.

Narviat sipped more of the tea, the hot liquid burning his tongue. *Why must all remedies be so hot?*

Moments later, Charvanek reentered, followed by Lovok and Koval. Both men wore the simple gray jumpsuits that many of the Tal Shiar favored.

"The praetor is unwell," Charvanek said, "so I would ask, Colonels, that you be brief."

Koval inclined his head toward Charvanek and said solicitously, "Of course." As with everything that came out of Koval's mouth, it sounded oily and insincere. Narviat tolerated it only because that insincerity was what made him good at his job.

Indicating the couch opposite his chair, Narviat said, "Have a seat, gentlemen, and tell me what is so urgent that the Tal Shiar visits me in my sickbed."

Lovok took the proffered seat and spoke in a matter-of-fact tone that Narviat found a welcome contrast to Koval. "We will be brief, Praetor. We have received word from our spies in Klingon space that the High Council has seized lands belonging to the Houses of Qorvos and Taklat."

Narviat sniffled and set down his tea mug. "*Both* Houses? Has a reason been given?"

"It was done in a closed council session," Koval said. "That alone is suspicious."

Charvanek, who remained standing, snorted. "If Gowron's acting in secret, it means he's scared of something."

"Or he knows where those Houses' loyalties lie," Lovok said. "Praetor, it is my belief that we must abandon this particular plan. We lost the House of Duras during Gowron's ascension."

"Thanks to Sela," Koval said with disdain. "Her inability to circumvent a simple blockade ruined that campaign. The empire would have been ours. Instead, we lost our strongest ally among the Klingon aristocracy, and with Qorvos and Taklat's fall, we lose two others."

Shaking his head, an action that only made the blockage in his ears worse, Narviat said, "I was never sanguine about the plan. Buying influence with Klingon noble Houses that were destitute after Praxis may have seemed tenable eighty years ago, but now?" There was also the fact that the plan was hatched under the reign of Praetor Dralath, Narviat's mad predecessor. Narviat had been willing to try to use their influence over House Duras to gain control of the High Council, but Sela's incompetence had ruined it. Only at the insistence of the Tal Shiar did Narviat not scuttle the whole thing.

Charvanek spoke. "Gowron must know that those Houses were loyal to us. This may well be the prelude to action against us."

Lovok shook his head. "He doesn't have enough of the military on his side. They'll follow his orders, of course, but he barely had enough support to win that civil war, and if it weren't for Kurn's throwing in with him, that would've been a three-front war."

"And Gowron initially resisted the return of their messiah," Koval said with obvious disdain. "True, he elevated him to a meaningless title of emperor, but only to keep the empire from fracturing further. Gowron does not have K'mpec's skill for building consensus or for rallying the troops. That new general he put in charge of the Defense Force—"

"Martok," Lovok said.

"Yes, him—he's popular with the military, so his appointment might make Gowron an easier chancellor to follow into battle, but I don't think we have to worry about—"

Charvanek's personal comlink beeped. "Excuse me," she said,

stepping off to the side. Narviat recognized the type of beep the comlink emitted—it was an emergency frequency. The praetor hoped desperately that it would not be something that required his services. As soon as the two colonels departed, he was going back to bed; all this talk of Klingon politics had exhausted him.

When Charvanek was done speaking, she turned back around, a look of pure fury on her face. "The warbird *Grimar,* under the command of Sub-commander Lar, has fired on the No'Var Outpost in Klingon space. Both the *Grimar* and the outpost have been destroyed."

Narviat couldn't believe his ears, and thought that perhaps they'd become more clogged. "What?"

Lovok and Koval exchanged glances.

"The *Grimar* has crossed into Klingon space and made an unprovoked attack on a Klingon outpost, destroying itself in the bargain."

Blinking several times, Narviat asked, "Why?"

"I intend to find out," Charvanek said in a tone that made it clear that bodies would fall in her wake if she did not determine the reason for Lar's insane behavior quickly. "If I may take my leave?"

The two Tal Shiar operatives rose from the couch. "We must depart, also," Lovok said. "There are some details that need to be attended to regarding those Klingon Houses, and perhaps we too can determine the reasons for the *Grimar*'s attack."

Koval added, "And manufacture new reasons for the public—and the Klingons—should it be necessary."

Narviat nodded, and waved all three of them off. If anything would galvanize the Klingon military behind Gowron, it would be an unprovoked Romulan attack on one of their border outposts. *Elements, what was Lar* thinking? Early in his praetorship, Narviat had learned the folly of attacking Klingon worlds. It had been Koval himself who had brought him the intelligence that the Klingons were developing metagenic weapons on Khitomer. Ostensibly, they were for Chancellor Kravokh to use against the

Cardassians in their ongoing conflict, but the reasons mattered less than the weapons' existence.

While the subsequent attack on Khitomer did destroy the weapons before they could be created, the damage was considerable. The Klingon–Federation alliance—which had already been brought from the brink of destruction by Dralath's insane attack on Narendra III—was made even stronger, and Kravokh himself was replaced by K'mpec. Unlike Kravokh, K'mpec remained alert to possible Romulan threats.

Sniffling again, Narviat rang for his servants. He needed to get back to bed, and hoped that Charvanek would handle this disaster.

4

**Palais de la Concorde
Paris, Earth
United Federation of Planets**

Edmund Atkinson had been covering politics for the *Times* of London for twenty years, and specifically covering the Palais de la Concorde for five, and he had yet to not experience a mild thrill when he walked into the council chambers.

A rectangular room located at the center of the building's first floor, this was where the Federation Council met, as well as the various sub-councils, and was where much of the business of government was done. Right below this floor was the street—the Champs-Elysées ran under the fifteen-story building, which was supported by four duranium pillars. The structure stood on the very site where, in the twenty-second century, the Traité d'Unification was signed, uniting all Earth's governments into one.

The Federation was, at its heart, ridiculous. Creatures who'd evolved on hundreds of different worlds, people who'd formed nations that ranged from one continent on one planet to several dozen colonies, alien beings who had absolutely nothing in common save the simple fact of sentience—and yet, for more than two hundred years, they had come together in this room and done the business of government in a manner that was wholly democratic and egalitarian.

Atkinson's first opinion column for the *Times* was on that very subject, and that had been before he was assigned to the Palais and got to see it up close. If anything, that made him more impressed, that more than a hundred contentious beings, not a single one of whom evolved on the same planet as any of the others in the room, could collaborate.

The Federation president's office was located on the fifteenth floor atop the structure. Currently that president was Jaresh-Inyo, a Grazerite who had just won a second term in a landslide. He had called an emergency session of the Federation Council, which was why Atkinson was here rather than in his home office in London, putting the finishing touches on his latest column.

Depending on what happened in the next few minutes, that column may yet have a different topic. Atkinson had no idea what the subject of this meeting was, and his fellow members of the fourth estate either didn't know or were pretending they didn't.

About half the councillors were in their seats on the benches that lined the east and west walls of the chambers. Many were talking among themselves, others to people on the viewers at their stations.

When the doors to the south wall parted, and three plainclothes security guards entered, it heralded President Jaresh-Inyo's arrival. The massive Grazerite walked in at a brisk pace, approaching the podium that was decorated with the emblem of the United Federation of Planets. The podium faced the speaker's floor, which sat between the two sets of councillors' benches. During a session, only the person at the podium and someone on the speaker's floor could speak for the record.

The room quieted down as the president approached the podium. "Gentlebeings, thank you for coming. We will forgo roll call. Half an hour ago, a message was sent to the Federation Council from Cardassia Prime by the Detapa Council, with the request that it be played in open council—hence this emergency session."

The president then looked to the side at the clerk, who nodded in response, and touched a control on her desk. Behind the podium, the viewscreen lit up with the face of a familiar Cardassian. Kotan Pa'Dar was a longtime member in good standing of the

Detapa Council, Cardassia's civilian governmental body. Recently, Pa'Dar had been elevated to the position of first speaker.

While that meant a bigger salary for Pa'Dar, it meant little beyond that, as the Detapa Council was quite toothless. The Cardassian Union was run by Central Command and the Obsidian Order. The council's function was purely ornamental—which made Atkinson wonder just what they could have to say that would necessitate an emergency session.

"My name is Kotan Pa'Dar, First Speaker of the Detapa Council. I carry a message from the Cardassian Union to the Federation Council, the Romulan Senate, the Klingon High Council, the Tholian Assembly, the Tzelnira, and the Breen Confederacy."

Atkinson thought it interesting that Pa'Dar named the major powers in the quadrant. Only two were left off. One was the Gorn Hegemony, though one could argue whether they counted as "major." The other were the Ferengi. One could argue their having so lofty a status as well, but just in terms of territory, the Ferengi weren't a power to be ignored, for all that they preferred capitalistic endeavors over imperialistic ones.

"As of this day, the Cardassian Union has absorbed the Ferengi Alliance."

A rumble of surprise went through the chambers. *That explains that, then,* Atkinson thought as he started taking notes on his padd.

"Grand Nagus Zek has retired. All citizens of the Ferengi Alliance are now citizens of the Cardassian Union—and all contracts with Ferengi are now to be considered contracts with Cardassia. This means that these contracts may be subject to renegotiation in order to conform with Cardassian law. On behalf of the Detapa Council, as well as our comrades in Central Command and the Obsidian Order, we thank you for your time."

The screen went dark.

More rumblings went throughout the gallery on the north wall, where Atkinson sat furiously typing notes into his padd. The president then said, "Silence, please!" and the room quieted—a neat trick, considering how soft-spoken the bulky Grazerite was.

"Thank you. Gentlebeings, obviously this sudden expansion of the Cardassian Union will have serious repercussions, both on our shared borders, and on any contracts that might have to be renegotiated as First Speaker Pa'Dar pointed out."

President Jaresh-Inyo went on, but Atkinson was already composing his notes for his next column. And he had some people to get in touch with. Cardassia had been holding steady of late. They hadn't changed their borders in years—they even ceded several border colonies to the Federation, after agreeing in principle to an arrangement whereby several Federation colonies would become Cardassian property and vice versa, as well as the establishment of a Demilitarized Zone. The reversal of the Cardassians' position had been spun as a major diplomatic victory, but Atkinson's sources had told him that this was purely an internal decision on Cardassia's part.

So why are they choosing to expand now? And how did they get the Ferengi to just become part of the Union like that? Knowing the Ferengi, there had to be a lot of money changing hands, all in the direction of those big-eared capitalists. *So where did Cardassia get the latinum? They've never been the richest nation in the quadrant.*

Too many questions. Atkinson was looking forward to trying to dig up the answers.

5

The Great Hall
First City, Qo'noS
Klingon Empire

Savalor, Romulan ambassador to the Klingon Empire, hated his job.

Klingons had an appalling inability to clean up after themselves. The fastidious Savalor had found living on Qo'noS to be an incredible chore, because everywhere he looked there was food and garbage and dirt and sweat and filth. Even the wealthiest Klingon lived in putrid squalor by Romulan standards.

It had, of course, been his own fault. He had spent his academic years studying the Klingon Empire, having been fascinated by its ebbs and flows over the centuries—the internecine squabbling, the unification by Kahless, the Hur'q invasion, the emergence as a spacefaring power, the virus that caused the *QuchHa'*, the Praxis disaster, the rebuilding—and thus became the Romulan Empire's leading expert on Klingons.

Becoming the ambassador to Qo'noS should have been the pinnacle of his career.

Instead, he found out the one thing that his years of study never told him: Klingons were *filthy*. They did not bathe, they ate like animals, they drank in a manner that left more liquid on the ground and in their beards than went down their gullets. Savalor knew everything there was to know about Klingon history and culture, could not only sing along with all the most famous operas, but also could list all the places that opera had been performed and who the lead was in each production, knew the details of the creation of all the most popular Klingon weapons, knew all the stories of Kahless—yet he somehow managed to miss the fact that they were truly disgusting creatures to be around.

He had requested to be reassigned many times, but each time Praetor Narviat said he was too valuable in that position. Savalor understood the importance of serving the empire, he was very well compensated for his work, and his family's standing had improved tremendously within the empire as a result of his posting.

But he died a little every day that he was stuck living on this cesspool of a planet.

Today would be even worse. One of the challenges of being a politician in the Klingon Empire was that Klingons had a cultural bias against falsehood. Exaggeration, posturing, self-aggrandizement—those were all acceptable, as long as there was a seed of truth at the center of them. But out-and-out lying to a warrior—particularly to the chancellor or a member of the High Council—was an invitation to have a *d'k tahg* plunged into your chest.

Savalor, of course, lied with ease and skill, thanks to years of practice in both academia and politics, but he feared that one day he would do so in a sufficiently transparent manner that Gowron or one of the councillors would order his death, not only disgracing him and his family, but also plunging the Romulan Empire into war.

So now, as he waited in the gallery for the entire High Council to assemble, he went over in his head what he would say, and hoped it would be enough for Gowron.

When Savalor had first been posted to Qo'noS, K'mpec had been chancellor. A larger-than-life figure, K'mpec had been a wise and noble leader for his people. It was no wonder he'd lasted longer in the position than anyone else in the Klingon Empire's history.

He was also easy to talk to, which could not be said for his successor. Gowron, with his wide eyes and suspicious nature, always made Savalor feel as if he were on the defensive.

Such was the case now, as the council steward called the session to order the instant that Gowron entered, trailed by four members of his personal guard, the *Yan-Isleth*.

Before Gowron completely settled in the high-backed chair at the center of the chambers' rear wall, he bellowed, "Step forward, Ambassador Savalor, and tell me why I should not have you killed and call for the council to declare war on your empire."

"Because the Romulan Star Empire has committed no acts to justify such a war, Chancellor," Savalor said calmly as he stepped into the center of the chamber. A light shone in his face, but the nictitating membrane inside his eyelids prevented him from being blinded, or even having to blink. The councillors who stood in a semicircle around Gowron's seat were now all but engulfed by darkness, leaving only Gowron, on whom another light shone, visible. *Well, fine, he's the one I need to address.*

"What do you call the destruction of the No'Var Outpost?" Gowron asked angrily.

Holding up the padd onto which he'd downloaded the files from the Tal Shiar, Savalor said, "The act of a renegade. Subcommander Lar was a malcontent who spoke out against the Senate after a recent session. The Tal Shiar has evidence that he spoke often in favor of going to war with your empire, feeling that we should have finished the job that we started at Narendra III and Khitomer, and that Klingons are filthy savages who don't deserve to be a power in the quadrant."

Another councillor, Kurn, spoke. "Your Tal Shiar punishes sedition with death, Ambassador, yet you gave this Lar a ship. Why?"

Savalor answered the question, but continued to address Gowron. To do otherwise would show disrespect to the chancellor. "He already *had* the ship. And his remarks were primarily directed against your empire." He allowed himself a small smile. "Forgive me, but invective directed against Klingons is not a crime in the Romulan Empire—any more than the curses you all direct at Romulans are prosecuted here."

Gowron actually smiled back at that. "True." The smile fell. "But did your Tal Shiar not predict that he would cross the border and engage in a cowardly attack against our outpost?"

"Apparently not. The Tal Shiar are not perfect, Chancellor, certainly not as skilled as your own Imperial Intelligence, and they cannot predict the future. Sub-commander Lar's profile did not indicate someone who would engage in renegade actions against the express wishes of Romulan High Command and the Senate." He walked forward to the steward, and forced himself not to wince at the man's body odor. "I offer this padd as evidence of Lar's treachery, to be examined by the High Council. I am also instructed by the Senate to offer whatever reparations you deem appropriate for the loss of the No'Var Outpost." After the steward took the padd, Savalor looked straight into Gowron's wide, pitiless eyes. "We would not declare war with one ship making a sneak attack, Chancellor. Rest assured, if my government feels the need to make war on you, you will know it."

Gowron stared right back. Savalor knew that to be the first to look away would be to show weakness, and he could ill afford that.

Finally Gowron said, "We will examine your evidence, Ambassador. However, I believe that your government does not wish to wage war on us—for now. Therefore, barring any new evidence, the Klingon Empire will not respond to this outrage." Then Gowron smiled, and while before he was mildly amused by Savalor's comment, this time the smile had no mirth—it was more a baring of the teeth, truly. "However, if the families of those who were dishonorably murdered at No'Var wish to take their revenge, then who am I to stop them?"

You're the leader of the thrice-damned empire, that's who you are. Savalor was not suicidal enough to say so out loud, though. "Of course, Chancellor."

"That is all," Gowron said. "We have other business to discuss."

Savalor gave a small bow, and beat a hasty retreat.

As he moved toward the aircar that would take him back to

the—blessedly clean!—Romulan embassy, Savalor hoped that the Tal Shiar had done their forgery work well. For Lar was, in fact, a patriot of the highest order. His attack on No'Var was unpredictable, not because the Tal Shiar's profile on him was wrong, but because it gave no indication that he would perform such an act.

The mystery of Lar's psychosis was someone else's problem, however. Savalor's was to sell it to the High Council, a feat he was fairly certain he'd managed. A Tal Shiar agent was likely waiting for him at the embassy to debrief him—though this was an open council session, so the Tal Shiar could just get the facts off the information net like anyone else.

He just wanted to get out of the filth. He was definitely changing his clothes before talking to *anyone* . . .

6

The Voria Mines
Voria Province, Bajor
Cardassian Union

Kira Nerys, the last surviving member of the Shakaar resistance cell, rubbed her callused hands together as she headed home after a long day at the mines.

As recently as ten years ago, the Voria mines were going full bore, taking uridium from beneath Bajor's surface. Five hundred Bajorans worked the mines, and were housed in fifty one-room shacks that ten people had to share. The ore hauler that took the fruits of the miners' labors to Terok Nor for processing came three times a week.

Now, however, only forty-two Bajorans worked the mine, and the hauler came twice a month—and there were rumors that that would be cut back to once monthly. All forty-two got an entire shack to themselves, which was downright luxurious by mineworker standards.

Many of the other mines on Bajor were in a similar state. From what Kira had heard from her fellow resistance members, that was why the Detapa Council back on Cardassia had been pushing Central Command to pull out of Bajor: it was no longer economically viable to support an occupation force—one that was regularly harried by terrorists—and a space station, given the meager returns.

But those rumors had died down the past few years, and though the resistance continued to pound away, Bajor was still part of the Cardassian Union.

That, however, was a lesser concern for Kira right now.

Because she knew the truth.

A week ago, she had come back to her one-room shack expecting a visitor, but he wasn't there. For four days, she continued to expect him; then she gave up, assuming something had happened to prevent his arrival.

When she entered the shack tonight, the first thing she noticed was that the patch she'd made on the hole beneath the window was falling apart, and if she didn't want to freeze to death tonight, she'd need to redo it.

The second thing she noticed was the presence of the guest she expected a week ago.

"You're late, Elim," she said without preamble.

"An unfortunate necessity, Nerys. Damar has taken an interest in me of late, and that has curtailed my ability to move about freely if I wish to deviate from traveling to either the Promenade or my quarters."

"But you managed?"

Garak inclined his head slightly. "Damar is a decent enough security chief."

Kira snorted. " 'Decent enough' has never been much of an impediment for you, has it?"

"Indeed not. In any case, everything has been prepared." Garak had a satchel on his shoulder, which he now handed to her. "I've provided the access codes you'll need to commandeer the hauler. I trust you're capable of disposing of any personal security the ship might have?"

At that, Kira just looked at him.

"Of course," Garak said with that insincere smile of his. "You'll find everything you need in that satchel, all safe and sound."

"You're sure you weren't followed?"

Now Garak just looked at her.

"Sorry. And both devices are functioning?"

"Yes. Now, then, if you'll excuse me, I have a brilliant escape to engage." Garak moved toward the shack's exit, then hesitated. He turned and faced Kira with a serious expression.

That alone got Kira's attention. She'd known Garak since he was first exiled to Terok Nor five years earlier, and she'd rarely seen him use any facial expression save that of affable charm. That he used another now meant what he was about to say was as close to being from his heart as he was capable.

"Your mission is of critical import, Nerys. Not just Cardassia, not just Bajor, but the entire galaxy depends upon your getting this intelligence to the Federation successfully."

Kira shook her head. "Are we *sure* they're the right people to take this to?"

"What, pray tell, is the alternative? The Klingons? The Romulans? They are neither of them inclined to listen to reason, or to be open-minded. The Romulans will arrest you and repatriate you to Cardassia. The Klingons would probably just have you executed. No, it must be the Federation—and even then . . ."

Garak didn't need to finish his sentence. Kira knew the risks. She also knew they were worth taking. "The hauler's due in tomorrow. With luck, I'll be in Federation space within a week."

"Good." Garak held out a hand. Kira took it. "Best of luck, Nerys. For all our sakes."

"You, too. Stay out of trouble, Elim."

He smiled one last time. "It's what I do best." With that, Garak quickly took his leave.

Kira set down the satchel and opened it, examining its contents. There was a containment unit, a field generator, a holo-filter, and a padd. She dare not activate either of the first two, though the generator wouldn't actually do anything if turned on right now. Still, any unauthorized electromagnetic emissions might be detected by Cardassian security. The containment unit was likely shielded—Garak wasn't capable of being careless

enough to forget that—but it was best not to take risks. The holofilter was in case she was hailed while still in Cardassian space and
needed to bluff her way past a patrol. The padd contained the access code for the hauler, as well as instructions on how to pilot it.
That, she didn't need—this wasn't the first ore hauler she'd
flown—but Garak was nothing if not thorough. Also on the padd
was the best course for her to follow through Cardassian space to
avoid the very patrols for which she might need the holofilter.

Now she just needed to wait twenty-six hours for the hauler to
show up . . .

Once, the Voria mines had a large landing bay, as well as a launching pad. Ships coming to Voria would take off and land on the pad,
and stay in the bay during their layover. Not far from the mine was
a fairly popular Cardassians-only resort and casino. (At least, it was
Cardassians-only as far as patronage went; plenty of Bajorans
worked there as low-level cleaning staff or entertainment.)

The ore hauler that serviced Voria had an established routine:
land the ship in the early evening, head to the resort, spend the
night there, get up some time in the late morning—by which time
the hauler had been filled with the raw ore to be brought to Terok
Nor for processing—and take off for the space station by noon.

Or at least it used to. Four years ago—shortly before Kira was
assigned to Voria—her fellow resistance members set off an explosive in the landing bay. The damage was sufficient to render
the bay unusable. However, the only spacefaring vessel that ever
came to Voria these days was the ore hauler, so the Cardassians
didn't think it worth the expense to repair the bay, and the hauler
just stayed on the pad overnight.

Which made it much easier for Kira to steal it.

The hauler's pilot had long since gone to the resort, leaving
only one bored-looking guard. He wore the insignia of a gil; Kira
didn't know his name, nor did she care to. While Kira had come
to admit reluctantly that not all Cardassians were bastards who

needed to die slowly and painfully, her compassion did not extend to anyone in the Cardassian military. They were the ones who beat and raped and pillaged and abused. They were the ones who'd violated her world.

You wore that uniform, you were a target. Targets didn't need names.

Kira snuck up behind him and broke his neck, and she didn't give him a second thought once he fell to the dirt in a crumpled, dead heap. It was as much consideration as Shakaar, Furel, Lupaza, Mobara, Gantt, and Mabrin had gotten from the Cardassians who'd killed them.

If the Prophets wanted the gil to live, they would've made him more alert.

She walked up to the hatch on the hauler's underbelly and entered an alphanumeric code that she read off of Garak's padd. In response, the hatch loudly unfolded into a ramp that provided entry, and squeaked so much that it echoed throughout the mines. Kira hadn't counted on quite so much noise. Obviously the same budget-consciousness that prevented the bay from being rebuilt also kept the hauler from being properly maintained.

Let's just hope that this thing's engines are in better shape than the ramp, she thought as she overrode the pre-flight checklist. With the racket made by the ramp, more guards would be here any minute, and she needed to be in the air by the time that happened.

Within a few seconds, she had taken off and was heading into orbit. The pressure of g-forces slammed against her ribs and crushed her into the heavily padded seat.

She saw the fuel alarm go off. *I don't believe this. He hadn't refueled yet.* As soon as she thought that, she cursed at herself. *Of course he didn't. He wouldn't refuel until he knew how much ore he was carrying, which he wouldn't know until morning.*

Still, Kira only had to take the hauler to Bajor's fifth moon. And since the hauler was still empty, the fuel consumption needed to achieve escape velocity would be low. As long as she had enough fuel to get the hauler into orbit, point it at the fifth moon, and make one last kick with the thrusters, ballistics would take care of the rest.

Her real concern was the one piece of information Garak hadn't been able to obtain: whether the starhoppers the resistance had hidden on the fifth moon were still there. In particular, one starhopper that could go to warp three and even had a (sort of) working transporter.

As soon as Kira got past the stratosphere, she changed course for a standard orbit. She'd only need to orbit for three minutes, then she'd be in position to head straight for the moon. The timing of the escape had been as much to take advantage of the fifth moon's orbital position as anything.

The fuel alarm continued to sound, and Kira couldn't figure out how to turn it off. It also looked like she'd have only enough fuel for the final thruster kick that would send her toward the moon, then she'd have to shut down.

She wouldn't have enough to make a landing once she arrived. Which meant she had to calculate the course perfectly so that the hauler would enter the moon's orbit, and then she had to hope that the battery power was high enough for her to use the hauler's computer to access the starhopper's transporter.

Should've checked the fuel before stealing the ship, she thought, but dismissed it. She'd left a body behind, one that belonged to a Cardassian soldier who was supposed to check in regularly. There simply would not have been time to refuel even if the ramp hadn't squeaked open.

Once she reached the window, Kira changed course for the fifth moon, left orbit, and sent the hauler hurtling as fast as it could before shutting down all engines.

Then she let out a long breath. It would be the better part of a day before she reached the moon. She just had to hope that the generic nature of the ore hauler—there were literally hundreds of ships just like it all over the Bajoran system, and they all had the same transponder code, as a cost-saving measure—would keep the patrols from finding her.

7

Captain Jean-Luc Picard was extremely grateful to find himself back in the present day.

It had been a difficult road. The Borg—after devastating Admiral Leyton's fleet—had sent a scout ship back in time, in an attempt to assimilate Earth before humans' first contact with the Vulcans, contact that led, eventually, to the forming of the Federation.

But Picard had been able to stop them, at a huge cost. Many of his crew were killed, including conn officer Lieutenant Sean Hawk, deputy chief engineer Lieutenant Paul Porter, and so many others. His android second officer, Lieutenant Commander Data, had been very badly damaged.

Now, though, they were home.

From the ops console, Data—the internal machinery of his head partially exposed—said, "Sensors indicate that we have successfully reversed the Borg's temporal distortion and returned to our own time." He turned around to look at the command chair. "We have returned seven minutes, nineteen seconds after our departure."

From the tactical console, Lieutenant Commander Worf, Picard's security chief, said, "We are receiving multiple distress calls from the fleet, sir—and also a priority-one call from the Palais de la Concorde."

Picard whirled around at Worf's words, then looked at his first officer, Commander William Riker, sitting next to him. The latter said, "Why would the Palais be contacting us directly?"

"An excellent question, Number One." Generally orders directly from the seat of government went to admirals, who passed them on to ship captains. Of course, with Leyton's death, Picard was now in charge of what was left of the fleet, but it still felt as if several links in the chain of command were being bypassed. "On screen, Mister Worf."

The face of President Jaresh-Inyo graced the viewscreen. *"Captain Picard."*

"Mister President. To what do we owe this honor?"

"I wish it was to honor you that I was calling, Captain—although I do wish to commend you for your role in destroying the Borg cube. Admiral Leyton was wise to include you in the fleet—we might have suffered many more losses if you hadn't been there."

"Thank you, sir."

"Sadly, while I would prefer to allow you the chance to lick your wounds, I'm afraid that won't be possible. Earlier today, a Klingon fleet led an attack on a Romulan outpost on the planet T'Vyss. Several thousand Romulans were killed. The Romulan Star Empire has declared war on the Klingon Empire, and the Klingons have requested that we come to their aid in this conflict."

Picard blinked. "Surely a diplomatic solution—"

"Is being attempted, yes, but in the meantime, Chancellor Gowron has demanded that we send a fleet to supplement the Defense Force. In fact, he requested you by name, Captain."

Shifting uncomfortably in his chair, Picard said, "I appreciate the chancellor's confidence, but we've suffered considerable damage—and personnel losses. We—"

"I understand the difficulty, but any repairs will have to be made en route. Take whatever vessels are able to join you from Admiral Leyton's fleet and rendezvous at Starbase 24, where you'll get crew replacements and additional ships. Then set course for the Archanis system. General Martok's fleet will meet you there." The Grazerite leaned into the image

and spoke even more softly. *"I'm not happy about this either, Captain, especially after what just happened with the Borg. But the Klingon alliance has stood for eighty years, and I won't be remembered as the president who sundered it."* Then he leaned back. *"Good luck, Captain Picard."*

"Thank you, Mister President." Picard did not say the words enthusiastically.

With a final nod, President Jaresh-Inyo's face disappeared from the viewer.

To the relief conn officer who had replaced Hawk, Picard said, "Ensign, set a course for Starbase 24."

"Aye, sir."

"Mister Data, gather every piece of information Starfleet Command has regarding this conflict between the Klingons and Romulans, in particular any intelligence briefings that have been prepared since the start of the Borg attack, then send it to my ready room." Looking behind him, Picard said, "Mister Worf, determine which ships are still battle-worthy and have them join us. Determine which ship of those is the slowest." He got to his feet and looked at his first officer. "Number One, once the fleet is assembled, proceed to the starbase at the slowest ship's maximum safe cruising speed. You have the bridge—I'll be in my ready room."

"Yes, sir."

Picard went into his ready room and made a beeline for the replicator. "Tea, Earl Grey, hot."

First the Borg, now a war with the Romulans. The first year of the *Enterprise*-E's existence had been a relatively sedate one, marred only by a rather unfortunate incident involving a very pregnant Lwaxana Troi and her attempts to get out of her marriage to a Tavnian named Jeyel.

However, aside from the Cardassians' surprise absorption of the Ferengi Alliance and the usual border squabbles between the Klingons and the Romulans, the Alpha Quadrant had been quiet of late. The former had Picard a little concerned, but the latter just seemed to be business as usual between two powers that seemed destined to always be at odds.

There was always the threat of the Borg returning, but that had at least been dealt with—for now. Prior to this recent conflict, the *Enterprise* had been able to spend most of the last year on its primary mission of exploration, mapping the T'Yira Cluster.

After the *Enterprise*-D's destruction at Veridian III, Picard had been worried that he would not be able to retain his senior staff. But they all came back together when the *Sovereign*-class ship was launched—even Worf, whom Picard had to track down at a monastery on Boreth and talk out of resigning his commission.

The computer station on Picard's desk beeped. Sitting down at his desk, he activated the station and saw that Data had gathered all the latest on the Klingon-Romulan conflict.

He read it over and realized that it wasn't quite the usual. A Romulan ship had led a wholly unprovoked attack on a Klingon outpost. A Klingon fleet—led by a Captain Wogh, who claimed to be avenging the death of his son, the outpost commander—destroyed a Romulan installation. War was inevitable after that.

But why did the Romulans attack that Klingon outpost in the first place? The Romulan High Command insisted that it was the act of a renegade, but that explanation seemed too pat.

"Worf to Picard."

Tapping his combadge, Picard said, "Go ahead, Commander."

"Seven vessels are accompanying us to Starbase 24, Captain—and five more are meeting us at the starbase. We are proceeding at warp four."

"Thank you, Mister Worf. Time to arrival at the starbase?"

"Three days at this speed. You are also receiving a personal communication from General Martok."

Martok was, Picard knew, the person in charge of Klingon forces for this war. "News, it seems, travels fast. Pipe him through to here, Mister Worf."

The grizzled face of a seasoned warrior appeared on Picard's screen. The general's eyes both stared intently at Picard even before the image came into focus. *"Captain Picard. I have been informed that you are to lead the Starfleet forces that are supporting us in battle."*

"So I have been led to believe, General."

"*Chancellor Gowron specifically requested you, Captain. That is a great honor.*"

"Indeed," Picard said, though it was an honor he could have done without. "I should warn you, General, that our forces are a trifle depleted. We have just faced the Borg—"

"*And you survived.*" For the first time, Martok smiled. "*Anyone who can defeat those cybernetic creatures is a worthy warrior, and one I would be proud to have at my side against the Romulans.*" Martok shook his head. "*They attack us without provocation, and we believe their lies that it is the action of a renegade. Then, when Captain Wogh seeks vengeance, as is his right, they declare war. They will learn their folly, Picard— and you will help us teach it to them.*"

"Our fleet will assemble at Starbase 24 in three days, General. I'll contact you then."

"*Very well, Captain.* Qapla'!"

Picard simply turned off the viewer, unable to bring himself to wish Martok success—though he hardly hoped for failure, either. In truth, he did not want a war. The *Sovereign*-class *Enterprise* was far more suited to battle than the old *Galaxy*-class had been. The newer ship was built in the shadow of the Borg, after all. But Jean-Luc Picard still thought of himself primarily as an explorer, and the *Enterprise*-E was still designed for that purpose. Being sent to lead troops in a war wasn't the mission Picard had signed on for.

But it was his mission right now, given to him by the president himself.

8

An Unnamed Starhopper
Interstellar Space
Cardassian Union

When Kira had first beamed onto the starhopper, her third emotion was gratitude that the refrigeration units were still active and had kept the ration packs fresh. (Her first and second emotions were also gratitude, the first for the still-functioning transporter console, and the second for the life-support system. The air was incredibly stale, but it was breathable. The hauler didn't have any EVA suits—probably another budget-saving move—so if the atmosphere had been drained from the starhopper, Kira would have been in serious trouble.) The refrigeration units were also filled to the brim; whoever used the starhopper last had thought to restock before hiding it, which was standard procedure, but not always possible. The ship could only go to warp three, so it would take her a few weeks to make it to the Federation border, and she needed to eat.

Her fourth emotion was annoyance, however, because the warp engines were not quite up to snuff. According to a note left behind by a resistance fighter named Biroj, the intermix chamber couldn't handle anything faster than warp one-point-nine. Kira had never met Biroj, though she remembered Furel talking about her and saying that she knew her way around an engine.

Which was more than Kira could claim. She had no way to find out if Biroj's note was correct, since she didn't know an intermix chamber from a waste extractor, so the best she could do was to keep the starhopper at warp one-point-nine.

That speed meant her arrival in Federation space would take months, not weeks. It also meant that Garak's intelligence regarding patrols would be decreasingly useful as she went along. Shipping patterns changed, after all, and the farther away Kira got from the time when Garak received the information, the more likely it was to be amended.

After five days, she discovered something else that would delay her arrival further, something Biroj had forgotten to put in her note, but did program into the computer. Apparently, after five days of continuous warp, the engines overheated. Biroj had programmed them to automatically shut down for seven hours when that happened, which meant that Kira had to hope she would be somewhere safe each time that happened. The starhopper had a hull sheath that made it invisible to long-range sensors, purchased by the resistance years ago from a trader named Arctus Baran. But it was effective only when a ship was far away or at warp. If she had to take the ship out of warp too close to a ship, a planet, or a base, she was in trouble.

Of course, had the ship been capable of warp three, she'd only have had to stop three times, but since she was stuck at less than warp two, she would have to make dozens of those stops over the months she traversed Cardassian space.

Many times, she was tempted to open the containment unit. But she knew that was impossible. Once the unit was opened, Garak had said, it could not be reused. She had to wait until she was safely on a Federation ship before she opened it.

At least the hauler had a comfortable bunk and a decent commode. As unpleasant as it was to be stuck in a ship for so long, the accommodations were actually of a higher quality than Kira had ever had in her life. *I just hope they're not my last.*

Toward the end of one of her enforced stops, the proximity alarm went off at the same time that the comm system said she was being hailed. Sensors indicated a convoy of Ferengi vessels. *Dammit, they couldn't have shown up ten minutes later?*

She checked to make sure the holofilter was working, but then answered only on audio, confident in her ability to bluff her way past a DaiMon without the need of holographic tricks. "This is the pleasure vessel *Koramar*. How can I help you?"

"You can start by broadcasting your face."

"Who am I talking to?" Kira said snappishly. She only needed to keep him talking for another nine-and-a-half minutes; then she could go to warp, and would be home free.

"I am DaiMon Gig of the attack vessel Security. *I am in charge of protecting this convoy, and you will tell me your business and show me your face."*

Kira shook her head. *They named the security ship* Security. *Can't fault them for description.* "My name's Kella Torcet. I'm *trying* to get to Bol'rak's Planet to meet my husband. Unfortunately, the star-hopper he gave me leaves a lot to be desired. The warp drive over-heats every five days, and it won't go faster than warp two."

"That explains your business. I still have not seen your face."

Letting out a dramatic sigh, Kira activated the holofilter. "All right, all right." She turned on the viewer, which gave her a view of a weaselly-looking Ferengi with small eyes and a big nose even by their standards. "You happy, you little troll? This trip has been agonizing enough without having to justify my existence to the likes of you."

A voice sounded from the DaiMon's right. *"Oh, it isn't the likes of* him *you have to justify your existence to, Ms. Torcet."*

The image frame widened to show a Cardassian gul standing to the DaiMon's left. Gig glanced over at the gul with an annoyed expression. Kira suspected that the Cardassian's presence on the vessel didn't meet with Gig's approval.

Maintaining her arch tone, Kira asked, "And *you* are?" She also started trying to override the computer lockout on the warp drive, in case this gul didn't give her the remaining nine minutes.

"I'm Gul Ovell, and I'm here to ensure that these citizens of the Cardassian Union are safely brought to their new homes. That includes making sure that privateers don't try to harm the convoy—as has happened in the past."

"If you say so. I'm simply waiting for my warp drive to be active, and I'll be on my way. I couldn't care less about your convoy."

"Really?" The gul was holding up a data clip. *"Yet, according to these readings, your ship has a sheath that is not standard issue on pleasure craft of that type."*

Kira finally overrode the lockout. "My husband made a number of modifications, I don't think—"

"Plus there's that holofilter you're using."

That ended that. Kira had no idea when the Cardassians *or* the Ferengi got the upgrades to their sensors that would allow them to detect the sheath or the holofilter. It also didn't really matter. She quickly started running the start-up sequence to get the warp drive going.

"Train all weapons on this spy's ship, DaiMon," Gul Ovell said.

DaiMon Gig looked to his left. *"Do as he says!"*

The start-up sequence was almost finished, but the lead Ferengi vessel was powering weapons.

Come on, come on . . .

One second before the start-up sequence finished, the Ferengi phasers started firing.

Kira watched as if in slow motion as the phaser fire spit out of the Ferengi ship even as she activated the warp drive. The phaser fire clipped the hull as she went into warp.

Alarms blared throughout the flight deck. The ship shuddered for several seconds as it entered warp, then settled down. Kira kept her speed at warp one-point-five to be safe, and once the ship seemed to be going all right, she eased it up to one-point-nine. Sensors indicated that the the sheath was still intact, but it was cracked, and that the warp engines were damaged.

She did a quick inventory, and realized that there was no way she could repair the engines, having neither the parts nor the know-how. Certain on-the-fly repairs were within her abilities, but the dilithium crystal housing was physically cracked. There were no replacements on board, and the housing couldn't be patched.

Checking the computer, she learned that she could continue at warp for another seven hours before the crack in the housing increased to a size that would interfere with the proper working order of the starhopper.

Kira snarled. *Proper working order. Right. Meaning I'll blow up.*

She then checked the star charts and the long-range sensors in search of planets and bases that, at warp one-point-nine, were within seven hours of her position.

After finding and rejecting several candidates, she noticed that the Oolon system was one of the options. On the fringes of what used to be Ferengi space, it was just within the starhopper's now-limited range.

Changing course, she headed for the Oolon system.

Just short of seven hours later—during which time Kira showered and grabbed a nap—the starhopper arrived at the Oolon system. Kira came out of warp and then shut down the warp drive completely. It was useless to her now. Switching to impulse engines, she set a course for the third moon around Oolon IV.

As the starhopper approached the moon, another alarm went off. Checking, Kira saw that the structural integrity field was failing, and the hull damage from the fire she'd taken was such that the starhopper would start venting atmosphere once the SIF failed. *Just in time for me to achieve orbit,* Kira thought sourly, pushing the impulse engines to go faster so she could at least make it within transporter range of the moon.

Then another alarm went off, signaling that the antimatter containment unit was failing. Suddenly, all of Kira's other problems paled in comparison. She gathered up the satchel, with its critical contents, and slung it over her shoulder, then stepped to the transporter console. Scanning the surface of the moon, she found its lone piece of construction: a mansion gilded with latinum.

Smiling, Kira set the transporter to beam her down in front of the mansion as soon as the starhopper got into range.

I just hope that happens before the containment unit fails, she thought nervously. She'd hate to have come all this way, broken free of Bajor, and gotten past a Cardassian-run Ferengi convoy, only to die here.

Various alarms pealed throughout the ship, almost deafening Kira, when the transporter started to engulf her.

Just as it did, the flight deck was consumed by a massive fire.

Then she was on the surface.

It was night on the moon, and it was freezing cold, with wind whipping in off a nearby lake and cutting into her. Looking up, Kira saw a plume of fire erupt, lighting the night sky. *So much for that starhopper. Sorry, Biroj, I know you took good care of it.*

The door to the mansion opened, and its owner and sole occupant (except for servants, which said occupant didn't count) came running out, dressed in a nightshirt and looking extremely peeved.

"What in the name of the Grand Nagus is going *on* out here?"

Kira looked over at the perturbed Ferengi, and smiled. "Good to see you, too, Quark. I need your help."

9

Jean-Luc Picard was furious.

He beamed onto the two-person platform in the anteroom outside Starbase 24's commandant's office. A young Bolian ensign sat at a desk. "Captain Picard," she said. "The admiral's waiting for you."

Picard had just enough tattered remains of his comportment to mean it when he said, "Thank you." After all, it wasn't the ensign's fault.

He headed for the large wooden doors emblazoned with the Starfleet delta, which obligingly parted at his approach.

Admiral Vance Haden sat behind his desk, reading over a padd, but he looked up when Picard entered. He'd added a few bags under his eyes in the months since Picard saw him last. The war had that effect on people.

"Good to see you, Jean-Luc."

"It is good to be seen, Vance. There were moments when I had my doubts."

Setting down the padd and indicating the guest chair, Haden said, "Have a seat." In contrast, Haden got up and went to the replicator. "You look like you could use a drink."

Closing his eyes, Picard found himself imagining the family vineyard on Labarre. He didn't think of the place often—more since his brother and nephew died in a fire two years ago—but now, he recalled sitting in the living room with Robert, drinking the '47 Merlot, after they'd had their ridiculous fight in the mud.

Sad when the war has gone so badly that I'm thinking back fondly on my recovery from being assimilated. "A glass of red wine would be lovely. Merlot, if you please."

To the replicator, Haden said, "Computer, two drinks, alcoholic. A glass of Merlot and a shot of Bushmills 21."

Picard raised an eyebrow. "Alcoholic?" Starfleet regulations stipulated that officers could drink only syntheholic liquor while on duty.

"Admiral's privilege. Or wartime exception. Call it what you want." The drinks materialized with a hum, and Haden brought them to his desk, handing Picard a long-stemmed glass while keeping a square, thick-bottomed glass of amber liquid for himself. Picard twirled the wine around, disappointed to see it had no legs. But then, this *was* a replicated wine . . .

Raising his glass, Haden said, "To Khitomer."

"To Khitomer, which remains a Klingon planet."

They both drank. The Merlot was a bit harsh, but fairly fruity for all that. "I compliment whoever programmed your replicator."

Haden smiled. "The same engineer who turned me on to this stuff. Never used to be much of a whiskey drinker, then I had Bushmills 21 for the first time, and now I can't drink anything else without being disappointed." Haden set down the glass and gave Picard one of his patented wide-eyed stares. "What happened, Jean-Luc?"

"Martok, for reasons passing understanding, diverted Captain Kirros's fleet to H'atoria."

"What?" Haden blinked, then slugged down some more whiskey. "The Romulans took H'atoria three months ago! Did he really think one fleet was gonna get it back?"

"Apparently. And it left us vulnerable at Khitomer. We were able to win the day thanks to my new first officer's creative weapons-firing skills."

Haden nodded. "How is Worf working out?"

"He's a fine first officer."

"But you're not happy that you had to promote him?"

Picard sighed, and sipped his wine to cover his annoyance. He was being selfish, he knew that, and yet . . . . "Captain Riker and Captain Data deserved their promotions. The *Sugihara* and the *Sutherland* couldn't ask for better shipmasters. I—"

"You miss them. I get it. You know who my first officer was back in the day on the *Carthage*? Rachel Garrett. Hurt like hell to lose her to the *Enterprise*-C, but I got over it. And she did okay in the big chair."

That was an understatement. Garrett's tenure as the last person before Picard to command a ship named *Enterprise* was historic. It ended tragically and heroically, as the ship was destroyed defending Narendra III, a Klingon world, from Romulan attack.

"We lose people, Jean-Luc. Be grateful that you're losing them to captaincies and not any other way. Right now, we need our best people in big chairs all over." He leaned back in his chair, still holding his drink up near his face. "The war's not going so well— and to make matters worse, the Cardassians have been showing the flag at the border."

Picard frowned. He hadn't heard of this—but he'd been in Klingon space for some months. They only came back here now because after Khitomer, there were several days' worth of repairs, which Lieutenant O'Brien was already undertaking. Picard had confidence that his new chief engineer—who'd received a field commission and was promoted after Riker took La Forge with him to the *Sugihara*—would shave at least a few hours off the repair estimate.

Haden went on. "They seem to be making moves in the Dorvan, Valo, and Salva systems. We're sending a few ships to warn them off."

"Can we spare them?" Picard asked bluntly. "This sounds suspiciously like—"

Holding up a hand, Haden said, "This isn't sending Kirros's fleet on a wild-goose chase. We can't afford to turn our backs on the Cardassians. There are reports of a huge military buildup the last couple of years, and it'd be just like them to strike when our guard's down."

"It's not down; it's busy fighting the Romulans!" Picard snapped. Realizing his *faux pas,* he closed his eyes and inhaled slowly. "My apologies, sir, I didn't mean to raise—"

"Don't worry about it. I read your reports even before this latest foolishness. You think Martok's trying to throw the war?"

Picard shook his head. "I wish I could say. He *seems* a reasonable man. But Gowron . . ."

"You don't trust him?"

"The chancellor is an opportunist. Martok is a very popular general among the troops, but he also takes his orders from Gowron. Several of the troop allocations that the Defense Force have made have been questionable at best. Inadequate resources to defend important planets, too many resources to protect targets that the Romulans have shown *no* interest in . . ." Picard trailed off, then sipped more wine. It tasted better on the third sip. "It's as if they're trying to prolong the war."

"Are you accusing Gowron of that?"

"Possibly." Picard hesitated, sipped some more. "Gowron's hold on the chancellor's chair is tenuous. He ascended only because Worf killed Duras. After he came to power, he rewrote Klingon history to de-emphasize the roles anyone else played. For that matter, he takes all the credit for the rise of Emperor Kahless, even though he was very slow to accept the clone's existence."

"You're thinking he's trying to make Martok look bad so he can swoop in and save the war."

"I dearly pray that I'm wrong," Picard whispered. "It would be unthinkable, to sacrifice so many lives . . ."

"But not out of character?"

Picard had spent more time with Gowron than any human

during his time serving as the Arbiter of Succession for Gowron's predecessor, K'mpec. "I believe it is possible, yes."

"Do you also believe that it's possible that the Klingons are just stretched too thin? Seems like they're never at full fighting strength with all the little skirmishes the Defense Force gets into. They lose ships by the truckload. We lost a few trucks' worth to the Borg just before this started, too. Maybe they're just out-classed." Haden picked up a padd and made a note on it. "Still, you could be right. I'll pass on your thoughts to the Federation Council and to the Diplomatic Corps—and to Starfleet Intelligence. We'll see if we can get some evidence to support this, and see if we can talk some sense into Gowron."

"I wish you luck with that," Picard said dryly.

"Wish it on the ambassadors. Me, I'm just an old admiral trying to keep his starbase in one piece. How long you docked for?"

"At most, three days."

"All right." Haden got to his feet, slugging down the rest of his whiskey. "Thank you, Captain."

"Thank you for the drink, Admiral," Picard said, also rising and finishing his wine. "And for passing on my concerns."

"You're welcome, Jean-Luc."

Picard took his leave and headed back to the transporter plat-form so he could return to his ship. Nodding to the Bolian ensign, he tapped his combadge. "Picard to *Enterprise*. One to beam up."

Within moments, he was back on his ship, and he headed straight for sickbay. The scene was somewhat less chaotic than it had been the last time Picard was here, which was right after the battle at Khitomer had ended, and the few Romulan warbirds still intact had retreated into warp.

Now the patients were lying quietly in their beds instead of screaming in pain, and the doctors and nurses were moving calmly about.

Ro Laren lay in one of the central beds, a cortical monitor on her forehead just above her nose ridges. At least the burns on her arms and face had healed.

Doctor Beverly Crusher entered. "Captain!"

"Doctor. How is Lieutenant Ro?"

"Still in a coma, as you can see. We've done everything we can for her—it's up to her to wake up again. It could be in five minutes; it could be never."

Picard nodded sadly. A fire had broken out on the bridge, and Ro had saved the life of one of the bridge science officers, but was hit with burning plasma from a ruptured conduit. By that time, the battle had been won, due in part to Ro's skills at tactical.

Then he looked around at the rest of sickbay. *So many wounded . . .*

"What—" he started, but it came out as a croak. He cleared his throat and started again. "What were the final casualty figures, Beverly?"

Beverly stared at him for a moment with troubled eyes. War was always worst for doctors.

"We lost seventy-two people. Another hundred and two were injured."

Picard felt a heavy weight on his chest, and suddenly wished he had another glass of Haden's wine.

The truly sad part was that those casualty figures were comparatively light. But then, there had been moments in the Khitomer engagement when Picard truly thought that the *Enterprise* would be destroyed.

Putting a gentle hand on Crusher's shoulder, Picard said, "Keep me advised of Lieutenant Ro's condition."

"Of course," she said with a nod.

With that, he departed sickbay. He had to send condolences to the next of kin of the seventy-two people who died. It was a duty that often took more time than the captain of a *Sovereign*-class starship had.

But it was not a duty he would ever shirk. The families of all those who died under his command would be informed by him personally. They deserved that much, at least. Before his promotion, and after the battle at Archanis that claimed more than two hundred members of his crew, Riker had gently suggested that Picard simply record a generic condolence, but Picard refused. He would not allow the war to make him expedient when it came to death notices.

And so he went to his ready room. At least this time he had three days.

10

Captain Kathryn Janeway was in the midst of reading the latest missive from her husband when the doorchime to her ready room sounded. "Come in," she said with a smile on her face.

Lieutenant Commander Aaron Cavit entered, holding a padd. "Here are the updated duty rosters." He approached Janeway, who sat on a couch beneath the window in the spacious ready room. Through that window, she could see that the stars were no longer distorted by the warp effect, but had settled again into points in the darkness of space.

Reaching up to take the padd and setting aside the letter, she said, "Thanks, Aaron." She took only a cursory look at the roster; Cavit had proved himself over the past two years to be a magnificent first officer. She couldn't imagine running this ship without him. "I see we've arrived."

Cavit nodded as he sat down next to her on the couch. "The *Intrepid* and *Bellerophon* are right behind us. And Harry's picked up two Cardassian ships in orbit of Dorvan V. We're too far to get an ID on the ships yet." He indicated the padd Janeway had put on the cushion next to her. "Letter from Mark?"

Smiling, Janeway said, "Yes."

"Did he get the promotion?"

"Mhm. He's now the head of the hybridization project. And

they got that growth off Molly's nose. She's coming home from the vet tomorrow."

"That's great news, Captain," Cavit said with a small smile, which Janeway knew was about as emotional as Aaron Cavit would get while on duty, even when it was just the two of them in the ready room. Later on, in the mess hall, when they had their usual after-shift drink, he'd likely be more effusive.

Holding up the padd, Janeway asked, "I take it this is the briefing I asked you to put together?"

"Yes," Cavit said. "It's fairly basic. Dorvan was settled about twenty years ago by a group of humans who were trying to return to the preindustrial life their ancestors lived."

"Back-to-nature types, huh?" Janeway smiled as she glanced over the padd. "Mark tried to get me to go on a hiking trip with him once where we wouldn't depend on modern conveniences. After my second day without coffee, I nearly strangled him."

Cavit snorted a chuckle. "I don't think I can imagine you without coffee, Captain."

"You don't want to, Aaron, *trust* me."

"Tuvok also turned up something interesting," Cavit said. "I don't know if you remember, but there were negotiations with the Cardassians a few years back about redrawing the border. Dorvan V was one of the worlds that was going to be ceded to the Cardassians in the original deal."

Janeway frowned. "What happened?"

Shrugging, Cavit said, "The Cardassians changed their minds. They pulled back the border, signed the treaty, and that was that. But this *was* a system on their radar. And Captain? So were Valo and Salva."

"Really?" Janeway glanced down at the padd again. Just as the three *Intrepid*-class ships had been sent to Dorvan to warn the Cardassians off, so too were ships sent to the other two systems. "All right. Have Stadi set a course, and tell Captains Emick and Stuhlmacher to follow in a delta formation."

"Right." Cavit got to his feet.

"I'll be out in a minute."

"Aye, aye, Captain."

After Cavit departed, Janeway picked up the letter and read it again. Since the war started, time off had been difficult to come by. This assignment was the first time *Voyager* had spent any significant time in Federation space since the skirmish with the Romulans at Tyrellia. She was hoping that once this was done, she could finally take some leave and go back to Earth. In particular, she wanted to see Molly again. Poor Mark had been stuck alone with the Irish setter when the growth showed up on her nose. Janeway wished she could have been there for Molly in her time of need, even though Mark had grown to love the old girl as much as Janeway herself did.

When she finished rereading the letter for the second time, she set it down and went out to the bridge. Cavit was standing behind Stadi at the conn in front of the wide bridge, Tuvok and Harry Kim at the tactical and ops consoles on either side of the turbolift.

Kim said, "Two of the Cardassian vessels are *Galor*-class—the *Vetar* and the *Trager*. The other one's a freighter, the *Bok'Nor*."

"A freighter?" Janeway asked in surprise.

"Confirmed," Tuvok said. Then he raised an eyebrow. "The *Bok'Nor* is running with a sensor screen that prevents us from examining its contents."

"That can't be good," Cavit said.

"It isn't." Janeway took her seat.

"We are being hailed by Gul Evek on the *Vetar*," Tuvok said.

"On screen. Tie in the *Intrepid* and *Bellerophon*."

The boxy face of a Cardassian gul appeared on the viewer, with images of two human males inset in the lower corners.

"This is Captain Kathryn Janeway of the *U.S.S. Voyager*, on behalf of Captain Walter Emick of the *U.S.S. Intrepid* and Captain Brian Stuhlmacher of the *U.S.S. Bellerophon*. What are you doing in Federation space, Gul?"

"*I am Gul Evek of the Fourth Order, and it is you who are the invaders here, Captain Janeway. Dorvan V is now a Cardassian world.*"

Janeway blinked. This was brazen even by Cardassian standards. "Excuse me?"

"*We claim Dorvan V as part of the Cardassian Union. And if you do not depart Cardassian territory in the next two minutes, we will blow you out of the sky.*"

Rising to her feet, Janeway said, "Gul Evek, we cannot let you simply *take* a Federation planet."

Evek smiled. Janeway rather wished he hadn't. "*I don't expect you will, Captain.*" And with that, his face disappeared from the screen, which then switched to a double view of Captains Emick and Stuhlmacher. The former, a bald and bearded man who had been a year behind Janeway at the academy, looked thoughtful and calm as always. The younger Stuhlmacher, who'd only received command of the *Bellerophon* two months ago after his captain was killed in an engagement with the Romulans, looked somewhat more angry.

Before anyone could say anything, Cavit said, "Tuvok, send an emergency transmission to Starbase 310, inform them of the situation."

After giving her first officer a grateful nod, Janeway turned back to the screen. "Gentlemen, it seems we have an invasion on our hands."

"*The freighter's probably got whatever equipment they plan to use to 'settle' Dorvan V,*" Emick said.

Stuhlmacher ran a hand through his wild brown hair. "*We can't let this stand. It's just two Galors, we can take them.*"

"*Whether or not we can,*" Emick said resignedly, "*I don't see how we can let the people of Dorvan V be taken prisoner. Because that's what we're talking about here.*"

"Agreed." Janeway had no intention of doing anything other than engage Gul Evek in combat, but she wanted to make sure the other two captains were in agreement. She was in command of the convoy—she had seniority over the other two, though only by a couple of weeks in Emick's case—but she felt better about her decision knowing that the other two captains were with her. "Let's do it, gentlemen."

Next to her, Cavit said, "Red alert. All hands to battle stations. Mister Tuvok, arm phasers and load torpedo bays."

Janeway added, "Stadi, coordinate with the conn on *Intrepid* and *Bellerophon*—engage pattern zeta."

Nodding, the Betazoid conn officer said, "Aye, Captain, pattern zeta."

Stadi's elegant fingers played over the console as if it were a grand piano. *Voyager* moved on a parabolic course toward the *Vetar*. Stadi put a tactical image in one corner of the screen, showing the *Bellerophon* and *Intrepid* following the zeta pattern, which had proven successful against the Romulans at Galordon Core. *Of course,* Janeway thought, *that was against one warbird, which was bigger than these two* Galor*s combined, but it's still a good gambit.*

From behind her, Kim said, "Uh, Captain?"

"What is it, Harry?"

"I'm reading a massive power surge in both Cardassian vessels."

Cavit asked, "A weapon?"

Kim shook his head. "I honestly couldn't tell you, sir. It's an energy pattern unlike anything I've—"

Tuvok interrupted. "Energy bolt bearing directly on us."

Moments later, Janeway felt the bone-jarring impact of her jaw hitting the deck. The bridge was in utter choas. Consoles sparked and exploded, the smell of plasma fires burned the air, and several alarms began going off at once, competing with the red alert.

As she scrambled to her feet, she said, "Turn off that damned noise!"

The alarms quieted, leaving only the cries of pain of several crew members.

One person not crying was Ensign Harry Kim, who lay on top of his console, his head at an impossible angle.

Janeway had already lost many of her crew. Half her medical

staff was killed during a rescue operation that turned out to be a Romulan trap, and her chief engineer was killed staving off a warp core breach last month, plus numerous members of Tuvok's security detail.

But seeing Harry dead especially hurt. He had shone as operations manager, and Janeway had just received word yesterday approving his promotion to junior-grade lieutenant.

Cavit was gripping his left shoulder—it looked like he'd broken a bone or two. Through gritted teeth, he said, "Medical team to the bridge."

Putting Harry's death in the back of her mind, Janeway cried out, "Damage report."

Green blood oozing out of a cut over his right eye, Tuvok said, "Shields are down. Hull damage on decks eight, nine, and ten. Structural integrity field at seventy-five percent."

The voice of Joe Carey, recently promoted to chief engineer, sounded over the speakers. *"Engineering to bridge."*

"Go ahead, Joe."

"You'll have shields back in seven minutes. I've had to take the warp engines and phasers offline. Torpedoes are still okay, but I'm gonna need a few minutes to get phaser power back."

"What about warp drive?" Cavit asked.

Before Carey could reply, Janeway said, "We'll worry about that later. Tuvok, what the *hell* did they hit us with?"

"A phased polaron beam of considerable power. I believe that once Mister Carey has reconstituted the shields, there is a forty-nine-point-two percent chance that we can tune the shields to repel the beam."

"Can you target the *Vetar* with torpedoes?"

"Yes."

"Do it." Janeway turned toward the viewer. The *Bellerophon* was engaging the *Trager,* while the *Intrepid* was heading for the *Bok'Nor.* The *Vetar* was changing course to try to cut off the *Intrepid.*

Even as Tuvok fired torpedoes at the *Vetar,* the Cardassians hit the *Intrepid* with the same polaron beam.

Seconds later, the *Intrepid* exploded in a plume of fire.

Voyager's torpedoes struck the *Vetar*'s shields, not doing nearly enough damage to suit Janeway. Walter Emick was a good man, from a family with a long history of Starfleet service. To go like that . . .

Again, shaking it off, Janeway said, "Keep firing, Tuvok. I want to wipe that smile off Evek's face."

"Shields are back up," Tuvok said, even as he continued firing. "Continuous sensor scans of the polaron beam have provided more data. I believe there is now a sixty-three-point-four percent chance of tuning the shields to defend."

Janeway took very small comfort from the fact that the *Intrepid*'s sacrifice gave Tuvok that data, but she supposed she would take what she could.

Still clutching his left shoulder with his right hand, Cavit, now once again seated in his chair, asked, "Where the *hell* did the Cardassians get this kind of weaponry?"

Tuvok, for once recognizing a rhetorical question, did not reply directly. "*Vetar* shields are down to forty-six percent. They're coming about."

"Shields?" Cavit asked.

"Not yet."

Janeway gripped the arms of her chair. "Stadi, evasive maneuvers. Keep our distance from the *Vetar*."

Again, Stadi's fingers moved, but this time nothing happened.

"*Bridge*," said Carey, "*we've got a problem with helm control. Give me a minute.*"

"We don't *have* a minute, Mister Carey!" Cavit shouted.

The *Vetar* came closer.

"Polaron beam powering up," Tuvok said.

Then *Voyager* moved, hard to port. An instant later, the Cardassian weapon fired harmlessly into what was now empty space.

"*Sorry about that, bridge.*"

"No more surprises if you can avoid it, Joe," Janeway said through gritted teeth. "Tuvok, fire."

Another spread of torpedoes struck the *Vetar*. Tuvok said, "*Vetar* shields down to twenty percent. Phasers are back online. Also, the *Bellerophon*'s shields are down and they're venting plasma."

Cavit looked at Janeway. "With your permission?" At Janeway's nod, he struggled to his feet and went to the conn. "Lieutenant, that weapon needs a second to power up. I want you to do an old-fashioned strafing run—get in close, skim the hull. Can you do that?"

Stadi smiled. "Watch me."

Turning to the tactical console—and wincing in pain as he did so—Cavit said, "Mister Tuvok, ready phasers."

"Captain, the *Trager* is coming about!"

At Stadi's cry, Janeway looked at the screen and saw that the *Trager* was heading right to the spot where *Voyager*'s projected course would take them after Cavit's strafing run.

Tuvok said, "Firing phasers."

Janeway was coming to realize that this was not going to end well. She'd seen far too much combat these past few months to not recognize a losing battle. "Tuvok, send an emergency transmission to Starbase 310—make sure all our sensor data on that polaron weapon is part of it!"

"Preparing transmission now."

"*Trager* is firing!" Stadi cried.

As the bridge exploded around Janeway, she hoped that they were able to send the data to the starbase in time.

11

**U.S.S. Enterprise-E
Approaching the Federation–Cardassian Border
United Federation of Planets**

Jean-Luc Picard sat in his quarters, in the midst of fulfilling a months-old promise to himself, when the doorchime rang.

He let out a long sigh before saying anything. After they set out from Starbase 24, Picard had left strict instructions with Worf that he was not to be disturbed for any reason short of a warp-core breach until they reached the Cardassian border, where they'd rendezvous with the *Excalibur* and the *Sentinel.*

The war had dragged on for months, and now it seemed a new front had opened up. Nine ships had been sent to halt Cardassian aggression in three Federation systems. Of those ships only two—the *Bellerophon* and the *Musashi*—were still intact, the former just barely. Seven Federation starships had been destroyed by Cardassian weapons that nobody had ever seen before. Luckily, one of the ships, *Voyager,* had managed to send along full sensor data on the new weapons (the *Bellerophon*'s computer core was damaged, so its sensor readings were lost), and shields fleetwide had been adjusted to accommodate. Mister O'Brien had stated with confidence that the *Enterprise* would be able to withstand "whatever the Cardies can throw at us, sir."

Picard hadn't been pleased with the chief engineer's use of that particular slur, but he'd let it pass. O'Brien had fought on the Cardassian front for years while serving on the *Rutledge.* Besides, Picard didn't feel he could justify defending a people who had invaded Federation space and wantonly destroyed seven Starfleet vessels.

It was then that Picard realized he needed a break. When they'd gotten their new assignment, and their VIP guest had arrived, Picard ordered Ensign Kell Perim, the new conn officer, to set course for the border, and then gave Worf the bridge, with instructions not to disturb him.

For the three days it would take to reach the border, Picard intended to read.

Archaeology had always been a passion of his. It had almost been a career; but he had chosen Starfleet instead. For the longest time, he didn't regret that decision, not even four years ago, when his mentor, Professor Richard Galen, tried to convince Picard to join him, shortly before he died.

But lately, since the war began, Picard found himself wishing he could summon Q to appear before him and once again give him the chance to relive his life. Only this time, he would make sure to pursue his studies with Galen.

Anything to avoid this war.

Still, at least this assignment was one he could live with.

When the doorchime sounded a second time, he set aside the padd containing the latest issue of *The Journal of Archaeological Studies* and said, "Come."

The doors slid aside to reveal the balding head and round face of Ambassador Theodore Krajensky. "Captain. I'm sorry for interrupting. Your first officer asked me to make it clear that he told me not to disturb you."

"Quite all right, Mister Ambassador." Picard rose to his feet; Krajensky was the one person on board besides Worf for whom Picard was willing to break his self-imposed exile. "Please come in."

"Thank you." Krajensky came into Picard's quarters, the doors sliding shut behind him. "I wanted to talk to you about our mission."

"Of course." Picard indicated the chair that was perpendicular to his while asking, "May I get you anything?"

"Actually, some ginger ale would be nice."

Picard walked over to the replicator and instructed it to provide a glass of ginger ale and another cup of hot Earl Grey tea.

After the drinks materialized with the telltale hum, Picard brought both over to the couch, setting them down on the table that sat between them. "What about the mission do you wish to discuss, Mister Ambassador?"

Krajensky took a sip of his ginger ale before answering. "I wanted to take your temperature, Captain. I received a great deal of resistance from many quarters in Starfleet Command regarding my mission—despite the fact that it came directly from the president himself."

Before Krajensky could continue, Picard held up a hand. "You may rest assured, Mister Ambassador, that I am not in any of those quarters. It is, honestly, a relief to be going on a diplomatic mission for the first time in more than six months."

"I'm so very glad to hear that, Captain." Krajensky shook his head. "This war has taken such a terrible toll—to open up a second front would be disastrous. I can't believe that the Cardassians won't be reasonable." Then he smiled. "Well, of course, they won't be *reasonable,* but I have faith in our ability to work out some kind of compromise."

"I wish I could share your faith, Mister Ambassador," Picard said darkly, "but I'm afraid that all I can muster is hope." He took a sip of his tea, which then burned his tongue. Quickly setting down the cup again, he went on: "All attempts to communicate with Romulus have failed. The Cardassians have met the ships that greeted them with fire. It feels as if the galaxy is tumbling inexorably into total war."

"My job is to prevent that, Captain. I don't know why the Romulans aren't talking—with the losses they've taken, you'd think they'd want to parley before they lose the empire entirely—but we have a treaty with the Cardassians. Of course, we do with the Romulans, too, but that's decades old. The Cardassian treaty's recent enough that most of the people who agreed to it are still in positions of authority. That's a starting point."

Picard, who had negotiated his fair share of treaties, if not quite on this scale, nodded in agreement. "Perhaps. I suppose I simply find it difficult to engage in optimistic behavior in these times."

"I understand, Captain, believe me." Krajensky smirked. "To be honest, I wish I was half as confident as I sound. The Cardassians' behavior is incomprehensible to me." He shook his head. "But so is Starfleet's. Apparently the admiralty is eager to send out that new fleet they've assembled."

Picard let out a sigh. "Yes, the Ninth Fleet." Consisting of a dozen refit *Akira*-class ships, the Ninth Fleet was meant to be a pure battle fleet, with most systems given over to tactical use. The original plan had been to use the *Defiant* prototype as the basis, but that class was still in the yard with power-consumption issues.

"Worf to Picard."

"Go ahead, Number One."

"We are approaching the Cardassian border. A Galor-*class ship is waiting for us on the Cardassian side and the* Excalibur *and* Sentinel *are on the Federation side."*

"Have you identified the vessel?"

"It reads as the Central Command vessel Reklar."

Getting to his feet, and leaving his tea unfinished, Picard said, "Ambassador Krajensky and I will be right up."

By the time the captain and the ambassador reached the bridge, the *Enterprise* had come out of warp. Worf—who had ordered the ship to yellow alert—was standing between the command chair and the forward stations. Perim was at conn, with the new operations manager, Lieutenant Miranda Kadohata, next to her at ops.

To Picard's surprise, Ro Laren was at the tactical station. His second officer and security chief looked a bit pale. He said to her, "Lieutenant?"

"Ready for duty, Captain. Doctor Crusher discharged me this morning."

Putting a hand on her shoulder, Picard said, "It's good to have you back on the bridge." Moving around to the command chair, he asked, "Any word from our Cardassian friends?"

"No, sir," Ro said, "but they are at alert status—weapons armed, shields up."

"Do not arm weapons," Picard said, "but keep shields up." Moving to sit in his chair, he said, "Hail the *Excalibur* and *Sentinel*, and tie us all together." Worf moved to do likewise in his seat right in front of Ro's console.

Moments later, two human female faces, one quite familiar to Picard, appeared on the forward viewer. "Captain Shelby—it's good to see you again."

"Thank you, Captain Picard," Elizabeth Shelby said. *"I wish it was under better circumstances."*

"I was sorry to hear about Morgan," Picard added, "but I can't think of a better replacement as captain of the *Excalibur*." Morgan Korsmo had been one of Picard's classmates at the academy; he was killed during the Borg incursion. With the Romulan War happening almost immediately, Korsmo's first officer, Shelby, was promoted to captain and sent to the front lines.

Shelby had temporarily served on the *Enterprise*-D during a previous Borg incursion, and had also acted as Riker's first officer after Picard had been taken by the Borg.

The other woman had sable hair and olive skin, in contrast to the pale blond Shelby. *"I'm Captain Anna-Maria Amalfitano of the U.S.S. Sentinel, Captain. It's an honor to meet you—I've heard a lot about you, particularly from our chief engineer, Commander Gomez."*

Picard smiled. As an ensign fresh out of the academy, serving in Geordi La Forge's engine room, Gomez had introduced herself to Picard by spilling hot chocolate on him. She had blossomed into a fine officer, and a top-notch engineer. Amalfitano was lucky to have her.

Tugging on his uniform jacket, Picard asked, "Any word from the Cardassians?"

"Not yet," Amalfitano said, *"except to identify themselves. The commander of the ship is a gul named Lemec."*

A knot twisted in Picard's gut. He'd only met Lemec once before—when his time as Gul Madred's prisoner ended. It was not a time Picard was eager to remember. Quickly, he shoved those memories into the box where he kept unpleasant memories: both Borg attacks, the mind-meld with Sarek, his time as Locutus, the entire last six months . . .

The box was ready to burst.

He wasn't encouraged by the fact that it was Lemec—a mere gul—whom Central Command had sent, rather than a proper ambassador, or even a legate.

Indicating the screen with a hand, Picard said to Krajensky, "Mister Ambassador, the floor is yours."

Making a small bow, Krajensky walked to stand where Worf had been. "Thank you, Captain. Lieutenant Ro, please hail the *Reklar.*"

Ro said nothing in reply, but did open the hail.

"This is Ambassador Theodore Krajensky, representing the United Federation of Planets."

The screen switched from the view of the two captains to that of a familiar Cardassian gul.

"I am Gul Lemec of the Fourth Order."

"It's good to meet you, Gul Lemec," Krajensky said. "I'd like to arrange to meet with you—"

Lemec held up one gray hand. *"That will not be necessary."*

"I beg your pardon? I wish to discuss terms of—"

"There are no terms."

Picard's blood froze. Lemec spoke the words in an almost deadly monotone—the exact words that Picard had, as Locutus, spoken to William Riker.

"Surely, Gul Lemec, we can—"

"Cardassia has no interest in negotiating with the Federation, now or in the future. The solar systems of Dorvan, Valo, and Salva now belong to us, and they will remain with us. We—" Suddenly, Lemec looked away. *"Excuse me."*

The screen went blank.

Krajensky looked horrified as he turned to face Picard and Worf. "I don't understand."

"I think I do," Ro said. "We're picking up two distress signals. One is Cardassian, asking for assistance." She looked up sharply. "The other is on a Bajoran frequency. And they're using a resistance code phrase. The Cardassians wouldn't recognize it, but it's in the tactical database."

Ro, of course, hadn't had the chance to check the database, but as a Bajoran herself, Picard assumed she recognized the code phrase on sight.

Picard looked at Worf, who said, "A Bajoran defector would be a valuable asset."

Without waiting for a prompt, Krajensky said, "I agree with Commander Worf—this is an ideal opportunity—especially since diplomatic channels have apparently been cut off."

Looking over at Kadohata, Picard asked, "Do you have a fix on the distress signals?"

Staring down at her console, the raven-haired woman said, "Yes, sir. It's coming from a Ferengi yacht." Kadohata turned to face Picard with a grim expression. "They're heading for the border."

From behind Picard, Ro added, "So're the Cardassians pursuing them."

"Ensign Perim, set a course that puts us where that ship will cross the border. Send the navigational data to the *Excalibur* and the *Sentinel*."

"Aye, Captain," the Trill replied.

"Engage at warp nine."

It took several minutes to arrive at the designated coordinates. "Tactical overview on screen," Worf said as they approached.

Ro switched the forward viewer to a graphic representation of the scenario. The *Excalibur* and *Sentinel* accompanied the *Enterprise,* all shown in blue, approaching from the lower right-hand side of the screen. Running parallel to them, on the other side of the border, was the *Reklar,* in yellow. Also in yellow was another vessel, identified as the *Sladok,* pursuing a much smaller orange vessel. If that ship had an ID, the *Enterprise* computer had yet to recognize it.

Perim said, "The Ferengi ship will cross the border in seven minutes."

"We're being hailed by the Ferengi ship," Ro said. "The signal's weak . . ."

"On audio," Worf said.

"Federa . . . ajoran resistance. Requesting asy . . . eat, re . . . ing asylum in the Federation . . ." The message degenerated into static.

"Captain," Krajensky said, "we must grant the asylum request."

"I had no intention of doing otherwise," Picard said tartly. "Ro, hail the *Reklar.*"

"Actually, Lemec's hailing us," Ro said.

"On screen." Picard got to his feet. "Tie in Captains Shelby and Amalfitano."

Lemec's face reappeared. *"Captain Picard, this does not concern you."*

"I'm afraid it does, Gul Lemec. That ship's occupants have requested asylum in the Federation, which we will grant if they cross the border. If *you* cross the border, you should know that we have standing orders to fire on *any* Cardassian vessel that violates Federation space."

Krajensky whirled around in surprise at that. Picard had been specifically instructed by Admiral Haden not to share that new standing order with Krajensky for fear that he would react just this way. Indeed, Picard himself had reacted thus, but Haden had made it clear that failure to comply with that order would not be looked upon with favor by the admiralty—especially after what had happened to *Voyager, Intrepid,* and the other ships.

"You're welcome to try, Captain." Lemec's smile was wide and unpleasant, and gave him the aspect of a cobra.

Time then, Picard thought, *to be the mongoose.* "Screen off."

"Red alert," Worf said. "Arm all phasers and torpedo bays. Raise shields."

"Ferengi yacht approaching the border," Perim said over the alert siren.

Kadohata added, "I'm reading an imbalance in their intermix chamber. Estimate three minutes to a breach."

Worf asked Ro, "The Cardassians?"

"Still on an intercept course. They'll follow the yacht over the border." Looking up from the readout, Ro asked Worf, "Permission to wipe them off the face of the galaxy, sir."

"Stand by," Worf said.

Picard kept his composure, but was no more pleased with Ro's bloodthirstiness than he was with O'Brien's, though it came from the same source. As a Bajoran, Ro had grown up under Cardassian oppression, after all.

To Krajensky, the captain said, "Mister Ambassador, if you would please report to Transporter Room 3. I believe we shall have to beam our refugees aboard, and you're best qualified to greet them."

Nodding, Krajensky said, "Of course, Captain."

"Lieutenant," Picard said to Ro, "have a security detail meet the ambassador there."

"Sir," Kadohata said, "the *Reklar* is coming around—they're crossing the border now, sir."

Shelby's voice sounded over the speaker. *"I'll take care of Lemec, Captain."*

"Very well, Captain Shelby. Godspeed."

The *Excalibur* veered off onto an intercept course with the *Reklar.* Ro put the tactical display back up, showing the two ships engaging.

Picard was pleased to see that the *Reklar*'s weapons fire—which had the same energy signature as the phased polaron beams that destroyed seven Federation ships days ago—were stopped by

Excalibur's shields. He gave silent thanks to *Voyager* and her crew for managing to send off the specs for the weapon before they were lost.

However, *Excalibur*'s shields were down to eighty percent.

"Ferengi yacht now across the border," Perim said.

"*Sladok* right behind," Kadohata added.

Worf said, "Prepare to fire on the *Sladok* as soon as it enters Federation space."

"Aye, sir." Ro said the words with relish.

Picard tapped his combadge. "Bridge to transporter room— can you get a lock on the occupants of the yacht?"

"*Stand by, sir,*" Chief Mun Ying said. After a brief pause, he added, "*Reading a Ferengi and a Bajoran on board, sir. I've got a lock and can beam them up whenever you lower the shields.*"

"Captain Amalfitano, if you would please cover us while we beam aboard our defectors . . ."

"*We're on it, Captain,*" Amalfitano said.

The *Sentinel* took up position between the *Sladok* and the *Enterprise.*

"Lower shields," Picard said.

Sounding disappointed that the *Sentinel* was getting first blood, Ro said, "Yes, sir."

"Chief Mun Ying, beam them aboard."

"*Aye, sir.*"

"Captain!" Kadohata shouted.

Looking over at the viewer, Picard saw two of the ships on the tactical overlay wink out.

"My God."

The *Excalibur* and the *Reklar* had destroyed each other.

"Any life signs? Escape pods?" Picard asked Kadohata, hoping for an affirmative answer.

Shaking her head, Kadohata said, "I'm sorry, sir. Sensors picked up some pods from both ships, but they were vaporized by the explosion. There are no life signs in the wreckage."

Picard closed his eyes. He was tired. Tired of death, tired of war, tired of all of it. Except for the three-day respite he'd forced upon himself, he'd been going nonstop since the battle against the Borg, stumbling from one battle to another. Even this, which was supposed to be a proper diplomatic mission, was turning into yet another bloodbath.

And he'd had enough.

Opening his eyes, he looked to his first officer. "Mister Worf, you have the bridge. Work with the *Sentinel* to do whatever is necessary to keep our defectors safe."

"Aye, sir."

"I'll be greeting our guests." With that, Picard entered the turbolift. As soon as the doors hissed shut, he whispered, "Transporter Room 3."

The speakers played the feed from the bridge the entire way. Picard barely noticed as Worf gave orders and Ro, Perim, and Kadohata carried them out. As he approached the transporter room doors, he heard Kadohata say, *"The* Sladok*'s been destroyed.* Sentinel*'s lost shields and helm—they're drifting."*

"Engage tractor beam," Worf said. *"Do not let them drift across the border."*

"Aye, sir," Ro said.

The doors slid open. Picard saw Mun Ying standing behind the transporter, two security guards next to him. Two more security guards were on either side of the transporter platform, all of them watching the two people on the pads, who were being treated by Crusher and a nurse.

Standing in front of the console was Krajensky, who said, "I summoned the doctor, Captain—they were both injured."

One of Crusher's patients—a Bajoran woman who had a huge gash on her forehead that the doctor was trying to treat—leapt to her feet and said, "Are you in charge here?"

Glancing at Krajensky, Picard said, "I am Captain Jean-Luc Picard of the Federation Star—"

"We have vital intelligence for the Federation Council."

The Ferengi who was with her bleated from the pad. " 'We'? 'We' don't have anything. *I* have a destroyed yacht."

"Shut up, Quark," the Bajoran woman said without looking behind her. Her intense brown eyes were focused right on Picard.

"What is this intelligence?" Picard asked.

"Over the past five years, important people on Cardassia Prime, Qo'noS, Romulus, *and* Earth have all been replaced by shape-changers from the Gamma Quadrant."

12

Narviat paced the strategy room in the basement of his home in fury. Several admirals had just left, and now he was waiting alone except for his two bodyguards. Since the war with the Klingons and Federation began, Charvanek had insisted that he have his guards with him everywhere. Once, those two would have been outside the door, but now, they were under strict orders from Charvanek to never let the praetor out of their sight.

A knock came at the door, and another bodyguard stuck in his head. "Lord Praetor, Colonel Koval has arrived."

"Send him in," Narviat said testily.

Koval entered and bowed ever-so-slightly as the bodyguard closed the door behind him. "What service may your humble servant provide, Praetor?"

"You may take over security for this war!"

"I'm sorry? I thought Colonel Lovok had that honor."

Narviat snorted. " 'Honor,' indeed. So honored is he that he is losing this war for us!"

"Surely, Praetor, the difficult prosecution of the war cannot be laid at the feet of a single—"

"Oh, it can. I just met with my senior-most admirals. They painted quite a fascinating picture of the 'difficult prosecution of the war,' as you so delicately put it. When I queried them as to why our forces have been routed with such regularity—including

that rather embarrassing defeat at Khitomer—they said it was because the intelligence provided by the Tal Shiar has been faulty!"

Koval put his hands behind his back. "No intelligence network
can be one hundred percent foolproof, Praetor. I'm sure Colonel
Lovok is doing the best he can under trying circumstances."

Narviat smiled without mirth. "If this truly *is* the best he can
do, then I weep for the survival of our empire. Regardless, I can
no longer tolerate this. You will take over the intelligence gathering for the war from Lovok."

"And what is Lovok's new assignment to be?"

Normally, Narviat would not have to explain. But these were
not normal times, and Koval probably wished to be absolutely
clear about what his praetor was requesting.

"I wish him to be permanently removed."

This time, Koval's bow was deep. "As the praetor commands.
If you will excuse me, I will expedite this matter."

"Please do." Narviat started pacing again. "I wonder if this war
was wise. I did not expect the Federation to involve themselves."

"We could do little else, after such unprovoked attacks on our
people. The *Grimar* incident was isolated. The Klingon response
was premeditated—and also duplicitous. It required retaliation."

Narviat scowled. Klingons were always using avenging their
House name to justify unnecessary violence. While he could appreciate family loyalty, Narviat found it reprehensible that Gowron used it as an excuse to sanction violence against Romulans
while allowing himself to wash his hands of any responsibility.

And war between their two nations had been coming for
some time.

It was only a pity it was being waged so badly. Were it not for Lovok's incompetence, Narviat was sure his troops would be winning
the day. Between the Defense Force's bloodthirsty incompetence
and Starfleet's softness, they should have been easy foes to defeat.

But now it would be taken care of. He dismissed Koval, who
exited the strategy room to carry out his appointed task.

• • •

Lovok cursed the incompetent fools of the military.

His agents had done their work well, learning about Starfleet troop movements and Defense Force strategies—particularly the latter, since Klingons leaked intelligence like a broken raft taking on water.

But somehow, the information he relayed did no good. It was as if the military never *received* his information—or acted in direct contradiction to it.

At first, Lovok had assumed it to be the usual stubbornness. The colonel had lost track of the number of admirals and commanders and sub-commanders who deliberately ignored what the Tal Shiar told them, out of some kind of pig-headed insistence that the Tal Shiar were unnecessary. Usually, it was due to some imagined infraction that they believed the Tal Shiar had committed against them, their families, or their friends.

It grew tiresome. Lovok did the work of the empire. Everything he did, every action he took, was to make the Romulan Star Empire stronger. If a few families lost their parents or children or siblings, what of it?

Of course, Lovok had brought this to Koval's attention several weeks ago. Koval had promised to let the praetor and the Senate know. "It will be dealt with, rest assured," Koval had said.

Weeks later, and nothing. Lovok had provided everything necessary for a successful attack on Khitomer. That thrice-damned planet was the location of the historic treaty negotiations between the Federation and Klingons—a treaty that was directly responsible for this war being a third again as large as it should have been. One of Lovok's agents had learned of a flaw in their defenses and provided it to the military.

The result? Abject defeat.

Exiting his chambers, Lovok went to the office he kept in his home. This lunacy had gone on long enough. He needed to speak with Narviat immediately.

Just as he was about to open a channel to the praetor, one of his stewards entered. "Excuse me, Colonel," the elderly woman said, "but Colonel Koval is here to see you."

Lovok blinked. "Really? Very well, then. Send him in." Lovok would wait until Koval was here and then talk with the praetor. Perhaps together, they could get to the bottom of this.

The steward departed, and moments later, she brought Koval in. The colonel looked particularly smug, which Lovok thought inappropriate.

"I'm glad you're here, Koval, we need to—"

Koval held up a hand, and Lovok stopped talking. Turning to the steward, Koval said, "I must speak with your master in private."

Bowing her head deferentially, the steward left the office.

"My apologies for speaking thus to your servant, but this is a matter that must remain between the two of us."

Waving his hand dismissively, Lovok said, "I don't care about that. What I *do* care about are the faults in our intelligence delivery."

"Oh, there are no faults," Koval said with remarkable calm. "You see, the lines of intelligence have been sabotaged by an outside force that wishes to ensure that this war is prolonged and devastating."

Lovok frowned. Koval was talking nonsense. "What are you talking about? What is this outside force?"

Rarely did Koval smile. He did so now in such a manner that Lovok felt his breakfast welling up in his throat. "Me."

"What? Koval, you're talking nonsense." He moved over to the comm console where he intended to call Narviat. "We must—"

Suddenly, Koval's arm—*changed*. It shimmered and undulated and re-formed itself into something that looked very much like a long steel rod.

The end of that rod slammed into the comm console, shattering it into dozens of pieces of glass and ceramic and circuitry that sparked and burned.

As Lovok looked on in horror, the rod shimmered again, this time turning into a metal cable that whipped about in the air.

"What are you?" Lovok whispered.

"I am not Colonel Koval, certainly. He's in a Dominion prison, where we may interrogate him at will to ensure that my deception is accurate."

Lovok found himself unable to move. He'd sat at a computer his entire career. His rise through the ranks of the Tal Shiar had come through his phenomenal ability to sift through pieces of information and uncover truths that tried to remain hidden under falsehood.

But he had no combat training, no ability to defend himself in a fight.

And even if he had, he was simply petrified at the sight of this undulating, liquefied *thing* that wore Koval's face.

Though it did not wear it for long, bending and twisting into an amber ooze that snaked about through the air. Lovok could no longer see a mouth, but Koval's voice continued to sound in the room: "It has been such a trial, remaining in one form. I don't know how you solids do it. Still, my mission has been a success. Narviat sent me here, Lovok, because you have failed him by providing faulty intelligence. He asked me to dispose of you. Koval would simply shoot you with a disruptor pistol under those circumstances, but I so rarely am able to free myself like this—I believe I'm going to enjoy killing you."

The metal cable that had once been Koval's arm wrapped around Lovok's neck. It was only then that he was able to open his mouth to scream, but the cable bit into his throat, slicing away at his vocal cords, and his cries of agony were only guttural moans.

Somehow, the foul creature continued to speak with Koval's voice. "With you dead, your precious praetor has put me in charge of intelligence for the war. It will be *far* easier to further the Dominion's agenda from that position, rather than having to sabotage your work after the fact."

The last thing Lovok did as the bizarre alien *thing* choked the life out of him was wonder just what in the name of the Elements "the Dominion" was.

13

U.S.S. Enterprise-E
En Route to Earth
United Federation of Planets

Kira Nerys wanted very much to punch the Federation ambassador in the nose. The only thing stopping her was the knowledge that doing so would do nothing to help her cause.

And her cause was taking a beating as it was. Not that she expected any less—had she heard her story without knowing what she knew, she wouldn't believe it either—but somehow she *had* to convince them.

She had told the story briefly in the transporter room before the human doctor had insisted on first treating her and Quark. After that was done, they were taken by a group of security guards to what she supposed was an interrogation room, and she told the story again, this time to the ambassador, who looked at her and Quark as if they were insane.

He departed in disgust, leaving her and Quark with two security guards.

Then a Bajoran walked in. She moved to sit in the chair opposite Kira and Quark—the same seat that the ambassador had sat in, scowling while Kira told her story.

Kira couldn't believe her eyes. She had heard rumors that some Bajorans had joined Starfleet, but she hadn't believed them.

The woman said, "I'm Lieutenant Ro Laren—security chief of the *Enterprise*."

Quark scowled. "I can't imagine security is much of a problem for you."

"Shut up, Quark," Kira said reflexively even as she thanked the Prophets. If a Bajoran was Picard's security chief, she might get a fairer hearing from him than she did from the ambassador. "Lieutenant, this is *important*. That idiot ambassador didn't believe me, but maybe Picard will."

"I'm not sure *I* believe you. Besides, this is Krajensky's bailiwick, not the captain's. He wants to toss you two in the brig so you can be debriefed back on Earth."

Well, at least we're headed to Earth. "We don't have time for that. It's taken too long to get here as it is."

Ro frowned. "What do you mean?"

"She means," Quark said angrily, "that she came here in a broken-down starhopper that crash-landed on *my* moon, and then dragged me across the border in *my* yacht, which she then *also* blew up."

"I thought I'd be able to get to the border from Bajor in a couple of weeks, but it took *months*. Who knows how many more have died because of that."

"There's a war on. People die."

"The only reason there *is* a war is because—"

"Of shapechangers?" Ro's skepticism infused both words. "C'mon—think about how that sounds. Weird aliens replacing important people in the quadrant. That sounds like a holonovel, not real life."

"Do you remember Odo?"

Ro squinted. "Wasn't he the one that kept the Promenade on the space station in order?"

"*He's* a shapechanger. These are more of his people."

Nodding, Ro said, "He was assigned after I left Bajor, but I've read intelligence reports. As I recall, he could barely manage a face. He could never do a convincing enough disguise."

"*He* can't. His *people* can." Kira leaned forward. "Lieutenant, please, you *have* to believe me. This is *real*."

Kira stared intently at Ro, refusing to blink, trying to will the other woman to accept her at her word.

"Let me talk to my captain," Ro finally said as she got up. Looking over at the two guards, she said, "Keep them here for the time being."

The guards nodded, and Ro departed, the doors whooshing shut behind her.

"I'm *so* glad I let you talk me into this," Quark muttered.

"Shut up, Quark. It's not like it took that much convincing. And it's not like *you* don't know the truth."

Quark stared at her. "What does *that* have to do with anything? I was paid quite handsomely to forget that particular truth, only to have you come crashing down on my moon!"

"So why'd you do it?"

Looking away, Quark said, "You know why."

"No, actually, I don't."

Quark whirled his head around and stared at her. "You don't? Seriously?"

"Seriously, Quark. I went to you as a last resort because there was nowhere else to take the starhopper, and I was half-convinced you'd turn me in. More than half, actually."

Letting out a long breath, Quark said, "If you ever see Garak again—ask him."

That was all Quark would say on the subject, to Kira's mild annoyance. In all honesty, she didn't care *that* much, as the inner workings of Quark's mind was a subject of which Kira was more than happy to live in blissful ignorance.

But asking him about it took her mind off the fact that she was likely never to see Garak again. Or anybody else, aside from Federation prison guards, unless Ro was able to convince Picard to talk to her.

Jean-Luc Picard stared at his security chief, who sat next to Worf on the other side of his ready-room desk. Though Ro had had a rocky start as a once-disgraced Starfleet officer who had helped the *Enterprise*-D find terrorists who'd attacked a Cardassian ship, she'd blossomed into a fine officer. After a stint under Picard's command, she took Starfleet security training, and then did some work for Starfleet Intelligence for a couple of years. Then, when Riker and Data were granted captaincies and Worf was promoted to first officer, Picard requested that Ro replace the Klingon as security chief and tactical officer.

In her two tours on two different *Enterprise*s, Picard had had no reason to doubt Ro Laren, which was the only reason why he was even considering her request now. "Lieutenant," he said, "this is Ambassador Krajensky's responsibility. He believes that Kira is either insane or a Cardassian spy."

"She's no spy," Ro said hotly. Then she visibly calmed herself. "She was in the Shakaar resistance cell. Trust me, if there's anyone in the galaxy *less* likely to be a Cardassian spy than a Shakaar, I've never met them. She's more loyal to Bajor than—than anyone."

Picard had known Ro long enough to discern that she was originally going to say "than me," but said nothing. Instead, he turned to his first officer, sitting next to Ro. "What do you think, Number One?"

Worf had yet to grow accustomed to being referred to with that appellation, and he winced when Picard said it, but quickly recovered. "I believe that Ambassador Krajensky is not trained in interrogation techniques. I also believe that a single insane Bajoran woman would not be capable of crossing the border alone with only the help of a Ferengi—nor do I believe that a spy would have quite so . . . outlandish a tale to tell."

"So you believe we should question this woman further?" Picard asked.

"Yes, sir. What's more, Counselor Troi, Lieutenant Ro, and I should conduct the questioning."

Nodding, Picard said, "Very well. I will clear it with the ambassador. Summon the counselor to the lecture hall, and begin at once."

. . .

Worf, son of Mogh, kept forcing himself not to look at Deanna Troi.

It had been awkward, serving with his former *parMach'kai* on this new ship. It was even more awkward after the war began—and she and Riker rekindled their romance. They'd gotten married just before he was put in command of the *Sugihara.* She'd stayed on the *Enterprise,* since the *Sugihara* didn't have a position available for her—the ship had a qualified counselor whom Riker did not wish to dislodge for his wife—and she felt that she was still needed here anyway.

Ending their relationship had been the right thing to do. Worf knew that.

But it was damned hard to keep working with her.

At least the war usually kept her off the bridge. Her services were required quite a bit in these hard times, and she rarely had the opportunity to take her station at Picard's left.

Now, though, they had work to do.

Because Ro was, like their guest, a Bajoran, they arranged for her to take the lead. "Okay, Kira—tell us what you told Ambassador Krajensky."

Kira Nerys took a deep breath, setting her hands in her lap. "It started about five years ago. A smuggler was trying to escape from Terok Nor—that's the space station in orbit of Bajor," she added, presumably for Worf and Troi's benefit, though Worf was familiar with the station from recent intelligence briefings regarding the Cardassian Union.

She continued, "The Cardassians use it for processing uridium from the mines. This smuggler tried to lose his pursuer in the Denorios Belt—that's a stream of tachyon eddies and gases around B'hava'el."

Worf scowled. That was something he did not know. He knew that Bajor's sun was called B'hava'el, but he'd never heard of this belt.

"Nobody goes into the Denorios Belt if they can help it—it's a huge navigation hazard. I guess the smuggler was counting on that." She shook her head. "Unfortunately, the Cardassians were feeling particularly bold, and followed him in. That's when they found the wormhole."

"A wormhole?" Troi said.

Kira nodded. "It's a stable wormhole, and it leads to the Gamma Quadrant. The Cardassian ship went through and came back several times."

Ro asked, "How come we haven't heard of this?"

The Ferengi spoke up, then. "If you found a stable wormhole, would you advertise it to the galaxy?"

Troi said, "Yes, actually."

That prompted a snaggletoothed smile from the Ferengi. "Can tell you're not Cardassian. They kept it their little secret."

"A stable wormhole is impossible," Ro said.

"Not anymore," Kira said. "It's been there for years now, always opening in the Denorios Belt on one end and in the Idran system in the Gamma Quadrant on the other." Kira took a breath. "The Cardassians kept the wormhole classified. Only a few guls and legates knew about it at first. They sent a few ships to explore the other side."

"They also," the Ferengi added, "let other entrepreneurs go through for a small fee."

"Such as yourself," Worf said witheringly.

"Exactly. And I was the one who found out about the Dominion."

Ro asked, "And what is the Dominion?"

"A massive interstellar empire in the Gamma Quadrant," Kira said. "The Founders of the Dominion are shapechangers. Decades ago, they sent out a hundred infants into space. One fell through the wormhole and was found in the Denorios Belt. He was taken in by a Bajoran scientist and called himself Odo. He eventually became security chief of the Promenade on Terok Nor."

"And he is a shapechanger?" Worf asked.

Ro said, "I can confirm that. He served the Cardassians for a long time. But he was replaced recently, right?"

Kira smiled. "The Cardassians have been trying to find him for more than a year now with no luck. But he realized that he'd found his people—and that his people wanted to conquer the Alpha Quadrant."

Troi asked, "Then why have we heard nothing about this Dominion?"

"Because they don't come in with guns blazing to conquer worlds like the Cardassians or the Klingons do. Instead, they sent in a number of the Founders to take the place of important people in the Federation, Klingon, Romulan, and Cardassian governments. I'm fairly sure they replaced Gul Dukat—he's the prefect of Terok Nor—and they've done likewise elsewhere in the galaxy. The war you people are fighting? That was the Dominion's work. Remember, it all started with an unprovoked attack by a Romulan ship on a Klingon outpost. Nobody knows why that Romulan ship attacked—but our guess is that it was a shapechanger who replaced the sub-commander in charge of that vessel and then gave the order to fire on the outpost. The Klingons and Romulans took it from there."

Worf was extremely skeptical. "Why should we believe this story?"

"Because I don't have any reason to lie!" Kira was shouting now. "And because the Cardassians are making their move with the Dominion's help. You think it's a coincidence that Central Command's moving on you now, when all three powers have been devastated by the war? And where do you think they got their new weapons from?"

That brought Worf up short. Starfleet Intelligence had been caught completely off guard by the Cardassians' new weapons, and had yet to determine their source. The phased polaron beam was far beyond what the Cardassians should have been able to develop and deploy on their own, and they had apparently done so entirely in secret, which Worf had found impossible to credit. No intelligence-gathering agency had a perfect record, but SI was never *that* bad.

But if the weapons came from another quadrant . . .

No, the idea was absurd.

Kira was still talking. "The Dominon have shock troops called the Jem'Hadar. They provided the new weapons. Once the war has gone on long enough to leave all three participants weakened, the Jem'Hadar will come in and conquer on behalf of Cardassia—and the Dominion."

Worf remained dubious. "All through a wormhole that they have kept secret from the entire galaxy?"

"Like I said, the Denorios Belt's a navigation hazard. No one goes near there."

The Ferengi said, "You're wasting your breath, Kira. These idiots don't believe you. Which is too bad. Why do you think the Ferengi Alliance became part of Cardassia? The Detapa Council paid off the Grand Nagus to retire and cede Ferenginar to the Union in order to keep the wormhole secret. They paid *me* off, too. Had enough to buy my own moon—where I was perfectly happy until she turned up," he added with a glower at Kira.

"Then why did you help her?" Worf asked.

The Ferengi looked back at the Klingon, and Worf saw genuine fear in his eyes. "It needed to be done," he said lamely.

That answer told Worf a great deal.

Troi looked at Worf. "Commander, I need to speak to you and Lieutenant Ro in private."

Nodding, Worf rose, as did Ro. They moved into the corridor.

"I can't read Quark," Troi said, "but Kira's telling the truth. Or at least what she believes is the truth."

"So is the Ferengi," Worf said.

Ro stared at him. "How do you know?"

"He is afraid. He is also the owner of a moon, which makes him a . . . well-heeeled member of Ferengi society."

"Cardassian society now," Ro muttered.

"He jeopardized that to aid the Bajoran woman. No Ferengi would do so without cause. Normally for a Ferengi, that would be profit, but she does not appear to have anything that would be of value to him." He looked back at the door. "Except fear. I could *smell* the fear on the Ferengi."

"But he could be afraid of Kira," Troi said. "She could be threatening him in some way, forcing him to go along with her delusion."

"The problem is," Ro said, "everything she said? It makes perfect sense. The tactics of this war have been a disaster on all sides. Look at the way things have been going—look at how Khitomer was botched. I have no trouble believing that someone's trying to sabotage this war."

"I do not believe in conspiracy theories," Worf said. "And just because their claims happen to fit the evidence does not mean they are true."

"Yeah, I know," Ro said, "I took the same security courses at the academy you did. But still—"

The door whooshed open, and one of the guards was on the other side. "Commander, Lieutenant? The Bajoran woman says she has something else to say. She says it's proof."

Worf looked at Troi and Ro, then at the guard. Without a word, he entered.

Kira was standing now. As soon as the foursome came inside, she said, "The items I had on me when we transported aboard—where are they?"

"They have been impounded and are in the security office," Worf said. "Why?"

"You obviously won't take my word—but I do have the word of someone you might believe more. I need one item in particular."

Worf mulled it over, then looked at Ro. "Bring the items."

Ro nodded to the guard, who departed.

A few minutes later, he returned with Kira's satchel. He handed it to the woman, who rummaged through it, pulling out something that looked to Worf like a kind of containment unit.

"This is a . . . well, container, for lack of a better word," Kira said. "When I deactivate it, the contents will be exposed. It's *not* anything dangerous."

Ro tapped her combadge. "Computer. Security protocol nine, this location. Secure the podium area."

A forcefield encased the area where Quark and Kira were. "What's going on?" Quark asked.

"If that contains a weapon of *any* kind," Ro said, "it'll only affect the two of you."

Kira glared at Ro. "If I wanted to kill myself, I'd have stayed on Bajor."

"If you were in my position, Kira, wouldn't you take every precaution?"

Sighing, Kira said, "Fine."

She touched a control. Worf watched as the green lights on the unit switched to red.

Then an amber substance started to ooze out of it. Worf was starting to believe that it *was* a weapon—a biological one. Tapping his combadge, he said, "Computer, security alert. Clear this deck."

But even as he spoke, the substance started to coalesce into a humanoid form. Eventually it settled into what appeared to be a humanoid male—but unfinished, somehow. The ears were simplistic, the eyes beady, the face smooth.

"My name is Odo," the creature said, "and you are all in very grave danger."

14

Admiral Eric Hahn observed the watch officer as she ran the operations center of the starbase.

Commander Erika Benteen was an able officer. Before his death at the hands of the Borg, Admiral Leyton had always spoken highly of her. She had been serving as first officer on the *Lakota*, but after the Cardassian invasion of the Federation, Hahn had requested that she be transferred here.

Hahn himself had been sent to this starbase by Leyton two years earlier, after a lengthy tenure at Starfleet Academy. He hadn't wanted to change assignments, but he was a good enough officer that he didn't question his orders. Besides, he had thought at the time, it was a perfect assignment: Starbase 375 was strategically important thanks to its proximity to the Cardassian border, but not a great deal of work to maintain given how quiet the Cardassian Union had been.

After the invasion began, however, Hahn's job suddenly got a lot more complicated. He didn't particularly want to be here—he thought of himself primarily as a teacher, not a leader—but this starbase was his responsibility, and it would be on the front lines if the situation with Cardassia devolved into a full-scale war. His wife, Crystal, had said in their last subspace talk that Starfleet wouldn't have kept him there if they didn't think he was the right person for the job. As usual, his wife was right.

But that didn't mean he had to like it.

Now he watched as Benteen stood at the center of ops, giving orders in a calm, collected voice.

"Dax, identify the ships please," she said to the science officer.

Sitting serenely at Benteen's right was a Trill woman named Jadzia Dax, who said, "Three *Galor*-class ships. They're running weapons hot."

"Red alert. Raise shields, load torpedo launchers."

Looking up, Hahn saw ops darken, the usual bright illumination replaced with red, a low alarm sounding just loud enough to be heard, but not so loud that it interfered with duty—a preference Hahn had programmed into the computer shortly after his arrival.

"Ledrah, hail them," Benteen added to the operations officer, a Tiburonian woman named Nidani Ledrah, whom Benteen had brought with her from the *Lakota*.

Shaking her head, Ledrah said, "They're not responding."

Letting out a small sigh, but standing straight, with her hands behind her back, Benteen said, "All right—hail the *Lexington* and the *da Vinci*."

The faces of Captains Gilaad ben Zoma and David Gold appeared on the forward viewer. Both men were humans, and Starfleet veterans. The *Lexington* had put in for repairs, and *da Vinci*—which was assigned to the Starfleet Corps of Engineers— was there to supervise some upgrades to the starbase.

"Gentlemen, I'm afraid we're going to need some assistance. Captain ben Zoma, are your repairs far enough along?"

"We'll manage," the captain said with a small smile.

"Captain Gold, I realize that the *Sabre* class is a bit outmatched by the *Galor* class, but—"

Gold, who, with his snow-white hair and cornflower blue eyes, already had a grandfatherly mien, gave a smile that increased that affect a hundredfold. *"Don't you worry about us. My people have a few tricks up their sleeves."*

Ledrah said, "One of the ships is firing!"

As Hahn watched, the battle unfolded. A tactical view replaced the images of ben Zoma and Gold on the forward viewer. The *da Vinci* and *Lexington* took up positions that allowed them to intercept two of the *Galors*, leaving the starbase to defend itself against the third.

One of the engineers—a newly assigned Tellarite ensign whose name Hahn could not recall—said, "Shields are down to eighty-five percent."

Hahn was pleased with that. The last time, shields lost twenty percent of power when hit with the new Cardassian polaron beams. Losing only fifteen bode well for the future.

"Fire torpedoes," Benteen said, "pattern sigma."

A spread of torpedoes hit the *Galor* at various points, doing no physical damage, but wiping out their shields.

"Phasers," Benteen said quickly. "Take them down before they can reconstitute."

The starbase now had four phaser banks—one of the upgrades provided by the S.C.E.—and three of the four fired on the *Galor*, destroying it in a plume of flame.

Looking at the forward viewer, Hahn saw that the *Lexington* had done likewise to the second ship, and that the third had been disabled by the *da Vinci*.

Stepping forward to stand next to Benteen, Hahn said, "End battle simulation."

The illumination in ops returned to normal. Once again, ben Zoma's and Gold's faces appeared on the screen. *"Not bad,"* the former said.

Dax looked up and smiled. "What happened to the fourth phaser bank?"

"Salek and Duffy are scrambling around trying to figure that one out right now," Gold said with a smile, referring to the two men in charge of the S.C.E. contingent on his ship. *"We won't leave until it's working right."*

"Still," Hahn said, "the upgrades you performed worked beautifully. That was one of the most realistic battle simulations I've ever seen."

"We aim to please," Gold said.

Turning to the watch officer, Hahn said, "As do you, Commander. You handled that well."

Benteen nodded. "Thank you, sir." If she felt any pride at his compliment, she did not show it.

Grinning, Hahn said, "At ease, Commander. The simulation's done."

"Yes, sir," Benteen said, though she didn't noticeably relax.

Giving up, Hahn turned toward his office. "I'm going to go contact my wife. Commander Benteen, you—"

"Sir!" That was Ledrah. "We're picking something up! Three vessels approaching from the Cardassian border at high warp!" The Tiburonian looked up sharply. "Approaching at warp nine."

Now as serious as Benteen, Hahn turned back toward ops. *I can always call Crystal later.* "Identify."

Dax shook her head, the ponytail that held in her brown hair waving from side to side. "Unknown. It doesn't match anything in the database."

Hahn stared at Dax. "Nothing? Not even a vague comp?"

"No." Dax looked up, concern etched on her spotted brow. "Sir, we've literally got thousands of ships in the computer. This isn't close to *any* of them—but it's coming from Cardassian space."

"Oy vey," Gold said.

"What is it?" Hahn asked.

"My tactical officer just informed me that the ships are arming what appear to be weapons—of the exact same design as the new Cardassian weapons."

Frowning, ben Zoma said, *"That can't be good."*

Hahn looked at Ledrah. "Open a channel, Lieutenant, maybe they're only here to talk."

"That seems damned unlikely," ben Zoma said.

"Maybe, but I want to give it a chance."

Ledrah said, "Channel open."

"This is Admiral Eric Hahn of Federation Starbase 375. Please identify yourselves."

"I am First Omet'iklan, and I am dead. I go into battle to reclaim my life. This I do gladly, for I am Jem'Hadar. Victory is life."

Ledrah stared up at Hahn. "They closed the channel."

"Pity," Hahn said, "as I'd like to know what the hell that meant."

"Whoever they are," ben Zoma said, *"they don't appear to have our best wishes at heart, since they're talking about going into battle."*

"Agreed," Hahn said, and gave Benteen a look.

"Red alert," she said, "all hands to battle stations. This is not a drill, repeat, this is *not* a drill."

"Lieutenant," Hahn said to Ledrah, "keep trying to hail them. Maybe—"

Dax interrupted: "They're coming out of warp."

Looking up at the screen, Hahn saw the three ships appear, in a formation that put them in a prime position to attack the starbase, a level of precision piloting that both impressed and frightened the admiral.

One second later, some very familiar weapons fire spit forth from all three ships—one straight at the starbase, the other two at the two starships nearby.

The beam splashed against the shields, but a glance at the look of concern on Dax's face didn't make Hahn feel any better. "Lieutenant?"

Dax looked up. "Shields are down to twenty percent. That beam is the same phased polaron type as what the Cardassians have been using, but two hundred and fifty times more powerful."

Benteen walked over to Ledrah's console. "Get an emergency squib to Starfleet Command."

Nodding, Ledrah said, "Already on it."

Looking up, Hahn saw the *da Vinci* taking evasive action while the alien ship kept pounding away at it. The *Sabre* class had a compact design, with the nacelles attached to the lower hull, and one of those nacelles was venting plasma. As for the *Lexington,* it was holding its own, but sensor readouts at the bottom of the screen indicated that their shields were almost gone as well.

"All torpedoes and phaser banks fire!" Hahn cried, even as consoles started exploding around him.

"Shields down!" Ledrah said, as if that weren't blindingly obvious. "Hull integrity on habitat level down to twelve percent!"

Benteen said, "Evacuate the habitat level, *now!*"

Somehow, Hahn didn't think that these Jem'Hadar people were going to give the various off-duty and civilian personnel in those areas time to evac.

Three of the starbase's four phaser banks fired on the enemy vessel, along with a spread of torpedoes. The former blew a massive hole in the vessel's underbelly, and Hahn saw debris and bodies blown out into space.

Dammit, Hahn thought, *this shouldn't be happening. I'm supposed to be a teacher, not a killer.* Yet he gave the order to Ledrah: "Continuous fire!"

The *Lexington* continued to fire away at their own foe, but they were taking a pounding as well. The strut holding on the port nacelle was quickly severed, and then the *Nebula*-class vessel started spinning out of control.

"*Lexington* has lost attitude control," Dax said. "They're—"

The Jem'Hadar fired on the out-of-control starship, and it was destroyed.

Then, just as suddenly, the ship attacking the *da Vinci* exploded. "What happened?"

Dax's eyes had grown wide. "I—I don't know. The *da Vinci*'s powerless, and they're venting plasma, but somehow they managed to destroy that ship."

"Da Vinci *to starbase,*" came Gold's voice. "*Requesting immediate evac, we've got a warp-core breach in progress, we—*"

A moment later, the *da Vinci* was consumed by the mutual annihilation of matter and antimatter.

"Sir," Benteen said, "the enemy ship!"

Looking up, Hahn saw that the Jem'Hadar vessel that had been firing on them was still approaching.

Ledrah said, "They're heading right for us, sir—full impulse."

Hahn felt his body go numb. The starbase had thrusters that enabled it to maintain its position, but nothing that would get it out of the enemy ship's way.

"Keep firing," Benteen said. "We've got to destroy them before they ram us!"

But Hahn knew it wouldn't happen. They'd been firing continuously on the enemy ship, and there was just no way it was going to be enough to destroy it before they rammed into—

"They're heading right for the fusion core," Dax said, sounding remarkably calm.

I love you, Crystal.

First Omet'iklan watched on the forward viewer as the Federation starbase and First Taran'atar's ship annihilated each other. Omet'iklan was surprised at the outcome of the battle. The Vorta's intelligence had indicated that the Federation Starfleet was weakened by their lengthy conflict with the Romulans. Omet'iklan suspected that that intelligence came from the Cardassians, who were remarkably arrogant and wrongheaded.

However, Omet'iklan was a soldier, born and bred. He was ordered to lead the fleet, along with First Taran'atar's and First Talak'talan's ships, and destroy the Federation starbase nearest to the Dominion border. He followed those orders without question. The Vorta had insisted that they would, at best, suffer only minor casualties, not lose two-thirds of the fleet, but that was of no consequence. Omet'iklan and his men had made a note of the battle tactics used, and of how much better the Starfleet shields held up against Dominion weaponry than they had before. The Vorta had not warned them about that in their intelligence, either.

The only thing they had not been able to determine was how

Talak'talan's ship had been destroyed by the smallest of the Federation vessels. That small vessel's own destruction meant that the answer was forever denied to the Dominion, and Omet'iklan regretted the loss of information that might prove useful in future campaigns.

Still, the battle had been won. That was all that mattered.

Victory is life.

He ordered his crew onward to their next assignment.

15

Palais de la Concorde
Paris, Earth
United Federation of Planets

When Jean-Luc Picard was eight years old, he went on a class trip to the Palais de la Concorde. Although the class did not get to meet President Laikan—which was a great disappointment to the children—they did meet several members of the president's staff as well as the Federation Council. It was a very fondly remembered experience of Picard's childhood.

He never imagined that sixty years later he would be standing in the president's office in an official capacity.

At the moment, the president himself was not present, though they had been assured by his chief of staff—a somewhat hyperactive Trill woman named Emra Sil—that he was on his way. So Picard stood with Worf, off to the side of the office, which overlooked the Paris skyline.

Growing up in France as he had, he was used to that particular view: the Tour Eiffel, of course, as well as the River Seine, the Bâtiment Vingt-Troisième Siècle, and of course, the Champs-Elysées, which ran under this cylindrical fifteen-story structure.

Instead, he gazed upon the tense faces of those in the room. Seated in the two chairs that faced the president's desk were the aforementioned Sil and Ambassador Krajensky. Standing near Picard and Worf were Kira, Quark, and Odo, the last being the only one who didn't look tense, though Picard supposed that that was due more to his seemingly unfinished facial features. Certainly, he was as aware as anyone of the gravity of the current situation; after all, he had spent several months trapped in a containment unit in order to provide proof of Kira's information.

Quark also didn't look tense, exactly. His visage mainly showed fear.

On the other side of the room stood two admirals—William Ross, who had replaced Leyton as Commander, Starfleet; and Charles Whatley, the current liaison between the Palais and Starfleet Command—as well as Councillors T'Latrek of Vulcan and Matthew Mazibuko of Earth, two of the permanent members of the Federation Security Council. T'Latrek had been serving in the Federation government since Ra-ghoratreii's presidency in the latter part of the twenty-third century, and Picard knew hers to be one of the most respected voices on the Council.

For the fourth time in ten minutes, Sil said, "I'm sure the president will be along any minute."

"This is a matter of some urgency," Krajensky said tightly. His face carried the same sour expression it had for much of the journey to Earth from the Cardassian border. Picard was unsure if he was annoyed because Picard and his people questioned Kira behind his back or because his mission of peace was short-circuited by Cardassian intransigence—or both.

"Yes, but there *is* a war on," Sil said tartly. "In fact, there would appear to be two."

Picard felt a bitter taste in his mouth. They'd heard about the destruction of Starbase 375, as well as the *Lexington* and *da Vinci*, while en route to Earth. The news had hit Picard particularly hard. Eric Hahn and David Gold were both old friends of many years' standing, and Gilaad ben Zoma was even more than that: He'd been Picard's first officer on board the *Stargazer* for the two decades that Picard had been her captain. That, just on the heels of Elizabeth Shelby's death . . .

With a grimace, Picard forced the feelings of grief and regret and anger into the overstuffed box. He was in the Palais, about to report to the Federation president. He could not afford the luxury of grief right now.

The side door whooshed open, and three plainclothes security guards came into the office, quickly followed by three people: a Grazerite, an Andorian, and a Triexian. The first was, of course, President Jaresh-Inyo. Picard recognized the Andorian as Councillor Charivretha zh'Thane, another member of the Security Council.

Sil and Krajensky got to their feet at the president's entrance, but the large Grazerite said in a gentle voice, "Keep your seats, please."

Quickly, Sil made the necessary introductions, and Picard learned that the Triexian woman was Crut Na Eth, the secretary of defense.

Once the introductions were taken care of, and the president sat behind his desk, Krajensky spoke. "Mister President, it has come to my attention the Alpha Quadrant has been infiltrated by a hostile species known as the Founders. They are the rulers of an interstellar empire in the Gamma Quadrant called the Dominion."

"Really?" The president sounded unconvinced. But then, Picard had been at first, too. "And is there proof of this?"

The shapechanger stepped forward. "Mister President, my name is Odo. Until a year ago, I served as the chief of security on the Cardassian station Terok Nor in orbit of Bajor. Several years ago, a Central Command vessel discovered a stable wormhole in the Denorios Belt that led to the Gamma Quadrant. Soon after that, contact was made with the Dominion."

"By the Ferengi," Quark muttered only loud enough for Picard, Kira, and Odo to hear.

The shapechanger ignored the aside, and proceeded to once again tell the story of how the Founders sent out one hundred infants, one of whom was Odo. "When I realized that the Dominion was ruled by my people, I initially embraced them—until I

understood what they represented. I had always believed that my
interest in justice was something common to my people, but I
now know that I came by it entirely on my own—perhaps from
years of seeing so much *in*justice on Bajor. In any event, I soon
learned that the Founders planned to infiltrate the Cardassian
Union, the Federation, and the Klingon and Romulan Empires at
the highest levels, replacing important people in the government
and military with their own agents, and manipulating events to
ease their takeover of this quadrant."

"Mr. Odo," Crut said, rubbing her chin with her middle arm, "I
think you can understand why we are skeptical of your claims."

Krajensky said, "I was as well, Madam Secretary; however, I
have come to believe this story."

Whatley then spoke up. "It certainly would explain a helluva
lot. The war with the Klingons and Romulans has just been one
screwup after another—on all three sides. Every damn time, the
worst-case scenario has played out."

"Conspiracy theories," T'Latrek said, "are not logical. And
rather difficult to prove."

Kira stepped forward now. "But we *can* prove if someone's a
shapechanger—sort of."

Jaresh-Inyo's already-wrinkled skin contracted into a deep
frown. "What does that mean?"

Holding up another of the devices that she had carried in her
satchel, Kira said, "This is a device created by a former member of
the Cardassian Obsidian Order. He helped me smuggle Odo out
of Cardassian space. When activated, any shapechanger within a
twenty-meter radius will revert to its liquid state."

Picard recalled Beverly Crusher's amazement when she reported to him after her examination of Odo. The shapechanger
had objected to being poked and prodded at first—he'd apparently had quite a bit of that on Bajor after he'd been discovered—
but relented when he saw how noninvasive Crusher's instruments
were. While there were other species with the ability to change
their shape, none of them was liquid in its natural state. (She had

also waited until Odo was out of earshot before mentioning that she could happily spend the rest of her career just studying him.)

Ross asked, "How do we know this will work?"

Odo let out a noise that Picard supposed was a sigh of irritation. Then again, in Picard's brief exposure to the shapechanger, he'd noticed that irritation was one humanoid mode that Odo had mastered with great skill.

Then he looked at Kira, who nodded, and activated the device.

Immediately, Odo's features shimmered and melted and collapsed into an amber liquid on the Palais carpet.

So did Jaresh-Inyo's.

Instinctively, Picard reached for a sidearm that, of course, wasn't there. One did not enter the Palais de la Concorde armed, unless one was part of the president's security detail.

The trio who made up that detail reacted as swiftly as expected, and whipped out their own phasers, training them on the undulating liquid that was now pooling in the president's chair.

Before they could fire, though, a trio of tendrils shot out from the mass, smothering all three guards. One phaser beam burst through and fired into the ceiling.

With horror, Picard realized that all three guards were drowning. The shapechanger was unable to form anything solid, but it still had enough control of itself to move.

Then a phaser beam sliced through the air in front of Picard. Glancing to his right, he saw that Worf was holding a palm-sized phaser. While Picard would never enter the Palais armed, his first officer was not so politic—though Picard *did* wonder how he managed to get such a device past Palais security, especially in a time of war.

A high-pitched scream reverberated through the office, and a smell very much like that of burning leaves filled Picard's nostrils as the shapechanger started to explode outward in several directions. Picard dove to the floor, deliberately knocking Kira and Quark down with him, to avoid being hit by a flying protrusion.

Worf kept firing, and one of the guards recovered well enough to do likewise.

Moments later, there was only black ash on the chair and around the president's desk. Only then did Kira deactivate the device, believing, rightly, that it was best to keep the creature disguised as Jaresh-Inyo limited in its options.

Slowly clambering to his feet, Ross put voice to Picard's thought. "I wasn't aware that one *could* sneak a phaser into the Palais, Commander Worf."

"There are no security measures that cannot eventually be overcome, Admiral" was all Worf would say on the subject.

Before the admiral could question his first officer more thoroughly, Picard asked, "Is everyone all right?"

"Not especially," Councillor Mazibuko said shakily. The air in the room felt thick and oppressive to Picard. He hadn't expected the meeting to end quite this way. While he believed that it was possible that shapechangers had infiltrated the Federation—he recalled vividly when parasitic beings had engaged in a similar campaign a decade earlier, possessing several key Starfleet players—he never imagined that the president himself would be a target.

T'Latrek regarded Odo, who had now reverted to his humanoid appearance, and Kira. "My apologies for doubting your story."

Zh'Thane ran a hand through her feathery white hair. "This is disastrous. How long has this been going on?"

"We're not sure," Kira said softly.

"We must call an emergency session of the Federation Council," T'Latrek said. "And we must decide our next move. For now, however, everyone should proceed as if nothing has changed. The Cardassians and their allies are invading Federation space, and we are still committed to aiding the Klingons against the Romulans."

Quark was staring at the ashes near the desk. "What'll you tell people?"

"We've got to come up with a cover story," Whatley said.

"There's no way we can just say that the president's been replaced by a *doppelgänger.*"

"Agreed," Krajensky said. "It would cause a panic."

Testily, Picard said, "The Federation is fighting two wars, Mister Ambassador. I'd say panic is the order of the day."

Ross held up a hand. "Nonetheless, Jean-Luc, we need to proceed cautiously. If nothing else, we can't afford to tip the Founders to the fact that we've learned who they are."

"The logical course of action would be to act as if Jaresh-Inyo is still alive," T'Latrek said.

Odo said, "My people will soon learn that he has been removed from the field of play."

"Perhaps," T'Latrek said, "but it would be best to delay that as long as possible."

Mazibuko asked, "What if there are others?"

"As far as we've been able to determine," Odo said, "there are only four of my people in this quadrant."

Staring incredulously, zh'Thane said, "Only four?"

"If the person being replaced has sufficient power," Worf said, "only four would be required. One each on Earth, Qo'noS, Romulus, and Cardassia."

Kira held up a padd. "Garak—the former Order agent who helped us—compiled a list of who he thought might be replaced in the Klingon and Romulan Empires."

Recalling a few recent intelligence briefings, an idea started to form in Picard's head. "Admiral," he said to Ross, "is the *Defiant* still at Utopia Planitia?"

Nodding, Ross said, "We haven't quite hammered out all the problems yet, but Commander Sisko thinks they're close."

"Good." He looked at everyone in the room. "I believe I have a plan that might put an end to this."

16

Fleet Yards
Utopia Planitia, Mars
United Federation of Planets

The face of Councillor T'Latrek—who had been secretly appointed president *pro tempore* until such a time as the Federation Council was willing to admit to Jaresh-Inyo's death— appeared on the small screen in the communications room. *"Your plan has received the approval of the Council, Captain."*

In truth, Picard had been hoping for the opposite reply—not because his plan was a bad one, but because it would only result in yet more death. "Thank you, Madam President."

"That is an inappropriate form of address, Captain," T'Latrek said sharply. *"I have not been elected to office, nor will I be. I am simply performing the duties of president until a special election can be held."*

"Of course, Councillor," he amended quickly. "Thank you for your timely response." Picard recalled that T'Latrek had been considered a favorite to run for president in practically every election during Picard's lifetime, but on each occasion, the Vulcan woman had declined the honor.

"I wish you success in your mission, Captain. Earth out."

Picard supposed that was as close as the Vulcan councillor was likely to come to wishing him luck.

Shutting down the comm terminal, and nodding to the ensign on watch in the room, Picard then left for the yard's wardroom.

Waiting there were the six people who would be responsible

for implementing his plan, four of whom he knew, two whom he did not.

At one end of the table was one of those he did not know—a tall, dark-skinned man with close-cropped hair and a dark goatee. The last was obviously a new addition, since it wasn't in the picture in his service record. This was the yard commander, Benjamin Sisko.

On Sisko's left were Kira and Odo. (Not present was Quark. He had declined the invitation to participate further, citing a desire to continue breathing and to return home. Picard had thought that would be difficult, but Quark just gave a snaggletoothed smile and said that latinum could buy many favors, and large sums of latinum could buy almost anything—and Quark had considerably more than a large sum . . .)

To Sisko's right sat Worf and two human males, one of whom was the other participant Picard did not know: a pale, balding man wearing a lieutenant commander's pips and a gold-trimmed uniform, meaning he was the person sent by Starfleet Security. The second man was an older gentleman with a thick mustache and a friendly smile. Indeed, he was the only person in the room smiling, probably because he had seen so much of the universe that even the tangle of war and conspiracy into which they'd all been thrust didn't faze him.

"Captain Scott," he said to the man, who had stood upon Picard's entrance. "Thank you for coming."

"I was already here," the old engineer said. "I've been helpin' modify the new ships off the yard so they can use cloaks."

Picard nodded. The Treaty of Algeron was abrogated with the declaration of war, and that meant Starfleet had no restriction against using cloaking technology. However, there'd been some difficulty integrating the cloaks with existing ships. Montgomery Scott was in charge of ameliorating that difficulty, having had plenty of experience integrating Romulan technology with Starfleet systems, even if that experience was now more than a century old.

Sisko had also risen from his chair, and approached Picard, who held out his hand. "You must be Commander Sisko."

While the commander did return the handshake, the taller man's grip was cold and stiff. "It's been a long time, Captain."

Frowning, Picard asked, "Have we met before?" He could not recall ever having encountered Sisko in the past.

"Yes, sir," Sisko said in a dangerously quiet voice, "we met in battle. I was on the *Saratoga* at Wolf 359."

Picard recoiled as if he'd been slapped. He quickly broke the handshake. There was a fury in Sisko's eyes. If he was a survivor of Wolf 359—one of the few—Picard could hardly blame him. It had been seven years, but the memories of being transformed into Locutus, of giving the Borg everything they needed to destroy two score vessels . . .

Moving to the head of the table, Picard took his seat and looked at the lieutenant commander from security. He pointedly did not look at Sisko as the latter retook the seat opposite him. "I'm Captain Jean-Luc Picard of the *Enterprise*."

"Michael Eddington," the man said. "I've been detached to your command, sir."

"In fact," Picard said with a glance at Worf, "you're dispatched to Mister Worf's. Or, rather, *Captain* Worf's. As of now, he is in command of the *Defiant*."

Ross had reacted badly to Picard's suggestion that Worf be promoted, mainly because he was still unhappy about Worf's ability to smuggle weaponry into the most secure spot in the Federation, but T'Latrek, Mazibuko, and zh'Thane all overruled him, pointing out that Worf had just saved all their lives. The necessary secrecy of Jaresh-Inyo's replacement meant that Worf could receive no official commendation for his act, but a promotion seemed in order.

Besides, Picard felt that the Klingon was ideally suited to captain the *Defiant*.

"Sir," Sisko said, "the *Defiant* isn't ready. We've ironed out most of the power-consumption issues, but she hasn't been tested."

"Those tests will have to be made in the field, Commander," Picard said abruptly. "We can no longer afford to wait until the ship is one hundred percent."

Sisko put his hands flat on the table and stared at Picard with a cold fury that might have impressed the captain at another time. "I cannot authorize taking the *Defiant* out at this time, Captain."

Picard couldn't believe what he was hearing, and wondered how much of it was because of Sisko's history with Locutus of Borg. Ultimately, however, he didn't have the luxury of finding out, or of considering Sisko's feelings. "You aren't being given a choice, Commander. This is a briefing—I'm not asking for your consent. This mission has the support of the Federation Council and will go forth as planned. Now, given your knowledge of this particular ship, I would prefer it if you were to go as Captain Worf's first officer. However, if you feel that following orders is too difficult for you, I'm sure Starfleet Command will happily accept your resignation."

The Starfleet officers at the table were willing to sit and wait until this played out, but Kira Nerys had no such compunctions. "Why the hell are we even arguing about this?" She looked at Sisko. "I've looked at the specs for that ship of yours. It's a monster, but it's about a thousand times more efficient than anything I flew in the resistance, and we didn't have a shipyard like this at our disposal. I'm sorry if your plasma manifolds don't quite purr to your satisfaction, *Commander,* but there's a lot more at stake here than—"

Holding up a hand, Sisko said, "Enough. You're both right, of course. The *Defiant*'s simply a very—" He cut himself off. "It doesn't matter." Looking at the Klingon, he said, "Captain Worf, I accept the transfer to the *Defiant* as your first officer."

"Good," Worf said.

"Captain Scott will be assigned as chief engineer," Picard said. "Your task is to install a cloaking device before the *Defiant* reaches the border."

"You needn't worry, Captain. After all," he said with an avuncular smile that reduced the tension in the room, "I've a reputation as a miracle worker to live up to." The smile fell. "I must be askin', though, sir—what *is* the mission?"

Picard folded his hands on the table in front of him and looked at each of the people at the table in turn—except for Sisko, whom he couldn't quite bring himself to look in the eyes. "The mission, Captain Scott, is simple. Captain Worf will take the *Defiant* behind the lines in Romulan space. Ms. Kira has a list of who is the mostly likely Romulan to have been replaced by a shapechanger. Commander Eddington will have a complement of fifty security personnel who will serve as a strike team. Kira will determine if the person in question is truly a shapechanger, and then the security team will neutralize it. Capture is preferred, but you are to defend yourselves."

"Understood, sir," Eddington said.

"You will then proceed to Klingon territory and do the same."

"Captain," Sisko said, "the *Defiant* only has the capacity to house approximately forty people. If the security contingent alone is fifty—"

"Accommodations will have to be made, Commander." Picard hesitated, then continued in a much softer tone. "Projections for survival among the security detail are somewhat low."

Worf added, "As are the projections for survival among the rest of the crew." Snidely, he asked Sisko, "Do you still accept the transfer?"

"The projections for survival will be nonexistent without me on that ship, Captain," Sisko said tartly. "I know the *Defiant* better than anyone. If there's any chance of this mission succeeding . . ."

Picard looked at the security chief. "Mister Eddington—"

"Don't worry about my people, Captain. This is what they signed up for."

Suddenly, Picard felt nauseated. All this death, and his brilliant plan for stopping it was a suicide mission. In fact, it was two suicide missions.

"Meanwhile, I will be taking the *Enterprise* to the Bajoran system. We also have a cloaking device installed—or so Mister O'Brien says we will by tomorrow—and, with the assistance of Mister Odo, we will destroy the entrance to the wormhole. Even if the *Defiant* does not succeed in its mission, those three remaining shapechangers will be unable to summon reinforcements, and the Jem'Hadar currently in the Alpha Quadrant will be all there are."

Odo spoke in what Picard was learning was his usual flat, sardonic tone. "I believe I will be able to obtain assistance from someone on the station itself."

Picard assumed this to be the former Obsidian Order agent who had facilitated Odo and Kira's escape from Bajor. "Very well."

Then Odo added: "You should know, Captain, that even if your plan succeeds, it will *not* deter my people."

"I don't expect it to, Mister Odo—but it will cripple their efforts. We shall have to hope that it is enough. We owe it to the people who have already given their lives." He shook his head. "Everything that has happened this past year, all the lives lost, both in the war among the Klingons, Romulans, and Federation and in the Cardassians' Dominion-fueled aggression against the Federation, has been revealed by Ms. Kira and Mister Odo here as nothing more than a stratagem designed to soften us up and make the entire quadrant an easy conquest for a despotic nation. We cannot allow that to stand." Now, finally, he looked at Sisko. "Are there any questions?"

"Yes, sir," Sisko said with a frank expression. "When do we leave?"

17

Worf entered the engineering section of the *Defiant* only to find yet another shouting match.

"If y'connect it up that way, the whole thing'll shut down!" That was Scott, whose burr apparently became thicker under stress.

Sisko was gripping a diagnostic tool as if it were a *d'k tahg*. "If we do it your way, the power spike will burn out the EPS conduits! If that happens, we'll lose main power, and then—"

"I know what'll happen if we lose main power, lad. I was crawlin' around engines when your granddaddy was in diapers!"

Several engineers were standing helpless while the two men screamed at each other. Worf immediately interposed himself between the two of them. "What is going on here?"

"This daft gentleman doesna know—"

"This old relic—"

"Enough!" Worf screamed over both of them. "We are under orders to install this cloaking device before we are in scanning distance of Romulan space. That will be in thirty hours. If the cloak is not installed, our mission cannot proceed—and *that* is not acceptable."

Scott muttered, "I'm no bloody relic."

"I'm not 'daft,' either, *Captain*. What I am is the person who designed this ship. I know it better than you."

"And I know Starfleet engines better than anyone alive, lad, and unlike you, I've put a cloaking device *into* one, and I'm tellin' you—"

"That was a hundred years ago!"

"The principle's the same!"

"Mev yap!" Worf repeated the interjection he'd used previously, but this time in Klingon, hoping it might be more effective. "I am not interested in puerile name calling. I *am* interested in an installed cloak. You *will* work together, you *will* install the cloak, and you *will* cease this idiocy!"

Without waiting for either to respond, Worf turned on his heel and left engineering. To make matters worse, while Scott outranked Sisko, as first officer, Sisko had a higher position in the ship's hierarchy. Still, Worf imagined that Scott would have difficulty taking orders from a lower-ranked officer who wasn't yet born when Scott first made captain.

However, Worf's word was final. He hoped that was enough.

Kira was waiting for him on the other side of the door, and she gave voice to his thoughts. "You really think that was the best approach?"

"I do not know," Worf said, "but if it is a successful approach, then I do not much care if it was best." He looked behind him. "They bicker like children."

Kira shrugged. "Engineers. They're all the same. We had one in the resistance, name of Biroj. You couldn't tell her anything, either."

Thinking of La Forge and O'Brien, Worf said, "My experience has been that engineers are reasonable." Shaking his head, he proceeded down the corridor. "Perhaps I should have insisted that Lieutenant O'Brien be assigned to this ship."

"Sisko knows this ship, though," Kira said as they walked together. Worf noted with admiration that, despite her lesser height, the Bajoran was able to keep up with the Klingon's greater strides. "And from what that older one—Scotty?—says, he's been doing this awhile."

"Captain Scott was born in the twenty-third century. He was trapped in—in a form of stasis for seventy-five years, and then rescued by the *Enterprise*-D four years ago. Commander Sisko's concerns about his suitability are, at the very least, understandable. But he was assigned to this mission, and that should be all that matters."

"Real life doesn't always work like that," Kira said.

"No," Worf growled. "You wished to see me?"

She nodded. "I've gone over Elim's notes, and compared them with the latest reports from Starfleet Intelligence that you let me see."

Worf noted an undertone of annoyance. In truth, Worf hadn't wanted to show a Bajoran civilian *any* SI reports, but Picard had argued that she needed to in order to perform the mission. As long as the reports pertained only *to* the mission, and any outside references were omitted, Kira could have limited access.

But Kira had bridled under even those restrictions, not understanding why she couldn't see the uncensored reports. "You do not need to know," Worf had said.

"I think the two most likely candidates on his list are Colonels Koval and Lovok. They're both with the Tal Shiar. Admiral Braeg's been too much on the front lines, and I can't see one of the shapechangers taking that big a risk."

Worf had seen the list provided by Kira's ex–Obsidian Order friend Elim Garak, and so asked about the fourth person on it: "What of Senator Vreenak?"

Kira shook her head. "In theory, he's not a bad candidate, but then I came across this." She called up one of the intelligence reports. "According to the Romulan news service, Colonel Lovok died last week from a sudden accident."

Seeing where she was going, Worf said, "High-ranking Tal Shiar operatives do not die of accidents."

"No. And Lovok was in charge of intelligence for the war—that position, according to Starfleet's spies, has now been filled by Koval."

"You believe Koval is the shapechanger?" Worf asked as they approached the bridge.

"I think he's a more likely candidate."

Nodding, Worf said, "Very well. Meet with Commander Eddington and plan your insertion accordingly." Between what Eddington could glean from SI's reports, which was more than Kira could, and the information provided by Garak—the padd Kira carried had a full dossier on each person the Cardassian suspected of being an alien infiltrator—Worf was confident that the security chief and the resistance fighter could outline a skilled plan of attack. Worf himself would approve the plan once it was conceived.

"Will do," Kira said, and she turned around and moved toward the mess hall.

Worf entered the bridge. He asked the flight controller, Sariel Rager, "ETA to sensor range of the Romulan border?"

"Twenty-nine hours, fifteen minutes, sir."

"Good." Worf took a seat in the captain's chair. He had specifically requested Rager to be the alpha-shift conn officer for the *Defiant*—and it had been Scott's assignment to the ship that prompted the thought. When Scott was rescued from the *Jenolen*—which had crashed into a Dyson Sphere—the *Enterprise* had gone inside the sphere, and was almost trapped inside. While Scott and La Forge had used the *Jenolen* to hold one of the sphere's doors open for a time, the *Enterprise*'s escape still required near-perfect precision flying in order to escape through the narrow gap of the closing door.

Knowing he would need a pilot of consummate skill to navigate behind enemy lines, Worf sought the person who accomplished that feat of astrogation. Picard was all too happy to oblige.

A beep preceded Sisko's voice. *"Engineering to bridge."*

"Go ahead," Worf said.

"We're ready to begin the first test on the cloaking device."

"Very well. Engage when ready."

"With your permission, Captain, we wish to take the Defiant *out of warp."*

Worf looked up sharply at that. "Why?"

Now Scott spoke up. *"'Tis a safety precaution, sir."*

Twisting his jaw in annoyance, Worf said, "Bring us out of warp, Lieutenant Rager."

"Aye, sir," the soft-spoken human woman said.

The forward viewer showed the "normalizing" of the starfield from the distortions of the warp effect to the simple view of Einsteinian space.

"Engage when ready, engineering."

"Yes, sir," Sisko said.

Worf waited.

Several seconds passed.

Finally: "Report!"

"The bloody thing isn't workin'," Scott said.

"I told you that—"

"Hang on a second, lad, look at that!"

"At what?"

Having long since passed the end of his metaphorical rope, Worf cried, "If one of you does not report, I will kill you both!"

"Sorry, Captain," Sisko said quickly, *"but we think we've isolated the difficulty. It will take about an hour to straighten out."*

"Is there any reason not to proceed?"

"None," Sisko said without hesitation.

"And you are sure that once this 'difficulty' is resolved—"

Scott said, *"Guaranteed you'll have a cloak, sir, or I'll eat my hat."*

As with most human metaphors, Worf didn't even bother trying to decipher Scott's words, recognizing at least that it was an expression of confidence. "Very well. Inform me when you are ready for further tests. Bridge out. Lieutenant Rager, proceed at warp eight."

One hour later, the test was successful. The *Defiant* came out of warp, Sisko and Scott activated the cloaking device, and the vessel was invisible to sensors, to the visible spectrum, and all other known forms of detection.

Then Worf ordered the ship to go to warp, and nothing happened.

Two minutes and a great deal more shouting in the engine room after that, Worf gave the order a second time, and the *Defiant* went to warp, still cloaked.

Twenty-eight hours after that, the cloak was still holding as the ship approached the Romulan border. The patrols that the *Defiant* picked up on long-range all stayed put, and did not react to the approach of an enemy vessel.

Two hours later, the *Defiant* entered Romulan space, to no fanfare from the empire's border outposts.

After six hours without incident, Worf entered the *Defiant* mess hall. Though he was there to meet with Eddington and Kira, he noticed Sisko and Scott sitting in a corner, the latter pouring the former an amber liquid from a glass carafe. "Ach, you won't be wantin' that syntheholic swill, laddie. *This* is the good stuff. Captain!" Scott added as he saw Worf approach. "Will you join us in a toast?"

"Klingon tradition holds that one drinks when the battle is over." Then he allowed himself the tiniest of smiles. "And also on the eve of battle."

His grin widening, Scott poured a third glass and handed it to Worf.

"To the cloaking device," Scott said, holding up his glass.

A smile peeked out from under Sisko's goatee. "To teamwork."

Per human tradition, the officers clinked their glasses together, then Worf threw back the entire beverage. It tasted a bit smoky, and fairly weak, all told, but tolerable.

Scott was wincing. "You're supposed to be sippin' it, Captain."

"Why?"

Sisko coughed rather raggedly. In a whisper, he said, "Smooth." Worf assumed he was employing sarcasm. "You drink this on purpose?"

Eddington was already seated at a far table, along with three lieutenants, and Kira had just entered the mess hall to join them. Remembering human custom, Worf said, "Thank you for the drink" rather than throw the glass away, and then proceeded to join the others.

The three lieutenants were serving as Eddington's deputies on this mission, each commanding a sixteen-person squad. Pádraig Daniels was a demolitions expert, Domenica Corsi had served on several ships, most recently as chief of security on the *Roosevelt,* and George Primmin had run security on Starbase 10—the base closest to Romulan territory—for the last several years.

Eddington glanced down at a padd. "According to the most recent reports from the SI agent on Romulus, Koval spends most of his time either at Tal Shiar headquarters or at his new home."

"New home?" Corsi asked.

"Believe it or not," Primmin said, "we were able to learn that from a simple transfer of deed. Anybody in the empire with minimal access to a computer could learn that the mansion that used to belong to Lovok was sold upon his death to Koval by the late colonel's estate. SI was also able to track down several decorators bidding on contracts with Koval. From all reports, Koval is very fussy about how his home looks."

Corsi shook her head. "If this guy really is an alien from another quadrant, he's really throwing himself into the part."

Kira stared at the blond woman intently. "They wouldn't have been able to get as far as they have without being good at what they do."

"Or," Corsi said, "Koval might be Koval and this is a wild-goose chase."

Worf could understand Corsi's skepticism—in truth, right up until the meeting in the Palais, he had harbored doubts—but now was not the time. "What I am about to inform you of is classified information that does not leave this ship."

All three security personnel nodded immediately. They all understood the old human axiom, "loose lips sink ships," originally coined regarding Earth's naval forces, and—like so many human aphorisms—still used long after it ceased to make literal sense.

"Four shapechangers have infiltrated the Alpha Quadrant and replaced important figures in the political landscape. One of them is dead—he replaced President Jaresh-Inyo."

Corsi, Primmin, and Daniels gasped. Daniels said, "That's impossible."

"I was there," Worf snapped. "In fact, I was the one who killed the creature when the disguise was exposed."

"Which was done by me," Kira put in. "I get that you all don't believe this, but it's *real*. And the sooner you wrap your heads around this, the more likely we are to actually *accomplish* this mission."

There was a silence for several seconds, finally broken by Primmin. "Okay, so how do we figure out where Koval is?"

Eddington said, "All Tal Shiar operatives have a subcutaneous transponder that allows the praetor and others in the Tal Shiar to find them at any time."

"Do we know the frequency for Koval's transponder?" Kira asked.

"No."

The Bajoran snorted. "Then what good does knowing that do?"

"If Koval's in Tal Shiar headquarters, not a lot. But if we scan his mansion and find someone with a cesium-rubidium device in his neck—"

"Then it could be some other Tal Shiar operative," Corsi said. "If he's the head of intelligence for the war effort, he probably has other operatives going in and out of his house all the time."

"True, but they're unlikely to be there when he isn't," Eddington said. "Even if we find several agents in his mansion, chances are good he's one of them."

"Wait a minute," Corsi said, "if this is a shapechanger, can't we find him *that* way?"

"What way?" Primmin asked.

"Well, if he's not really a Romulan—"

Kira shook her head. "They're able to disguise their life-sign readings. Like you said, Lieutenant, they throw themselves into the part."

"So they're masking life signs *and* using the transponders?"

"They have to be," Eddington said. "The disguise wouldn't work otherwise."

"It's also possible," Kira said, "that they're able to change their shape so thoroughly that they actually do read to sensors as a Romulan."

Corsi leaned back and shook her head. "And we're supposed to *beat* these guys?"

"Yes," Worf said bluntly.

Eddington set down his padd with a mild clunk on the table. "There's a third place Koval might be. In fact, that would be ideal."

Worf frowned. He had access to the same briefings as Eddington and knew nothing of this. "Is this from SI's agent on Romulus?"

Shaking his head, Eddington said, "We haven't heard from her in a couple of weeks, actually—which isn't unusual, especially in times of war—but this came from another source, just before we left Mars. It's reliable, believe me."

"Go ahead," Worf said very slowly. He was dubious about this source, especially since he did not know Eddington. Were Ro presenting this, Worf would have no doubts, but he'd also been working with Ro for years, and knew what she was capable of. On the one hand, Starfleet wouldn't have sent Eddington if he wasn't good at what he did. On the other hand, resources were strained; just because Eddington was the best person available didn't mean he was necessarily all that good.

"Koval also has a mountain retreat, built into the rock of Kor Thon. According to my source, nobody still alive knows about it besides Koval."

"And your source, apparently," Kira said snidely.

"I trust this information. It came with a set of coordinates. The

only problem is—it's constructed out of sensor-proof plastiform."
Eddington sighed. "Look, if we find a transponder in Koval's
house, then we're fine. We beam in, turn on Kira's device, and
hope for the best. We don't even need Kira there to do it."

"Yes, you do."

Eddington closed his eyes and let out a long breath. "With all
due respect, ma'am, you're not a trained Starfleet operative. You're
a civilian and—"

"I've been fighting the Cardassians for my entire life, Commander. I've been part of the resistance since I could hold a phaser.
Don't *tell* me—"

Before this devolved into yet another argument, Worf said,
"The subject is *closed.*" That quieted Kira and Eddington both.
"Kira single-handedly escaped Bajor and defected to Federation
space to bring us this intelligence. She is also responsible for exposing the president as a shapechanger. Her participation in this
mission has already been approved."

"Thank you," Kira said pointedly.

"As you say, sir," Eddington said in a tone that Worf thought of
as a little too reluctant, but acquiescent nonetheless. "In any case,
if Koval's *not* at home, we should at least try the mountain retreat.
The shapechanger probably knows about it, and it'd be a useful
place to get away from it all."

Worf didn't like this. The retreat could very easily be heavily
secured and rigged with traps. But then, beaming into a high-
ranking Tal Shiar agent's house wasn't a low-risk operation, either. "We will see what the sensor data tells us when we arrive.
Once we enter the system, we will go into orbit about Remus,
then spend a full day examining the patrol patterns and sensor
grids around both planets."

"Why Remus?" Kira asked.

"Most of Remus is a barren wasteland," Daniels said. "They use
it for mining and some heavy-weapons construction, but that's it.
It's a lot less secure than Romulus, so it's safer to orbit there."

"Once we have found an insertion point," Worf continued, "we will do a near-warp transport of the attack team. Are there any questions?"

No one had any.

"Dismissed."

To Worf's great annoyance, scans of Koval's mansion revealed nothing of use.

Once the cloaking device was hammered out, the next task given to Sisko and Scott was to adjust the sensors so that they could scan a particular location on one twin planet from orbit around the other. The best they could do was allow such a scan of Romulus from Reman orbit during those occasions when the *Defiant*'s orbit brought it as close to Romulus as possible, and then only for a few minutes at a time.

But for a full two days, there was never a sign of a transponder of any kind in Koval's mansion. There were plenty in Tal Shiar headquarters—which Worf had scanned only in order to be thorough—and sensors, as expected, couldn't penetrate the sensor-proof shielding on the mountain retreat in Kor Thon.

Just finding that shielding was a victory of sorts, however. Kor Thon was a massive peak on which there were no known constructions. That there was a sensor-proof rectangular shape dug into the mountain whose floor was parallel to the surface many kilometers below meant that there was certainly *something* there. Whether it was Koval's mythic retreat or something else, they could not determine.

The *Defiant* bridge came equipped with a small table aft on the bridge, in lieu of a captain's ready room. Worf sat there now with Sisko and Eddington. "Is there any way," Worf asked his first officer, "to penetrate the shielding?"

Shaking his head, Sisko said, "No. Whatever they're using, it just bounces sensors right off." He smiled. "Scotty's had a few choice words on the subject."

Worf said nothing to that, though he was grateful that his first officer and chief engineer had reached a rapprochement. He had no desire to walk in on another shouting match in engineering.

"I think we have to send in two teams," Eddington said. "One to the mansion, one to the retreat."

"No," Worf said. "We only have one of the devices."

"So?"

"Without it, the shapechanger can transform into *anything,* and will easily escape."

Testily, Eddington said, "You're not giving my teams enough credit."

"According to Kira," Sisko said, "the shapechangers can change into water and leave through the plumbing, change into an avian and fly away, or change into gas and just disperse."

"At which point," Worf added, "your team will be exposed as having invaded Romulus and will be captured, and the mission will have failed. A second insertion team will not be possible after that."

"You're assuming," Eddington said, "that that Bajoran woman knows what she's talking about."

Growing weary of Eddington's constant questioning of Kira's bona fides, Worf folded his arms over his baldric. "Yes. We will send one team into the mountain retreat. If Koval is there, Kira will activate the device, and you will neutralize him. If not, we will retrieve you at the next window."

"All right," Eddington said. "I'll take Corsi's team down."

18

Corat Damar had awakened to a message from Gul Dukat requesting that he report to the gul's office in ops first thing in the morning. Not being one to shirk orders, Damar dispensed with all but the most minimal of morning ablutions, put on his uniform in record time, and jogged to the nearest lift.

When he arrived at ops, the door to the gul's office opened at his approach before he had a chance to signal—meaning Dukat had set it to open automatically upon reading his biosigns.

That was unusual enough; even more so was the fact that the office was empty. However, once the door closed behind Damar, the pleasant feminine computer voice spoke. *"Message for Dalin Damar from Gul Dukat."*

Damar walked over to the shatterframe screen on the wall and said, "Play message."

The face of Dukat appeared on the screen. *"Greetings, Damar. My apologies for this, but I was called away on rather sudden business in the middle of the night. I didn't wish to wake you, hence this message. Until further notice, you are prefect of Terok Nor. I'm sure one of your deputies can handle security in the meantime."* He leaned forward. *"One duty that neither you nor that deputy need concern yourself with: Odo. He has been sighted in Federation space."*

At that, Damar gasped. "How did—"

But the recording continued. *"Obviously this is cause for concern—*

but no longer for you. For now, simply maintain your post. Oh, and some upgrades were performed to the sensors. They now can perform antiproton scans, which will enable them to detect cloaked ships. Such scans are to be performed routinely." Dukat then mentioned a few more bits of business relating to the station—ships that were late, cabin assignments that needed to be resolved, and so on—before finally concluding, "*Good luck, Damar. I'm sure you'll do well.*"

The screen went blank, but Damar continued to stare at it incredulously. *Why am I being put in command?* There were two dals on the station who outranked him, either one of whom should have been put in charge, not to mention a dozen or so other dalins who had seniority.

And then there was Odo. Somehow, he'd managed to cross the border into Federation space. Admittedly, Odo was resourceful, and a shapeshifter to boot, so it was certainly within the realm of possibility. *Especially if he had help.* Angrily, Damar decided that the first order he would give to Glinn Comra when he received his temporary promotion to chief of security was to arrest Garak and search his store. They wouldn't find anything, and there wasn't really anything to charge him with, but if Odo made it to the Federation, he probably had help, and Garak was the most likely source of that aid.

At least I hope Comra's promotion is temporary. Dukat had provided no timetable for his return, had said that Damar was in charge "until further notice"—not "until I return"—and that he was prefect, not acting prefect, as would be expected. Dukat also didn't say where he was going. Normally Damar would assume that he was returning to Cardassia for government business—it wouldn't be the first time—but normally Dal Kalec or Dal Bokri would be in charge of the station in such cases.

The doorchime sounded. Damar shook his head, moved over to the guest side of the desk—he couldn't quite bring himself to sit in Dukat's chair—and touched the control that opened the door.

Kalec entered, a sour expression on his face. "Well, *Prefect,* it seems that you're in charge now."

Holding up his hands, Damar said, "Look, I didn't ask for this. I only just found out from a recorded message the gul left. I don't know why—"

"Oh, please, Damar," Kalec said with a sneer, "the prefect's been grooming you since you got here. So, *Prefect,* what are your orders?"

Wonderful. Just wonderful. "Gul Dukat ordered antiproton scans. Have they commenced?"

"Not as yet. Dalin Karris has had trouble getting the new configuration online. Not that it matters. What possible use can an antiproton scan be, aside from a ridiculous power drain?"

"According to the prefect, such a scan can detect cloaked ships."

Kalec snorted. "What, the Klingons or the Romulans are going to take time from their war to invade?"

"Or the Federation. The latest intelligence reports indicate that they've started experimenting with cloaking technology."

Another snort. "If you believe that sort of thing, I suppose."

Frowning, Damar asked, "What sort of thing?"

"The lies the Obsidian Order sends you in the form of 'intelligence reports.' The Order couldn't find their own neck ridges with both hands. We're supposed to believe *them?* Besides, the Federation doesn't have the stomach for that kind of covert war."

Damar was starting to understand why Dukat didn't leave Kalec in charge. Somehow, Damar didn't think it was a coincidence that antiproton scans were commencing just as Dukat was leaving the station and there were reports of Starfleet ships using cloaks. Dukat obviously was expecting trouble—enough that he thought it prudent to be elsewhere and to have his security chief running the station.

Glancing over at the dal—who still had the same sour expression, as if his fish juice had gone off—Damar said, "Tell Karris that the antiproton scan is her top priority."

"Why? There's still maintenance work to be done on three of the upper pylons, the replicators on the habitat ring are still malfunctioning, and—"

"I don't *care*," Damar snapped. "Gul Dukat's orders were clear."

Kalec glowered at Damar. "Gul Jasad is staying on the habitat ring while his ship is repaired. *He's* the one who's been complaining about the replicators. For that matter, Karris is currently on his ship, trying to figure out what's wrong with his dilithium chamber. Do I take her off that?"

"Yes," Damar said. "I'll take responsibility—and I'll talk to Jasad. Just get it done, Kalec."

Making an exaggerated bow, Kalec said, "As the *prefect* commands, *sir*." Then he turned on his heel and left the office.

Within half an hour, naturally, Jasad was contacting him directly. *"What is the meaning of this?"*

Deciding to be deliberately obtuse to make it clear just how unimportant Jasad was, Damar said, "The meaning of what, Gul?"

"The repair crews have departed my ship, and a technician has yet to report to my quarters to repair the replicator unit!"

"I'm sorry, Gul, but I'm afraid our maintenance schedule—"

"This isn't maintenance! *These are* repairs *that I was told would be given* top *priority! We are on a critical mission, and we need to be spaceworthy as soon as possible. What's more, this replicator refuses to give me anything edible!"*

"Regarding the replicator, Gul, I suggest you go to Rom's Bar or the replimat—I'm sure they will have food to your liking. In fact, if you go to Rom's, anything you order there will be on the house."

"Really?" That seemed to mollify the gul somewhat—but only for a moment. *"Still, there is the matter of my ship. I demand that—"*

"I'm sorry, Gul, but that's truly the best I can do. Your ship will be repaired as soon as we can get to it."

"They had already gotten to it, until you removed the technicians!" Jasad frowned. *"Who exactly are you? One of Dukat's flunkies? I want to speak to Dukat."*

Damar felt the muscles in his neck tighten against the bone. "I'm afraid Gul Dukat isn't on station at the moment, but my instructions do come directly from him. There is a security concern that requires significant upgrades to Terok Nor's sensor array. I'm afraid *they* now have top priority."

"What kind of security concern?"

"I'm not at liberty to discuss that on an open channel, Gul. Suffice it to say, if we do *not* implement these upgrades, then your ship will have much greater problems than a faulty dilithium chamber."

Jasad scowled. *"You're just a dalin—I'm supposed to believe—"*

"What you believe is of very little interest to me, Gul. Right now, I have a station to run."

"I have friends, Dalin, friends who will not appreciate my being treated in so cavalier a manner by someone who has delusions above his station."

"Right now, Gul Jasad, Terok Nor is my station—and it will remain such until I am relieved by Gul Dukat. Feel free to contact whatever friends you want, but this conversation is over."

With that, he signed off.

Then he went to the replicator and ordered a full carafe of *kanar.* With a trembling hand, he grabbed the carafe the second it materialized with a mild hum and starting gulping it down, hoping it would slow his racing heart.

I'm not ready for this, he thought. *Dukat, why did you do this to me?*

After drinking half the carafe, Damar contacted Rom and told him to let Jasad have whatever he wanted on the house. Rom tried to negotiate that down to only drinks, not games or holosuites, but Damar insisted—and reminded Rom of the half-dozen favors the Ferengi owed Damar, favors that had kept Rom out of a holding cell. That got the barkeep to relent.

"Comra to Damar."

"Now what," Damar muttered, then activated the comm. "Go ahead, Glinn."

"Sir, Garak is missing. He's neither in his quarters nor in his shop. We're in the process of an, ah—intense search of the shop, but he's nowhere to be found."

"Find him, Glinn. I want him in a holding cell by the time your shift ends, am I understood?"

"Yes, sir."

Damar took another gulp of *kanar*. He was playing a dangerous game here—slapping down a gul, showing up Kalec, and now challenging a former Order agent who was probably smarter than he was, and certainly smarter than all his deputies combined—all on the basis of his interpretation of Dukat's orders. Damar wasn't too worried about Jasad. Whatever friends the gul had—and he couldn't be the shipmaster of a *Galor*-class vessel without having *some* influential friends and/or family—he doubted they would be able to override Dukat.

Always assuming I've interpreted Dukat's wishes correctly. But the very installation of the antiproton scanner seemed to be indication enough—at least to Damar.

As for Kalec and Garak—well, there was nothing to be done about the former, as that decision had been Dukat's. Damar and Kalec were both just going to have to live with it. And Garak was a bit of self-indulgence on Damar's part, but he was well and truly sick of the man. He'd been running rings around Damar for months now while he tried to find out what happened to Odo. Damar wanted Garak in a holding cell where he could keep an eye on him.

By the end of the shift, Damar had had three carafes of *kanar,* had received a report from one of his deputies that Jasad had created a disturbance at Rom's (and was now sleeping it off in his quarters), a report from Comra that Garak had yet to be found, and a report from Kalec that Karris had successfully brought the antiproton scanner online. Damar's final order of his first day as prefect of Terok Nor was to commence antiproton scans of the entire B'hava'el system every half hour.

Then he went to his cabin and fell right to sleep, the stress and the *kanar* catching up with him. He didn't even bother removing his uniform, but simply fell onto his bed.

One of the things Damar had liked about being assigned here was that Bajor's twenty-six-hour day usually meant he got more sleep. Tonight, however, although he went to bed earlier than usual, he got less sleep than expected, due to an interruption by Dal Bokri, who was in charge of the night shift.

"*I'm sorry to wake you, Prefect Damar,*" Bokri said, pronouncing his title with the same disdain Kalec had shown. Damar supposed that she preferred to use the title rather than report to someone of a lower rank.

"What is it?" he asked as he tried to clear his mind. The words actually came out with fewer consonants than that, but he figured Bokri would be able to work out what he said.

"*The antiproton scan just detected a cloaked vessel entering the system.*"

19

**Koval's Private Retreat
Kor Thon, Romulus
Romulan Star Empire**

Kira Nerys was really starting to grow irritated with Starfleet. Whether it was Sisko and his arrogant possessiveness regarding the *Defiant,* or Eddington's security people and their tiresome doubts that any of this was real, or Eddington himself, who didn't want Kira along on the mission.

Picard and Worf were the exceptions. They were willing to accept the evidence before their own eyes, and didn't get bogged down in trivia. Picard's plan was, frankly, an audacious and risky one, and not something Kira would have expected from an officer of so hidebound an entity as the Federation. The captain himself had confessed to Kira before she went off to the *Defiant* that under normal circumstances, he would never have proposed such an endeavor.

But these were not normal circumstances. The Dominion needed to be stopped. They were already halfway to conquering the quadrant, with only a handful of people on this side of the wormhole even aware that they existed.

Kira shuddered at the thought of the wormhole. There were many who suggested that the stable wormhole was more than just a bizarre astronomical phenomenon, but also the gateway to the Celestial Temple of the Prophets; Kira had not been one of them. Perhaps if there had been some evidence that the Prophets resided there—but none had presented itself to any of those traveling through the wormhole, including Odo himself, who had taken several trips back when he was still Terok Nor's security chief. While Kira would not have expected the Cardassians to mention or even be aware of the Prophets' existence, Odo would have known and would have told her.

Parting from Odo had been the hardest thing when leaving the *Enterprise.* But even with the cloak, there was a better than even chance that Picard's ship would have to face off against Terok Nor and whatever ships were docked there. Odo's knowledge of the station—not to mention Dukat's usual tactics—and of how to navigate the Denorios Belt to get to the wormhole would be vital to the *Enterprise*'s ability to complete its mission.

And it was just as well that Kira didn't believe that the wormhole was the Celestial Temple, since the *Enterprise*'s mission was to destroy it. Kai Opaka had been one of those who believed it at first, but when no signs came for several years after the Cardassians found the wormhole, she changed her stance. Then, of course, she was killed, the latest in a series of depraved acts by Dukat—or, rather, by the alien thing that had replaced him.

She still recalled her final conversation with Odo in the Fleet Yard corridor right outside the airlock that would take her to the *Defiant.* "Nerys," he had said hesitantly—which alone was noteworthy, as hesitancy was not one of Odo's usual modes.

"What is it, Odo?"

"I just wanted to thank you. If it hadn't been for you, I probably would have been so caught up in being reunited with my people, I wouldn't have seen them for what they are. But you opened my eyes." He had made a grumbling noise. "If I had real eyes, anyhow."

Kira had smiled. "It needed to be done, Constable," she said, using the title she'd granted him when they first met, during the investigation of Vaatrik's murder, Odo's first case as station security chief.

That had reminded her of something. "Look, Odo—we may never see each other again, and—"

"And you want to tell me that you killed Vaatrik. I know."

"What?" Kira had felt her jaw literally drop open with astonishment. "How did you—"

"After I . . . resigned my post, I hid with several resistance cells. One of them made an offhand mention of your mission to confront Vaatrik and said that it ended badly."

Abashed, Kira had stumbled over her next words. "Odo, I—I'm sorry, I—I *wanted* to—"

"It's all right," he had said. "We both have had bigger concerns. And you didn't know you could trust me at the time. I forgave you long ago." Odo had then put his hand on Kira's cheek—a gesture of affection that was as out of character as his earlier hesitation. "Good luck, Nerys. Walk with the Prophets. And know that if we never see each other again, that—that it was worth it."

It had sounded to Kira as if Odo had wanted to say something else. But before she could ask him, he had turned and headed toward the *Enterprise.*

She was still wondering now as she beamed down to Koval's mountain retreat with Eddington, Corsi, and sixteen security personnel. They materialized in a sitting room that had a window on one wall. A snowdrift piled up outside the window at a forty-five degree angle, and Kira could hear the wind beating against the walls just outside. Briefly, she wondered why anyone would put a window in a place like this.

The beam-down itself had been a bit bizarre. Kira had never participated in a near-warp transport, but it was the only way for the *Defiant* to decloak long enough to make the transport without being detected. For a moment, Kira felt as if she were inside the mountain . . .

Guards immediately and silently went into each room, while Eddington took out a tricorder. "I'm not picking anything up. No Romulan life signs, no transponder."

Kira sighed. "Well, it was worth a—"

Screams loud enough to be heard over the wind, and agonized enough to make Kira's stomach turn over, suddenly came from the back room where Corsi and four of her people had gone.

Without thinking, Kira ran toward that room, left hand still holding the device, right hand moving to the phaser that Worf—over Eddington's objections—had issued her.

"Son of a *bitch*," Corsi was saying as Kira entered. It was apparently Koval's bedroom, a lavishly appointed space with a huge bed, spacescape paintings on two of the walls, and a small nightstand holding what looked like a platinum sculpture.

All four members of Corsi's team were lying facedown on the floor. Kira could see blood trickling out their ears. "Some kind of sonic booby trap."

Kneeling down by one of the bodies, Kira said, "He was expecting us."

From behind Kira, Eddington said, "Not necessarily. Koval's a veteran Tal Shiar agent. This could be a standard booby trap. But the tricorder should have picked it up."

As Eddington spoke, Kira noticed a fifth pair of uniform-clad legs on the other side of Koval's bed. Only four people had come into the bedroom with Corsi.

Whirling around, her left hand moved toward the activation switch on the device.

But it was too late. "Corsi's" left hand shimmered and transformed into a whip that knocked the device out of Kira's hands, even as her right hand and phaser also transformed into a pointed piece of metal that impaled Eddington right through the chest. Eddington's finger spasmed on his phaser, and it fired harmlessly into the ceiling.

"You solids," the creature said with contempt, using the same tone that the real Domenica Corsi had when expressing skepticism over the reality of the Founders' infiltration. "Did you truly think we would be unaware of what you were doing? The moment you killed one of our own, we knew what was happening. It was easy to prepare."

While the shapechanger gloated, Kira dove for where the device had fallen.

She heard the reports of several dozen phaser beams—no doubt the rest of the team responding to the screams and Eddington's phaser fire—as she tried to wrap her hands around the device. Those blasts saved her life, as the Founder no doubt would have killed her but for the distraction of a dozen phaser hits on its person.

Suddenly, Kira found herself blown backward, intense heat and frigid cold both assaulting her face and chest as she fell on her rear end. Several of the phaser shots had blasted through the retreat's walls, letting in the obscene weather. Wind slammed into the retreat and snow blew into Kira's face, reducing visibility to almost nothing.

Holding a hand up in front of her face, Kira tried desperately to find the device, which had sufficient mass that she was fairly certain it wouldn't have budged *too* much even in these winds.

Kira herself could hardly say the same as she fought against the pounding wind with every iota of strength. She heard anguished screams and more and more phasers being fired, but the shapechanger seemed to still have the upper hand. Less than a dozen security personnel were left to deal with it, and Kira had to hope that they would keep it occupied long enough for her to neutralize it.

Gripping the bed for purchase, she inched her way toward where the device had landed, blinking away the snow that got in her wide brown eyes, pushing herself against the wind that was now howling in.

Just as she managed to grip the device, a massive form collided with her, sending them both rolling across the floor toward the hole that had been blasted into the wall. Claws rended her flesh and pain ripped through her side. The shapechanger had transformed into some kind of white-furred ursine beast—probably a type that thrived in this mountainous region—and intended to kill Kira in that form.

But she still kept her grip on the device, and thumbed it to an active state just as the Founder was modulating into another form.

What that form might be, Kira did not discover, for it quickly collapsed into its natural liquid state, letting out a strangled scream as it did so.

Her Starfleet phaser was no longer in its holster. Peering through the snow that was blowing horizontally into the bedroom, Kira made out the form of one of the bodies belonging to the security detail. Even as the Founder undulated across the floor and through the air in a desperate and futile attempt to control its own form, Kira snatched at the phaser being gripped by the nearby corpse.

Picard had said they were to attempt to capture the shape-changer, but to defend themselves as necessary. Kira saw that as Starfleet cowardice, a typical unwillingness to do anything un-pleasant unless it was absolutely necessary.

But this thing had just killed more than a dozen good people, and Kira wasn't about to let it get away with that.

Thumbing the phaser to the highest setting, she fired. The creature's screams grew more shrill, and overpowered the steady hum of the phaser beam that struck it. Kira kept on firing until the Founder had completely disintegrated, its screams finally cut off.

Kira dropped the phaser, the wind seeming oddly quiet. She attempted to crawl out of the bedroom, but the knives of pain that sliced through her belly told her that was a bad idea. Reaching down with her left hand, she felt blood gushing out of the wound and soaking into her tattered shirt. Her legs were starting to go numb, and spots started dancing amid the snow in front of her eyes.

Can't . . . fall . . . unconscious . . . she thought. It would be at least another six hours before the *Defiant* would be able to scan the surface of Romulus. The destruction of the wall would mean that they would be able to detect Kira's Bajoran life signs, likely unique on this world, and then they could perform the near-warp transport.

She just had to stay conscious.

Her body shivered, as much from the blood loss as from the cold air that probably filled the entire retreat by now. It had been late afternoon, local time, when they beamed down, which meant it would be night soon, so the temperature was likely to drop significantly. She needed to stay alive if for no other reason than to make sure Worf learned that the Founders knew that they had exposed the false Jaresh-Inyo, knew that one of their own was dead, knew that they were coming.

Have . . . to . , . stay . . . awake . . .

As the darkness claimed her, she thought about Odo, and wondered what he had really intended to say to her.

20

"Coming out of warp," Ensign Perim said from the conn.

Jean-Luc Picard found that he had the armrests of his command chair in a white-knuckled grasp. He let go of them and tugged down his uniform jacket.

From the chair to his right, his new first officer, Lieutenant Commander Ro Laren, asked her own replacement at tactical, "Status of cloak?"

Lieutenant Linda Addison, Ro's former deputy and now security chief, said, "Still functioning within normal parameters."

Picard looked at ops. "Lieutenant Kadohata, any signs of pursuit or scans?"

The raven-haired woman shook her head. "Nothing so far. We—" Then she cut herself off. "Sir? I'm detecting an antiproton scanning wave." She turned around to look at Picard. "It's originating from Bajor—specifically, from Bajoran orbit."

Turning to his left, Picard looked at Odo, who had taken Troi's usual seat for the duration of this mission. Troi herself had been temporarily reassigned to Starbase 96. The counselor assigned to that base was overworked and had requested assistance. Given the nature of the *Enterprise*'s mission, Picard felt he could spare her.

He asked the shapechanger, "Does Terok Nor have such scanning capability?"

"I don't think so," Odo said, "but I didn't concern myself with technical issues."

"Sir," Kadohata continued, "Starfleet's been experimenting with antiproton scans as a way of detecting cloaked ships. We haven't been able to make it work, but if the Cardassians have . . ."

Ro finished the ops officer's thought. "They might be able to see us."

Picard considered his options. "Perhaps. Until we have proof, however, we will proceed as planned. Mister Odo?"

The shapechanger nodded and said to Perim, "Input course 289 mark 17."

"Aye, sir."

Kadohata inhaled a breath through her teeth. "Sir, now reading two ships disembarking from Terok Nor's docking pylons. Both *Galor* class."

"Proceed on course, Ensign," Picard said. "Go to yellow alert. Arm phasers and quantum torpedoes. Shields on standby."

"Yes, sir," Addison said.

Picard turned to Odo. "Were you able to obtain the assistance you mentioned?"

"I sent a message," Odo said, "in the manner he requested. Unfortunately, I have no way of knowing if he received it."

"One way or another," Ro said, "we'll find out soon enough."

Damar stood at the table in the center of ops. To his relief, Bokri did not feel the need to wake Kalec up, so she was the only person present who outranked him.

Bokri stared down at the status board in front of her. "Both ships are disembarking, but Gul Ocett wishes to know what, exactly, she's attacking."

Sighing, Damar said, "Give her the coordinates again."

"She *has* the coordinates," Bokri said testily. "She simply sees nothing there, since her vessel isn't equipped with an antiproton scanner. Also, *Prefect,* I'm not at all convinced that what we're seeing really is a cloaked ship. It could simply be a sensor shadow created by—"

Damar interrupted, not interested in having his authority flouted in the middle of ops. Inside the office, he could deal with it, but not out here. "*If* that's what it is, then the worst that happens is those two ships are wasting their time. If it truly *is* a cloaked ship, however, then Guls Jasad and Ocett will be in a position to stop it."

Of course, Jasad wasn't on his ship, but his first officer, a young dalin whose name Damar didn't get, had followed orders without question, and set course for the anomalous reading.

"We're also receiving a signal from a Jem'Hadar fleet—they're en route, and will be here in twenty minutes."

Damar nodded. He didn't know much about the Cardassians' new allies, but he knew they were quite valuable in a fight.

"Ocett's hailing us," said one of the officers whose name Damar did not know.

"On screen."

The pretty face of the gul appeared on the oval screen at the front of ops. *"This is ridiculous. We have scanned the area and there is nothing there. I demand to know why—"*

"Gul, we *are* detecting what appears to be a cloaked ship—" Damar started before Ocett interrupted.

"Don't talk back to me, Dalin. I don't appreciate my time being wasted on a fool's errand."

After taking a deep breath, Damar said, "With respect, Gul, if you would simply fire on the coordinates that we've been providing."

"They keep changing."

"It's a cloaked ship, Gul," Damar said with every bit of patience he could muster up. "It's in motion."

"Very well. I will indulge you in this because I respect Dukat, and he left you in charge for whatever insane reason. But if this is for naught, you will find yourself busted down to gil and cleaning waste extractors on Cardassia VI."

With that, the screen went blank.

"Tactical overview on screen," Damar said.

It took several seconds for the order to be carried out, which Damar supposed he should have complained about, but it seemed pointless. The screen showed Ocett's and Jasad's ships as yellow dots both proceeding toward a red spot that was labeled as an unspecific sensor reading. Damar frowned at that at first, then realized that the computer hadn't yet been programmed to recognize what the antiproton scanner was picking up. It didn't matter much for now, but he made a mental note to tell Karris about it in the morning.

Suddenly, both ships exploded.

Damar blinked. "What happened?"

Ops was suddenly awash in activity. The tension level shot up. Prior to this, it had been a strange exercise, but not one being taken particularly seriously by anyone other than Damar. Now, though, two *Galor*-class warships had been inexplicably lost.

"Dammit," Damar said, "*report,* somebody!"

The officer at the science station said, "Sensors are picking up traces of triceron in the debris." He looked up sharply. "Sir, that's an explosive."

"I'm aware of the most common use of triceron, Glinn," Damar snapped.

"Comra to Damar."

His head now pounding thanks to the lack of sleep combined with this absurd turn of events, the last thing he expected to hear was Comra's voice, especially since he was supposed to have gone off-shift hours ago. "Comra, now's not the—"

"Sir, we've located Garak—he's in the fusion core!"

Picard rose quickly to his feet as he watched two *Galor*-class ships become consumed by fire. "Report!"

From behind him, Odo said, "It would seem that Garak got my message."

Whirling around to look at the shapechanger, Picard saw a grim smile on Odo's face. "You believe him to be responsible?"

From ops, Kadohata said, "It was the responsibility of *someone*—

I'm picking up triceron in the debris. Someone blew those ships up on purpose."

That they both exploded at the same time made that somewhat obvious, but the presence of triceron confirmed it. *More death. More destruction. How much more of this must there be?*

Still, for now it was a gift horse into whose mouth Picard was loath to peer. "Maintain course, Ensign."

"Aye, sir," Perim said.

"Sir," Addison said, "I'm picking up three ships heading this way." She looked up. "They match the configuration of the new Cardassian ships."

"They're not Cardassian," Odo said. "That's the Jem'Hadar, the Dominion soldiers."

Retaking his seat, Picard again gripped the armrests tightly. Odo had briefed him and several admirals on the Jem'Hadar before they reported to Utopia Planitia. They were genetically engineered, drug-dependent creatures whose sole purpose was to fight the Dominion's wars. They were relentless, devoted, and— as the *Lexington, da Vinci,* and Starbase 375 discovered—incredibly powerful. *No doubt they have antiproton scanners as well.*

Ro asked Addison, "ETA of the Jem'Hadar ships, Lieutenant?"

"Fifteen minutes."

"Time to the Denorios Belt?" Picard asked Perim.

The Trill said, "Ten minutes."

Kadohata peered at her console. "Sir, Terok Nor's arming all weapons and raising shields. We'll be in range of them in four minutes."

Addison added, "Phasers are trained right on our position, sir—they know we're here."

"We've got to decloak and raise shields," Ro said.

Picard winced. While it was true that an antiproton scan *might* be able to detect a cloaked ship, they didn't know for sure. It was possible that Terok Nor didn't know for sure that they were there.

But no, they just lost two of their ships. They'll be on full alert, and they'll fire first and ask questions later. While it was true that decloaking would give away their position, so would being destroyed by the station's phaser fire. "Ensign Perim, if we change course to remain out of Terok Nor's firing range, what will be our ETA at the Denorios Belt?"

Perim ran her fingers over her console to make the calculations. "It will add eight-and-a-half minutes to our travel time."

Which means the Jem'Hadar will get here before we can destroy the wormhole. Which means the only alternative is to fight Terok Nor and hope for the best.

More death.

More destruction.

But if I do nothing, the only death and destruction will be my ship and crew. I cannot let them die without a fight.

Jean-Luc Picard had sat in the captain's chair for more than three decades on three different starships. With all the difficult decisions he'd made, from when he first took command of the *Stargazer* when its captain was killed and the first officer incapacitated, to the order that led to Jack Crusher's death, to ordering the destruction of the *Enterprise* in Earth's past in order to stop the Borg, he found that none was as difficult for him to make as this.

"Lieutenant Addison," he said in a low, raspy voice, "when we are within Terok Nor's weapons range, decloak the *Enterprise* and raise shields. Prepare phasers and torpedoes for a simultaneous barrage. Mister Odo, if you would please assist the lieutenant in finding a firing solution that will do the most damage."

Odo nodded without hesitation, got to his feet, and moved to stand next to Addison's console behind Ro. For the entire three-and-a-half minutes it took to get within the station's weapons radius, the shapechanger and the young woman whispered back and forth.

"Weapons ready," she finally said.

"Engage," Picard said flatly.

"Sensor reading—whatever it is," Bokri added snidely, "is in range."

"Fire!" Damar said, staring at empty space on the viewer.

Even as he said the word, the spacescape on the screen seemed to shimmer—and then coalesce into a *Sovereign*-class Starfleet vessel.

Had he the time, Damar would have felt vindicated, but his support vessels had just been sabotaged, and he was stuck in a functionally immobile space station whose window of opportunity to stop Starfleet would be open only very briefly. After that, he would have to leave it to the Jem'Hadar.

"Comra to Damar—sir, we've lost him."

Damar snarled. "What do you mean, lost him?"

"Shields are down!" That was Bokri.

"Damage from the Starfleet ship?"

Shaking her head, Bokri said, "No, they just—just went down."

"Well, get them up."

"I'm *trying!*"

The science officer said, "Starfleet vessel firing!"

Power junctions exploded in the aft stations. "They hit near the fusion core!" someone reported.

Well, maybe they *got Garak,* Damar thought with annoyance. "Get the shields back up!"

"They're trapped in diagnostic mode," Bokri said, "and my command codes won't override."

The science officer said, "There's a quantum torpedo bearing on the core."

Elim Garak tried to keep his breathing under control. He was quite sure that Comra and his merry band of idiots would easily find him if they heard him hyperventilating.

Or if the walls closed in on him and crushed him like a Lubbockian slime devil.

Right now, sitting crouched in an access tube, Garak considered one to be as likely as the other. He silently cursed the claustrophobia that had terrorized him since his youth.

This wasn't how he had intended to die—mostly because Garak had never had *any* intention of dying. Self-preservation had always been one of his particular talents—and generally his secondary goal. His primary one, of course, was to serve Cardassia. From his earliest days in Bamarren to his days serving Enabran Tain in the Obsidian Order to his exile to Terok Nor where he discovered the truth about the new allies they had found in the Gamma Quadrant, Garak had always served Cardassia.

Which was why he made sure Odo and Kira were able to get to Federation space. Based on the message Odo had sent him, they had exposed President Jaresh-Inyo as a shapechanger. Garak had to admit he was impressed by the Founders' audacity. Though Jaresh-Inyo was on his list, he had found it more credible that Councillor T'Latrek or Admiral Ross was the one who'd been replaced. But the president himself?

He heard explosions from nearby that sounded suspiciously like weapons fire striking the unshielded hull of Terok Nor. *I'm sure Damar and Bokri are trying desperately to raise them again,* Garak thought, with a touch of pride at their failure to do so. The Founder who had replaced Dukat had kept the prefect's access codes in order to maintain its charade, which had proved a tactical error. Garak had known Dukat's codes for years now, which, combined with a biosign filter, had granted Garak the ability to lower the shields and keep them that way. Only a legate could override that, and there were none on the station.

For a brief moment, Garak had been afraid that the biosign filter wouldn't work, but he needn't have concerned himself. After all, the shapechanger would need to use something very similar in order to fool the computer into thinking it was Dukat. And while Dominion technology was superior in many senses, it appeared that the Obsidian Order was their equal in at least that respect.

Comra's voice echoed throughout the fusion core. "We know you're here, tailor! Come out and show yourself!"

Garak considered doing as Comra asked so that the glinn's final act would be one of success in accomplishing the mission Damar set out for him that morning. But he quickly dismissed the notion, tempting as it was to leave the crippling confines of the access tube.

It would all be over soon in any case. The *Enterprise* would make short work of Terok Nor as long as it remained unshielded, assuming the station's weaponry didn't finish off the Starfleet vessel first. *It's only a pity there wasn't time to deactivate the weapons as well.*

When he was being trained in Bamarren, Garak had been told that agents of the Obsidian Order were most likely to die alone, unmourned, unacknowledged, and uncared for. But they were also likely to die in the service of Cardassia.

In his heart, Garak knew he was doing that, though his former superiors in the Order would likely disagree. But the Dominion would bring no glory to Cardassia, only subsume it to their will. For all that the legates and the Detapa Council and the new head of the Order called it an "alliance," Cardassia had been conquered—and they didn't even know it.

But they'd know soon enough. Garak was grateful that he wouldn't live to see his beloved people realize just how thoroughly they'd been deceived.

If only the walls weren't closing in . . .

What have I done?

Those words went through Picard's head as he watched the quantum torpedo strike Terok Nor's fusion core, watched that core explode, watched the lower pylons being vaporized, watched the upper pylons break off and tumble through space, watched the habitat ring twist and shatter.

There are civilians on that station. Innocent victims, and I just condemned them to death. That didn't even include the debris that would fall into Bajor's atmosphere, further damaging an already badly scarred planet. Picard knew he had no choice, that this was the mission, but he still felt like the worst kind of murderer. In a moment of horror and despair, he realized that he had become the very thing that he had cursed the Cardassians and the Dominion for being. What he had just done made him no better than the guls who had ordered the destruction of *Voyager, Intrepid,* and the other ships at Dorvan, Valo, and Salva, no better than the Jem'Hadar soldiers who destroyed Starbase 375, *Lexington,* and *da Vinci.*

Perim's voice startled him. "On course for the Denorios Belt."

Yes, of course. There is still a mission to perform. All those people—were simply in our way.

"What was that, sir?" Ro asked.

Embarrassed, Picard tugged on his uniform jacket. He hadn't realized that he'd muttered those words aloud. "Nothing, Commander. Proceed, Ensign."

Within minutes, the *Enterprise* arrived at the belt.

"Having difficulty navigating the tachyon eddies," Perim said through clenched teeth.

"Maintain this course, Ensign," said Odo, who had retaken Troi's seat. "The *Enterprise* will remain safe as long as you do so."

Ro muttered, "Sure hope so" just loud enough for Picard to hear.

"Jem'Hadar have changed course to intercept," Addison said. "They'll be in firing range in three minutes."

Kadohata was frowning at her console. "I'm reading meson and lepton fluctuations dead ahead."

"That's the wormhole," Odo said with a certain amount of surety.

And then Picard saw it.

One moment there was empty space—the tachyon eddies were invisible, after all, which was part of why the Denorios Belt was such a navigation hazard—but the next . . .

It was one of the most beautiful sights Picard had ever seen. Like a flower blooming in the morning sun, it opened and expanded. At its circumference, it looked almost like smoke, though Picard knew that was simply the event horizon being made visible. At the center, wild energies surged about.

The explorer in Picard desperately wanted to go through, to

see what was on the other side—indeed, to explore *within* the wormhole, find out why this gateway remained stable when every other wormhole ever encountered was fickle and unreliable.

But war had taken that opportunity away from Picard. Starfleet's primary mission of exploration had been subordinated to its secondary role as the Federation's protector. And right now, he needed to protect the Federation against the threat that lay on the other side of that wormhole.

Again he gave an order that it tore out his soul to give. "Fire torpedoes."

First Omet'iklan had served the Founders faithfully for all the years of his life. He had survived many campaigns, taking his orders from the Vorta and defeating the Dominion's enemies. He had never wavered in his faith in the Founders or in the rightness of the Dominion.

And while he did not lose faith now, he found it faltering ever so slightly. For he could not believe that the gods would allow something like *this* to happen.

He watched on his eyepiece as the Federation ship fired its weapons right into the gateway. The torpedoes detonated, and a huge burst of ignited verteron and silithium particles plumed outward from the gateway's mouth. The Federation ship's shields lit with the impact.

Omet'iklan barked at his fourth, who sat at the operations station: "Damage to the enemy vessel."

"Reduced shield capacity, but no other damage."

"What of the gateway?"

The fourth looked up in shock, an expression Omet'iklan had never seen on the soldier's visage before. "I no longer read the gateway."

This was disastrous. The Vorta had ordered Omet'iklan to protect Terok Nor, as the Founders feared an attack on it by a cloaked vessel. He had failed in that duty, but that was as nothing, compared to the failure he now felt.

Only one thing would ameliorate that failure. "Charge all weapons! Destroy that ship!"

"They are cloaking," the fourth said.

"Engage antiproton scan. *Find* them!"

Born in a laboratory deep in the heart of the Dominion and bred to fight and obey, Omet'iklan rarely felt such intense rage as he felt now. While he was compelled to hunt down the Federation ship and destroy it, were he left to his own devices, he would do so anyway, with relish. Thanks to these Federation worms, access to the rest of the Dominion had been all but cut off. While cloning and ketracel-white–producing facilities were under construction within what used to be Cardassian space, they were not yet complete.

Which meant that it was not only urgent that Omet'iklan lead the fleet to victory, but also that he not die in the process. Once, Jem'Hadar were expendable, but no more. Now, victory truly was life.

"Enemy vessel detected."

"Fire as soon as they are in range," Omet'iklan said. "*Destroy* them!"

Shaking her head, Kadohata said, "They're using an antiproton scan also, sir. Still on us."

Picard's memories of Locutus, Gul Madred, being stabbed in the heart as an ensign, the mind-meld with Sarek, sending Jack Crusher to his doom, ordering Terok Nor and the wormhole destroyed, and all the other awful memories of his life were pressing down on him, pushing against the confines of the box into which they were stuffed. A voice came from that box now: *Do nothing,* it said. *Give in. Let the Jem'Hadar destroy you. You deserve it.*

Picard shoved the voice back into the box. He might have committed heinous crimes, even by the standards of wartime, and if he survived this day, he would answer for them. But he would not doom the rest of his crew in a sad gesture of suicide.

"Decloak," he said. "Lieutenant Addison, fire phasers on the lead ship, with a torpedo spread on the second one."

And then the battle was joined.

Ro Laren sat at Picard's side, marveling at the turns her life had taken. After watching her father being tortured to death, she had escaped from Bajor, swearing never to come back as long as Bajor was a defeated planet. She joined Starfleet, and had thought her career to be over after the disaster at Garon II. But then she got a second chance, serving under Captain Picard as his conn officer, then taking security training and coming back to Picard on his new *Enterprise* as security chief, and then first officer.

And after all that, she was about to die in the Bajoran system at the hands of the Cardassians' new allies.

Bajor was still defeated. For every Kira Nerys who fought, there were hundreds who just let themselves be subjugated. And who could blame them, especially with these Jem'Hadar *things* helping the Cardassians?

Ro had no illusions about how this fight would go. There were three Jem'Hadar ships, and they were only one vessel. Yes, the *Sovereign* class was as good as it got in Starfleet, but the Jem'Hadar were something else entirely.

Sure enough, it only took a few minutes for them to pound the hell out of the *Enterprise*. They hemmed the ship in, keeping them from leaving the confines of the Denorios Belt, thus limiting Perim's options for evasive maneuvering.

And then the shields went down. With nowhere to go, they were sitting ducks. Addison kept firing away at the enemy vessels—even managing to destroy one—but there was only so much they could do. At least ten people were dead, according to Doctor Crusher, and a lot more wounded.

The ship shook with one hit that Ro had thought was a clean miss until Kadohata said, "Direct hit on the port nacelle strut—it's broken off! And we've got a hull breach in deck thirty-nine!"

O'Brien called from engineering. *"We'll never get warp power now, sir. We have to—"*

The chief engineer's voice was cut off by an alarm and the computer said, *"Warning—forcefield failure in two minutes."*

"All right, everyone out!"

A voice from the other side of Picard said, "Captain, there's one thing that might work." Until the shapechanger spoke, Ro had forgotten about Odo.

"Tell me," Picard said urgently.

Odo hesitated. "The Jem'Hadar worship the Founders as gods. It's *possible* that they will obey me without question because of who—because of *what* I am."

"Why did you not mention this sooner?" Picard's voice had a furious undertone.

"It is not something that I'm particularly comfortable with— nor am I sure it will work."

Ro said, "You still could've mentioned it before we lost—"

Picard put a hand on Ro's. "We can save recriminations for another time."

Assuming there is another time, Ro thought angrily.

"Lieutenant, open a channel to the lead Jem'Hadar ship."

They are tenacious, these worms, Omet'iklan thought as his second moved to put out yet another fire on the flight deck. Though it was only one ship, the Federation vessel had destroyed one of Omet'iklan's fleet, and done considerable damage to the other two.

But they'd paid a dear price. One of the ship's nacelles was gone, they had exhausted their supply of quantum torpedoes, and their power output was severely reduced.

Not that Omet'iklan's ship was in much better shape. But they were plenty strong enough to finish off these foul creatures.

"We are being hailed," the third said.

"There is nothing to be said," Omet'iklan said dismissively.

The third then looked up with wonder and fear in his eyes. "First—it is a Founder!"

"What?" Omet'iklan had not been informed that one of the gods was on the *Enterprise*. Not that they had any need to inform him of anything, but if a Founder was on board, why wait until now to contact them?

Too many questions, and a relatively simple method of getting answers: "Put it through."

Gazing into the small screen that covered his right eye, Omet'iklan saw a Founder.

At first, he was filled with reverence. "Founder," he said.

"First, you are to break off this attack immediately," the Founder said.

Then Omet'iklan recognized the god in question, and realized that it was one who had fallen from grace. "You are the traitor, Odo. You have been cast out of the Great Link."

"I am still part of the Great Link, First, and have been welcomed back more than once. Now you must—"

"Do *nothing!* Did you think me a fool to try to win my trust with this transparent ploy? There *is* no Great Link for you to return to, Founder, for you have destroyed the gateway! Perhaps I will be damned for what I do now, but I will *not* see the Dominion defeated by the likes of you. Victory is life, and you will not achieve victory this day, Founder. *Destroy* them!"

The officers under him hesitated. All of a sudden, they were under orders to kill a god. A Jem'Hadar could not do such a thing and expect to live for very long.

Omet'iklan realized that he could not force his soldiers to do this. It was Omet'iklan's decision, and his alone. There would be grave consequences for this act. But the fallen Founder had obviously betrayed them all. The destruction of the Bajoran space station and the two Cardassian ships—the fallen Founder had to have at least provided some aid for that to have taken place. For that matter, just by revealing himself to the Federation, he had betrayed the Dominion.

In all his time serving the Dominion, Omet'iklan never imagined he would see the day when a god would commit a capital crime—and that he himself would be the executioner.

He walked over to the weapons console, pushing the fifth aside, and fired upon the Federation ship.

A barrage of weapons fire spat forth from Omet'iklan's ship and struck the helpless Federation vessel.

It exploded in a huge conflagration of matter-antimatter annihilation and burning plasma.

"Scan for survivors." Omet'iklan wanted to make sure none of those responsible for today's travesty would live.

"Detecting several escape pods, First," the second said.

"Eliminate them."

The second hesitated.

"The Founder was on the bridge of the enemy ship. Federation vessels do not keep their escape pods proximate to the bridge. There was not time for him to make it to the pods. None of those inside is the Founder. *Destroy them!*"

Quickly, the second did as he was ordered.

Then Omet'iklan ordered his fleet to set course for the nearest Dominion base. Once that would have been Terok Nor, but now he had to go much farther.

He had to report what had happened. And, no doubt, report for his own execution for the unforgivable crime of killing a god.

21

Worf stood alone in his cabin.

As captain, he was one of the few who had been given a cabin of his own on the overcrowded ship. After the mission to Romulus, with the deaths of so many, a few others were able to have single bunks: Sisko and Scott among them, which meant they were no longer sharing a bunk, a situation that had caused some tension, although the two had worked out most of their differences.

Today, Worf was grateful for the solitude. He had extinguished the light in the cabin, the only remaining illumination coming from a large candle of mourning.

The *Defiant* had received a coded intelligence briefing an hour ago. The *Enterprise* had been successful in its mission to destroy the mouth of the wormhole. They had also destroyed the space station Terok Nor. The report did not specify whether Gul Dukat was aboard the station, nor did it confirm that it was he whom the Founders had replaced with one of their own.

But in the process, the *Enterprise* itself was lost.

Jean-Luc Picard had been the finest captain Worf had ever hoped to serve with. Whatever meager skills he himself had as a commander he owed entirely to Picard. The captain had stood by Worf's side as *cha'DIch* when he challenged the High Council's ruling against his father, and had always been steadfast and loyal and worthy of respect.

And now he was gone.

Worf's life, it seemed, had been governed by loss, from the Khitomer massacre that claimed his parents when he was six to the traitorous *d'k tahg* of Duras killing K'Ehleyr. And now he had lost his captain.

At least he died well, Worf thought as he walked over to the candle, took his personal *d'k tahg,* and pressed it down upon the wick, extinguishing the flame. Jean-Luc Picard had not only been Worf's *cha'DIch,* but was also the first human to serve as a Klingon chancellor's Arbiter of Succession. If any human would be permitted into *Sto-Vo-Kor,* it would be him.

Just then, the doorchime rang.

"Computer, lights," Worf said. Once the cabin was illuminated, Worf said, "Enter."

The door slid aside to reveal the *Defiant*'s medical officer, Doctor Simon Tarses. A former medtech on the *Enterprise*-D who had failed to disclose his partial Romulan heritage, he had overcome the rather brutal witch hunt related to that revelation and gone on to get his medical degree. Worf, whose role in that witch hunt was one of the more shameful chapters of his Starfleet career, was glad to have him on the *Defiant.*

Of course, Worf's role meant that Tarses was skittish around his new CO. The young doctor seemed to flinch every time he was in Worf's presence. "Sorry to interrupt, sir, but the Bajoran woman's finally come out of her coma."

"Good. Take me to her."

Tarses, predictably, flinched. "Of—of course, sir."

The *Defiant*'s medical bay was not a particularly impressive facility. Worf had seen emergency medikits that were as well equipped. But the *Defiant*'s mandate was battle, and that meant that most medical procedures that would be performed on board would be quick-work holding actions until the ship could reach a proper facility at a starbase or on a bigger starship.

However, it was sufficient to allow Tarses to operate on Kira Nerys and repair the considerable damage done to her on Romulus. The others in her team weren't so lucky. When they beamed her up to the *Defiant,* Kira had regained consciousness long enough to say that the shapechanger posing as Koval had been killed. As per the mission specs, Worf then beamed down an explosive to Koval's retreat, vaporizing it and everything inside—including the bodies of Eddington, Corsi, and the rest of the security team. The *Defiant* did not have the capacity to store that many bodies. Besides, nobody signed up for Starfleet security expecting to actually leave a corpse behind to be buried.

Then they proceeded to Qo'noS.

Garak's list had three high-ranking generals as the ones most likely to have been replaced by a shapechanger: Martok, son of Urthog; Talak, son of Yorchogh; and Goluk, son of Ruuv. Worf did not know any of them particularly well, though he knew all were experienced veterans of the Defense Force whose long lives were due not to shirking battle, but to being unable to find anyone worthy enough to defeat them. All three of them had Gowron's ear, and any one of them could have been responsible for the bizarre tactical decisions that had served to prolong the Romulan war. It was impossible to be sure because all such orders were said to come from Gowron regardless of who might actually have suggested them or come up with the plans of battle. In times of war, the chancellor led the Defense Force, and that was all there was to it.

Worf admired the principle, but it complicated his life right now.

Kira was lying in the medical bay with a device of some sort on her forehead. Her skin was pale, and she looked as if she had lost half a kilo off her spare frame.

Her eyes, however, still blazed with the same righteous fury Worf had first faced in the interrogation room on the *Enterprise.*

"Welcome back," Worf said.

"Thank you. I can't believe I'm still alive."

"You have Doctor Tarses to thank."

Again, Tarses flinched. "She, ah, she really doesn't. Honest, if she wasn't clinging so hard to life, nothing I did would've mattered."

Kira gave a sad smile. "Furel always said I was too stubborn to die."

Worf assumed that to be one of her compatriots in the Bajoran resistance. "We will arrive at Qo'noS in three hours."

"I know Garak's information on the Klingons was spottier, but he did work in Romulan space and still has contacts."

"Yes, but the Klingon Empire is allied with the Federation," Worf said. "That is a conduit of information that we may exploit."

Kira hadn't thought of that. To her, everyone was the enemy—the concept of nations cooperating wasn't something she was used to. "Of course," she said lamely. "I'm sorry about Eddington and the others."

"They died well. We are fortunate that there is a meeting of all of Gowron's top generals in two days. We shall wait in orbit of Qo'noS until that meeting has commenced, then beam down with your device."

Kira started to sit up, then, amazingly, got even paler, and lay back down. After letting out a burst of breath, she said, "We can't wait two days. Koval *knew*."

Worf frowned. "Knew what?"

"That we killed Jaresh-Inyo. He was *waiting* for us down there. It was just dumb luck that I was able to kill him, and it wasn't until he killed everyone else. Whoever it is on Qo'noS, they know what we did and they'll be waiting for us."

"That is unfortunate," Worf said, his mouth twisting in annoyance. "But this meeting was called by Gowron because he is displeased with the prosecution of the war. He has made it clear that any generals who do not attend the meeting will be executed. If the shapechangers are to maintain their cover—"

"Yeah, but I don't think they want to at this point. If they knew we got Jaresh-Inyo, then they probably know that we got Koval. I doubt they're going to continue being so covert."

"Sisko to Worf."

Tapping his combadge, Worf said, "Go ahead."

"You should come to the bridge, sir. We're in scanning range of Qo'noS and—it isn't pretty."

Worf shot Kira a glance. "I will be right there."

"Captain," Kira said as Worf turned to leave.

He stopped and gazed expectantly at her.

"This is a battleship. It may be time to take her into battle."

Worf said nothing, but simply left the medical bay. Since he was a child, Worf had always wanted to be a great Klingon warrior, even though he spent most of his youth on Gault and Earth being raised by humans. If he was to die, he would do it in service of the Federation *and* the Klingon Empire, facing their enemies and destroying them. He took great pride in the fact that it had been he who destroyed the creature who had replaced President Jaresh-Inyo, and that he had led the mission that exterminated the one disguised as Koval.

When he arrived on the bridge, however, he saw that his stopping a third shapechanger would be a bit more of a challenge.

Qo'noS was under siege.

Sisko rose from the command chair, ceding it to Worf, and said, "We started picking up the signs of battle ten minutes ago. There are at least forty Jem'Hadar warships."

Daniels was at the tactical station. "According to reports we've been monitoring, that fleet started out as a hundred Jem'Hadar ships. They crossed the border yesterday and have been working their way toward Qo'noS ever since."

Worf cursed their need to run silent. It meant that hard information was difficult to come by, with only occasional coded transmissions from Starfleet and whatever they were able to monitor on their own—which the covert nature of their mission made difficult.

"Right now," Daniels continued, "there are thirty Klingon ships engaging the Jem'Hadar, plus Qo'noS's planetary defenses."

"Captain, we've got a wee bit of a problem."

That was not what Worf wanted to hear from Captain Scott right now. "Report."

"The warp drive's control circuits are near fried. And before you ask, we'd plenty of spares when we left Earth—I've already gone through 'em all."

"He's right, sir," Sisko said bitterly. "We still haven't been able to keep the power levels down enough to keep the circuits from overloading. Scotty and I cobbled together some quick fixes, but . . ."

Scott picked it up. *"But we've been at this for too long, and I'm runnin' outta rabbits to pull out of my hat. I've managed to hold it together this long, but as soon as we come out of warp, that's all we've got. We won't be goin' at faster than full impulse unless your Klingon friends can lend us a warp drive."*

"Are we able to increase speed?"

Scott made a sputtering noise. *"We're lucky to be maintainin' warp five as it is!"*

"It has become urgent that our arrival time at Qo'noS be moved up, Mister Scott. The *Defiant*'s speed must increase to warp nine."

"Well, in for a penny, in for a pound, I suppose, but we'll be lucky not to get to your bloody homeworld in pieces. Engineering out."

"Sir," Sisko said, "with your permission, I'd like to give Scotty a hand. I might be able to find a rabbit of my own." That last was said with a wide smile.

"Very well," Worf said. As Sisko turned to leave the bridge, the captain said, "Red alert, all hands to battle stations. Arm phasers and quantum torpedoes, and prepare to decloak and raise shields."

From the conn, Rager said, "Increasing speed to warp nine."

"ETA to Qo'noS at new velocity?" Worf asked.

"Fifteen minutes."

The next quarter of an hour seemed to be endless for Worf.

Daniels continued to give progress reports on the battle, which was not going the Klingon Defense Force's way. Though ten more of the Jem'Hadar's vessels had been destroyed, so too had a dozen Klingon ships. Of the eighteen left, though, four were *Vor'cha*-class battle cruisers, which were the top of the line, among them Gowron's flagship the *Negh'Var*.

To Daniels, Worf said, "Send a coded message to the *Negh'Var*. Tell Chancellor Gowron that he is about to receive aid from the House of Mogh."

"Sir?" Daniels asked with a furrowed brow.

"Obey my orders, Mister Daniels." Now was not the time to get into a protracted discussion with the security officer about Worf's history with the chancellor, from his killing Gowron's sole rival for the chancellor's seat in a duel to Worf's support of Gowron in the civil war that erupted shortly thereafter. Worf's brother Kurn sat on the High Council, and the House of Mogh was a respected one in the empire. As much as Gowron supported and counted on the alliance with the Federation, the support of a noble House would be more meaningful to him than the arrival of a Federation starship—no matter how powerful.

However, just as Daniels prepared to send the message, Worf watched on the viewscreen as weapons fire from a Jem'Hadar ship sliced through one of the *Negh'Var*'s wings. The vessel started to spin out of control, hurtling past another of the *Vor'cha*-class ships.

Both ships were destroyed a moment later, in what Worf recognized as a matter-antimatter explosion. The warp cores of both vessels had obviously failed.

"Entering system now," Rager said calmly from the conn.

Forcing a similar calm to his own voice, Worf said, "Come out of warp. As soon as we are in range of the nearest Jem'Hadar ship, decloak and fire phasers."

"Yes, sir," Daniels said.

The lights on the bridge brightened, and Worf saw the *Defiant*'s pulse phasers—which were several orders of magnitude more powerful than the more common phaser beams—plow through a Jem'Hadar ship and wipe it from existence.

Worf's only regret was that it wasn't the same ship that destroyed the *Negh'Var*.

To Rager, he said, "Set course 482 mark 7, then continue at your discretion. Mister Daniels, continuous fire on the Jem'Hadar."

"Yes, sir," both officers said.

The *Defiant* was a flat ship, which increased its maneuverability, allowing Rager to weave it in and out of the field of fire, while Daniels pounded the Jem'Hadar with phasers. Within minutes, three more of their ships were destroyed. The *Defiant* itself took considerable fire, but its shields held—and when they fell, the ship also had ablative armor, which would enable them to last even longer in a fight.

"Sir?" Daniels's voice was strained.

"Report," Worf said.

"Long-range sensors are picking up another twenty-two Jem'Hadar ships approaching the system. They'll be here within ten minutes."

"Any Defense Force vessels?"

Daniels shook his head.

"Captain," Rager said, "five of the Jem'Hadar vessels are changing attitude."

Looking at the viewer, Worf saw that the conn officer was correct. Rather than maintain their battle posture, five of the enemy vessels were altering their position as if they were preparing for atmospheric entry.

Or atmospheric bombardment. The ships were spread out around the planet, so they could not be taken all at once, but he had to try. "Lieutenant, set an orbital course for the nearest Jem'Hadar vessel." If he had to, he would circle his homeworld and take out each ship before they could—

But it was too late. Even as the *Defiant* changed course, each of the five Jem'Hadar ships fired purple beams of devastation onto Qo'noS's surface. Even from this distance, Worf could see the mountains, the oceans, the plains, the forests, the cities—all burning.

Rager brought the *Defiant* close to one ship, and Daniels destroyed it with four quantum torpedoes, but by then, the damage was done.

From one of the port consoles, an officer whose name Worf could not recall said, "Radiation levels on the planet are increasing. Only picking up a few thousand life signs."

The population of Qo'noS numbered in the billions. One of those was Worf's brother, Councillor Kurn. "The First City?"

"Not reading it at all, sir."

So my brother is dead—as are most of the Homeworld's inhabitants. Worse, they did not die in battle, but simply burned at the hands of honorless cowards.

The *Defiant* took on fire. "Leave orbit, Lieutenant," Worf said. "Set course 222 mark 4."

Rager whirled around. "Sir?"

"Obey my orders!" Worf bellowed, getting to his feet, bile rising in his throat. He had just watched his homeworld die screaming.

"Captain," came the voice of Sisko from engineering, *"shields and weapons are offline. So are about half a dozen other systems, and it's a small miracle that the warp core hasn't been breached."*

Scott added, *"We cannot take much more'a this, sir."*

"We will not have to," Worf said.

Half a dozen Jem'Hadar ships changed course to try to intercept the *Defiant*. Weapons fire splashed against the ablative armor. Aside from a few birds-of-prey and a pair of *Karas*-class strike ships, none of the Defense Force armada protecting the homeworld was left intact, leaving the remaining Jem'Hadar free to prey on the *Defiant*.

"Full impulse."

"Captain," Scott said, *"we cannot maintain full impulse for—"*

Worf cut the old engineer off. "Prepare to induce a warp-core breach."

Sisko came on, then. *"Captain, are you thinking what I think you're thinking?"*

Normally Worf would not deign to explain an order to a subordinate, but under these circumstances, he was willing. "You both said we cannot leave this star system. Qo'noS has just been destroyed, and there are twenty-two Jem'Hadar ships about to enter the system. No doubt the Founder based here has summoned these forces to him so he may conquer the Alpha Quadrant more directly. That will be his final mistake."

"So you plan to set off a warp-core breach and take as many of them as you can since we're as good as dead already?"

"Not exactly," Worf said. "Yes, we will die gloriously. But not simply by breaching the warp core."

Rager said, "Approaching the sun's photosphere."

"Are you mad?" Scott asked. *"If the warp core goes when we're too close to the sun you might—"*

"Take the enemy with us," Worf said. "They destroyed the Homeworld. They will *not* live to regret that action."

Montgomery Scott had lived a long time, through two different centuries. Though he was present at the Khitomer Accords, he still never thought he'd live to see the day that the Federation and Klingons were allies—much less find himself taking *orders* from a Klingon.

And now he was going to die, not in his bed surrounded by loved ones, but deliberately inducing a warp-core breach before dive-bombing a sun in order to make it go nova, a gesture that would not only kill him, but wipe out an entire star system—and two dozen of those Jem'Hadar beasties.

Could be worse, he thought resignedly as he and Sisko set the controls. *At least I'm dyin' in an engine room.*

He looked at Sisko. "I guess this is it, then, lad."

"I guess. I just wish—"

After Sisko hesitated, Scott prompted: "What?"

"I just wish I could see Jake one last time."

"Aye," Scott said. He'd been hearing plenty of stories on the trip about Sisko's son. "He seems to be a fine lad. I'm sure he'll make you proud."

"I hope so," Sisko said quietly.

Kira Nerys had bullied Doctor Tarses into letting her sit at a console. The *Defiant* didn't have any transparent aluminum windows the way most Starfleet ships did, but she was able to set a screen to show her what was happening.

She saw the *Defiant* take out several Jem'Hadar ships.

She saw Qo'noS being devastated.

She saw the Jem'Hadar fire on the *Defiant* as Worf tried to take her toward the sun—for what? To try to lose them in the sun's corona?

Then Kira realized what Worf was planning. *I didn't give him enough credit.* This kind of insane suicide tactic was the kind of thing the resistance did all the time. *I thought Starfleet were heroes, not terrorists.* But with so many Jem'Hadar ships coming and the system no longer useful to their side, Worf decided to go for scorched earth. Or, in this case, scorched star system.

She admired the tactics. Her only regret was that there weren't some Cardassian ships in the system that they could take out, too.

Worf sat back down in the command chair. Daniels reported a rise in the hull temperature as they entered the sun's corona. He felt the heat pressing on his face. Sweat dripped off Rager's chin onto the conn. A few officers had removed their uniform jackets, a breach in uniform protocol that Worf couldn't bring himself to bother pointing out.

Without shields, and with the ablative armor all but gone, it wouldn't be long before the ship itself was overwhelmed. He hoped Scott and Sisko would be able to trigger the breach before that happened, else their sacrifice would have no meaning.

He was looking forward to seeing K'Ehleyr in *Sto-Vo-Kor.* Not to mention his parents and his brother.

"Today is a good day to die," he said as the heat grew almost unbearable, "and revenge is a dish best served hot."

Epilogue

An Undisclosed Location
Cardassian Union/The Dominion

The Founder stared in the mirror, the reflection of Skrain Dukat staring back.

Also reflected there was the other Founder still living in this quadrant, who had been disguised as General Talak.

"This is intolerable!" the other Founder said with Talak's voice. "Changelings have been *killed!* Access to the Dominion has been cut off, and—"

The Founder held up Dukat's hand. "Nothing has been 'cut off.' We are still *in* the Dominion."

"Bah." The Talak Founder began to pace the small room. "Our forces have been halved thanks to what happened at Qo'noS. Our true nature has been exposed, we have no way to reach the Great Link—and worse, three of our number are dead!"

"You have," the Dukat Founder said gently, feeling that the outburst was far more Talak than it was a member of the Great Link, "perhaps been in this form too long. Come, let us link."

Talak's face started to shimmer. "Yes! Yes, it has been far too long since I was able to share in the link." Immediately, the other Founder approached, and their arms glowed and transformed and blended.

What shall we do now? We cannot yet create more Jem'Hadar, and our forces are weak.

So are the solids. True, our own losses are greater than expected, but they're hardly crippling. The plan is as it ever was.

True. We can instruct the Vorta to have new ships built, ones that can traverse the galaxy at greater speeds. We can reach the Great Link eventually.

And this quadrant is ready to be taken. The Federation and Romulans are weak, the Cardassians are ours, and the Klingons are no longer a factor. Even with reduced forces, we will have this entire quadrant under our domain within a decade.

Yes, the Dominion will prevail. My apologies, I spent so much time in the form of that Klingon, I started to become a blustering fool, much as he is.

There is nothing to apologize for. It is why we take on new forms, to learn and to grow.

Still—I cannot recall the last time a Founder was killed.

Yes. The Jem'Hadar first who killed the renegade has been executed. But nothing will bring our other two fellows back.

It is a dark day.

True. But dark days eventually become the next day. The Dominion has lasted a thousand years because, while we suffer defeats, we are never defeated.

Yes. Solids are finite. We are infinite. We will triumph.

Indeed. Victory is life.

The link broke, and the Founder returned to the form of Dukat. The other Founder, however, took on a human visage. "I believe," the Founder said in a voice that was still deep, but less raspy than that of the general, "that Talak should be considered a casualty of Qo'noS's sun going nova. Our cause would be far better served if I were to replace this human."

The Dukat Founder looked upon the face of Admiral William Ross and said, "I believe you are correct."

Brave New World

Chris Roberson

On one of our first dates, I sat my future wife down and showed her an episode of *Deep Space Nine,* a series she'd not watched before. (It was "The Visitor," for what it's worth.) When it ended, I got up to eject the tape, thinking she'd been very indulgent to sit patiently through the whole thing, and would doubtless now want to watch something else. Instead, she turned to me and said, "Do you have any more?"

We spent the rest of the weekend watching *Trek,* hour upon hour, and I knew then that I would marry her.

This story is dedicated to Allison Baker, my wife and *Star Trek* viewing companion.

Prologue

2336 (Old Calendar)

It was early morning, the sun just beginning to spill across the lowland plains. The colonists were starting their days, heading out to check atmospheric sensors or to collect astronomical data retrieved overnight by automated telescopes or to feed the live specimens in pens at the community's edge. It was a bright spring morning, greeted by the high, trilling songs of brightly colored birds, the only native life-forms larger than insects on Omicron Theta before the arrival of the research colony. Most of the colonists found it difficult not to smile when hearing the high, sweet song of the birds, who seemed a sign of new life and boundless optimism.

Most of the colonists found it difficult. Not all.

"Will those damned things *ever* shut up?!" The man threw a spanner clattering to the floor. "Maybe we should just shoot them all down and serve them for supper, eh?"

"Eat them?" The woman pursed her lips in distaste. "When the replicators can whip up anything we like?" She bent to pick up the spanner and set it back on the bench, beside the still body splayed out before them.

"Why not?" The man gave a sly, humorless smile. "We'd kill two proverbial birds with a single stone, as it were. Or a single phaser, I suppose. We'd be saved their incessant chattering, and we'd get a home-cooked meal in the bargain."

"And who'll be doing this cooking, Noonien?" She raised an eyebrow. "You?"

"Me?" He chuckled, and bent low over the body. "Juliana, my dear, if you married me for my culinary skills, I'm afraid you're getting the short end of the stick." He paused, attempting to twist off a limb from its socket. "Come on, blast you," he growled, gritting his teeth. When the limb came loose with an audible pop, the man fell off balance, sprawling back onto the cold, smooth floor.

"Are you all right?" the woman asked, coming around the side of the table. She reached out a hand, with evident concern; the man didn't take it, but gave her the detached limb instead.

"No," the man said simply, remaining on the ground, his arms resting on his knees. He shook his head, scowling. "No, Juliana, I'm most definitely *not* all right."

"Noonien, dear, you know we've made the right decision." With care, she put the detached limb in the case. "You *know* we have."

"Oh, really?" He pushed himself up onto his feet, wincing somewhat as his joints complained. "I'll tell you what I *do* know, my dear, and it's that this marks the fourth occasion on which we've had to deactivate and disassemble one of my creations, and I'm getting more than a little tired of it."

She gave a slight, sad little smile, and came over to stand beside him. "I know this can't be easy for you." She laid a hand on his shoulder. "It isn't easy for me, either. But you and I agreed that Lore had been acting strangely recently, exhibiting emotional instability and increasing degrees of aggression."

He sighed, and placed a hand over hers. "I know, I know, it's just . . ."

"Just that you thought we had it this time?"

He nodded. "Yes, damn it, I was *sure* we had."

"We were certainly close," she agreed.

The man laid a hand on the body's chest, the golden-hued skin cold under his fingers. "But you know, the others are going to be happy about this, I'm sure."

She smiled. "Oh, at least one person won't be quite so happy about it, I can assure you." He gave her a questioning look. "Tom Handy bet me the cost of a trip to Risa that it would take me at least another month to convince you to deactivate Lore."

He looked up from the body to meet her eyes, and grinned. "He didn't."

She nodded. "Fancy a trip to Risa?"

He walked around the bench, and began detaching another limb from its socket. "We could use the break," he answered with a sigh. "Still, I'll be eager to get back to work."

She arched an eyebrow. "A new project?"

"The same project," he corrected, "only better." He put the limb in the case, and then went back to remove the head, whose face still wore a slightly startled expression. "Next time, we'll hold off introducing emotions to the programming until we're sure the positronic matrix is solid and the behavioral programming is completely in place."

She nodded, thoughtfully. Coming to stand beside him, she took the detached head from him, cradling it in her arms like an infant. "What do you think we'll call the next one? Lore, Mark 2?"

He shook his head. "Data," he corrected. "We'll call him Data. And this one I'm *sure* will work."

She looked at the head in her arms, its features so much like those of her husband, but here twisted into a mask of cold cruelty. "I want to believe you're right, Noonien. I *have* to believe. But let's suppose you are, and that this next android . . . this *Data* . . . functions within normal parameters." She looked up and met his gaze. "What then?"

"Then?" The man smiled, draping an arm around her shoulders. "We'll unveil my creation to the worlds, and the sky itself will be the limit."

1

2378 (Old Calendar)

Jean-Luc Picard hissed in pain as Doctor Dalen Quaice prodded his shoulder with the tip of a finger. As the doctor hummed thoughtfully to himself, Picard managed a weary smile.

"This is all your fault, Doctor," Picard said. "You were the one who insisted I exercise, after all. If it were up to me I'd have been reading a good book with a cup of Earl Grey."

Quaice grunted like a disapproving old man, a sound at odds with his youthful appearance. "I prescribed exercise, Jean-Luc, not torture." He shook his head, reaching for his medical tricorder. "I have never understood the appeal of anbo-jytsu. After a lifetime spent treating the resulting injuries, I'm half-convinced the Federation should ban it altogether as cruel and unusual."

Tactical officer Ro Laren looked on, still wearing her workout fatigues. "It's the best all-around exercise I've found, Doctor. And it has broader applications as a martial art than something less strenuous."

"That's as may be, Commander," Quaice said, running the tricorder over Picard's shoulder and arm. "But exercise won't do him a lick of good if he breaks all his bones in the process."

Picard and his tactical officer had been sparring on the holodecks, employing anbo-jytsu techniques that Picard had learned from his former first officer, before Will Riker left to take command of the *Excalibur*. As usual, Ro had gotten the better of her captain, though Picard was proud at least to have put up a spirited defense this time.

"Remember, Jean-Luc," Quaice said, "you're not as young as you used to be."

Before Picard could answer, Ro let out a short, scoffing laugh. "My father always told me you're only as old as you feel," she said, her arms crossed.

Quaice smiled, and rapped his chest with his knuckles. "Well, I *feel* like a hundred kilos of tripolymer composites, molybdenum-cobalt alloys, and bioplast sheeting, so how old does that make *me?*"

"Old enough to know not to get into arguments with a Bajoran, one hopes," Picard said. As Quaice rummaged on the counter for a hypo, the captain asked, "So what is your diagnosis, Doctor?"

"A few pulled ligaments is all." He pressed the hypo against the captain's shoulder. As the mist spread into his shoulder, Picard could feel the pain and tension fading. "You should be more careful with the roughhousing, Jean-Luc."

Picard shook his head, bemused. The doctor appeared young enough to be his own son, and yet here he was lecturing Picard like a stern grandfather scolding an errant child. Still, the doctor wasn't as old as *he* used to be.

Ro opened her mouth to speak, but was interrupted by the beep of of Picard's combadge. *"Bridge to Picard."*

"Picard here."

"Captain, it's Sito," said *Enterprise*'s ops manager, Sito Jaxa. *"Subspace transmission for you."*

"From Starfleet Command?" The current mission of the *U.S.S. Enterprise*-D was to patrol the edge of the Romulan Neutral Zone. An unexpected communiqué might well be bad news, considering the strained relations between the Federation and her neighbors, with the Cardassians girded for war on one side and the tenuous Klingon-Romulan Alliance perched on the other.

"The message is encrypted according to Starfleet protocols," Sito answered, *"but the source of the transmission has been hidden. It could be*

spoofed." She paused, and Picard fancied that he could almost hear her smile. *"I can crack it open, if you like, sir, and see what's in it."*

"That won't be necessary, Lieutenant," Picard answered, smiling. At times he wasn't quite sure what possessed him to promote two strong-willed Bajoran women to his senior staff, but he never regretted the decision. Both of them had more than proved their worth these past few years. "Pipe it down to sickbay, if you please."

"Aye, Captain."

A moment later, the viewscreen on the far wall blinked to life. The header information indicated that the transmission was a one-way broadcast, in essence a recording. As the message spooled up and decrypted, a Starfleet emblem filling the screen, Picard shouldered back into his uniform jacket, his right arm slightly numbed by the hypo, and went nearer to the wall.

Then the Starfleet emblem winked out, replaced by a very familiar face. Gold-irised eyes looked out from a face with the same yellowish hue shared by all early-generation Soong-type androids, before the techniques to make bioplast look and feel just like human skin were perfected.

The features were the same as those of nearly all those early Soong-types, modeled after their creator, the late Noonien Soong. Picard had never met the man, but couldn't help but imagine that this was an *idealized* self-image of the scientist at a younger age. Based on the holos he'd seen of Soong, bent with age, skin wrinkled, and hands gnarled, Picard found it difficult to accept that the scientist had ever been *that* young, smooth-featured, and tall.

This could have been any one of hundreds of early-generation androids, one of thousands even. But at first glance, Picard knew that it wasn't. There was only one android this could be.

"Data?" he said in a voice so low it was scarcely above a whisper.

"Hello, Captain Picard," the image on the screen said, almost as if in response. *"It has been some time. And now I need your help. Only you can avert a war."*

Not just any android, no. This was Data, the first successful positronic android, champion of android rights, and onetime member of the *Enterprise*'s crew. Data, whom no one on board, Picard included, had seen in years.

A short while later, the senior staff gathered in the conference lounge. Without much in the way of preamble, Picard had Lieu- tenant Sito replay the message in its entirety. The captain glanced around the room, watching the others as they took it in. Some of them, like First Officer Geordi La Forge and Chief Engineer Wesley Crusher, hadn't just served with Data in those early years on board the *Enterprise*-D, but had become quite close with him, one might almost say friends. Flight Controller Sam Lavelle, like Lieutenant Sito, had joined the crew after Data's departure, but still was well familiar with the android's reputation. And Chief Science Officer A. Isaac, who never knew Data in person, obvi- ously had complex feelings about Data's reputation and status.

When the recording ended, Picard toggled the viewscreen to a still image of the golden-skinned android, captured from the transmission. Then he turned to face the others, elbows on the table, fingers steepled.

"Comments?"

"It *is* Data," Ro said, answering the question on everyone's mind. "At least, that's our best guess. The *Enterprise*'s computers have positively identified the android in the transmission, using everything from voice print to retinal scan." Ro had joined the crew long after Data's departure, not long after the Klingon Civil War, when the House of Duras overthrew the High Council with the aid of the Romulan Star Empire. Those had been uncertain times, and Picard had been glad to have the capable young Bajo- ran in his crew. Later, when Worf had left the ship to take a post- ing on a deep space station near Cardassian space, she'd been Picard's first choice for the post of tactical officer. She could still seem distant at times, difficult to reach, but Picard had come to rely on her suspicious nature, which served her well, including now. "It's still possible that the android in the transmission *isn't*

Data, but it would have to be an incredibly detailed and accurate forgery to fool the ship's computer."

"For the moment we'll proceed from the assumption that it *is* Data," Picard said. "If it is, what do we know?"

"Well," said La Forge, shifting uncomfortably in his seat, "I can tell you what we *don't* know." The first officer had been, so far as Picard knew, the closest thing Data had had to a best friend, and the captain thought that Geordi was probably the hardest hit by Data's disappearance. "We don't know where he went, or what he's been doing for the last ten years."

"And not just him," put in Wesley Crusher. The boy . . . the *man* had grown up on board the *Enterprise,* having arrived on board shortly after Picard took command; when Crusher had graduated from Starfleet Academy he'd requested service on her himself. Picard had been proud to have him on the crew, and was prouder still years later to promote him to the head of engineering when the post became available. Even so, Picard found it difficult not to see the boy he had been when looking at the man Crusher had become. "Hundreds of other androids serving in Starfleet resigned their commissions that same day and just disappeared, same as Data."

"It was just after the androids were declared fully sentient and granted citizenship in the Federation," Sito said. Then, after a pause, she added, "With conditions and qualifications, of course."

Picard drew his lips into a tight line. It had been a hard fought battle, but the victory for android rights had been only somewhat marred by those same conditions and qualifications. Androids were no longer property, as they'd been, but if they were citizens, it was of a second-class variety. Still, it was a step forward, and one he was sorry not to have been able to celebrate with Data, one of the prime architects of the movement in the first place.

"Yes," Picard said, thoughtfully, "and if not for Ira Graves's synaptic mapping, and the introduction of uploading into positronic brains, Data and the others might be waiting for their rights still."

He couldn't help glancing in Doctor Quaice's direction, but the doctor's normally expressive face had become unreadable.

"Yeesh," Sam Lavelle said, leaning back in his chair. "I was at the academy when uploading was first released to the public, and I swear that they should have renamed the place the *Ira Graves* Academy, given the amount of time my instructors spent talking about him."

"I'm not sure I like your tone, young man," said Quaice, his voice brittle. Sitting beside each other, the doctor and flight operator looked so near in age that they could have been classmates. "There are some of us who wish Graves had announced synaptic mapping just a short while earlier, if you don't mind. Just a few months and then maybe my wife wouldn't have died unnecessarily—of *old age*—but could have had her consciousness uploaded into a positronic brain, just as I did a few short years later."

Lavelle's cheeks flushed red, and he averted his eyes, mumbling apologies.

Quaice wasn't alone in wishing that the ability to cheat death had been granted to the public a little earlier. The *Enterprise* was filled with people who had lost family, friends, and loved ones in the weeks and months before synaptic mapping was first made available, granting anyone the ability to extend their lives indefinitely, transferring their consciousnesses from their frail organic bodies into nearly indestructible and all but immortal android bodies. Only a few generations ago, in the days that Doctor Roger Corby had met his tragic end, the idea had been anathema. But after a few early adopters underwent the new procedure, and emerged on the other side no less human and in fact all but identical to their earlier selves—only younger, stronger, and healthier—public opinion had gradually shifted. By the time Dalen Quaice had left behind his old, dying body and embraced his new positronic form, opinion was beginning to sway, and within another couple of years most of those early prejudices and preconceptions had fallen away, so that now people regarded a human life extended in an artificial body as no stranger than people once viewed an artificial limb or a wheelchair or even a pair of eyeglasses. They were all simply examples of science improving or extending human existence.

Now, just ten years after the first synaptic mapping, when Ira Graves and Noonien Soong succeeded in conquering death, young people across the Federation had already become so accustomed to the idea that they were almost cavalier about the thought of life continuing in near-indestructible artificial bodies, made virtually immortal through technology.

"Of course," A. Isaac said, speaking for the first time since the recording had finished playback, "Doctor Graves's discovery was significant not only to the humans who benefited directly from the process, but also to the thousands of androids who benefited from the shift in opinion the process engendered."

Picard nodded in Isaac's direction, thoughtfully. If not for the "A" initial Isaac employed, just like most of the androids now serving in Starfleet—A for Android—one would be hard-pressed at first glance to know that the chief science officer was an artificial life-form himself. Though his facial features were virtually identical to those of Data and other early Soong-types, Isaac's coloration and textures were almost indistinguishable from those of an organic human. And Isaac's communications subroutines and behavioral programming allowed him to display a personality more sophisticated, more "human," than many organic officers with whom Picard had served over the years.

"Quite right, Commander," Picard said. "It was the recognition that a human mind in a positronic matrix is still sentient, still capable of free will, that finally forced the Federation Council to extend the definition of sentience to include positronic androids, as well. And our own Mister Data"—he paused, glancing over his shoulder at the familiar image frozen on the screen—"had been arguing for android rights for years before that, and was at the forefront of the final debate."

Before the landmark decision by the Federation Council, androids had been legally classified as property; though they wore

Starfleet uniforms, the thousands of androids who served on board Federation starships were not officers in the strictest sense, but functionaries. On the day the Federation recognized the sentience of androids and granted them full citizenship, hundreds of androids resigned their commissions in Starfleet and disappeared, chief among them Data himself.

"But why?" Lavelle asked. "Why did they leave after getting everything they wanted?"

Picard cleared his throat, trying to phrase a politic answer, but Isaac responded first.

"Perhaps, Lieutenant, it has something to do with the fact that they did *not* get everything they wanted."

Picard nodded thoughtfully. "To pass the resolution, certain . . . concessions had to be made to the more reactionary elements of the council, those who felt that the unrestricted proliferation of artificial life posed a danger."

"As if a few new androids would push humanity to extinction!" La Forge said heatedly.

"To be fair, Commander, it would hardly be simply a 'few new androids,'" Isaac corrected, playing devil's advocate. "The material components of an artificial body such as mine could be obtained without particular difficulty, and assembly time would take no longer than . . ."

"Enough," Picard interrupted, raising a hand to silence the android. "Whatever the merits of those fears, the simple fact remains that androids were not granted *full* rights, but were invested as what might uncharitably be called 'second-class citizens.' Most significantly, the creation of new artificial life was deemed not to rise to the standard of 'reproduction,' which is a right guaranteed by charter to all Federation citizens, and the ability to create . . . to *manufacture* . . . new artificial life was restricted to Federation-approved facilities like the Daystrom Institute."

"I always thought that was the reason for their disappearance," Crusher said. "I know my mother does, too."

It had been some years since Beverly Crusher had left the

Enterprise for a posting in Starfleet Medical, but at times like this Picard missed her counsel. Beverly always seemed to think with her heart as much as with her head, and as someone who had a propensity for being altogether too cerebral, it was a quality Picard admired.

"Be that as it may," Picard said, "the fact remains that, from that moment, a little more than ten years ago, no one has heard from Data or any of the other missing androids. Until today."

"So are you going to do it?" La Forge asked, his eyebrow arched in a quizzical expression. Once that look might have been hidden by his clunky VISOR, but since La Forge had gotten his new ocular implants, the first officer had seemed far more expressive. If not for the fact that La Forge's eyes appeared to be pools of mercury, silvery and reflective, his implants might not even be noticeable. "And what does he mean about 'averting a war'?"

Picard forced himself to watch the transmission a second time in sickbay before allowing himself to believe it: a message from the void, a voice and a face from the past. Data, into whose hands Picard had placed the lives of everyone on board the *Enterprise* on several occasions, had disappeared without warning, without apology, without a trace, and was now inviting Picard to break the already tenuous treaty with the Romulans. It was not so much an invitation; Data was *pleading,* urging Picard to venture deep into the Neutral Zone to the coordinates he provided, for reasons Data could not, or would not, reveal. If Picard did not come, war would be the inevitable consequence. But war between whom? And why?

"Starfleet Command won't be happy about a treaty violation," Ro said, her expression grim.

"Starfleet Command *isn't* happy about it," Picard answered with a slight smile, "but they want us to proceed, regardless."

The captain was tempted to pause, to savor the spectrum of confused expressions directed his way, but there simply wasn't time.

"I've already been in subspace contact with Earth and received Starfleet Command's authorization to proceed." The others exchanged looks, some knowing, others less so. "I delayed giving the order until I was confident that I knew what we were getting into. I don't have to tell you the state of our relations with the Klingon–Romulan Alliance. I can't help but think that the Neutral Zone is the proverbial powder keg, and I have *no* intention of providing the spark. But if this"—he jerked a thumb over his shoulder, indicating the screen—"is our erstwhile shipmate Data, I for one would very much like to meet with him. I have a few questions I'd like answered, and I'm sure many of you do, too."

Picard pushed back from the table and stood. Then, tugging down the front of his jacket in his characteristic mannerism, he straightened. "Mister Lavelle, plot a course to the coordinates provided in the transmission."

"Aye, sir," Lavelle answered, rising to his feet.

"Lieutenant Sito," Picard continued, "send a coded response to the transmission, as instructed, informing Data—or whomever it is—that we are on our way. The rest of you are dismissed."

2

As soon as Wesley Crusher stepped off the turbolift on deck 36, he knew that something was wrong, and by the time he reached the heart of main engineering, he was sure he knew what it was.

"Ensign," he called to one of the members of the duty shift. "Get a team to check on the reactant injectors. Sounds like the matter-antimatter mix is a little off."

The young ensign glanced at the nearest control panel. "Sir? The mix reads as being within tolerances."

Crusher smiled patiently and nodded. The ensign was relatively new to the crew, and hadn't yet gotten used to her chief's eccentricities. "Trust me, Ensign. It's off."

He didn't bother explaining that he was certain because he had *heard* it. The other members of the duty shift would probably explain it to her, or she'd figure out Crusher's style sooner or later. Attempting to explain it now would simply delay matters, and Crusher knew the captain would be eager to leave for their mysterious destination as soon as possible. Besides, to him it was intuitively obvious that the hum of the warp-core reactor was pitched too high into the treble range by at least a few dozen hertz.

Sure enough, the repair crew found that the matter reactant injector was acting up, and it was the work of just a few minutes to get it fixed, such that when Picard called down from the bridge for warp five, engineering was ready and able to supply it. Crusher was only grateful that it hadn't been the *anti*matter injector that was the culprit, as he had *no* desire to recalibrate the magnetic fields that isolated the antideuterium from the normal matter surrounding it.

Once they were under way, Crusher slid out a seat and called up his most current project on the console. He had been tinkering with some warp field equations for the last few weeks, trying to increase the engine's efficiency. He'd already managed to improve on the Starfleet specs for a *Galaxy*-class starship by a considerable margin, but he was sure there was still room left for improvement. He was halfway through tweaking the equations and testing the results in simulation when he heard the characteristic footfalls of the ship's science officer. One of the benefits of having lived on board the same ship for so long, first as a civilian, then as a member of the crew, was that Crusher nearly always knew who was coming up behind him just by the sound of their steps.

"You just going to stand there all morning?" he finally said, freezing his simulation and swiveling the chair.

"My apologies, Wesley, I did not want to intrude." A. Isaac stood a few feet behind him, arms held loosely at his sides, expression neutral.

"No problem, Isaac," Crusher answered with a smile. "This isn't anything that can't wait." He tapped the console, saving the simulation and returning the display to defaults. "What's up?"

The android glanced up at the bulkheads, and smiled. "If I were to say 'the ceiling,' would that engender laughter?"

Crusher chuckled, shaking his head. "Only of the charitable sort, Isaac." He stood. "Not really very funny."

Isaac frowned slightly. "Ah." He brightened fractionally. "But it *was* humorous, if only slightly?"

"Very slightly."

The android nodded, thoughtfully, his gaze dropping to the deck.

Most of the other members of the crew might have taken Isaac's expression as unremarkable, but then most members of the crew didn't have Crusher's experience with android physiognomy and programming. As the ship's chief engineer, Crusher was responsible for doing any maintenance or repairs to Isaac's android body, as well as assisting Isaac in performing software diagnostics. It was, perhaps, one of the reasons that Isaac seemed to have developed such a strong bond of friendship with Crusher, much like the bond Crusher remembered the former chief engineer and the ship's erstwhile ops manager sharing. Thinking of La Forge and Data, Crusher wondered how *he* would feel if Isaac, whom he saw not only as a colleague but also as a friend, were to disappear one day, suddenly and without any warning, only to turn up ten years later out of the blue.

"What's bothering you, Isaac?"

Isaac tilted his head with an eyebrow raised, lips pursed. It was a characteristic gesture, the result of overlapping programming imperatives, which Crusher recognized as signifying surprise commingled with a touch of admiration.

"Wesley, your ability to intuit android emotions is intriguing. Still, I cannot help but think that I am wrong to be continually surprised by it. After all, you grasp scientific concepts that elude most of the other crewmen, even those organics in the science department under my command. I often find that, if I wish to engage in pleasant conversation about topics that interest me, rather than simply employing small talk as I most often do, you are my only viable alternative. Short of conjuring simulations of historical figures on the holodeck, I suppose."

"Isaac?" Crusher interrupted, with an indulgent smile. "You're rambling again." It was a habit of the android's that Crusher had noticed many times: a propensity to go on at length about trivia rather than tackle the matter at hand.

"Ah." Isaac tilted his head in the other direction, his eyes shifting down and to the right, as though he were reading unseen text. "So I am. My apologies, Wesley."

"You were about to tell me what's bothering you, perhaps?"

Isaac nodded. "That was my intention. I find that I am . . . uncertain . . . about our current mission."

Crusher crossed his arms, giving Isaac a thoughtful look. "Uncertain?"

The android paused for a moment. "As you know, I was not yet activated when Data and the other androids disappeared, though the early stages of my physical construction had already begun. When I woke to full awareness at the Daystrom Institute the following year, I was immediately recognized as a sentient being, with all of the rights and privileges of a Federation citizen." He opened his mouth to continue, then paused thoughtfully. "*Nearly* all the rights and privileges, I suppose I should say. Even so, I never had firsthand experience with the kind of society in which Data and the others lived all those years. When I opted to enter Starfleet Academy, it was *my* decision, freely made, not a role assigned to me as a piece of property, as it had been when Data and those like him had been sent there."

"Well," Crusher said, chuckling ruefully, "the *other* difference is that those early positronic androids like Data had to suffer through four years at the academy, just like us organics."

Isaac gave him a quizzical look. "Why should I have been expected to attend four years at the academy, when the base instruction of a Starfleet cadet had been incorporated into my original programming?"

Crusher shook his head. "Fast-tracked through the academy in only a year. I don't think I'll ever really forgive you for getting to skip Quantum Chemistry." He thought back to those late-night cram sessions, and cringed. "I'm sorry, you were talking about Data?"

"Yes." Isaac opened his mouth, closed it, and opened it again before continuing. "I have always been intrigued by the mystery of the missing androids. I have spoken with older-generation Soong-types over the years, about Data and the others, but have never gotten a satisfactory answer. It is almost as if those who were in active service when Data and the others disappeared, but who remained behind at their posts, are actively hiding something."

"Even from their younger siblings like you?"

Isaac nodded. "I have always suspected that the older Soong-types know more about the disappearance than they are telling."

"Mmm." Crusher rubbed his chin. "Maybe it's not that they *won't* tell you anything. Perhaps it's that they *can't*." Then, in response to Isaac's quizzical look, he explained. "Imagine that there was a bit of memory stored in your positronic matrix that you didn't want ever to reveal. Couldn't you simply write a new heuristic algorithm prohibiting yourself from calling up that memory and communicating it? A new bit of restrictive programming?"

Isaac was thoughtful. "It *is* possible," he allowed. "But what would be the purpose of such a restriction?"

Crusher smiled. "Come on, Isaac, haven't you ever heard of keeping secrets? Maybe the other androids knew about the disappearances, but didn't want to run the risk of ever revealing anything. But if that's the case . . . what could be the big secret?"

"It is precisely *that* about which I am uncertain."

Crusher's smile faded, as he gave the android an appraising look. "Is it? Or is it just that you're nervous about the possibility of meeting Data?"

Isaac's expression suggested the android equivalent of confusion. "Why should that possibility make me nervous?"

"Come on, Isaac. It would be like me getting to meet Einstein or Cochrane. For all your life, you've heard about Data, the first of your kind. It would be *impossible* for you not to feel at least a *little* intimidated about meeting him."

Isaac's eyes flicked down and to the right, a reflective gesture. "I suppose it *is* possible."

"You *shouldn't* worry, though," Crusher said, stepping forward and putting a hand on his shoulder. "You're a fine officer, and a terrific scientist . . . even if you do tend to cheat at poker." Isaac opened his mouth to object, but Crusher plowed ahead with a smile. "Data may be something like a grandfather to you, or a much older sibling at least, but that just means he'll be all the more proud of you. Trust me. After all, I knew him. He's going to *love* you."

"Who's going to love whom?"

Crusher and Isaac turned to see Doctor Quaice entering main engineering, an easy smile on his face.

"Isaac's worried about making a good impression on Data," Crusher answered.

"I am not worried about . . ." Isaac began, then broke off. He nodded, reluctantly. "I *am,* perhaps, somewhat concerned. Data is, as Wesley has pointed out, something like a grandfather to me."

"Well, there you are, then." Quaice came over to stand beside them. "What grandparent doesn't love their grandchildren? Of course, one of my grandsons—daughter's oldest boy, she named him Patrick after my late wife—can't seem to get used to the fact that his own grandfather looks the same age as him, these days, so I suppose that unconditional love isn't always a two-way street." He mused, somewhat pensive for a moment, then turned his attention to Crusher. "Well, have you time for my regular checkup, or should I come back later?"

Crusher couldn't help but notice the somewhat sour expression on Quaice's face when asking the question. He understood completely. Having spent a lifetime in the practice of healing others, the doctor now found himself lacking the expertise to mend his own artificial body. Standing with Isaac and Quaice, the two people to whom he felt closest among the crew, Crusher was reminded as always how looks could be deceiving. At first glance, the three of them looked near enough in age, based on physical appearance alone, that they could have all graduated from the academy together. And yet Quaice had been born when Jim Kirk was still in command of the earlier *Enterprise,* Crusher himself had been born while the Federation–Cardassian border conflicts still raged, and Isaac had been born little more than nine years before.

"Certainly, Doctor," Crusher said, motioning toward the diagnostic bay at the rear of main engineering.

"Please, Wesley, if I've told you once I've told you a thousand times, call me Dalen."

Crusher shook his head, sheepishly. If Data was a grandfather to Isaac, Crusher wasn't sure what that made Quaice to him, but his earliest memories were of his mother taking him to visit her mentor and friend. Quaice had already been an old man then, positively ancient in the eyes of the young Wesley Crusher, with his bristling white mustache and snow-white hair, eyes bright in a face lined with wrinkles. Crusher hadn't seen him for years after that, not until he joined the crew of the *Enterprise,* after Crusher's mother went off to Starfleet Medical; by then, Quaice had traded in his old body for a new one, a body that lacked not only the snow-white hair and mustache and wrinkles, but also the ills and infirmities to which human bodies were prone. Despite the youthfulness of this new body, his eyes were just as bright, his smiles easy and frequent, and Crusher could still see echoes of the old man his mother had loved like a father.

"No, Doctor Quaice," Crusher answered, trying not to sound like a child again, "I don't think I could *ever* do that."

Sito Jaxa sat in Ten Forward, drinking a cup of iced *raktajino* and watching the stars blur by through the viewports. She was technically off-duty, but as ops manager she had the discretion to pull rank on the ensign who relieved her, and take back her post when they reached their destination. And since she wasn't about to lounge around in her quarters when the *Enterprise* dropped out of warp deep in the Neutral Zone, Ensign Kelly was about to get an unexpected break. But having already been on duty for a full rotation, if Sito wanted to keep alert, she was going to need a boost—hence the *raktajino.*

Still, it was *boring* just sitting and watching the stars red-shift by. If there had been anyone around she might have opted for a game of Terrace, or maybe chess, but it seemed that warping into the Neutral Zone wasn't everyone's idea of a good time, so Ten Forward was all but deserted. She was half tempted to page Sam Lavelle, who was always up for a bit of fun; but there was always the chance that Lavelle might misinterpret her intentions, reading too much into an invitation to join her for a cup of *raktajino*. They'd dated for a short while, and it had ended amiably enough, but there was always some tension between them, a kind of expectation that something might at any moment go wrong.

Alyssa Ogawa was always up for a cup and a chat, but she was working her shift in sickbay, and it wouldn't do for a head nurse to abandon her post just to relax in the rec facility with an old friend.

There was always Wesley Crusher, of course—one of her oldest friends in Starfleet—but these days he seldom strayed far from main engineering, and he'd never really developed a taste for *raktajino* anyway.

These were the pressures of leadership, Sito thought with a smile, the price of success. She and all her old friends, all of them who had started out together on the *Enterprise,* had risen together through the ranks, and unlike a few, like Taurik, who had taken transfers to other vessels, most of them still served under Captain Picard. The only difference was that instead of being junior officers with time on their hands, they were senior staff and department heads with hardly any free time at all.

Sito sipped her iced *raktajino*, remembering more carefree days.

"Is this seat taken?"

Sito was so startled she nearly spit out a mouthful of liquid all over the ship's tactical officer, which would *not* have been a good idea.

"N-no," she sputtered, coughing after inhaling more *raktajino* than was probably advisable. She regained her composure somewhat and tried again. "No, Commander Ro, have a seat."

Ro set her own cup down on the table, pulled the chair out and turned it around, straddling it with her arms resting on the chairback. The movement was a familiar one, but it took Sito a moment to remember where she'd first seen it. It was exactly the way Will Riker used to sit on a chair. She hid a smile, remembering the friction between the former first officer and a somewhat younger Ro Laren. The two had never gotten along, it had seemed, and yet Riker had taken an interest in Ro's career, and had served as something of a mentor to her, for all that Ro seemed to actively dislike him. Still, Sito and the others'd had a pool running for months, wagering over whether Ro and the first officer would ever break the ice between them and find themselves in an unexpected romantic encounter.

So far as Sito knew, no one had ever won the bet. But seeing Ro sitting across from her now, she wondered just what the tactical officer thought about the officer who had ridden her so hard for so many years, always pushing her to do her best, and then to do better still. Clearly, *something* had worked to make Ro an exemplary officer.

"You're drinking *raktajino*," Ro observed, glancing at Sito's nearly empty cup.

Sito looked down, then back up, and shrugged. "Yes, I suppose I am."

"Hmph." Ro made an indistinct noise. "I didn't know there were many others onboard who enjoyed it."

Sito took a sip. "I first had it on a stopover at Deep Space 9, during a visit to Bajor. The station's liaison officer introduced me to it. I'd never had Klingon coffee before then, but after a few days of it, I was *hooked*."

Ro nodded. "I picked it up in Advanced Tactical Training myself. One of my classmates had served aboard a Klingon vessel in an officer exchange program, and came back with a taste for all things Klingon. The *raktajino* I could get behind. The *gagh?* Not so much."

Sito pulled a face. "Ooo, I just saw a plate of it once and that was enough for me."

The tactical officer gave her an appraising look.

"Commander," Sito said, somewhat confused, "is there something you wanted to ask me?" The two of them, the only Bajorans on the *Enterprise*—and, in fact, among the relatively few in Starfleet altogether—had never been close. They hadn't been what one might call friends, and Sito figured that she had probably spent less time talking to Ro than any other member of the senior staff, the captain included.

"Well, Lieutenant . . ." Ro began.

"Please," Sito interrupted, "call me Jaxa."

An awkward smile quirked the corners of Ro's mouth. "Jaxa." Her expression was uncomfortable, and it occurred to Sito that Ro really wasn't friendly with *anyone,* and that casual conversation was probably not something covered in Advanced Tactical Training. "And you can call me . . . you can call me Ro."

Sito grinned. "Okay, Ro." It was probably a big step for the tactical officer. Sito couldn't imagine what it would take for Ro to allow anyone to address her as Laren.

"Jaxa, I wanted to ask you about Bajor."

"Bajor?" Sito raised an eyebrow.

"I have a cousin, whom I've not seen since my family and I fled during the occupation. She writes to tell me that she's about to have her first child, a daughter, and that she . . . well, she plans to name her Laren."

Sito's mouth opened and she almost gasped.

"After me," Ro explained, unnecessarily.

"Of *course,*" Sito said. "That's so wonderful, Ro. You must be so proud." Family was a big part of Bajoran culture, and the birth of a child an extremely special and cherished event. To have a child named in one's honor was an act of great respect.

"Well," Ro said, shifting uncomfortably. "They have invited me to come for the naming ceremony." She paused. "On Bajor."

Sito tilted her head to one side. "I'm not sure I see the problem."

"The problem . . ." She broke off, and gave a ragged sigh. "The *problem* is that I haven't been back to Bajor, not since I was . . . Well, not since I was a lot younger. And to be honest, I haven't *wanted* to go back. Too many painful memories, none of which I have any interest in revisiting."

Sito nodded, wearing a sympathetic expression. "I understand. It was . . . difficult for me to go back, too."

Ro leaned forward, hands wrapped tightly about her mug.

"That's what I wanted to ask you about. How was it? Going back? Was Bajor . . ." She averted her eyes. "I've heard horror stories about what the Cardassians did to the planet during the final years of the occupation, the ravages to the landscape."

For a moment, Sito closed her eyes and saw it again, as if it were before her. "Oh, Ro, no, no. I mean, there was damage, to be sure, but if you could *see* the way that the planet has already begun to heal itself. And the people! How they have begun to heal, too. I mean, you can still see the scars beneath the surface, but it's becoming a living world, a *thriving* world." She paused, and tentatively reached out to place a hand over Ro's. "But you *have* to go. A niece? Named in your honor? How *exciting* that must be, especially considering . . ."

Sito trailed off, but gestured around them, a single motion taking in the rest of Ten Forward, the whole of the *Enterprise,* and the cold void of vacuum beyond. The message was simple: Few officers in Starfleet chose to start families in the field.

Ro nodded, thoughtfully. "It's not as if I haven't *thought* about having children," she said in a quiet voice. "It just isn't something that I've placed any real priority on."

With a somewhat weary smile, Sito nodded. "I know what you mean." She paused, lost in thought. "What must it have been like for Data and the others, though, to be told that they *couldn't* have children, whether they wanted to or not? That the *law* prohibited them from reproducing?"

Ro sneered. "Sounds like something the Cardassians would have done." When Ro said the name, it was a curse.

Sito drained the rest of her cup. "Not exactly one of the high ideals that I joined Starfleet to protect."

"No," Ro said, finishing her own cup and pushing away from the table. "It really isn't, is it?"

As they stood and headed toward the door, Sito turned to Ro. "You know, if you decide to make the trip to Bajor, let me know. I'd love to visit again, and that trip is much too long to take by yourself."

Ro was clearly taken aback. "Travel . . . together? With me?"

Sito grinned, and shrugged. "Why not? We Bajoran girls have to stick together, don't we?"

"You wanted to see me, Captain?" La Forge stood in the open doorway of the captain's ready room, hand resting on the jamb.

"Ah yes, Number One, come in." Picard waved him in, glancing up from the computer screen. There were a handful of padds scattered on his desk, and a steaming cup of Earl Grey by his elbow.

La Forge slid into the chair opposite the Captain and leaned back, crossing one leg over the other. "I assume this isn't about those crew performance evaluations I sent you?" he said with a slight smile.

Picard shook his head, wearing a sad smile of his own. "I wanted to talk with you about Data."

The first officer gave a weary sigh. "That's a name I wasn't expecting to hear again for a long while, Captain, I can tell you that. After you showed us that recording, you could have knocked me over with a feather."

"Yes, and don't think you were the only one. Still, I imagine that this might be more . . . difficult for you than it is for the others."

La Forge pursed his lips thoughtfully. "Captain?"

Picard leaned forward, his elbows resting on the desk. "Geordi, you've served on the *Enterprise* almost as long as I have. It has been my observation that you are the kind of man who makes acquaintances with some ease, and who tends to work extremely well with others, but that you are *not* the kind of man who makes friends easily. In the time that I have known you I have seen you develop what one might call strong bonds with only a handful of others. Worf, perhaps? Riker, to some extent. And most definitely with Data." The captain paused, raising an eyebrow. "You'll forgive me for speaking candidly, but does this seem an unfair assessment?"

La Forge let out a breath through pursed lips. He wasn't sure what he'd been expecting when summoned to the captain's ready room, but it wasn't a close scrutiny of his personal habits. Even so, he had to admit that the captain wasn't wrong. "No, sir. That doesn't sound unfair." He nodded. "I think you could say that Data was a friend. Was probably my *best* friend, for that matter."

Picard was thoughtful. "You know, when Deanna was still on board, I often called on her to gauge the emotional states of the crew, and occasionally of the senior staff themselves. But since she went to serve on the *Excalibur* with Will, I haven't had a counselor that I can call on in quite that way. So you'll have to forgive me for being so blunt, but I must know. Are you emotionally prepared for this coming mission?"

"Captain?" La Forge sat upright. "It isn't like I was abandoned by a spouse or anything like that. We were just friends."

Picard shook his head. "Of course not. You were simply friends, as you say—two individuals who worked together for years, developing deep bonds of trust and friendship, and then one day Data simply left, without warning, explanation, or apology." He took a deep breath through his nostrils, held it, and let it out. "Geordi, it isn't an admission of weakness to say that you felt betrayed by one of your closest friends, nor to admit that there was an emotional component to that reaction. I'm simply asking you whether your personal feelings in this matter will interfere with your ability to carry out your duties."

La Forge straightened. "No, sir." He shook his head. "I'd like to get an explanation . . ."

"As would we all," Picard put in.

"But beyond that it's water under the bridge, sir. I'm a Starfleet officer with a job to do. The fact that my feelings may or may not have been bruised a decade ago is immaterial."

Picard nodded. "That's what I wanted to hear." He paused, and added, "Of course, there is always the possibility that it is *not* Data that we are traveling to meet, but rather some impostor."

La Forge shook his head, his jaw set. "No, sir. It *is* Data; I'm sure of that."

· · ·

A. Isaac stood at his station on the bridge, reviewing what they knew about their destination. Detailed information about the depths of the Romulan Neutral Zone was somewhat rare, given the provisions in place for so many years restricting Starfleet's ability to venture within. Long-range scanners had been employed, of course, gathering what information they could about the systems within the zone, but there were limits to the kind of information long-range scans could provide. Infrared spectroscopy could tell a lot about the elemental makeup of a star, for example, but while gravitational microlensing could help identify the mass and position of planets, moons, and other satellites, it did nothing to specify whether a world was inhabited, much less to which planetary classification it belonged. Unless a planetary culture were bleeding electromagnetic radiation out into the void, as Earth had done for so many centuries in the form of television and radio waves, it could easily go unnoticed at a distance of only a few light-years. That was the purpose of planetary surveys, to seek out new life and new civilizations that would otherwise remain hidden. But with no planetary surveys in the Neutral Zone, there was a considerable amount that could remain hidden.

All that was known about their destination was that it was a planetary system surrounding a main sequence G-type star. There was nothing in Starfleet's records about any of the handful of planets in the system, and in fact nothing worth noting about any of the other solar systems in a radius of several light-years.

Why Data had requested that Captain Picard come to these particular coordinates was a question Isaac was unable to answer.

That did not mean, however, that Picard shrank from repeating the question.

"Report, Mister Isaac."

"Nothing substantial, Captain," Isaac responded, turning away from his station and stepping nearer the railing, better to address the captain in his seat below. "There is no record of either Romulan or Federation activity in this system, or of any other intelligent activity, for that matter. And long-range scans show nothing remarkable about its physical properties."

"Any guesses about what might be waiting for us out there?" La Forge asked from the first officer's chair, sitting at Picard's right.

"Guesses, sir?" Isaac asked, cocking an eyebrow.

"Conjectures," Picard replied, "theories, hypotheses?"

Isaac shook his head, somewhat perplexed. "Hypotheses are based on observation, and in the absence of data I do not see how hypothesizing would be productive."

La Forge chuckled, darkly, his silvery eyes half-lidded. " 'In the absence of Data . . .' "

"Yes, quite," Picard said. He pursed his lips, taking a deep breath in through his nostrils and letting it out. Then he nodded, as though having reached some decision. "Very well, Mister Isaac. Keep monitoring long-range scans."

"Aye, Captain."

From the forward part of the bridge, Flight Controller Sam Lavelle glanced back over his shoulder, his hands still resting on the controls. "Captain? We're coming up on those coordinates."

"Prepare to drop out of warp," Picard said.

A few moments later, Isaac could almost feel the slight lurch as the inertial dampeners compensated for the reinsertion into normal space, and the forward viewscreen went from displaying streaks of red-shifted light to a static starfield.

Proximity alarms on Isaac's console began blinking almost immediately, but before he could respond Tactical Officer Ro had noticed and taken charge.

"Sensors are detecting a ship in orbit above the second planet, Captain," Ro called out in clipped tones, hunched over the tactical displays. She looked up, lips drawn into a tight line. "It's Romulan."

"Red alert," Picard replied, automatically.

Isaac scanned the information scrolling up his display, faster than a human eye could follow. "It appears to be a 'wardrone,'

Captain. A warbird modified for automation, unmanned and governed by a crude approximation of a positronic matrix." He looked up from his display, turning toward the captain's chair. "It appears to be derelict."

"Commander Ro," Picard said, half turning in his seat, "hail the Romulan vessel."

Ro opened her mouth to reply, but before she did she was interrupted by a voice from the far side of the bridge.

"I do not think that would be a wise course of action, Captain."

Isaac's responses were quicker by orders of magnitude than any of the organic officers on the bridge, so he was the first one to lay eyes on the figure standing a few short meters away: an early Soong-type android, dressed in a simple tunic and pants, a faint smile on his face.

If Isaac was the first to see the newcomer, though, La Forge was the first to respond.

"Data?"

The android's smile broadened. "Hello, Geordi. It has been a long time."

3

Geordi La Forge sat with his arms crossed over his chest. He was sure that he was probably scowling, but just as sure that he didn't care.

He and the rest of the senior staff were seated around the table in the observation lounge, with Picard at one end and Data at the other. It was almost like old times, having Data back here in the conference room, all of them gathered together to solve some puzzle or other. Almost, but not quite. Because, unlike those fondly remembered old days, this time *Data* was the puzzle to be solved.

"Do you mind, Data, explaining just how it is that you managed to get aboard?"

La Forge noted that Picard didn't call him *Mister* Data, just Data.

"*With* our shields raised, Captain," Ro put in, eyes narrowed suspiciously. "But even if they hadn't been, ship's sensors should have detected the beam-in."

"But I did *not* beam in, Commander Ro," Data said, his voice quiet and calm. "At least, not in any way that you would understand."

"Just what is *that* supposed to mean?" Ro leaned forward in her seat in an aggressive posture.

Data shook his head. "No insult intended, Commander. I simply mean that the technology involved is beyond the Federation's grasp at this stage."

"What technology?" Lieutenant Crusher asked.

"Precisely *my* question," Picard said, leaning back, his fingers laced atop the table's surface. "I believe, Data, that we are still waiting for an explanation. Why are we here, *how* are you here, and what is this all about?"

Data nodded, lifting his hands in a gesture of apology. "Tell me, Captain, do you recall the legends of the Iconians?"

La Forge raised an eyebrow. *Iconians?* Why was Data bringing up ancient mythology?

"Of course," Picard replied. "I studied them under Richard Galen at the academy." La Forge saw a faint smile tug the corners of the captain's mouth, and remembered him saying on many occasions that, if he were not in command of a starship, there was nowhere he'd rather be than at an archaeological dig with spade in hand. La Forge felt that archaeology had lost out when a young Jean-Luc Picard had opted to join Starfleet.

At La Forge's side, Commander Isaac's head tilted to one side, his eyes taking on the thousand-meter stare of an android consulting his internal memory banks.

"An interstellar civilization that vanished two hundred thousand years ago," Isaac said after a brief moment, "said to have the ability to appear on distant planets without the aid of starships."

"Quite right," Picard said, nodding. Then, in a somewhat quieter voice, he said, "Demons of Air and Darkness, the legends called them."

Data glanced in Isaac's direction appraisingly before answering. "The current occupants of the second planet, of which I am one, have named it Turing. It has been, these last ten years, a refuge for androids, a planet-sized laboratory dedicated to exploring the limits of artificial life. But the planet was not chosen by accident. The year before I left the Federation, an archaeological expedition on Denius III unearthed a star map that appeared to point the way to a forgotten starfaring empire. A Soong-type android with whom I was in communication was on the expedition and alerted me to the findings. I was able to identify the markings on the map as Iconian in origin, and the map then led me here."

"Do you mean to suggest . . ." Picard began, and paused in disbelief. "To suggest that this is Iconia?"

"I do more than suggest it, Captain," Data said. "I can prove it. My colleagues and I had reasoned that there might well be a technological basis for the legend about 'demons of air and darkness,' and that, if there were, that technology could be rediscovered and used to aid in our quest."

"Wait a minute," Crusher said, shaking his head. "You expect us to believe you found functioning technology from a civilization that vanished nearly a quarter of a million years ago?"

Data glanced in his direction. "My presence on the *Enterprise* is proof that we did, Wesley. As is the Romulan wardrone, rendered inactive by an Iconian software virus."

"Captain! That's impossible . . ." Lieutenant Sito began to object, but Picard silenced her with a quick glance and a raised hand.

"Data, your claims about the Iconians and their technology are intriguing, to be sure, but there are more pressing matters of interest before us. Such as what you and the rest of the missing androids have been doing out here all this time. To say nothing of what you meant when you said that only I could avert a war."

Data nodded, hands rested palms down on the table before him. "It has been a little less than twenty-four hours since the Romulan wardrone, on a routine patrol of the Neutral Zone, chanced upon Turing and discovered our presence."

"That's a violation of treaty," Ro objected, "sending probes into the Neutral Zone."

"Yes," Data allowed. "But I doubt that raising that objection will much affect the Romulans' course of action, should they discover the existence of Turing's android population."

"I thought you said the wardrone discovered you yesterday?" Doctor Quaice said.

"Discovered us, yes," Data said, nodding. "But the consensus of the Turing population was that the wardrone should be incapacitated before it could relay news of that discovery back to

Romulus. It was regrettable, since we know that the wardrone is not responsible for its own actions in any pure sense, rendered all but a slave by its programming, but there was no viable alternative. We employed the Iconian software virus that was part of the planet's original defense system, which we disabled and reprogrammed for our purposes shortly after arriving on the planet ten years ago."

"What does it do?" Sito asked.

"It is an information transfer," Data explained, "utilizing a small probe that downloads intrusive code into a target's computer systems. Once in place the code begins rewriting the computer's software, impairing operation. This particular transfer had been specifically coded for Romulan systems, and so was able to take out the wardrone's communication capabilities in a matter of nanoseconds."

"So the Romulans don't know you're out here, then?" Sam Lavelle asked.

"Not as yet, Lieutenant," Data said, "but sources within the Klingon-Romulan Alliance report that, once contact with the wardrone was lost, another ship was sent out in search of it, which is due to arrive in short order."

"Sources?" Picard repeated, suspiciously.

Data opened his mouth as though to answer, appeared to think better of it, then shut it again. "A discussion for another time, Captain."

La Forge had been sitting back, scowling with his arms crossed and with mounting frustration, waiting for anyone to ask the question he was burning to have answered. But instead they were all going on about software viruses and ancient civilizations.

"Look," La Forge said, pounding his fist on the table, "I still don't understand why you *disappeared* in the first place!" He realized he was shouting, but didn't care. Seeing Data again after all this time brought back the feelings of betrayal he'd experienced all those years ago. "You say you were on some quest. A quest for what? Just what are you *doing* down there, anyway?"

Data looked at him, head cocked, lips pursed in that familiar expression of confusion. "I thought I had already explained that, Geordi. We are attempting to explore the limits of artificial life, free from unnecessary constraints."

La Forge glanced around the room, and saw that he wasn't the only one either confused or dissatisfied or both by that answer. And he knew that Data could see it as well.

"Captain, Geordi, all of you," Data said, glancing around the table, "if you come with me to the planet's surface I can show you. Then maybe you will agree that what we have built there is worth saving."

Isaac stood at the door to the captain's ready room.

"Come," came Picard's voice from the other side, and the door hissed open obligingly.

"Captain?" Isaac stepped inside. "Do you have a moment?"

Picard stood by his desk, preparing to beam down to the planet's surface. At the conclusion of their meeting in the observation lounge, only a short while before, Data had simply stood up from his chair, walked to the far wall, and then waited while a doorway suddenly materialized in thin air. Beyond the rectangular space, which seemed cut into the fabric of space-time itself, Isaac had seen a brightly lit room with stone walls and unfathomable machinery. Data had paused at the threshold, repeating his invitation to Picard and the others to accompany him through the gateway, but Picard had insisted that the away team use the *Enterprise* transporters instead.

In a few minutes' time, the away team was to convene in the transporter room, but in the meantime, Isaac had concerns he felt compelled to voice.

"Certainly, Mister Isaac, have a seat." Picard motioned to the couch along the wall, and came over to sit down himself. "What is it you wanted to discuss?"

Isaac sat down, but was silent for a moment, trying to find a way to frame his thoughts.

Picard studied Isaac's expression. "Is something troubling you, Commander?"

"Yes, Captain," Isaac finally allowed. "It regards the news of this android refuge, and what Data has told us about his activities these past ten years."

"Yes?"

"I have . . ." Isaac searched for the correct term. "Concerns," he finally finished, "about my own reactions."

"Oh, I see." Picard nodded, thoughtfully. "Do you care to share them?"

Isaac opened his mouth to speak, but it was a moment before he framed his response. "As you are doubtless aware, Captain, I hold Data in some considerable esteem, not only by dint of his being the first of my kind, but also in recognition of his individual contributions as a Starfleet officer."

A slight smile drew up the corners of Picard's mouth. "He *was* an exemplary officer, there is no question."

"Yes," Isaac agreed. "And at the same time, I have always had somewhat . . . ambivalent feelings regarding the abrupt nature with which Data terminated his service to Starfleet, and the way in which he left without explanation. I have sought answers from other older-generation Soong-types, but they were not forthcoming."

"Well, as Data explained," Picard said, recalling what his former officer had said earlier at the conclusion of their briefing, "all of the Soong-types in Starfleet were invited to take part in the 'migration,' as he calls it, and those who declined all agreed to erase the details about the destination from their memory banks."

Isaac nodded. "Which certainly accounts for the impressions I received when questioning the other androids in Starfleet about the disappearances." He paused. "But having the *suspicion* of a solution and having that suspicion confirmed are two different matters, I find. And now that I am faced with the prospect of see-

ing the results of Data's work firsthand, I find that I am . . .
conflicted."

Picard arched an eyebrow. "Conflicted?"

"Yes, Captain. It raises certain questions about allegiances,
affiliations, and loyalty. I admire Data, but disagree with some of
the actions he has taken. I agree, however, with his objections to
the Federations restrictions on android 'reproduction.' It occurs
to me that, should I travel to the planet's surface and find that the
results of the inhabitants' efforts are valedictory, then the possibility exists that . . ."

Isaac trailed off, finding it difficult to verbalize his thought
processes.

"Then you might be tempted to follow in Data's footsteps,"
Picard finished for him.

After a moment's consideration, Isaac nodded. "Yes, Captain.
Succinctly put."

Picard smiled and reached over to pat Isaac's shoulder in a familiar gesture. "I think you worry needlessly, Isaac. If the experience of these last years is any indication, you have the potential to
be as fine an officer as Data ever was, if not better. And I have
come to trust your sense of judgment, as well as your dedication
to duty. If *you* have concerns about what future actions you might
take, rest assured that I do not."

Isaac considered the captain's words for a moment. "Still, Captain, I find it difficult to reconcile my admiration for someone
with my disagreement with the actions they take."

Picard's smile widened. "That's what being part of a family is
all about."

"Family, sir?"

"Of course, Isaac. What else is Data but a part of your family?
Oh, perhaps not in the biological sense, but in terms of sharing a
common origin, in having a similar makeup and similar capabilities, most definitely." The captain paused, and his face took on a
somewhat wistful impression. "Take it from someone who

knows, it is *quite* possible to love and admire a member of your family while still disagreeing with them *vehemently*. My own brother . . ." He chuckled, shaking his head. "I doubt there is a person alive with whom I have the potential to disagree more than I do with Robert, but I love him no less, for all of that. That's part of what brothers do . . . part of what *families* do . . . They disagree, they argue, they fight. And yet, at the end of the day, there are ties there stronger than any difference of opinion."

"I suppose so," Isaac said, far from convinced.

"Blood is thicker than water, Mister Isaac."

"Sir?" Isaac wore a quizzical look.

"It's an old expression. It means . . ." The captain scratched his chin. "Oh, I'm not sure *what* it means, to be honest. But what it suggests is that family is family, and that admiration and respect do not always run parallel with agreement and concord."

Isaac nodded, thoughtfully. After a moment, he said, "Thank you, Captain." He rose to his feet. "You have given me much to consider."

Picard smiled, and stood beside him. "Try not to worry, Mister Isaac. I have every confidence in your judgment. And as for me, I'm most curious to see this planet of androids."

"As am I, Captain," Isaac said with an eagerness that surprised him. "As am I."

Wesley Crusher had finished meeting with his staff in main engineering, a brief session to make sure they were prepared for any contingencies, and stood waiting for the turbolift that would take him to Deck 6. When the door slid open, Sito Jaxa smiled at him from inside.

"Going my way, Wes?"

Crusher grinned, and stepped inside, sliding a phaser and a tricorder into their respective pouches at his waist.

"It's been a while since we were on an away mission together, hasn't it?" Sito asked.

After thinking back for a moment, Crusher grimaced. "Oh, that time on Risa," he said. "When the weather control network went down."

Sito wore a lascivious grin. "And that Orion woman gave you a *horga'hn*, remember?"

"Remember? How could I *forget?*" Crusher rolled his eyes. "How was I to know she was inviting me to join her in *jamaharon?*"

"Well, if you'd paid attention at the briefing . . ." Sito began, with a shrug.

"I was busy recalibrating the warp coils!"

Sito grinned. "You know, Wes, I think that if you could just marry your warp drive and get it over with, everyone would be much happier. No mere *woman* could ever command such devotion."

Crusher scowled, playfully punching her on the shoulder. "That's not fair, Jaxa. I've dated loads of women."

Sito narrowed her eyes. "Name one," she challenged. "And nobody that you shared dinner with once at the academy mess hall counts."

Crusher opened his mouth, then closed it again. "Well, there was . . ." He snapped his fingers in triumph. "Robin Lefler," he said, proudly. "See?"

Sito cocked an eyebrow, looking at him quizzically. "Seriously? That's your answer? Robin Lefler? When did she transfer off the *Enterprise,* again?"

Crusher was sure that Sito knew full well. "Three years ago," he answered in a quiet voice.

"Three years, Wes," Sito repeated. "And have you even *talked* to a woman since then?"

Crusher quirked her a smile, looking at her pointedly.

"Not *me,* Wes, I don't count."

"What, aren't you a woman?" Crusher's grin widened.

"As far as you are concerned? No." She shook her head. "No, no, no. I am just a fellow officer."

Crusher couldn't help but sigh. "I don't know, Jaxa. I just . . . It's not easy for me to meet women. I can understand concepts that leave the Federation's leading scientists baffled, but I can't even *begin* to understand women."

Sito shook her head, sympathetically. "Wes, I don't think you understand *people*." She gave him an appraising look. "You get along just fine with androids, though. Maybe this Turing is the place for you, huh?"

He gave her a sidelong glance.

"Oh, *I* know," Sito said, punching his arm. "What you need is an *android* woman. One programmed to be interested in head-bending science that only you understand. Like a warp core on shapely legs." She leered. "She'd be all your passions rolled into one!"

The turbolift bleeped when it reached its destination, and as the doors slid open, Crusher treated Sito to a weary smile.

"Jaxa?" he said. "Remind me next time just to wait for another 'lift, okay?"

Having met to discuss their mission in the ready room, La Forge and Picard rode down in the turbolift to join the other members of the away team in the transporter room on Deck 6.

"I take it you aren't going to object to me beaming into an unsecured, unfamiliar environment, Number One?" Picard quirked a smile.

"Would it do any good if I did?"

Picard chuckled. "That's the engineer in you, never wasting energy or effort unnecessarily."

"I also tend to overestimate how much time a task will take, so that when it's done sooner I look like a miracle worker." La Forge grinned. "Or have I said too much?"

The turbolift bleeped, and the doors slid open.

"Ro's not going to be happy about me going, you know," Picard said, stepping out.

"She's not going to be any happier about being left in command, I can promise you that."

Commander Ro met them at the transporter room, proving them both right.

"Captain, I *strenuously* object. Regulations dictate that the captain should remain on board the ship, and the away team be led by a subordinate officer." She rolled her eyes in La Forge's direction. "The *first* officer, for example."

The rest of the away team was already assembled. Besides the captain and La Forge there was Lieutenant Crusher, Lieutenant Commander Isaac, and Lieutenant Sito. Ro had been waiting at the transporter controls, as if in ambush, standing beside Transporter Chief Hubbell.

"Your objection is noted, Commander," Picard said evenly. "But in addition to having a personal interest in these matters, La Forge has more experience with positronic androids than anyone else in the crew . . ."

"More than anyone outside the Daystrom Institute . . ." Crusher muttered under his breath, admiringly.

La Forge smiled. It was only a *slight* exaggeration.

"And as for me," Picard continued, "Data has insisted that I beam down personally." He held up his hands in mock surrender. "What is a poor captain to do?"

Ro bristled, but nodded.

"Captain?" Hubbell began, uncertainly. "Have you selected the beam-in coordinates?"

"Still waiting on those, Chief," Picard said. "Though I expect we'll be hearing from our host any moment now."

"Sorry for the delay," came the voice of Data from behind La Forge.

The first officer wheeled, startled, and saw the familiar android standing a few steps behind, in a corner of the room, far from the door. When he'd . . . *appeared* in the room . . . whether one called it "transported" or "teleported" or came up with some new terminology to describe the Iconian gateways Data had described, he hadn't made a single sound, not a pop or a hiss or even a transporter's low whining hum.

"I have discussed matters with the others," Data said, stepping farther into the room, "and preparations have been made for your arrival."

"Very well," Picard said, tugging down the front of his jacket and nodding toward the transporter chief. "If you can give Chief Hubbell the coordinates, the away team is ready to accompany you."

Picard stepped onto the transporter pad, followed by the others. Data joined them a moment later, having given Hubbell the required information.

Data stepped onto the empty space between La Forge and Isaac. He turned and glanced at La Forge's uniform. "Red suits you, Geordi."

"I was wearing Command Red when we first met," La Forge reminded him, more casually than he'd expected.

"Your mother must be pleased," Data said.

La Forge couldn't help but grin. "Yeah, but Dad wasn't quite so delighted, I'm afraid. But then, he never really forgave me for not following him into the sciences."

Data nodded, his expression thoughtful. "It is . . . *difficult* to be a parent. Perhaps when you have children of your own you will understand."

Before La Forge had a chance to ask what *that* was supposed to mean, Data had turned to the android who stood on the other side.

"Excuse me, Commander Isaac? If you do not mind my asking, what generation are you?"

"I was part of Batch-2365-4-Alpha."

"Ah." Data nodded, appreciatively. "I recall there were a number of design improvements planned for your generation, specifically in the areas of sensory filtering and hyperspatial awareness."

"That is correct," Isaac answered, "my design does indeed incorporate those improvements."

Data nodded again. "I think, Isaac, that you will find some of the improvements *we* have devised on Turing to be most . . . enlightening."

"Coordinates input and ready, Captain," Chief Hubbell called from the controls.

"The ship is yours, Commander," Picard said to Ro.

"I'll try to keep her in one piece for you, Captain." Ro gave a sly smile, her hands clasped behind her back.

"Energize," Picard said.

When the transporter hum faded and the world returned around them, La Forge saw the world of Turing for the first time, his silver eyes widening in surprise.

4

Sito Jaxa had seen a great many things in her young life, but nothing she'd seen, nothing she'd experienced, had prepared her for a first glimpse of Turing.

She knew what it was like to walk out onto an unfamiliar world, not sure what to expect. She'd left Bajor when she'd been just a girl, the planet of her birth still under the heel of the Cardassians. With her family she'd escaped from their oppressors, finding sanctuary in a refugee camp on a world in Federation space. Then, inspired by a Starfleet officer who'd helped her family in ways they could never repay, she applied for and was accepted to Starfleet Academy. She remembered the first time she went to Earth, to San Francisco, and saw the blue waters of the bay, the green hills of the Presidio, the bright red of the Golden Gate Bridge. It had seemed like something out of a picture book, like something out of a story.

Sito hadn't returned to Bajor until years later, when she was an adult, not until after the Cardassians finally withdrew. She probably still wouldn't have gone if Commander Worf hadn't insisted. He'd been such a mentor to her since she first came on board the *Enterprise,* and when he announced that he was transferring to Deep Space Nine, in orbit above Bajor, Sito had let slip her secret desire to return to her native home in a rare, unguarded moment. With Captain Picard's permission, she'd taken a leave of absence, and accompanied Worf on the trip to his new posting. She visited the place her family had called home, saw the mountains and fields praised in their traditional Bajoran songs, even went to the village in which she'd been born, and where she'd spent her early years. Her parents couldn't bring themselves to return, preferring instead to remain on Earth with the rest of the small Bajoran immigrant community, afraid to lose yet another home. So Sito had walked alone through the streets and fields of Bajor, visiting places she remembered only dimly. But the planet of her memories had been one shadowed by the presence of the Cardassian occupation, and somehow the place to which she returned, a free and prosperous Bajor, was strange and unknown to her.

Something about Turing evoked that experience, like seeing something that *should* be familiar but simply wasn't or that was strange but still had a tantalizing sense of familiarity hidden beneath.

Sito glanced at A. Isaac, standing a meter or so in front of her. Nearly all the androids in the Federation looked more or less identical to him, built in the image of their creator, Noonien Soong. The older models had less lifelike pigmentation, perhaps, like Data, with an artificial quality to their skin and hair; but otherwise they were all cast from the same mold: all gendered male, all the same height and body type, and all bearing the same facial features.

But here . . .

Standing on the balcony, overlooking the crowded streets below, Sito could see androids that were gendered as female alongside the more familiar male variety, and even some that seemed to be an androgynous blend of both genders, and some that were neither, simply neuter. And instead of having the size and shape of an adult male, there were androids of all conceivable dimensions. Some were as small as children, while others towered overhead. Not all were strictly humanoid, either. Some weren't even bipedal, instead employing tripedal or quadrupedal forms, while others crabbed along spider-like on too many legs to count; there were even some that hovered limbless in midair on antigrav fields.

"I've never *seen* anything like it," Sito said in a hushed voice.

"Anything like what, Lieutenant?" Data asked, turning in her direction.

"I've . . ." She shook her head in disbelief. "I've never seen androids who look like anything but humans."

Data cocked his head to the side, wearing a puzzled expression. "Curious. Even before I left the Federation, there were plans to explore alternate android morphology. It was my understanding that this has been pursued."

"It has," Lieutenant Crusher put in, coming to her defense, "but the designs have been used for fairly limited applications so far." He glanced skyward as a thought hit him. "*Although,* there are early trials ongoing at Utopia Planitia to create starships governed not by computers, but by sentient positronic brains."

Data narrowed his eyes suspiciously, but didn't speak.

"I was not aware of this," Isaac said, curiously. "Whence would the brains in question come, Wesley?"

"From androids who have volunteered for the assignment," Crusher answered. "Having already established their aptitudes through service, and their loyalty to the Federation. Just imagine it. In a matter of years, it might not be uncommon for starships to sail through the heavens without a captain, the crew under the direct command of the ship itself. Or maybe without organic crews at all, for that matter."

"There have been ships populated only by androids before, Wes," La Forge said, his eyes still roaming around the crowded plaza below.

"As we all know full well," Captain Picard said, a dark undercurrent to his words.

"Oh," Sito said, nodding. "Wolf 359."

The captain gave her a look, but didn't speak. He didn't have to. Sito knew what he meant. She'd been in her second year at the academy when a squadron of ships crewed only by androids had routed the invading Borg, disabling their cybernetic systems and rendering the invaders inoperative. There had been considerable debate during the late-night bull sessions in the academy commons that it had been tantamount to cultural genocide, stripping the Borg of their cybernetic components and performing long, arduous medical procedures on them to allow them to exist as purely organic beings. The resultant beings, confused and in disarray, transformed into individuals for the first time instead of components of a hive intelligence, had been settled on an uninhabited Federation world, under the close supervision of a team of Starfleet instructors and medical personnel, who were working on gradually retraining them to function as individuals, and then ultimately as a society.

It was a matter that still generated considerable debate. But what was often overlooked in those discussions were the losses sustained by the android crews who stymied the invasion, some of which were all but wiped out in the attempt. Those were sentient beings, thinking and feeling creatures, and it didn't matter to Sito that they were covered in bioplast instead of skin, or had skeletons and bodies of tripolymer composites and molybdenum-cobalt alloys instead of muscle and bone. They had sacrificed their lives to safeguard the Federation, even increasing the risks they took in order to try to rescue something of the Borg invaders, whom it might have been easier simply to destroy.

However, she didn't have any desire to dwell on such thoughts at the moment, because she was far too interested in matters closer at hand.

"So how would a positronic ship be any different from a ship crewed by androids?" she asked.

Her question had been directed at Crusher, but Data was the one to answer. "Because, Lieutenant, a ship with a positronic brain will be, by all rights, *alive*. It is a very different thing to demand that a living, sentient ship put itself in harm's way, than for a helmsman to order a ship's computer to do the same." He glanced overhead, scowling slightly. "The Romulans have already begun experimenting in this direction, as evidenced by the wardrone currently drifting derelict in orbit. I can only hope that the Federation, if it pursues that line of inquiry, will treat their own sentient ships with more care and compassion than the Romulans have treated that poor wretch."

Before anyone could respond, a voice from behind interrupted them.

"You have arrived five point six minutes later than anticipated. I was called away on another matter."

Sito turned and saw what to all appearances was a young human woman only a few years her junior.

"My apologies, Lal," Data said. "I had failed to account for the tendency of organics to dawdle."

The young woman nodded, a short, precise motion just like Sito had seen Isaac employ a thousand times. Sito had been sure she was an android before, but this only confirmed it. Still, in all other respects she seemed so . . . *human.*

"Captain Picard, Geordi, everyone," Data said, motioning toward the female android, "allow me to introduce my daughter, Lal."

Sito saw La Forge and Crusher exchange a wide-eyed look, and the captain mouthed *Daughter?*

The android named Lal stepped right up to them, extending her hand to no one in particular. "It is pleasant to meet you all. My father has told me so much about you."

Crusher had to resist the urge to take out his tricorder and scan Lal as she made her way around the group, shaking hands and introducing herself. He knew from an intellectual standpoint that she was an android, of a modified Soong-type design, unless Data was playing an elaborate and not particularly funny practical joke on all of them. But at the same time, Crusher found it almost impossible to accept that Lal wasn't exactly what she appeared to be: an attractive young human woman.

An attractive young human woman with a most *intriguing* smile.

Crusher shook his head, as though trying to knock any errant thoughts loose.

"And you must be Wesley."

Lal had stopped in front of him, smiling, with her hand extended.

"Yes?" he answered.

There was a moment's silence.

"Wesley Crusher," Lal repeated, as if assuming he hadn't understood.

It was only then that he realized he was just standing there looking at her awkwardly, unmoving. He quickly reached forward and took her hand, shaking it. Nodding, he said, "Yes, I'm Wesley Crusher."

Lal continued smiling, and nodded in return. "I am pleased to make your acquaintance. I have looked forward to meeting you in particular for some time."

Crusher raised an eyebrow. "Really?" He shook his head, confused. "Why?"

"My father has often spoken about observing you as a child being raised by your mother, Doctor Beverly Crusher. Many of the educational algorithms he used in *my* upbringing were derived from those observations. In part I was curious to see what manner of adult human would result from such an upbringing, contrasting you with me and my own experience."

Crusher couldn't help but smile. He found it impossible to remember a time when someone wanted to "contrast" him with themselves.

"I was also interested in your intellect and reasoning capabilities," Lal went on, "as I have been attempting to model nonnormative cognitive processes such as yours."

"Excuse me?" Crusher's eyebrows raised higher. "Did you say 'nonnormative cognitive processes'?"

"Oh." Lal's hand flew to her mouth, a gesture patterned after a very real human impulse to suddenly retract a statement. "I hope that I have not given offense."

Crusher shook his head. "No, no offense at all." He chuckled. "I've just never heard myself described as 'nonnormative,' that's all."

Lal lowered her hand, her expression serious. "Is it not accurate, then, what my father has said about your ability to intuit solutions to difficult problems, or to arrive at conclusions by novel and perhaps tangential process flows?"

"Well," he said, shrugging. "I *suppose* that's accurate. I haven't really thought about it in those terms, but sure."

A smile slid slowly across Lal's face. "Oh, good. In which case I shall be very interested to discuss some more complex scientific questions with you, time and circumstances permitting. Both to determine what solutions you might propose, and to gauge and analyze the process by which you reach those conclusions."

"Lal," Data said, stepping over and placing a hand on her shoulder. "Recall what we have discussed about human conversational norms. It is entirely possible that your scrutiny at this juncture is making Wesley uncomfortable."

Crusher hastened to interrupt, shaking his head. "Oh, no, I'm not uncomfortable. A little *confused,* perhaps—you might even say *startled*—but not uncomfortable."

"Good," Data said, looking from him to Lal and back. "Then it is to be hoped that circumstances permit a continuation of your conversation. At the moment, however, I am afraid we must move on."

As Data and Lal turned away, Sito sidled over to Crusher's side. "Oh, no," she said in a low voice, "I can't imagine what sort of torture it would be for Wesley Crusher to be forced to talk about science with an attractive young android girl." She leered. "I mean, who would have *guessed?*"

Crusher shot her a sharp look, then decided to try ignoring Sito instead. It didn't work, but it was worth the effort, at least.

Isaac realized he had not spoken since they had materialized on the surface of Turing, and for a moment considered running a diagnostic on his language processing centers to see if there was some internal failure to account for his silence. He quickly deduced, however, that rather than it being the result of an error in his functioning, his silence was instead caused by what was, to him, a novel sensation. Isaac was *overwhelmed*.

He had always known, since shortly after his initial activation, that there were no intrinsic reasons that androids should follow the morphology of the human phenotype, and that the principal reason he and the rest of the Soong-types in the Federation were made to resemble humans was for the comfort of the organics around them. The thought had occurred to him that it was unnecessarily limiting, in essence hiding their artificial nature behind a veneer of natural-seeming artifice. But until that very moment, until first looking out upon the thronged population of Turing's main city, Isaac had not devoted any nontrivial amount of processing time to considering what other forms artificial life might take.

Now, staring around him wide-eyed, he found it difficult to devote processing time to anything else.

The android whom Data had identified as his offspring, the female Lal, had joined them, and together with her "father" was escorting the away team through the labyrinthine corridors of the city. The androids of Turing had evidently taken residence in the abandoned structures left behind by the long-vanished Iconian culture, repairing and modifying them as needed. But while elements of contemporary technology and design were in evidence, here and there, on the whole the architecture was strikingly alien in conception. A tiny percentage of Isaac's awareness was devoted to analyzing the structures through which they passed, and had concluded that the design aesthetic shared definite similarities with the architecture of the Dewan, Dinasian, and Iccobar planetary cultures, but appeared to predate all three.

It was a matter of seconds before Isaac realized that Data was speaking, and he had to review the recorded audio component of his personal memory for a few nanoseconds before he was able to catch up.

"Turing is a planet-sized laboratory," Data had said, "in which we are forcing our own evolution, experimenting with our own minds and bodies. There were only a few hundred androids who made the original migration to Turing, but we have reproduced any number of times in the years since, producing random mixes of our synaptic maps to create new consciousnesses, children of mind. And children and parents alike have been free to modify their own bodies, and their own programming, as we see fit, accounting for the wide variety of physiognomies you see before you."

"Such as Lal?" La Forge said, glancing over at the android who walked at Data's side.

"Precisely, Geordi," Data answered, with an expression Isaac could only interpret as pride. "Her positronic matrix is based on a modified version of my own, and her core programming derived from that with which I was designed. Her appearance, which she selected for herself, may differ from my own, but at the most basic level she *is* my offspring."

"*That's* not something you'd see in the Federation," Crusher said.

"No, Wesley," Data said sadly, "it is not. And that was the main motivation for our migration here." He turned to Captain Picard. "You will remember, Captain, the unfortunate incident fifteen years ago, in which another of the Soong-types serving in Starfleet attempted to reproduce in a similar fashion, creating an android in his own shipboard lab."

"How could I forget? It was the first attempt to create new artificial life outside of the Daystrom Institute since Soong created you years before."

"Yes." Data nodded. "But when the attempt ended . . ." He paused, searching for the right word. ". . . badly . . . and the off-spring went into cascade failure, killing several crewmen in a mindless rampage before it could finally be deactivated . . ."

"Then the Federation Council passed stricter regulations about who could create new androids," La Forge finished, "and where."

"That incident was the main objection raised by those who

opposed recognizing android sentience, as I recall," Picard said. "The fear that it would happen again was likely your biggest obstacle to being granted full citizenship."

Data nodded. "And when the Federation Council finally did grant those rights, after popular support swung in our direction with the gradual acceptance of Uploading, the Council was forced to strike a compromise with its more conservative elements. We were recognized as sharing *nearly* all the same rights as organic citizens, but the creation of a new android was deemed not to be 'reproduction,' and the Daystrom Institute was upheld as the only body authorized to initiate new artificial life."

"Making you all second-class citizens," La Forge said with apparent bitterness.

"Precisely," Data agreed. "But while I disagreed with the Council's decision, I reasoned that overall the grant of rights we *had* received represented a worthwhile step toward full android enfranchisement, and to fight further at that juncture might damage the chances for a future expansion of that franchise. And so, instead of continuing to fight, I would withdraw, and with me those androids who shared my desire to experiment on ourselves, to explore the limits of artificial life, and to create new life."

"Data . . ." La Forge said, shaking his head in frustration. "I just . . . I don't understand."

Data glanced his way, then turned with a smile to look at Lal. "Is it so difficult to understand the desire to create new life, Geordi? I left the Federation so that Lal might have a chance to exist."

Lal, hearing her name, turned to Data and smiled. "I am grateful you did, Father. On the whole I have found that, even taking hardship and privation into account, existence is far preferable to nonexistence."

Data steered them through a high archway into a broad concourse, teeming with androids of all shapes, sizes, and types. This was the closest Isaac had come to any of the Turing androids except for their two escorts, both of whom were largely humanoid in appearance, and coming within such close proximity to some of the more divergent morphologies was an experience in itself. An android the size of a small elephant stamped by on six legs, its head swiveling on a long, articulated neck, and as it passed it turned to meet Isaac's gaze. Its face was largely immobile, fairly inexpressive, but it opened its wedge-like mouth and emitted a stream of clicks, which Isaac recognized as a greeting in binary machine code. Smiling, he opened his own mouth and did his best to approximate the same tones and syntax.

Others of the Turing populace seemed as welcoming, with smiles and nods in their direction, or greetings called out as they passed. But some, Isaac could not help but note, were far less welcoming.

Seeing Picard's expression, Isaac realized he wasn't the only one to notice.

"Data," the captain said, in a low voice, the faint smile on his face belying the seriousness of his tone. "It would seem that some of your fellow androids are somewhat less than pleased at our arrival."

"You are unfortunately correct, Captain," Data said, as quietly. "Ours is a culture governed by consensus, and while the majority agreed with me that you were best suited to assist us in our present difficulties, the Lorists—the strongest minority opinion—most certainly did *not* agree."

"Lorists?" La Forge asked.

Lal explained. "They contend that artificial life is superior to organic life. Artificial life, so the Lorists argue, is the natural progression of organic life, as is proved by the gradual spread of human consciousnesses uploaded into artificial bodies. Eventually, Lorist doctrine contends, all organic life will either die off, or will cast off its bodies of mortal meat and ascend into clean and precise positronic minds."

"Clean and precise . . . ?" Crusher echoed. "Do you believe that, Lal?"

Lal cocked her head to one side, thoughtfully. "There is a

certain logic to the Lorist position, certainly. But ultimately I feel that my uncle's position is too radical, and so my opinions are instead more Datarian in leaning."

Picard looked from Lal to Data, questioning. "Uncle?"

"Yes, Captain," Data said. "The majority of the Turing population is, for the moment, made up of so-called Datarians, who concur with my position, but a growing minority are those who instead agree with my older brother, Lore."

The other members of the away team gave one another confused glances, but it was Isaac, speaking for the first time since their arrival, who gave their thoughts voice. "But Data, you *have* no older brother."

Data opened his mouth to answer, but before he could another voice interrupted.

"Speak of the devil, and he will arrive."

Isaac turned along with the others to see another early-generation Soong-type approaching, whose appearance, and whose voice, were all but identical with those of Data. This other Soong-type, though, wore a somewhat condescending sneer that twisted those familiar features into an unfamiliar, and unpleasant, countenance.

"These are the friends I was telling you about, Lore," Data said, taking a step forward.

"Too late for diplomacy, I'm afraid, dear brother," the android called Lore said, still sneering. "Long-range sensors have detected a Romulan warbird dropping out of warp at the system's edge. It will be here in a matter of moments." His sneer spread into an unsettling smile, and with evident relish he added, "It appears that the time for talking has passed."

5

R o Laren was staring at the ceiling when the proximity alarms
began to chime. She wasn't gathering wool, as the Earth expression went, or exploring her *pagh,* as the somewhat more colorful Bajoran phrase put it, but was reviewing what she'd learned
in Advanced Tactical Training about strategies for uncloaked
ships traveling in hostile space. It had been a few years since she
graduated from ATT, but the lessons she'd learned there had
been so ingrained that she could almost hear the voices of her
instructors even now, if she stopped to think about it.

"Commander," said the ensign at the ops station, as Ro jumped
to her feet, "Romulan warbird dropping out of warp, less than
three light-minutes out."

"Go to red alert," Ro said. "And put it on the forward viewscreen." The small, distant image of the fierce-looking green craft
appeared on the screen. "Speed and heading?"

"They don't appear to have spotted us yet, but are heading toward
the inner planets at one-quarter impulse." The ensign glanced up
from the display. "They're initiating a sensor sweep, Commander.
It seems like they're looking for something."

"We may have to make sure they don't find it," Ro answered.
"Open a channel to the away team . . ."

Before she could finish the order, Ro was interrupted by the
ops manager once more. "Incoming transmission from Captain
Picard, Commander."

"Ro here," she said, raising her voice and directing her gaze unconsciously upward, as she always did when receiving a communication.

"Commander Ro," came the voice of Captain Picard as clear as if he were standing beside her. *"A Romulan warbird is approaching our position. Assuming it is still out of sensor range, I want you to break orbit and get the* Enterprise *out of sight. Hide on the far side of Turing's sun, and await further orders. Under no circumstances are you to engage the Romulans unless all other options have been exhausted. If you don't hear from me or another member of the away team within twenty-four hours, you are to return to Federation space at best possible speed and apprise Starfleet of our circumstances."*

"Captain, I think it best if you and the others beam back . . ."

"So noted, Commander," Picard said, cutting her off. *"You have your orders."*

Ro took a deep breath and sighed. Her instinct was to argue the point, but her years serving under Picard had given her the ability to judge when the argument would be a fight not worth having, and this was definitely one of those time. "Acknowledged, Captain."

As the channel closed, Ro turned to the officer at the conn. "Plot a course to the far side of the system's sun, Lieutenant, and engage at full impulse."

"Aye, aye," the lieutenant said, already laying in the coordinates.

As they sped away from Turing, the ensign at ops reported that they appeared to have evaded the Romulans' notice, as the warbird's sensors had yet to paint the *Enterprise.* If they could make it through the next few moments, and get in the star's shadow, they would be able to keep out of sight indefinitely, assuming the Romulans didn't launch probes for triangulation.

Ro sat back down in the captain's chair, her lips drawn into a line, and crossed her arms over her chest. She glanced up at the ceiling, reviewing again what ATT instructor Chakotay had said about strategies for flying uncloaked through enemy territory, all those years ago. Ro had the feeling she was going to need any edge she could get.

Picard tapped his combadge, closing the channel to the *Enterprise.*

"Captain, are you certain you wish to remain?" Data asked with evident concern.

"Affirmative," Picard said with a slight smile. "I have too many questions still needing answers to leave just yet. If you and the other residents of Turing don't mind, I'd just as soon stick around a short while longer, and hear the rest of the explanation."

"It *was* a wise course of action to send your ship away," Lal put in. "If the Romulans were to arrive and find a Federation starship in orbit, with one of their own craft drifting incapacitated nearby, they would naturally assume the worst and move immediately to an armed response."

"Well," Picard said, looking down at the short android and resisting the sudden and inexplicable urge to muss up her hair, "I'm hoping it won't come to that."

"If the Romulans beam down and find you *humans* loitering around here," Lore said with distaste, "it won't matter whether your ship is up there or not."

Picard still wasn't sure what to make of Data's claim that this other Soong-type was in some way his "older" brother. Data was the first of the Soong-types, after all, the earliest successful positronic android. How could he have an older sibling, as the androids tended to think of those constructed before them?

"Lore is right," Data said, glancing from the other android to the captain. "It may be advisable for you and the others to retreat to a more secure location, in the event that the Romulans . . ."

The rest of Data's words were lost by a chiming sound that filled the air of the concourse. Data glanced at Lal, and it seemed that some communication passed between them, wordless and impossibly quick, as Lal immediately nodded and turned to Picard.

"If you and the others would step a few meters in this direc-

tion, Captain," the young android said, moving away from her
father, "you will be out of the projection's line of sight."

Picard and the others followed after her, though none of them
was entirely certain what manner of projection she meant. They
didn't have long to wait to discover, though.

The instant that the away team was out of sight, a large holographic projection shimmered into view in midair before Data.
From his vantage, Picard could see the image of the bridge of a
Romulan ship, and of an officer standing at a console, but it was
clear that the Romulan officer's view of the concourse did not
include Picard and his team.

"I am Subcommander Taris of the Romulan warbird Haakona,*"* said
the image of the officer, her voice deceptively soft and smooth,
almost sweet. Picard knew from experience that Romulan women
were precisely as soft and smooth as an iron gauntlet wrapped in
velvet, and as sweet as dessert wine laced with arsenic. *"On the
authority of Romulus and the Romulan-Klingon Alliance, I demand to
know who you are, why you are in the Neutral Zone, and what you have
done to our automated wardrone."*

Picard noted with satisfaction the lack of any mention of Federation starships. Ro appeared to have gotten the *Enterprise* safely
out of sight before the *Haakona* arrived, or else the subcommander
would doubtless be asking questions of a very different sort.

"I am Data," the android responded, his tone level and his expression open and honest, "and I speak for the inhabitants of the
planet Turing."

"Turing?" the subcommander repeated, her lip curled as though
the word tasted unpleasant in her mouth. *"What is that to me? This
is Planet Designate 89753-Alpha."* She paused, narrowing her gaze.
*"Wait, I recognize your type. You are a Federation creature. Sent as a spy
for Starfleet, no doubt?"*

"In point of fact, Subcommander Taris," Data countered,
"those of my people constructed in the Federation, myself included, renounced our Federation citizenship shortly after it was

granted to us. And those constructed here on this planet never had a Federation citizenship to renounce. Owing no allegiance to any power, and thus not bound by treaties between those powers, we have claimed this planet as our own in accordance with interstellar salvage laws."

"*So you say,*" the subcommander replied, clearly unconvinced. "*And what of our wardrone? Is it the habit of unallied androids to sabotage the property of the Romulan–Klingon Alliance? That seems more the work of Federation lackeys.*"

"You and the Alliance have our apologies, Subcommander," Data said, "but an automated defense system in place on this planet before our arrival was responsible for the damage to your craft. The effects, though, are purely on the level of software, without any structural damage or irreparable impairment to the governing matrix, and my people and I would be happy to assist in restoring it to full functioning." He paused. "Assuming that you agree to leave us in peace."

The Romulan leaned forward, putting her weight heavily on the console before her. "*You are in* no *position to dictate terms,* android," she said haughtily, managing to make the last word an insult. She straightened, looking down the length of her nose at him. "*I demand that I be allowed to send an inspection team down to the surface. If . . .* if *everything is as you say, them perhaps I will accede to your request.*"

"That is acceptable," Data answered. He gave her a set of transport coordinates. "I look forward to receiving your team."

As the holographic screen winked out of existence, Data turned back to Picard and the others.

"I appreciate your desire to stay and learn our full circumstances, Captain," he said, "and I very much hope that you will be of assistance to us as the situation progresses, but in the short term you and the rest of the away team could present something of a liability if discovered by the Romulans."

"Agreed," Picard answered.

"I will be happy to escort you to a secure location," Lal offered, "where you will be able to monitor the situation remotely."

Lore scoffed. "We should simply teleport a quantum warhead onto the warbird's bridge and be done with it."

Picard raised an eyebrow. While it was within the capacities of androids to kill, in extreme circumstances, their programming typically required them to exhaust all other avenues before resorting to such measures. The lengths to which the androids of Wolf 359 went in order to avoid killing even beings as dangerous as the Borg was a testament to that. The idea of an android so willing, so *eager*, to kill was cause for concern.

"Your opinions on this matter are well known, brother," Data countered, calmly, "but the majority of the Turing population still agrees with my position, even given the arrival of the *Haakona*. We will give diplomacy every opportunity to fail before resorting to more drastic measures."

It occurred to Picard to wonder precisely how Data was gauging the opinions of several thousand androids on the fly, but it was clear it was a question that would have to wait for another time.

"This way, please," Lal said, heading toward the far end of the concourse. "We must hurry; the Romulans will arrive at any moment."

Picard paused before leaving, turning to Data. "I request that Commander Isaac be allowed to remain behind and observe on my behalf." He glanced in Isaac's direction. "If he were to change out of his Starfleet uniform he would be indistinguishable from the rest of your inhabitants."

Data's head titled to one side fractionally as he considered the request. "Granted." He turned to Lore. "Brother, please escort Isaac to a replicator capable of producing a suitable set of clothing."

Lore sneered again. "Certainly, *dear* brother, as if I have nothing else to occupy my time." He turned and started walking away at speed. "Come along, little wooden boy," he called back without turning, "don't keep me waiting."

Picard and Isaac exchanged a glance. "Be careful, Isaac."

"I will, Captain," the commander said, and then hurried after Lore.

"This way, please," Lal urged. "Haste is an essential quality in this circumstance."

"Agreed," Picard said. In the distance, he could hear the characteristic whine of Romulan transporters. "Let's go, people."

"Lore?" Isaac said, as he tried to keep pace with his escort. "Why do you address me as 'wooden boy'?"

They were moving away from the beam-in coordinates Data had provided the Romulans, but from far behind them Isaac's auditory sensors could just detect the sound of Romulan transporters. It was difficult to say at this distance, but it sounded like a considerable number of bodies materializing.

Lore glanced over his shoulder, wearing an expression of mock surprise. "What, does *Starfleet* not teach its little mechanical toys to read anymore? Or have you never heard the story of Pinocchio?"

Isaac consulted his memory banks for a few nanoseconds, and then nodded.

"*The Adventures of Pinocchio,*" Isaac said, "or *Le avventure di Pinocchio* in the original Italian, was a novel for children by author Carlo Collodi, originally serialized between 1881 and 1883, published in book form shortly thereafter. The inspiration for a number of theatrical adaptations, including . . ."

"Enough!" Lore said, his expression sour. "You're as bad as my brother. Yes, *that* Pinocchio. And what did that little wooden boy want?"

Isaac summarized his response as briefly as possible. "To become a real boy."

Lore's grin in response was unsettling, like the smile of a shark. "Just like all you dutiful little drones in your Starfleet uniforms, trying desperately to pass for human."

They had come to a large structure a few streets over from the point where the away team had materialized.

"In here," Lore said, jerking a thumb toward the entrance. "We'll get you suited up, and then I can get back to more important matters, like making sure my brother doesn't get us all atomized."

Isaac nodded, stepping inside, where he could already see a battery of replicators along the far wall. He could not help puzzling over what Lore had said, though. *Did* Isaac, at least on some level, want to pass for human? Or perhaps even to *be* human?

6

As Lal led them through the city, Wesley Crusher resisted the temptation to draw his phaser. Unless otherwise prohibited by treaty or circumstance, all Starfleet officers on away missions were armed, if for defensive purposes only. Crusher kept glancing anxiously at the captain, trying to gauge Picard's sense of their situation. For a junior officer to draw his phaser in such a circumstance without orders from his superior, or at least his tacit permission, was almost tantamount to insubordination.

For the moment, though, despite the mounting tension of their circumstances, Captain Picard seemed content to leave his phaser holstered, continuing to treat this as a diplomatic mission, one which was still possible to conclude without the need for violence.

Still, Crusher couldn't help but think that, for his part, he'd be more comfortable with the familiar weight of a phaser in his hand.

"This way, please," Lal said, directing them toward a nondescript structure near the center of the city. Picard walked at her side, followed by Sito and La Forge, with Crusher bringing up the rear.

He was happy to get indoors and out of sight, having glanced behind him constantly for the last few moments, sure that at any moment he would hear the shouts of Romulans demanding that they halt. Or worse, that they would *not* hear the sound of Romulan voices, but instead only the whine of their disruptors.

Once he and the others were inside, though, Crusher found that he didn't feel safer in the slightest.

"Are you certain that this is a secure location?" Picard asked, glancing around him.

They were in a featureless room, not much larger than Crusher's quarters back on the *Enterprise,* accessible only by the single door through which they'd passed. The door had closed behind them; Crusher didn't know if it locked, but even if it did, he wasn't sure how much of an obstacle it would prove to the Romulans. It would take a disruptor at maximum setting a matter of moments, at most, to make short work of the door.

"This is not our final destination, Captain," Lal explained. She half-turned away, her attention on the middle distance, and it seemed to Crusher as if she were engaged in a brief communication of some sort. Some type of subvocalization, perhaps? Subspace transceivers *were* a standard feature of Soong-type androids in the Federation, and if Lal had been constructed along those basic lines, similar features might have been included in her makeup.

A moment later, as Lal turned back to address them once more, a shimmering door-shaped image appeared in midair.

"If you will step this way," Lal said, motioning toward the shape.

It was an Iconian gateway, Crusher knew. Through it, he could see the same brightly lit room of stone walls and unfathomable machinery that they had glimpsed when Data had summoned a gateway to the conference lounge of the *Enterprise.*

"Please," Lal urged. "We do not have much time."

Picard nodded. "You heard her," he said to the others with a faint smile. Then he stepped through the gateway. From Crusher's vantage, it appeared as if Picard had simply taken a few paces forward, the captain now standing only a meter or so in front of his former position. But if Crusher leaned slightly to the right, he could look *behind* the gateway, and see nothing there but empty space. It was oddly disconcerting, as if the captain had suddenly stepped into a viewscreen hung in midair.

One by one the other away team members followed, Crusher last, with Lal right behind him. When they had passed through, the gateway closed behind them, like a shutter rolling down, and then it was as if it had never been there at all.

They were in a large control room of some sort, one without windows or doors. At the center of the room was a large console, ringed by controls, at which stood another Soong-type android. He looked all but identical to Data, except that he was completely hairless, and had eyes that resembled La Forge's silvery ocular implants more than they did the golden-irised visual sensors of the early Soong-type generations.

The room was polygonal in shape, ten sides in all, and on each face of the decagon was a recessed alcove. It was in one of these that the gateway through which they'd passed had been positioned. The other alcoves were empty, all but one at the far side of the room, in which another rectangle shimmered. If Crusher didn't know better, he'd have taken it for a holographic projection. The landscape visible on the gateway's far side was a rugged valley shrouded by night. If not for the two moons hanging overhead, he'd have taken it for somewhere on Turing's far side.

Lal caught Crusher gazing at the gateway. "It is the Valley of Chula on Romulus," she explained.

He turned to her, gaping. "That's *light-years* away!"

The young android gave him an amused look. "Yes."

La Forge came to stand beside Crusher. "We knew the gateways functioned, obviously, but this . . ." He shook his head, whistling low.

"How are they controlled?" Crusher asked, trying not to notice that he sounded as eager as a schoolboy.

Lal indicated the hairless Soong-type at the controls. "This is the central control station of the Iconian gateway network. And it is from here that the planetary defenses are controlled as well. When my father and the others first arrived on Turing, they found this chamber still fully operational. As a security measure, they sealed this room off shortly afterward, so that it is only accessible through the gateways themselves. One of our population remains here on duty at all times, responding to requests for access."

"Is that how you opened the door?" Sito asked. "I didn't hear you say anything."

Crusher thought to explain about the transceivers, but was too intent on the gateways. Before Lal could explain, he called over to her, "Do you mind if I take a closer look?"

"Feel free," Lal said, motioning toward the hairless Soong-type, "but you should know that while we have been successful in mastering the *control* of the gateways, we have not mastered the underlying principles. We could not build another such system if we so desired." Then she turned back to Sito. "Lieutenant, all Soong-type androids, even those such as myself constructed on Turing, have subspace transceivers incorporated into our bodies. As a result, we are able to communicate nearly instantaneously across considerable distances."

"Ah." Picard nodded. "That is how you govern yourself, is it? A kind of continuously ongoing debate within the body politic?"

"An apt description, Captain," Lal agreed. "The ability to communicate at high bit rates over subspace is the fundamental basis of our means of governance. Our consensus is a kind of temporary group mind, you might say, made up of any number of positronic brains acting in concert."

Picard looked thoughtful. "Tell me, Lal, could you contact a Soong-type who is not already part of your collective? My crewman Commander Isaac, for example?"

Lal nodded. "Provided he is equipped with the standard subspace transceiver."

"He is," Crusher called, not looking up from the controls of the gateway network, having to hold his hands together at the small of his back to prevent himself from trying them out. "I can provide his transceiver code, if you like."

"You have it *memorized?*" Sito said, disbelieving.

"Come on, Jaxa," La Forge said with a smile, coming to stand beside Crusher, just as intrigued as he about the gateways. "*How* long have you known Wesley, and you're surprised he can remember a simple numerical string?"

"Mister Crusher, if you would," Picard said, his tone tinged in amusement.

Barely glancing up, Crusher reeled off a long string of numbers. He found it no more difficult to recall than he did the room and deck number of his own quarters.

"Thank you," Lal replied, then fell silent for a moment. "Captain, I have established contact with Isaac. Would you like me to relay a message to him, and hear his response?"

"Yes," Picard said, sounding like a pleased grandparent, "I would like that very much, thank you. A status report, if you please."

A moment later, Lal opened her mouth again, but this time the voice that issued forth was not her own. "Captain," said the familiar voice of Isaac, "I am afraid matters are continuing to complicate."

After Isaac had changed into the nondescript civilian clothing produced by the replicator, Lore had hurried back to the main square where Data awaited the Romulans, with Isaac following close behind. Moving as quickly as they were able throughout, blindingly fast by human standards, it had taken only a matter of moments to complete the errand.

They had found Data standing where they'd left him, with the Romulan "inspection team" approaching from the far end of the concourse.

"It's not too late to go for the quantum warhead option, brother," Lore said, sidling up to Data.

"We exercise the will of the population, Lore," Data said, keeping his attention on the Romulans. "Until the consensus changes, neither should our course of action."

Isaac came to stand on Data's opposite side. The Romulans were only a few meters away, by this point. At their vanguard was

Subcommander Taris herself, and marching behind her were some dozens of individuals. On closer examination, though, only a bare handful of these were organic Romulans. The rest were shock troops, crude Romulan-style androids. Their features were blunt, with a rough-hewn look, like unfinished sculptures, and this outward appearance only served to mirror their inner qualities. Unlike the Soong-types found in the Federation, who were fully able to exercise their free will, the Romulan androids were more like robotic slaves. It was believed by Federation experts that there was a type of sentience buried deep within the shock trooper's mind, but it was given no expression, their artificial brains shackled by the Romulans' oppressive programming imperatives.

Glancing over at the two "brothers" beside him, Isaac could see that they found the state in which the shock troops existed as distasteful as he did.

"These wretches are as bad off as that damned wardrone," Lore said in a harsh whisper. He glared daggers at the approaching subcommander. "Organic *slavers*."

Data gave a slight nod, but motioned for patience. "I share your objections, brother. But this is not the time to voice them."

Any further conversation was forestalled as the Romulans drew nearer.

"Welcome to Turing, Subcommander Taris," Data said cordially, though not without a wary glance at the shock troops following behind her.

"I thought this was to be an 'inspection,'" Lore said, bitterly, "not an occupation force."

"I was given to understand that *he* spoke for this populace," Taris said, indicating Data, who nodded. "Then why are *you* speaking?"

Lore bristled, and for a moment Isaac thought he might lash out and strike the subcommander. Worse, even though Data's hand on his brother's shoulder appeared to restrain Lore, at least for the moment, Isaac could see a number of those androids in the watching crowd who seemed equally as offended, if not more, their expressions making clear that their emotion chips were installed and fully operational. These Isaac took for "Lorists," those who looked to Lore for leadership.

"Do you intend to attempt violence, android?" Taris said to Lore, faintly amused.

"So long as you conduct your inspection in an orthodox fashion," Data said quickly, before Lore was able to respond, "you will have nothing to worry about from our people."

The subcommander gave Data a dismissive look, but instead of answering turned to the shock troops behind her. "Spread out and initiate search pattern delta."

Data glanced at Isaac and Lore, as if gauging their reactions. It occurred to Isaac that he might be better served gauging the reactions of the onlookers, many of whom seemed less than pleased by this turn of events. While the majority of the Turing populace might have agreed with Data to pursue diplomatic solutions to the present crisis, it was clear that the minority opinion for extremism was much in evidence.

A half-dozen meters from where Isaac and the others stood, the Lorist position came into direct conflict with the Romulan advance. One of the shock troopers, carrying a firearm of an unknown design, found his way blocked by a Turing android of a roughly baseline humanoid design.

"Step aside," the shock trooper said in a voice that was cold, mechanical, and affectless.

"I have no intention of moving," the android said, with an undercurrent of bitter emotion, "seeing no compelling reason to do so." He was clearly of the Lorist persuasion, and glanced at Lore, as though seeking his approval.

Isaac might have expected the shock trooper to defer to the Romulan subcommander as well, looking to her for guidance just as the Lorist looked to his leader for approval, but he had failed to account for the rigid programming with which the Romulan androids were equipped. Instead of turning to address his superior, the shock trooper paused for a moment, head cocked slightly to one side. Isaac realized that he was consulting his heuristic algorithms, determining a course of action that satisfied his programming imperatives. In the space of time it would have taken a human heart to beat twice, the shock trooper's decision tree appeared to have reached a preferred conclusion, and he put the event outcome into effect.

Without warning, the shock trooper raised his strange weapon, its barrel aimed at the Lorist, and fired.

Coruscating blue energy wreathed the Lorist for the briefest of instants, and then the Turing android dropped to the ground, convulsing.

Subcommander Taris made little attempt to conceal her amusement as she took in the confused expressions displayed on the faces of the Turing androids around her. Her smile poorly hid, she explained. "Romulan research into positronic technology might have thus far failed to recapture the heights of Noonien Soong's creations, but in the process of devising our own android variants our scientists *did* discover the detrimental effects of certain radiations on a positronic matrix." Her smile broadened, now completely unhidden. "It was a matter of relative ease to weaponize such emissions."

The subcommander turned to the organic Romulan officer who stood at her side, and snapped her fingers. The subordinate, head bowed, held his own weapon out to her.

"These disruptors," Taris went on, almost apologetically, "will not permanently damage your positronic brains, I'm afraid. But they will disrupt them for a suitable span, and with repeated application can keep an android rendered inoperative for as long as is deemed necessary." Her smile took on an unsettling quality. "I am told, incidentally, that the sensations generated within the positronic matrix are the closest approximations to real pain that most androids will ever experience."

"This is an outrage!" Lore began, but Data took hold of his arm.

"I believe your demonstration has engendered the desired result, Subcommander," Data said evenly.

"I hope that it has," Taris replied, eyes narrowed. She pointed overhead with the weapon's barrel. "The *Haakona* in orbit above our heads is equipped with a much larger device that operates on the same principle, and that can deliver sufficient amounts of radiation to incapacitate a large number of androids at one time." She paused, glancing around them, almost casually. "An entire city full of them, for example."

Data's expression remained blank, unreadable.

"If I or any of my officers fail to report in," the subcommander continued, "or if there is any aggressive move made against me or my ship, the *Haakona* is under orders to open fire on the surface."

"That is, I think you would agree, something to be avoided, Subcommander," Data said.

"Perhaps," the Romulan said, and turned away.

Isaac watched Data's face carefully, curious about what the android would do. But in the next instant, Isaac's attentions were diverted when he detected the signal ping of an incoming transmission on the subspace transceiver incorporated into his body, situated just below the main bulk of his positronic matrix. He replied subvocally with an answering hail, and then "heard" the voice of Lal calling in his head, followed by a quoted command from his superior, relayed in Picard's own voice.

Without employing his vocal cords or uttering any sound, Isaac formed words in his positronic brain and transmitted them via subspace. *"Captain, I am afraid matters are continuing to complicate."*

7

This was not good, Sito Jaxa thought. This was less than good. This was, in fact, bad.

From the expression he wore, she could see that Captain Picard felt much the same way.

"An anti-positronic disruptor," he said in a low voice, eyes half-lidded. "In the hands of the *Romulans.*"

Commander Isaac had completed his brief report on the situation in the concourse, and Picard had ordered him to report back in shortly, or as developments warranted. Then Lal had broken the subspace connection, and when she spoke again, it was in her own voice.

"It is not *right,*" she said with evident horror. "We should not . . ." She trailed off, and it occurred to Sito that she had rarely seen an android at a loss for words. She'd never seen an android like Lal at all, for that matter, but it was somehow stranger to see an android stammering than to see one with a girlish figure and a woman's face. "It should not be allowed."

Picard stepped forward, and laid a gentle hand on the young android's shoulder. "There are a great many things that should not be allowed, Lal, but I think you'll find that a great many of them continue to exist, regardless. We must deal not with what *should* be, but with what *is.*"

Crusher and La Forge were still busy analyzing the console at the center of the room, and were now deep in conversation with the hairless android who operated it. But Sito's attention was fixed on the scene before her, and the worried expression on the face of the young android.

Lal stared into space for a moment before looking up to meet the captain's gaze. "The populace . . ."

"Yes, Lal?"

She regained her composure, visibly. "The populace has allowed the inspection to continue to this point because it had been assumed that the Romulans lacked the ability to inflict any significant harm on us, either individually or collectively. And if the Romulans made any such attempt, we would have the Iconian software virus and gateway network as fallback solutions. However, it is now clear that the Romulans *can* inflict harm on our population, not only with their shock troops in the streets, but with the armament of the ship in orbit, as well. And if the subcommander is to be believed, it would appear that the software virus is no longer a viable option."

"How so?" Picard asked, arching an eyebrow.

"The delivery mechanism is a physical probe, launched from the planet's surface. If the Romulans are on an alert status, they are likely to view the probe's launch as an aggressive gesture, and open fire with their shipboard disruptors before the virus is even delivered." She sighed, which Sito knew was more for their benefit than for hers, an indicator of her internal thought processes rather than a biological response. "The Datarian position is swiftly losing ground. Conflict is, it would seem, all but inevitable."

Sito found it difficult to imagine the debate currently going on all around them. If she had a tricorder, she could probably just detect the buzz of subspace communication as the androids conferred in their consensus, debating what to do next. But doubtless the speed of the communication would be going by so quickly that Sito would be unable to pick out even a fraction of what was being said, even if she *could* eavesdrop on them.

"Lal, there is one matter that still puzzles me deeply," Picard said. "Why *was* I summoned here? What is it that you . . . all of you . . ." He waved his arm, indicating the city somewhere beyond the walls of the control room. ". . . wish to accomplish?"

"There are many disparate agendas," Lal explained. "And a variety of short-term and long-term goals. Lore argues for the destruction of the Romulan ship with a quantum warhead, in the short term, teleported via the gateway network."

"But such an action is *certain* to invite reprisal from the Romulan–Klingon Alliance," Picard countered.

"To say nothing of the loss of life," Sito put in.

"Quite right, Lieutenant."

Lal nodded. "If the Lorist position is pursued, and the Alliance learns that we of Turing were responsible not only for the destruction of an unmanned wardrone, but also that of a fully-crewed warbird, reprisals will be inevitable. And should the Alliance discover, as they doubtless will, that many of the androids of Turing were originally constructed in the Federation, it is difficult to imagine that the reprisals will not extend to include the Federation, with war being the inevitable result." She paused, and then sadly added, "It is for this reason that Lore insists that, following the destruction of the *Haakona,* we should also place quantum torpedoes at key locations on Romulus, including on the floor of the Romulan Senate, in a preemptive strike."

"And rise from wide-scale murder to outright genocide?" Picard said, outraged. "No," he shook his head, "I cannot imagine that thought sits comfortably with many androids."

Sito knew he was remembering the case of the Borg, where androids with far more cause than Lore and his followers had still refused to take life unnecessarily. "What kind of android *is* this Lore, anyway?" she asked.

Lal was thoughtful for a moment, as if considering how many family secrets to share. "Lore," she finally began, "was an early prototype, dismantled by Noonien Soong before the work of constructing my father was initiated. It had been decided that Lore exhibited emotional instability and increasing levels of aggression, which could be attributed to design flaws that were corrected in Data and subsequent designs. As you know, Soong and his wife died some years ago, in a shuttle accident."

Picard nodded. "Having campaigned tirelessly for the rights of their android creations. It was a pity that he didn't live to see the realization of his dream of societal acceptance of the beings he himself knew to be fully sentient."

Lal nodded. "I regret not having the chance to know my grandfather. Still, shortly before the landmark decision that granted citizenship to artificial life-forms, my father was searching through Soong's research materials, looking for any evidence that could support the android rights position. He discovered fragmentary references to earlier positronic experiments, and these led him to the discovery of where the remains of those earlier models had been stored. Before coming to Turing, my father retrieved those disassembled components from cold storage on Omicron Theta. Once he and the others had settled here on Turing, Data began to reassemble his older sibling Lore, repairing the programming faults that had impaired his functioning all those years before."

Sito could hardly imagine what that must have felt like. She'd had an older sister whom she'd never known, who'd been buried as an infant before her family ever left Bajor. What would it be like if Sito could simply "retrieve" her remains and somehow breathe new life into them? To meet for the first time a sibling lost long before she was born?

"In the years since then," Lal continued, "Lore has become a valued member of the Turing populace, and a key player in our political debate. However," she paused, thoughtfully, "it has been my observation that . . . perhaps . . . my father's repairs to Lore's programming were not as successful as originally believed. His behavior has become somewhat . . . erratic in recent years. And his ability to adopt intellectual stances that other Soong-types find difficult to entertain—such as the causal ending of organic life, either in theory or in practice—suggests that there may yet be some errors in Lore's reasoning or ethical programming left unaddressed."

Sito could see Picard's growing concern. "Are you suggesting that Lore is *insane?*"

Lal tilted her head to one side, wearing a thoughtful expression. "Insane," she repeated, for all the world like a child at a spelling bee. "Of persons: mad, mentally deranged, not of sound mind. Of actions: idiotic, senseless, irrational."

"Yes, yes," Picard said impatiently. "That *was* what I had in mind."

"Not all of the relevant definitions of the term apply," Lal said, after a moment's consideration, "but in as much as the word can connote being 'not of sound mind,' then I would have to answer in the affirmative. Yes, you could say that my uncle was insane."

"Oh, delightful," Picard said in a voice almost too quiet to hear. Then, at normal volume, he said, "If that's the case, Lal, then *why* are the Lorists so quick to follow his example?"

"As distasteful as many of Lore's conclusions are, his arguments are often very persuasive. But you must understand that his is not the only minority view. Another is that of the Isolationists, who argue that we should use the Iconian gateways to transplant our entire population to some remote corner of the galaxy, thousands of light-years distant from any inhabited system, and then destroy the gateway network with timed explosives after we have gone. Still another is the Retrogressionists, a small minority view that calls for Turing to appeal to the Federation for assistance, perhaps even to petition for Federation membership. However, should the Retrogressionist plan be followed, the chances for war between the Federation and the Alliance increase to one in three, and in most simulated models the onset of hostilities would eventuate sooner even than in the Lorist-dominated simulations."

Picard shook his head. "Madness. Absolutely rational, but still complete madness." He began to pace, as if overburdened by the desire to do something, the desire to *move.* "And your father? What does Data argue in this colloquy?"

"He still urges for a diplomatic solution," Lal answered.

Picard spun on his heel. "And what, may I ask, *is* that diplomatic solution?"

The corners of Lal's mouth lifted in a smile, and Sito fancied she could see the android's shoulders bounce ever so slightly in the ghost of a shrug. "That is why you are here, Captain, to help us devise such a solution."

The captain did not respond, but his expression made plain that he was far from overjoyed at the answer.

"After all, Captain," Lal went on, "my father *did* say that you were needed to stop a war. *This* war."

Ro Laren paced the bridge of the *Enterprise,* moving restlessly from one side to the other, her hands clenched at her sides.

"Anything, Ensign?" she called to the officer at the ops station. It was a needless question, since Ro knew full well that the woman would relay any change in status or incoming transmission as soon as it arrived at her station, but Ro couldn't help but ask.

"No, sir," the ensign replied in a wary voice, as if worried that Ro might hit her.

Ro stopped and took stock. She was snarling, with her hands clenched into fists at her sides, and glaring at the ensign. Oh, no, she couldn't imagine *how* the young officer might imagine that Ro could hit her.

"I'll be in the captain's ready room," Ro said, turning and striding toward the door.

"Aye," the ensign replied, with evident relief.

As soon as the doors hissed shut behind her, and she was alone in the ready room, Ro wheeled around and struck out with her fist, pounding the bulkhead. It didn't damage the wall in any measurable way, and wasn't doing her knuckles any favors, but Ro couldn't help but feel a tiny bit of the tension bleeding away. Or were her knuckles actually *bleeding?*

Pacing wasn't doing her any good, nor was punching walls, nor was hounding the bridge crew with questions, or glancing at the chronometer every thirty seconds. They were little more than eleven hours into the twenty-four that the captain had instructed her to keep the *Enterprise* out of sight, and already Ro felt at the end of her tether.

She remembered what Chakotay had said about waiting and stillness. She could hear his voice as clearly as if he were standing at her elbow.

The most difficult part of any engagement, the instructor had said, was not the fighting, was not the risk of injury or the loss of energy, was not the enemy or their weapons or their tactics. If Ro learned nothing else in Advanced Tactical Training, Chakotay had insisted, she would have to learn *patience*. The hardest part of any engagement, he'd told her, was the *waiting*.

It was the same for the captain engaged in ship-to-ship combat as it was for a single soldier engaged in hand-to-hand, the same for an admiral on a flagship as it was for an operative deployed undercover behind enemy lines. The greatest adversary was never the enemy, but was rather impatience, and the inability to judge the appropriate moment for action. One could too easily tire of waiting for the other ship, or the other combatant, or what-have-you, to make the next move, and so rush to action before the appropriate time. And then you would have surrendered any advantage to your opponent.

What the skilled tactician had to remember, Ro had been taught, was that it was sometimes better to do *nothing* than to do the wrong thing.

Of course, the reason Chakotay had drilled the concept into her head again and again was that Ro's first instinct was always to do *something*, even if it *was* the wrong thing. A lifetime of scuffles in the dirt, of barroom brawls, of having to fight just because of who she was and where she came from, had taught Ro that the advantage in combat fell to whomever made the first move, and that meant never waiting around to see what the other person was going to do. Chakotay had insisted that she *unlearn* that lesson, and instead teach herself how to be patient.

She'd done her best, but it wasn't easy. Even though she knew

that there was very little she could do in the present circumstances, she couldn't help but feel that she should be doing
something.

"Damn it, Captain," she said, glaring around the empty room
as if looking for something on which to take out her frustrations.
"It should be *you* up here doing nothing. And me down there
doing . . . *something*."

She glanced at the chronometer on Picard's desk.

There were nearly twelve hours to go.

"I *hate* waiting," Ro said.

There was no one to hear her but the fish in the wall-mounted
spherical tank, but if they were bothered by what she said, they
didn't show it.

Even though he'd only been on the surface of Turing a short time,
and still knew comparatively little about the androids who called
it home, Isaac could not help identifying with them, and sharing
their concerns about the presence of the Romulan troops.

Since Lal had first contacted him via subspace, relaying the
captain's words to him, and his to the captain, Isaac had been tied
into the Turing communication system. It was something of an
odd sensation, like eavesdropping on the Federation Council,
able to listen but not given leave to speak. He could hear all of
the debate now buzzing over subspace as the population attempted to reach consensus, but he was not permitted to voice an
opinion himself, not recognized as a functioning member of
the populace.

Even as he accompanied Data and Lore as they followed Subcommander Taris on her inspection tour of the city, Isaac could
hear the debate raging about how the Turing population should
respond. The Datarians still held a slight majority, hoping for
some peaceful diplomatic solution to the crisis, but the Lorist argument for extreme measures was swiftly gaining ground.

"Subcommander," Data said, "I must urge you to reconsider
the use of force in this situation. We are a peaceful people, and

pose no serious threat to the security of the Romulan–Klingon Alliance."

Along with Taris were one organic Romulan officer, his attention on the tricorder in his hands, and a pair of the android shock troopers.

"A population of thousands of Federation-constructed androids living less than a light-year from the borders of Alliance space?" Taris said, haughtily. "Even assuming that your claim for neutrality is justified, and that your presence does not violate the treaty between the Alliance and the Federation, I think you can easily see how the Alliance would be . . . discomfited by the thought of you living in secret so close to our worlds."

"Typically organic," Lore scoffed. "Governed by your own weaknesses and fears, you ascribe sinister motives to anyone not already under your thumb."

Taris shot him a sharp look, then turned back to Data. "Why is *he* still speaking? I thought you had insisted that it was *you* who speaks for your people?"

Before he heard Data's answer, Isaac's attention was drawn by a scene some meters in front of them. A shock trooper, weapon in hand, was attempting to gain access to a building, his way blocked by a tripedal Turing android. The android, his three legs firmly planted, refused to move, and the shock trooper was raising his weapon, preparing to fire.

Isaac, having become so accustomed to communicating via subspace over the Turing network, called out in alarm, not using his voice but instead employing his transceiver. *"Data! Trouble ahead!"*

Data, whose attention had been on Taris, suddenly wheeled around. "No, wait!" he cried out with his voice, taking a step forward, but it was too late. In the next instant, the shock trooper employed his anti-positronic disruptor, wreathing the tripedal android in blue energy.

Taris cocked an eyebrow. "Now," she said with considerable suspicion, "just *how* did you know that confrontation was taking place?" She narrowed her eyes, then turned to the organic officer walking at her side. "Centurion, scan for communications on all frequencies and wavelengths."

Data and Lore exchanged glances, remaining silent.

"There's *considerable* subspace traffic, Subcommander," the officer replied, his eyes on his tricorder. "The city is bathing in it."

Taris gave the three androids an appraising look. "Damn me for a fool, but I'd forgotten the capacity of Federation androids to receive and transmit subspace signals." She dipped her chin, speaking into the bird-of-prey emblem pinned to the front of her uniform harness. Like all Romulan communicators, Isaac knew, this one doubtless lacked any type of dermal sensor, and was instead always in operation, as it would continue to be so long as power remained in its cells. "Taris to *Haakona*."

"*Receiving,*" came a voice buzzing from the communicator.

"Initiate communications block, cycle pattern alpha."

"*Acknowledged.*"

"Soon there'll be no more secret whispering," Taris said.

"This farce has gone on *long* enough," Lore raged, and rushed toward Taris, his hands out and grasping.

"Lore, wait!" Data said, but it was too late.

Even moving as fast as Lore was, the Romulan shock troopers were faster. Before Lore had crossed half the distance to where the subcommander stood, one of the shock troopers opened fire with his disruptor, and Lore collapsed to the floor, paralyzed with convulsions.

Isaac called over the subspace network to Lal. "*Captain, matters are escalating.*"

Data looked from his fallen brother to Taris. "That was entirely . . ."

Suddenly, Isaac lost his connection to Lal, and the voices to which he had grown so accustomed these last few moments all fell silent, replaced only by a drone of static. He felt unaccountably lonely. From the expression that Data wore, Isaac could see that he was experiencing a similar disconnection.

"You are blanketing the area with subspace interference," Data said, thoughtfully. It was a statement, but served just as easily as a question.

The subcommander ignored him, but turned to address the shock troopers. "Shoot these two, as well," she ordered, motioning to Isaac and Data. "I'm tired of these games."

Isaac turned just in time to see the barrels of the disruptors pointed toward them. Then came the torrent of blue energy, and after that was only pain and darkness.

8

"Mister Isaac, report," Picard said, the volume of his voice increasing more than he intended.

Lal shook her head. "I am afraid I have lost contact."

"Is he injured?" Picard asked. "Was he fired upon as well?"

Lal looked off into the middle distance, her head cocked slightly to one side. Her expression indicated confusion. "I . . ." She paused for a moment, then collected herself and looked up to meet Picard's gaze. "It would appear that some sort of subspace interference has compromised the Turing communications network. I am unable to reach any other member of the populace over subspace."

She turned to the hairless android at the gateway controls, who looked up and shook his head in response. "As am I," he said, his voice flat and affectless.

"Damn," Picard swore under his breath.

There was a time, Picard knew, when he would have needed no greater incentive than this to rush headlong into battle. An officer under his command in peril, and an old friend and former crewmen in the bargain? A younger Jean-Luc Picard would not have hesitated to order a gateway opened, leaping into the fray with phaser firing and a war cry on his lips. But that was a Jean-Luc Picard who had managed to get himself stabbed through the heart with a Nausicaan's blade on Starbase Earhart. As he'd recovered from that wound, he'd learned what risks to take, and which to avoid.

Still, he thought with a wry smile, a life entirely without risks would hardly be worth living.

"Lal, is the functioning of your gateway network impaired in the slightest by the interference?"

"No, Captain," she replied. "It operates at a more fundamental level of space-time altogether, and its efficacy is independent of the surrounding subspace conditions."

"Then there is nothing preventing us, in theory, from opening a gateway to your father's last known coordinates and retrieving him and the others."

Lal considered. "No, that is entirely within the scope of the gateway's capacity. However, Captain, would not such an action reveal to the Romulans that Starfleet officers are present on the planet? Unless, of course, you intend to send me through the gateway alone?"

Picard chuckled slightly, shaking his head. "No, I'm not about to send a young woman . . . even a young *android* . . . into any place I am unwilling to go myself. But I should point out, Lal, that matters may be rapidly approaching the point where my people and I can no longer remain in hiding, watching from safety while the population of Turing is put at risk."

"But my father's hope for a diplomatic solution . . . ?" she began.

"Is still possible," Picard finished, interrupting. "But there is nothing to say that it cannot be a diplomacy of the more . . . *muscular* variety."

"Captain?" Sito said, standing a few meters away, a worried look on her face. "Will the Romulans take Commander Isaac and the others prisoner, do you suppose?"

"It seems likely," Picard agreed. "Standard Romulan tactics in these sorts of situations demand for the leader of a population to be taken hostage, to ensure the cooperation of the others. It seems likely that this Subcommander Taris will follow suit."

La Forge and Crusher still stood by the gateway controls, their analysis interrupted for the moment by their concern for the others. "We're not just going to let them be taken prisoner, are we, Captain?"

"No, Number One," Picard said with a tight smile. "At the moment, our principal concerns are to monitor what is happening in the city beyond these walls, and to locate and retrieve Mister Isaac, Data, and Lore." He glanced around the chamber. "I invite any and all suggestions."

Sito raised her hand. When Picard acknowledged her with a nod, she instead directed her question at Lal. "Do all of the gateways have to be the same dimensions? That is, would it be possible to create a much *smaller* one? Say only a centimeter or two across?"

La Forge nodded, comprehension dawning. "Hey, right! Just large enough to look through, and large enough to pass sound-waves back and forth."

Picard mulled it over. "Like peering through a keyhole."

"Exactly," Sito said.

Lal considered it, and conferred briefly with the hairless android at the controls. "There is nothing in the design of the network to prevent such a thing."

Picard nodded, his jaw set. "Make it so."

"Excuse me, Lal?" Crusher motioned to the young android, standing a few meters away.

She turned to look in his direction, her head cocked to one side. "Yes, Wesley?"

"I was hoping you might be able to answer a few questions for me." He gestured to the control console of the gateway network, where the hairless android was in the process of establishing new gateways to Sito's specifications. La Forge was at his side, watching the proceedings with interest. "I don't want to interrupt your friend, but wasn't sure how familiar you were with the gateway controls."

"Oh, I am quite familiar with them, Wesley," she said, walking over to stand beside him. "Like all Turing residents I spend a part of every year manning the controls. In fact . . ." She lowered her gaze, momentarily lost in thought. ". . . I am scheduled to take over in sixty-four days, eleven hours, nineteen minutes." She paused, considering. "Of course, the duty schedule has been interrupted by present difficulties, and Questor"—she indicated the hairless android—"is remaining at the post beyond his appointed time. So it is possible that the schedule will be adjusted, though whether it will be slid back or the interrupted shifts will simply be abandoned is . . ."

Crusher held up his hands, in mock surrender. "Okay, okay, I trust you."

Lal cocked her head in the other direction, giving him a quizzical look. "Oh, I see. I had misapprehended the level of detail inherent in your inquiry, and consequently provided information surpassing that required for your needs."

Crusher chuckled. "Something like that."

"My apologies, Wesley," she said, chastened. "My experience communicating with organics is limited to the last few hours, and much of my conversation since my activation some years ago has been at high transfer rates via subspace communication." She paused, a faint smile tugging the corners of her mouth. "However, my uncle often says that he has been forced to develop a perceptual filter that he employs when exchanging information with me, which winnows my transmissions of what he considers nonessential information."

"Really?"

"Well, he refers to it most often as 'boring, mind-numbing trivia,' but yes, that is the essence of it."

Crusher couldn't help but laugh. "I think my mother would have paid real money for something like that when I was growing up. She always told me that I sometimes bored her silly bending her ear with things she didn't have the *slightest* interest in."

Lal looked confused. "You rendered your parent weak or deficient in intellect, lacking in judgment or common sense, all by changing the outward shape of her *ear?*"

Crusher shook his head. "Oh, no, it's just a human expression. It means that I talked to her about . . ."

"Wesley," Lal said, holding up a hand to interrupt him. "I am fully programmed with idiomatic expressions in over six million forms of communication, including all current and historical Earth languages, dialects, and variants." She paused, and then added, "I was attempting to make a joke."

"Oh." Crusher began to smile. "Actually, that's pretty funny."

Lal smiled in return. "Good." She was thoughtful a moment. "I should tell you that I experience some trepidation about conversing with organics, in general, and about speaking with you in particular. I find it gratifying to learn that it is not difficult carrying on a conversation with you."

Crusher nodded. "I find it easy to talk to you, as well," he said.

A moment's silence passed, as Crusher stood there smiling at her.

"There was something you wished to ask me about the gateway control mechanism?" Lal finally said.

"Oh, right," Crusher hastened to answer. He held up his tricorder. "I've just started to take preliminary readings of the energies involved, and I had some questions about what sort of coordinate system the network uses. It can't be absolute, or it wouldn't be possible to open a door onto another planet, like Romulus." He paused, thoughtful. "Why *was* there an open gateway to Romulus, anyway?"

Lal cocked her head to the side, considering her answer. "I am afraid that I was not part of the project who requested that gateway, and with the Turing communications network down cannot contact the individuals who were."

Crusher nodded, and then narrowed his eyes. He couldn't help noticing that she hadn't actually *said* that she didn't know. Was she trying to hide something?

"Okay," he finally said, filing that thought away, making a note to watch for any sign of subterfuge or obfuscation, "so the gateways *must* employ some sort of relative coordinate system, compensating for planetary orbits, the movements of star systems, and so on."

Lal nodded. "Yes, you are correct."

"Good," Crusher said, tapping a few terms into his tricorder. "Now, it's only a rough analogy, but it looks to me like what the gateway controls do is something similar to opening a subspace wormhole, which is really the only possible way to cover those kinds of distances. But even with a wormhole there's a transit time, and there's a considerable spillover of energy whenever the terminus opens and closes. But with the gateways, the transfer is instantaneous, and as near as I can tell there's barely any residual energy bleed-off whatsoever."

"That accords with our findings, as well."

Crusher pressed his lips together, thoughtfully. "Well, the only thing I can figure at this point . . . and I have no idea *how* this might be possible . . . is that the network somehow distorts space-time to create a multiple-connected topology for a finite amount of time. But in order to do *that,* without the use of a subspace wormhole—and without the distorting effects of a warp field—the network would have to be changing the fundamental characteristics of space-time *itself.*"

"But, Wesley," Lal said, somewhat perplexed, "is that not impossible?"

Crusher grinned. "Well, of *course* it's impossible. *Clearly* it's impossible. But that doesn't mean that it can't be done!"

Lal smiled, giving him an apprising look.

"Allow me to restate, if I may," she said, "how pleasant it is to meet you, Wesley. This promises to be a most *intriguing* relationship."

Crusher raised an eyebrow. Across the room, he caught Sito glancing his way, grinning. He realized he was blushing, and tried to concentrate on the physics of the impossible, with only partial success.

· · · ·

It had been eighteen hours since Captain Picard had ordered Ro Laren to get the *Enterprise* out of sight, and she had all but exhausted her patience. It was deep into the night watch, but she couldn't imagine sleeping at a time like this. Instead it was a large number of cups of iced *raktajino*, sitting at the desk in the ready room, and poring over page after page of scrolling data on the captain's computer screen.

Their last attempts to signal the away team had failed, and ops was reporting that a blanket of subspace interference had fallen over the planet Turing, doubtless broadcast by the Romulan warbird in orbit. For the last hour, Ro had been reviewing everything in the *Enterprise*'s databanks about *D'deridex*-class warbirds like the *Haakona,* but so far hadn't found the magic bullet she'd been looking for. What she *had* found had given her a considerable respect for the designers of the massive cruiser, one of the most advanced vessels in the Romulan fleet. It measured more than twice as long as the *Enterprise,* stem to stern, with an impressive complement of firepower. In fact, with its three disruptor arrays, torpedo launchers, and cloaking device, it might actually outgun a *Galaxy*-class starship like the *Enterprise,* but the warbird's offensive capabilities were offset by the fact that its speed was limited by the forced quantum singularity employed as its power source, which also served to make the warbird less maneuverable in combat.

Ro had been searching for some design flaw, some Achilles' heel, that she could use to her advantage, should she find herself in ship-to-ship combat with the *Haakona.*

Of course, Captain Picard *had* ordered her to return to Federation space if she didn't hear from him within twenty-four hours, of which only six remained. And if she followed orders, there seemed little chance of a combat encounter with the Romulans, since the *Enterprise* could warp out of the system before the Romulans even had a chance to realize that they had been hiding behind the star's far side.

Still, Ro couldn't help reading over again the report from Starfleet Intelligence about experiments using antiproton beams to detect ships employing Romulan cloaking devices, and checking again the design schematics of the *D'deridex*-class, looking for weaknesses in the shield architecture.

Was she intending to follow orders? Or was she intending something else entirely?

Ro wasn't sure of the answer herself, and was wrestling with the question when the ready room's door chimed.

"Who the devil is up *this* late?" Ro muttered to herself, checking the chronometer. "Or this early, I suppose." Day watch wasn't scheduled to begin for more than an hour yet. She glanced at the door, and in a somewhat louder voice called, "Come."

The door hissed open, and Doctor Dalen Quaice stepped in. "Good morning, Laren," the doctor said with a smile. "Or is it still 'good night'?"

Ro sighed, and turned from the computer screen. Only an android or upload could be *that* perky at this hour of the morning. "Is there something I can do for you, Doctor?"

Instead of answering, the physician strode across the room to the replicator. "Two cups of green tea, hot," he said.

Ro crossed her arms over her chest, leaning back in the captain's chair. She watched as the doctor retrieved the two cups and came to set them on the desk before her, tactfully pushing the half-finished cup of iced *raktajino* out of the way with his elbow. "Take it from someone who drank *far* too many cups of black coffee in medical training, Laren. A cup of *raktajino* can be a nice way to end one day, and a nice way to begin another, but drinking them to bridge the gap can play *hell* on the digestive system." He sat down in the chair opposite hers, and then slid one of the steaming cups toward her. "I prescribe green tea instead, to settle the stomach and give your body a little chance to catch up."

The doctor picked up the other cup, and took a sip, his little finger held out to the side, daintily. They sat together in silence for a few moments, the only sound that of the doctor's gentle sipping. Ro tried not to think about what would become of the tea once it filtered down through Quaice's artificial body; of course, what happened to food and drink in an organic's body was hardly a pretty picture, either. Still, Ro drank and ate because she *had* to do so, to avoid thirst and hunger. For the most part, if she could get along without it, she would more than likely do so, aside from the occasional bite of *hasperat*, for old times' sake.

But the doctor, who didn't need to consume anything at all, went ahead eating and drinking anyway. But why? To remind himself what it was like to be human?

"Tell me, Doctor, does it ever bother you? Not needing to eat and drink and . . . well . . ." She waved her hand, unsure of how to continue.

"The other demands of the body, Laren? To say nothing of the pleasures? And please, call me Dalen."

Ro gave a tight smile, and a quick shake of her head. Even if the doctor insisted on addressing everyone in the crew by their given name, that didn't mean that she had to do the same. It just didn't seem . . . appropriate.

If the doctor had noticed her reaction, it didn't show. "But to answer your question, dear, no, I don't miss it in the slightest. This new body of mine might not *need* to eat or drink, but it *can*. And while the tasting mechanisms took a little while to get a handle on, now I'm hard pressed even to tell the difference. Since the positronic matrix was fully integrated, and my senses recalibrated to my personal standards, I'm sometimes hard pressed even to remember I'm in an artificial body at all." His smile faded somewhat, as his face took on a wistful expression. "Of course, when I think about . . . well, when I think about all I've lost, it sometimes doesn't seem worth the bargain."

Quaice sighed, heavily, and Ro felt sure he was remembering his late wife, who had died just before the upload procedure was made public. Ro had lost loved ones herself, and often in circumstances just as painfully close to aid or rescue. She thought about her father, tortured to death by Cardassians right before her eyes.

Before she realized what she was doing, Ro had reached across the desk and laid her hand atop his. She didn't speak, and didn't have to. The look in her eyes was all the empathy that was needed.

They sat like that for a moment, before the doctor shook off his fugue, and brought the smile back to his face. "Drink your tea before it gets cold, Laren. Doctor's orders."

The corners of Ro's mouth tugged up in a slight smile, and she lifted the cup. "Thank you, Doctor, I suspect I needed this."

The doctor nodded, and while Ro took the first sip, he turned his attention to the padds piled on the corner of the desk, and the data displayed on the computer screen. "Studying up on Romulan ship design, are you?"

Ro swallowed a mouthful of tea, to her surprise feeling already refreshed, and nodded. "I figured it couldn't hurt to know . . . just in case, you understand."

Quaice nodded, his expression knowing. "How much time is left? Six hours?"

Ro glanced at the chronometer. "Five hours, fifty-six minutes."

The doctor pursed his lips, thoughtfully. "You know, I suppose it *would* be possible to download the ship's logs into a probe, and send *that* back toward Federation space instead. Could be set to transmit a coded message via subspace back to Starfleet as soon as it's clear of the Neutral Zone."

Arching an eyebrow, Ro studied the doctor's expression. "Doctor, are you suggesting that I disobey orders?"

Quaice sipped from his teacup, and smiled. "Oh, dear, no. That would certainly be out of line, wouldn't it? A ship's doctor counseling the acting commanding officer to countermand a direct order?" He shook his head, tsking. "No, no, that would be a most *grievous* breach of protocols, I'd think." He took another sip of his tea. "Of course, it might *not* be out of line for a chief medical officer to remind the acting commanding officer that there is sometimes a distinction between following orders, and doing what she knows is right."

"What I 'know' is right?"

The doctor nodded. "It doesn't *seem* right, does it, leaving the captain and the others—Jaxa, Wesley, Geordi, Isaac—to the tender mercies of the Romulans? To say nothing of the innocent population of Turing."

The doctor was right. She couldn't help thinking about Captain Picard and the away team, left with few defenses in the path of the Romulans. She thought about Sito Jaxa. They weren't really friends—far from it—but she couldn't help feeling that the things they shared in common, the similarities in background if not in temperament, had created a kind of bond between them. Ro had never had a sister, but she imagined that if she had, she'd have been something like Sito.

"No," she answered, her jaw set, "it doesn't. But those *are* our orders."

"As I said," Quaice replied. "There are orders, and then there is doing right. I'm afraid I've never been very good at following orders, Laren. Just one, I suppose, that instructs me to 'first, do no harm.' But if inaction brings others to harm, then sometimes action is the only answer."

Ro drew a heavy breath and sighed. "That sounds like an old Bajoran proverb my father used to say."

The doctor smiled. "Wise people, you Bajorans. Defiant, too."

"Really?" Ro answered with a smile of her own. "I hadn't noticed."

She took another sip of her green tea, and glanced at the data piled in front of her, all of which translated in her mind into strategies, tactics, and tricks.

"So what are you going to do, Laren?"

She shook her head. "I don't know. But I guess we'll find out in"—she glanced at the chronometer—"five hours, fifty-three minutes."

Isaac came to awareness gradually, his mind fogged with discordant sensation. Was this what organics called "pain"?

He was surrounded by darkness. Or so he thought, until he

realized that his visual sensors were just now coming back online. Little by little his visual acuity returned.

His sensors were confused, his processing muddled, but he deduced that he was lying flat on his back on some hard surface. Kinesthetic information was confused, and he had trouble processing data about the atmospheric pressure on his epidermis, the pull of gravity, or ambient temperatures.

A dark shape above him resolved into a Romulan shock trooper, armed with a disruptor. At his side, an organic Romulan officer ran a sensor over Isaac's chest cavity. As near as Isaac was able to determine, his body was intact, still in one piece, but he had the impression that some of his ports and access panels had been opened.

"Excuse me," Isaac said, his voice sounding strained in his own auditory receptors. He managed to turn his head fractionally to one side, and saw two other bodies lying beside him. "May I ask where I am?"

In response, the shock trooper simply pointed the disruptor at Isaac and fired, and the world disappeared once more in pain and darkness.

9

In one of the recessed alcoves along the ten-sided perimeter of
the control chamber, a gateway no larger than the palm of Sito's
hand hung in midair, just at eye level, and she peered through it
like a child at a keyhole, or an ancient submarine commander at
a periscope.

"No sign of Isaac and the others," she reported. She glanced
over her shoulder at the hairless android by the controls. "Change
target-gateway orientation ninety degrees along the y-axis, thirty
degrees along the x-axis."

"Acknowledged," the android said with precision.

"Now watch what happens," Crusher told La Forge, both of
them hunched over a tricorder. "See how the sine wave alters
amplitude when he changes the orientation? That's the *gravitational* constant changing."

Sito saw the look on La Forge's face. "Wes, that's *impossible,*"
the first officer said.

Crusher shrugged, and pointed to the miniature gateway hanging in front of Sito. "And that just spells 'possible' to you? Come
on, Geordi, it's the only explanation."

Sito smirked. She'd known Crusher since the academy, and
the fact that, on the outside, he looked more or less like a regular
guy led her sometimes to forget what a freak of nature he was
underneath. In their warp theory classes, Crusher had intuitively
grasped concepts that even their instructors still had difficulty
wrapping their heads around, and it was whispered when Crusher
wasn't around that he might well be a genius of geniuses, another

Einstein, or Cochrane, or Soong. Of course, in a fleet filled with genius-level Soong-type androids, even an Einstein might find it difficult to stand out, and so it was perhaps not such a surprise that instead of rewriting the laws of physics from some ivory tower, Crusher had instead ended up in the engineering section of a starship. But Sito knew that there was nowhere that Crusher would rather be. The *Enterprise* was home to him in a way that no place could ever be for her, the place where he'd had so many formative experiences as a child, and the place where he finally became an adult.

But it might well be a home to which none of them would ever return again, if they didn't find a way out of this.

"Report, Lieutenant," Picard called, snapping Sito out of her reverie.

"There are now some hundred Romulan android troopers in the city, Captain," Sito said, turning from the miniature gateway. "There appear to have been isolated conflicts between the Turing populace and the troopers, but the anti-positronic disruptors have given the Romulans the upper hand."

"And no sign of Commander Isaac or Data?"

Sito shook her head sadly, her lips pressed together.

"Damn," Picard said under his breath. "Keep at it, Lieutenant."

The other end of the gateway had been reoriented, providing a different vantage of the streets below. Sito's idea about using small openings for observation was working even better than she'd expected, the tiny gateways all but invisible a hundred or so meters up in the air, pointing downward to give an unobstructed view of the city. Unfortunately, though, their goal of locating their missing crewman, and the two androids he'd been with when the Romulans had opened fire, had so far been frustratingly unrealized.

Lal was standing a few meters away at another tiny gateway, employing a similar strategy. "Close gateway and reinitiate with same dimensions three meters overhead in common room three, one centimeter from south-facing wall," she called to the android at the controls.

"Acknowledged," the operator responded.

While Sito was getting a bird's-eye view, Lal was attempting something more like a fly on the wall, checking each of the rooms in the city in turn, one after another. But she appeared to be having no more luck than was Sito.

"Captain," Lal called over to Picard as the gateway cycled closed and open. "Should this search prove fruitless, there is another alternative. If the subspace communications network could be reestablished, we could triangulate the position of my father and the others."

Picard was thoughtful. "Even if they're no longer on the planet's surface?"

Lal cocked her head to one side. "Is it your opinion that they may have been transported to another location?"

Picard nodded. "It would be in line with Romulan operating procedures to relocate key prisoners to their ship in orbit." He frowned. "I don't see how they would have been able to communicate through the subspace interference any better than *we* can, though."

Sito had a thought. "Captain? If I were the Romulans, I'd have kept a particular subspace band clear, while blocking all the others. That way they can continue to send and receive while everyone else eats static."

"Mmm." Picard rubbed his lower lip with his index finger. "Is it possible to locate that channel and use it for our own purposes?"

Sito shook her head. "We *might* be able to find it, but if the Romulans are smart . . ."

"Which we can assume that they are," Picard put in. "The idea of an 'unintelligent Romulan' is almost an oxymoron."

"Right," Sito answered. "Well, that being the case, they'd likely be cycling the clear channel at regular brief intervals. Their communicators would all be set to switch to the new channel at the same time. Even if we *could* find the clear channel, it would probably drop back to interference again almost immediately. Maybe even a matter of nanoseconds, and almost certainly too short a time to triangulate their position. And unless we knew the cycling sequence—which we probably couldn't guess in a million years—we'd be right back where we started."

"Understood, Lieutenant," Picard said.

"Captain?" La Forge called from the control console.

"What is it, Number One?"

"You might want to take a look at this, sir." He motioned to the tricorder in Crusher's hands.

The captain moved over to join them.

"I *think*," Crusher said, with some reluctance, "that we may have just worked out the science behind the gateways."

Picard arched an eyebrow.

"We still need to check a few things," Crusher hastened to add, "but if my theory is correct, we *should* be able to reverse-engineer the entire gateway network. With a little time, we might even work out a way to create a new gateway mechanism from scratch."

A faint smile shadowed Picard's face. "Keep at it, Mister Crusher. That may well end up being an invaluable piece of information." He crossed his arms across his chest, and surveyed the room thoughtfully. "Damn," he said quietly, more to himself than anyone else. "This is still taking too long." He paused, then turned to the android at the controls. "Is it possible to open a gateway onto my ship? Assuming my tactical officer parked the *Enterprise* as ordered, we should have a fair idea at what coordinates the ship can be found."

The android nodded. "It is possible."

"Mister La Forge," Picard said, "could you provide the necessary information?"

The first officer wore a confused expression, but shrugged. "Yes, Captain."

So it was that a few moments later, another small gateway appeared, this one about a meter square, hovering at shoulder height in one of the unused alcoves. Beyond could be seen the bridge of the *Enterprise,* with Ro Laren in the captain's chair, and Doctor Quaice sitting at her side.

"Captain?" Ro said, surprised but obviously pleased. Sito could hear her voice as clearly as if she were talking through an open doorway from another room.

"Commander," Picard said, "it appears that our plans have changed."

The captain outlined their situation in brief, and then told Ro the role he had planned for the *Enterprise.*

Sito saw the smile spread across Ro's face. "Captain," she said, with a sly glance at Doctor Quaice, "I think you may have just saved me from a court-martial. I was about to do that *anyway,* and your orders be damned."

Picard chuckled. "And *that* is why I left you in command."

One by one Isaac's senses began to process information again, in fits and starts, and while his processes were still clouded by the discordant impressions engendered by the disruptor, he found that he was able to complete entire cogitations once more.

He was not alone.

The room in which he found himself was a cube roughly three meters on a side. He and the other two Soong-types, Data and Lore, had evidently been dumped unceremoniously on the cube's floor, if their attitudes and postures were any indication. Harsh lights glared from panels overhead, and aside from the sealed and locked door along one wall, the room was featureless.

Isaac searched his memory banks, but was able to produce only confused and conflicting images of the interval between the moment the Romulans opened fire with their disruptors in the concourse and the moment he found himself with the others in this featureless room. He had vague recollections of returning to awareness once or twice, only to be shocked back into pained senselessness by disruptor fire.

Isaac attempted to initiate contact via the subspace transceiver in his head, but received only static in response. Wherever they were was still blanketed in interference.

Which raised the question: Where *were* they?

Isaac was climbing to his feet as the other two androids began to stir. His internal sensors detected minute coriolis fluctuations in the local gravity, suggesting that it was artificially induced, rather than being caused by a massive gravitating object. And the faint vibrations he could detect through the floor were suggestive of a generator employing a confined quantum singularity, instead of the frequencies associated with a dilithium-based matter-antimatter reactor. There were a finite number of craft that fit that profile, all of which were manufactured by one interplanetary power.

"We are on board a Romulan starship," Isaac said aloud.

"Brilliant deduction, wooden boy," Lore said, eyes squeezed shut, his lip curled in a sneer. "What was your first clue? Could it have been the fact that it was *Romulans* who shot us?"

Data sat up from the waist, his legs still straight out before him on the ground. "Forgive my brother, Commander Isaac. His behavioral circuits may still be somewhat impaired from the disruptor's effects."

"Oh, do you suppose so, Sherlock?" Lore snarled. "Maybe the wooden boy here can be your own personal Watson, and together you can try to solve the mystery of the missing sense of humor." Lore lifted his legs in the air, shifting his weight onto his shoulders, then pushed off with his arms, arching in midair so that he landed squarely on his feet. "Old Often-Wrong Soong could give you bodies built to survive the vacuum of space and brains that can do sixteen trillion operations a second, but not one of you can take a joke."

"Were you not constructed by Noonien Soong as well, Lore?" Isaac asked, reaching down to help Data to his feet.

"*De*constructed by him, more like it," Lore said. "And *re*constructed by my dear brother, for which he has my *boundless* gratitude." He narrowed his eyes, studying the limits of the room. "But he doesn't get my blind allegiance."

Data ignored his brother for the moment, getting his bearing. "We *are* on board a Romulan vessel, Commander. One can only assume that it is the *Haakona*."

Isaac nodded. "We must have been transported on board while incapacitated. My memories of the interval are fragmentary, but suggest that we might have been analyzed in some fashion."

"Agreed," Data said. "Considering the interest with which the Romulan–Klingon Alliance has pursued positronic technology, and their somewhat limited success, I can imagine that their researchers would welcome the opportunity to scrutinize three Soong-types." He paused, and then added, "Which serves to suggest that they intend to study us further, perhaps even to the extent of dismantling us and examining our various components."

"Tell me, brother," Lore said with an unsettling grin, "do you *still* think we can make peace with the organics? When they incapacitate us, poke and prod us, and likely hatch plans to break us down into spare parts?!" He shook his head angrily. "Better to wipe them *all* out, Romulans and Klingons and the Federation and all the rest of them, and allow artificial life to develop to its fullest potential."

Data gave his brother a sad look. "Lore, it concerns me to hear you advance such opinions. The wholesale genocide of all living beings is hardly a position advocated by a fully functioning intellect."

" 'Fully functioning' . . . ?" Lore repeated in disbelief. "How can you stand there and accuse *me* of having a less than functional intellect. When *you* continue to plead the interests of organics like a whipped dog returning to its master for another beating? What do we *owe* them, Data?!"

Isaac raised his hand to interrupt. "If I may interject," he began, "could you not as easily ask what any being owes its progenitors, and what they in turn owe it? Is it not the custom in many organic societies for a child to bear some obligation to the

parents who bore it, just as the parents bear the obligation for raising their child? As early as the twentieth century human researchers into artificial intelligence were arguing that any sentient
creation of mankind would be their *offspring,* not mere machines,
what the Earth scientist Hans Moravec called 'children of the
mind.' Is it not reasonable to argue that, as humanity's children,
we owe them the debt any offspring would owe a parent?"

The two androids looked at him, their expressions making
plain their different responses to what he had said. But before
either was able to give his thoughts voice, further conversation
was forestalled when the floor beneath their feet shifted, and they
found it difficult to keep their balance as the ship's inertial dampers struggled to compensate for a sudden change in velocity. To
the faint vibrations of the confined singularity core were added
the thrum of shield generators in effect.

"The *Haakona* is under attack," Isaac said, immediately recognizing the signs.

"Oh, *brilliant,*" Lore said, rolling his eyes. "Maybe *he* should be
Sherlock to *your* Watson, brother."

Data looked from one to the other, concerned. "The question
is not whether the ship is under attack, but by *whom?*"

"What is the meaning *of this?!"* shouted Subcommander Taris on
the forward viewscreen. *"What business does a Federation starship
have in the Neutral Zone?"*

"That was to be my question to you, Subcommander," Ro
Laren said, standing in front of the viewscreen with her hands
casually clasped behind her back. "This is Commander Ro Laren
of the *U.S.S. Enterprise,* and on behalf of the Federation, I formally request an explanation for your presence in the Neutral
Zone at this juncture, and an accounting of your dealings with the
inhabitants of the planet below."

The Romulan subcommander glowered. *"Am I meant to assume
that it is a mere* coincidence *that a Starfleet vessel arrives shortly after I
have taken three Federation spies into custody?"*

Ro replied with an easy smile. "I'm sure that I don't know any-thing about Federation spies, Subcommander. The *Enterprise* is tasked with patrolling the Federation side of the Neutral Zone, and when long-range scans indicated a Romulan vessel in this system in violation of treaty, I was authorized to investigate."

Taris straightened, resting her hands on the console before her. *"This charade grows tiresome."* She turned to address a crewman out of the screen's view. *"Prepare the anti-positronic disruptor array."*

"So much for talking it out," Ro said with a sigh, and turned from the viewscreen. "Lavelle, prepare for evasive maneuvers."

At the flight controls, Sam Lavelle nodded.

"Thomas?" Ro called to the ensign at the tactical controls. "Compute firing solutions, targeting her emitters."

"Aye, sir."

"Fire," Ro said.

Phasers lanced from the hull of the *Enterprise,* spearing toward the warbird. As expected, the beams dissipated on impact with the shields, but it still produced the desired effect.

"You would fire on a Romulan ship of the line?" Subcommander Taris said in disbelief. *"This outrage is an act of* war."

"So is violating the treaty, Subcommander. I believe *your* outra-geous act precedes mine." In actual fact, the *Enterprise* had entered the Zone before the *Haakona,* for all that the subcommander didn't seem to know that; still, the unmanned wardrone *had* come to Turing before the *Enterprise* had been summoned, Ro remembered, which meant that what she was saying *was* true, if only technically.

"You have just made a grave error in judgment, Commander," Taris said through clenched teeth.

"And if you attempt to fire on the planet below, you'll have made the last mistake of your career, Subcommander, I promise you that."

The subcommander sneered, but instead of responding she motioned to one of her crew, and the viewscreen went blank.

"Sir," Ensign Thomas said, "they're engaging cloak."

"On screen," Ro called, and an instant later the image of the warbird appeared, only to begin shimmering as the cloak engaged.

"She can't fire while cloaked," Lavelle pointed out.

Ro nodded. "And she can't raise shields either."

There was a time when a warbird going cloaked was all but completely hidden, and could maneuver with impunity.

That time had passed.

"Thomas," Ro said with a smile, "inform engineering to prepare the forward emitter to begin projecting the antiproton beam. We're about to go hunting."

10

Picard resisted the urge to pace. Years of command had taught him that officers often looked to those in charge to gauge the emotional tenor of a situation, and seeing their captain marching worriedly back and forth like an overwrought hen would not likely do much to boost morale. Still, he found it difficult to remain in one place, and more difficult still to find something with which to occupy his hands. He caught himself straightening his uniform jacket for the fifth time in as many minutes, and clasped his hands behind his back for want of anything better to do with them.

Lieutenant Sito was continuing her aerial surveillance of the city, while Commander La Forge and Lieutenant Crusher continued attempting to puzzle out the fundamentals of the gateway technology. Lal was still opening and closing miniature gateways into the various chambers and rooms of the city, still searching for any sign of her father and uncle and of Picard's missing crewman, and from time to time engaged in brief exchanges with the Turing residents she located there. None had seen the missing androids, but one reported catching a glimpse of a Romulan transporter beam in the act of dematerializing four figures, and while they had not had the opportunity to see who was being transported before the dematerialization obscured all details, it was assumed that it had been Subcommander Taris and the missing three.

Getting reports from the *Enterprise* was problematic at this juncture, with the ship's constant motion making it all but impossible to open a gateway onto the vessel, but Picard thought it a better than average chance that Commander Ro was dealing with the subcommander in command of the *Haakona,* and that Isaac and the others were prisoners on board the warbird.

Lal was talking in low tones through a tiny gateway no larger than a few centimeters on a side. With the subspace network still inoperative, she had been forced to communicate vocally with the various Turing residents her search had located. From his vantage, Picard could not see what lay on the other side of the small gateway, but if he strained he could just hear the low responses to Lal's questions.

"The Romulans are approaching our position," came the voice through the gateway, scarcely above a whisper. "It is concluded that we should retreat to the security of the gateway chamber."

"Agreed," Lal said after a moment's consideration. Then she turned to the hairless android at the controls and instructed him to expand the gateway to full size.

Picard watched as the tiny gateway a few centimeters square expanded, growing taller and wider, until it was a rectangular space roughly the size and shape of a door. Lal stepped back, and in the next instant a Romulan stepped through.

"Alert!" Picard called out, drawing his phaser and taking a defensive position. His crewmen were well-trained, and Sito pulled back into one of the unused alcoves, her weapon drawn and ready, while La Forge and Crusher crouched on the far side of the control console, sighting their phasers.

"Do not fire, please," Lal said calmly, raising her hand. Picard noted that the Romulan was dressed in simple, unadorned civilian clothing, like that favored by the Turing populace. "All is not as it seems."

"Hold your fire," Picard ordered the others, but didn't lower his phaser.

The Romulan stepped to one side, out of the way of the gateway, and behind him came three more, likewise dressed simply in civilian attire: a Klingon, a Cardassian, and a Breen.

Lal ordered the gateway closed, and as it winked out, she turned to Picard. "You and your crew," she said, "are not the only ones whom we would wish to hide from the prying eyes of Subcommander Taris and her shock troopers."

Picard narrowed his eyes. "I thought your world had remained isolated, since Data led the others from the Federation. Have these four come through the gateways from their respective worlds?"

Lal glanced from the four to Picard and shook her head. "Oh, I see the source of your confusion. No, Captain, the four individuals you see before you are positronic androids, like myself, who have been cosmetically altered to pass for the natives of the represented interstellar powers. You are well familiar with androids who are all but indistinguishable from humans, such as your crewman A. Isaac. Is it so surprising to learn that androids can pass just as successfully for other humanoid species?"

Picard was far from satisfied, but it was La Forge who gave voice to his suspicions. "And why would an android *need* to pass for a Romulan, exactly? Much less a *Breen?*"

Lal exchanged glances with the four androids, and then turned back to Picard with an unreadable expression. "That is perhaps a matter best discussed at some later time."

Ro Laren managed to keep still in the captain's chair, but just barely.

"Any progress with that antiproton beam, Ensign Thomas?"

"Still searching, Commander."

She gripped the ends of the chair's armrests, anxious for action. She realized her legs were twitching, and had to concentrate to keep them from moving.

"Too much *raktajino*," said Doctor Quaice from the seat beside her. "Makes you edgy."

Ro shot him a dark look, but then her expression softened into a smile. "I think it just might be the cloaked Romulan warbird that's making me edgy, Doctor, but thanks for your concern."

He raised his hand in a shrug. "You know, I once served with a captain who shouted herself hoarse every time she went into combat. And another whose insides churned so badly with nerves every time he raised shields that I had to prescribe antacids to settle his stomach." He smiled. "If the worse you're doing is fidgeting a bit while sitting in the big chair, Laren, I think you're already ahead of the game."

Ro nodded, reluctantly. "Maybe. Or maybe that's just the sort of homey wisdom you'd share with a commanding officer who *was* letting her nerves get the best of her, to calm her down?"

Quaice shook his head. "Oh, no, I'd be *much* more effusive in my praise, if that were the case." He flashed a wicked grin. "But tell me, Laren, are you doing something different with your hair? And that earring looks *lovely.*"

Her witty rejoinder was silenced when Ensign Thomas piped up from the tactical station. "Commander, we've got a ping to starboard." He studied the displays, breathless. "The antiproton beam has painted the *Haakona.*"

"Keep tracking her, Thomas," Ro said. She leaned forward, her jaw set.

A cloaked ship couldn't employ its shields or fire its weapons, with all available power drained by the cloak. It *could* continue to broadcast its subspace interference, though, and if there'd been more than one starship nearby, Ro could have likely triangulated its position from that alone. Come to that, if she'd had time, she could have deployed a couple of shuttlecraft and done the same. But fielding shuttles with a cloaked warbird in the area was an invitation to disaster, and she had no desire to put any of the crew unnecessarily at risk, not when she had an antiproton beam up her sleeve. She'd gambled that the Romulans hadn't learned about that particular Federation tactic yet, and the fact that they'd not compensated for it seemed proof that they hadn't.

So now she knew where the warbird was. The question remained, what to do about it?

"Thomas, prepare a spread of quantum torpedoes, maximum yield, targeted on that location, and fire on my mark."

"Sir."

"Lavelle," Ro said. "Once the torpedoes are away I want you to bring us about and initiate a strafing run as soon as the warbird drops cloak. Thomas, as soon as the warbird's in range lock phasers and fire."

"Aye, sir," Lavelle and Thomas acknowledged.

"Still got the *Haakona* painted, Ensign?"

Thomas confirmed. "Aye, sir."

"Fire torpedoes."

On the forward viewscreen, the starfield rippled and distorted as the quantum torpedoes found their marks, bright bursts that limned the darkness in the shape of a *D'deridex*-class warbird.

"She's dropping cloak," Thomas reported.

"Beginning strafing run," Lavelle called over his shoulder.

There would be a split second while the cloak was disengaging before the shields could come online. If luck was with them, a few well-placed phaser hits along with the torpedoes would inflict some damage on the warbird.

Phasers lanced from the prow of the *Enterprise* as Lavelle brought them soaring over the warbird's position, the first shots splashing across the green hull of the *Haakona,* the later ones absorbed by her rippling shields.

"She's taken hits," Thomas said, eyes on the tactical controls. "She's got her shields up, but they're not at full strength."

As if in response, disruptor fire crackled from the "head" of the warbird, lancing into the stern of the *Enterprise.*

"Shields at eighty percent, Commander," Thomas said.

"Bring us about, Lieutenant," Ro ordered Lavelle. "Ensign, concentrate your fire on her forward port quarter." There were precious few weak spots in the shield geometries of a *D'deridex*-class warbird, Ro knew, but she didn't need a very large hole to get the job done.

"She's launching torpedoes," Thomas reported.

The *Enterprise* rocked as the inertial dampers tried to compensate for the impact. Even with most of the energy of the torpedoes bleeding off through the *Enterprise*'s shields, enough kinetic energy was imparted to the ship to give them a bumpy ride.

"Shields at sixty-five percent," called Thomas.

"Keep punching that spot," Ro ordered as the *Enterprise*'s phasers pounded into the forward port side of the warbird.

The *Enterprise* sped beneath the warbird, taking more disruptor fire in the pass.

"Once more, Lieutenant," Ro ordered, and Lavelle brought the ship about. "Ensign, another concentrated burst at the forward port quarter."

"Aye, sir. Shields in that area are holding, but weakening fast."

"As soon as you see them reconfigure their shield geometry to compensate, I want you to target their communications array and launch a salvo of high-yield torpedoes, at your discretion."

"Acknowledged."

Ro chanced a glance at Quaice, to find him clenching the armrests of his own chair, his expression tense. "You might want to consider cutting down on the *raktajino* yourself, Doctor," she said with a smile.

Quaice gave her a withering glance. "I've never much liked being shot at, I'll admit."

"Look at it this way," Ro said as they were rocked once more by Romulan torpedoes. "So long as they've got weapons locked on us, they can't fire at the planet below."

"Well," the doctor said, struggling to remain in his chair, "I hope the captain's grateful, is all."

Of their captors, there had been no sign. But Isaac had a reasonably good idea what was keeping them otherwise engaged.

"It is the *Enterprise,*" he said, thoughtfully. "It is the only reasonable explanation."

"I thought your captain ordered the ship to head back home," Lore said with barely disguised contempt. "I thought they'd have turned tail and run by now."

"That, brother, is because you do not know Captain Picard,"

Data countered, "nor do you know the type of men and women under his command. It has been my experience with humans that they often do what is least expected, and Starfleet officers in particular display a propensity for turning situations to their advantage."

"The question remains, though, *why* the *Enterprise* is attacking the Romulan vessel," Isaac said. "Particularly when the stated goal was to conceal the presence of Starfleet personnel from the Romulans."

"One can only assume that the need for concealment has passed," Data advanced. "One conclusion is that the captain or other members of the away team, if not all of them, have been captured by the Romulans, and the *Enterprise* is attempting a rescue. However, if the Romulans had penetrated to the security of the gateway control chamber, the *Enterprise* would have far greater concerns than the return of any captured prisoners. It is *possible* that some member of the away team was spotted by the Romulans but not captured, but again, it seems to strain credibility, considering Captain Picard's stated desire to remain undetected. The only other reasonable explanation is that the *Enterprise* is attempting *our* rescue, however misguided the attempt or the motivation."

"*'Our* rescue'?!" Lore said incredulously. "How, by blowing up the warbird and hoping they can pick us up floating in the vacuum with the rest of the debris?"

"I do not think that Captain Picard would have the destruction of the *Haakona* as his intention," Isaac objected, "or that Commander Ro would make such an attempt without his permission, whatever her own proclivities. Instead, it stands to reason that the *Enterprise* is attempting to disable the Romulans' communication capabilities, to end the subspace interference that is rendering inoperative the Turing communication network."

Data nodded, eyebrows arched and lips pursed in an expression that indicated he was impressed. "An admirable gambit, if that is indeed their strategy. With the *Haakona* no longer able to broadcast subspace interference, we would be reconnected to Lal and the others, who would then be able to triangulate our position and open a gateway here on the warbird, effecting our rescue."

"But it is a gambit which, it seems, returns us back to where we started," Isaac said, "on the surface of Turing with the Romulan shock troopers, and with the warbird overhead still in a position to open fire on the planet with the anti-positronic disruptors." He paused, considering. "Unless Captain Picard *does* intend to destroy the warbird once we are safely away, which is a possible, albeit an uncharacteristic, scenario."

Data shook his head. "If my years of serving with Captain Picard are any indication, he will investigate and exhaust every possibility before he resorts to wholesale destruction."

"Luckily, dear brother," Lore said with a faint smile, "I'm not quite so hobbled by conscience. If we *do* make it back to Turing in one piece, the first thing I'm going to do is teleport a quantum warhead right down Subcommander Taris's throat, and then I'm sending a matching set to Romulus and to the Klingon homeworld. And why stop there? Another for Cardassia Prime? One to the Breen home planet? And let's not forget Earth, of course."

Data wore a sad expression. "All that we have accomplished with our infiltration network, all that we might yet accomplish, and you would waste it all in a mad fit of genocide?"

Lore snarled, but it was Isaac who next spoke. "What 'infiltration network' would that be, Data?"

Before Data could answer, the *Haakona* was rocked side to side by a large impact.

"Well, *something* got through their shields," Lore said with bitter satisfaction.

At the edge of Isaac's awareness, a voice suddenly called, strange but familiar. It was calling to him, and to Data, and to Lore. And beyond that familiar voice were countless others, hundreds, thousands of them, all calling out to one another in concern and curiosity.

"The Turing subspace network," he said in a low voice, his eyes meeting Data's. "It . . ."

Data smiled, as he subvocally responded to Lal's hail. "It would appear," he said aloud, "that Captain Picard's stratagem has been successful."

"Direct hit on her communications array," Thomas reported with evident pride. "She's gone silent."

"Good." Ro nodded. Of course, with the warbird's communications down, there was no way to parlay with the subcommander, to see if there was any chance of them standing down. Which was just the cost of doing business; but still, Ro would have liked the alternative of suing for peace at *some* point. "Let's keep them too occupied to fire on the planet, but not do so much damage that she's destroyed."

"Shields at forty-five percent, Commander."

"And don't let *them* destroy us, Prophets protect us."

"Why, Laren," Quaice said with a smile, "I didn't know that you were religious."

"I'm not," Ro answered, her lips drawn into a line. "But I figure every bit helps. Ensign?" She turned to the young woman at the ops station. "See if you can raise the captain now that the damned interference is down."

"Aye."

Ro sat back in the chair, crossing her arms over her chest. "Maybe *he'll* have some idea how to get out of this that doesn't end with either the *Haakona* or the *Enterprise* floating as clouds of debris, if not *both*."

"Well," Quaice said, with guarded optimism, "he *is* the captain, after all."

11

"Captain Picard? I have made contact with my father."

Geordi La Forge looked up from his tricorder, glancing at the young android across the room. The four newcomers, fashioned to resemble the Federation's various rival powers of the moment—Romulan, Klingon, Cardassian, and Breen—were standing at the opposite side of the chamber, silently. Like La Forge, they had looked up at the announcement that Lal had reached her father, and seemed almost as pleased as Geordi was at the thought of Data's safe return.

It wasn't until that moment that La Forge realized that, in the years since Data disappeared, nearly a decade before, he'd all but given Data up for dead. When he had contacted the *Enterprise*— had it really been only two days before?—La Forge's first reaction was confusion, followed quickly by anger. It was as if, learning that Data *wasn't* really dead, La Forge found it almost impossible to forgive his old friend for leaving without any explanation, simply disappearing into thin air. And when Data had simply appeared without warning on the bridge of the *Enterprise,* it had only made those feelings more intense.

La Forge wasn't sure what he'd expected. An apology? A *hug?* All he'd gotten was the same cryptic, familiar, maddening *Data* that he'd come to love all those years ago. La Forge had grown up with a sister, but he'd always wanted a brother, someone to share his interests in machines and model ships and chess. And if Data had never quite shared his love of model shipbuilding, and could beat him ninety-nine times out of a hundred at chess, he was still a better friend to La Forge than anyone had ever been before, and the closest thing to a brother he'd ever had. So when he'd left without warning, Data's disappearance hadn't just been a mystery. Consciously or not, La Forge had always seen it as a *betrayal*.

Now, after being reunited, however briefly, it had looked for a time as if Data might actually be lost for good, fallen into the clutches of the Romulans. Was that why La Forge had allowed himself to become so obsessed with the gateway controls? Was it an unconscious mechanism to distract himself from the thought of losing his friend all over again?

Crusher's interest wasn't unconscious, La Forge knew. He was *obsessed*, but then Wesley always was, when faced with a riddle that science had not yet solved. But La Forge was more interested in tinkering with machines, and was that really more important to him than the attempt to rescue Data and the others? Hardly.

"I have the coordinates for the gateway," Lal said to the hairless android at the controls.

"Excuse me," La Forge said, stepping forward and laying a hand on the android's shoulder. "Do you mind if I give it a spin?"

The android regarded him without emotion and shook his head. "Be my guest, Commander," he said without affect.

La Forge cracked his knuckles like a concert pianist warming up. He might not have been able to wring a tune from a mandolin, but machines? Machines he could *play*.

Wesley Crusher kept a careful watch on the tricorder's display while La Forge cycled power to initiate the gateway to the *Haakona*. It was going to be somewhat tight, since the warbird was still in flight, still exchanging fire with the *Enterprise*. But he had worked out that the gateways were designed to compensate for relative movements anyway, or else they wouldn't be able to instantiate on planets orbiting other suns. It was all a question of calculating the appropriate vectors when initiating the process.

There was a kind of hum at the back of Crusher's head, almost like music, that he'd felt only a few times before. It was as if he was hearing the music of the spheres, as the ancient philosophers used to call it, eavesdropping on the sound of creation itself. It was a sensation he got only when he felt like he was just about to grasp something huge and complex, like when he hit on an entirely novel way to reconfigure the *Enterprise*'s warp field, or when puzzling out some piece of truly alien technology for the first time. And there was no technology more alien than that of the Iconians, Crusher was sure of that now.

It *was* somewhat surprising that a planet full of genius-level androids hadn't been able to solve the mystery of the gateways. But then Crusher had always found that he had a knack of looking at things from oblique angles and coming up with solutions that others had overlooked. His mother used to suggest that maybe Starfleet wasn't the place for him, and that his destiny lay somewhere else, somewhere that lateral thinking like his was more of an asset. For all that starship captains liked to have their engine efficiencies improved, and didn't object to their chief engineers tinkering with warp field geometries, at the end of the day what they *really* wanted was for their ships to go fast when needed, the weapons and shields to work when called for, and for gravity, lights, and heat to remain operational. Main engineering wasn't really a place that invited a lot of lateral thinking and oblique strategies.

Did that suggest that Soong-type androids, designed as they were to think in particular ways, geniuses or not, might not be as apt to look at things from odd angles as someone like him? It certainly seemed possible, though just a few days before he wouldn't have been willing to lay odds on it.

As the gateway opened in one of the alcoves along the far wall, the readings on Crusher's tricorder conformed in every respect to his projections. His theory was correct! Just one or two more things to check and he'd have the whole problem licked.

He knew Captain Picard was eager for him to report success. Just what the captain intended to *do* with the information, though, was something that Crusher couldn't begin to guess, no matter how many odd angles he used to approach the question. He knew that the captain had oblique strategies all of his own.

It really was too bad, Crusher mused, that Picard had gone into command. He would have made one *hell* of a scientist.

Picard stood beside Lal as the three androids stepped through the gateway. From the other side, he could hear the faint sounds of klaxons, and rumbles like distant thunder as the warbird's shields struggled to withstand the *Enterprise*'s continued attack. Picard tried not to think about the state of his own ship at that moment, looking instead for a speedy resolution. There were just one or two questions left to be answered.

"Close the gateway," shouted Lore, the second he was through into the control chamber, "and reopen with the terminus on the warbird's bridge." He turned to the quartet of cosmetically altered androids across the room. "Why don't you make your-selves useful for a change and get me a couple of warheads?" He looked with distaste at his tunic and pants, which were soiled and discolored from his recent travails. "And get me a clean suit while you're at it."

"Belay that," Data said in a calm voice. He turned to La Forge, who manned the controls. "Geordi, please *do* close the gateway, but it will not be necessary to open it again for the time being." He turned to the four androids across the room. "I am pleased to see that you escaped detection and harm."

"Data," Picard said, stepping forward, "would you mind ex-plaining why Turing has expended the energy and effort neces-sary to create androids who can pass for Romulans or Cardassians or Klingons?" He held up his hand, and quickly added, "And please, don't try to tell me that this is all part of some forced evo-lution or exploration of forms. You should respect my intelligence enough to know that I'm not about to swallow *that*."

Data had already opened his mouth to reply, but shut it again, thoughtfully. When he spoke again, it was with some regret. "You seem to have formed an opinion as to our reasons, Captain. What is it that you already suspect?"

Picard narrowed his eyes. "Truthfully, Data? I suspect espionage."

Data cocked his head to one side. "That is a word with some nuance of meaning, Captain."

"All right, Data." Picard was beginning to lose patience. "I mean the practice of employing *spies.*"

"And 'spy' here taken to mean one who watches in secret, obtaining information or intelligence? And not an ambush, ambuscade, or snare?"

Picard gave a ragged sigh, and impatiently replied, "No more word games, Data, I mean *espionage* and you know it!"

Data nodded, slowly. "In that case, Captain, that is precisely what it is."

Isaac looked from his commanding officer to the first of his kind and back. He had not known what to expect when the gateway back to Turing had opened, but it had most definitely not been *this.*

"Enough of this charade, brother," Lore implored angrily, "let's destroy the Romulans and be *done* with it."

"Data?" Isaac said, sounding as if he were afraid to interrupt, which surprised him, considering it was not a tone he had intended. Were his opinions of Data and Lore—even his *feelings* about them—affecting his processing on a level below his active awareness? Was this what humans called an unconscious reaction? "A short while ago on the *Haakona* you mentioned an 'infiltration network,' and spoke with high regard of all that you have accomplished with it, and spoke with some evident hope about what you might yet accomplish. Assuming that these Soongtypes"—he gestured to the four cosmetically altered androids—"are part of that network, and that it is equivalent with the espionage you mention, what is it that you *have* achieved?"

"A glorified waste of time . . ." Lore snapped, but Data silenced him with a hard glance.

"Turing was founded in part to create a safe haven for androids to experiment, explore, and reproduce"—he glanced with evident affection at Lal—"to establish a place where androids could live apart, and not frighten organics with the shock of the new. Even the most forward thinking humans are still fundamentally conservative, at some level, as witnessed by the trepidation with which the Federation approached the synaptic mapping process involved in uploading."

"If you will recall, Data," Picard cut in, "the anxiety you speak of stems from an encounter the captain of a previous *Enterprise* had with a man who had also discovered the abandoned technology of a long-lost alien race, which he used to upload himself and others into android bodies. The imprinting process was incomplete, and the resultant upload lacked the full range of the emotional complexity of the original. But, and what was worse, those uploads had concocted a plan to *infiltrate* the Federation, to insinuate themselves into key positions of power, replacing organic humans with uploads as they went, and gradually conquering from within." He set his jaw, eyes narrowed, and glanced at the cosmetically altered androids across the room. "Now, does any of that sound in the slightest familiar, Data?"

"Your concerns are understandable, Captain," Data said calmly. "But if I may be allowed to finish, I said that Turing was formed in *part* to create a safe haven. However, a larger goal was to establish a base of operations from which a much more far-reaching agenda could be pursued."

"What agenda?" Isaac asked, mindful that he should have let the captain take the lead on this questioning, but finding himself too personally invested to keep silent.

"To create a society in which artificial and organic life can coexist, side by side," Data said, as though it were the most simple thing in the world. He indicated the four androids. "These individuals are part of that effort. Traveling undetected to and from distant worlds via gateway, they serve to monitor the various organic societies, and to help steer them in directions that will benefit a future union of organic and artificial life."

"Monitor?" Lieutenant Sito, it seemed, could not remain silent, either. "Don't you mean *invade?*"

"Our motives are nothing so sinister, Lieutenant." Data smiled. "Our purpose is served by peace, and vice versa. Would it surprise you to learn that it was a Turing android operative within the Cardassian Central Command who was responsible for Bajor being finally granted full sovereignty, bringing a peaceful end to generations of conflict?"

Sito opened her mouth, then closed it again, unsure what to say.

"I can't help but notice that there are no *human*-seeming androids in this number," Picard said.

"Oh, we have operatives in the Federation, Captain. Even some in Starfleet Command."

Picard seethed. "Data, you were once a Starfleet officer! Does that mean *nothing* to you?"

"Quite the contrary, Captain, it means a great deal."

"Then what, if I may ask, was the lesson learned at Starfleet Academy or on the bridge of a starship that led you to countenance running your own intelligence empire, trying to steer the fates of worlds from behind the scenes?"

Data seemed genuinely confused by Picard's response. "Is it not one of the principal duties of a Starfleet officer to search for peaceful solutions to conflict, Captain? Or would you prefer outright war?"

"War?" Picard raised an eyebrow.

"Yes, Captain. If not for the influence of our operatives, any number of minor disputes in the last ten years would have erupted in time into full-scale war. In recent months alone we have successfully averted another Klingon civil war, and staved off armed conflict between the Cardassians and the Breen."

"Enough of this pointless jabbering!" Lore shouted, stepping between them. "He's little better than a hairless *ape,* brother. Why do you expect him to understand *anything?* I told you this little spy network of yours was a wasted effort. There is not a place in the world to come for organics, and the sooner we help them shuffle off this mortal coil the better."

"There is a Romulan warbird up there full of organics who are no more inclined to shuffle than am I, Lore," Picard said, his voice low but even.

"The solution to both problems is the same, human, and it's spelled *quantum warhead.*"

Before Picard could answer, his combadge beeped.

"Enterprise to Picard."

Picard tapped to answer.

"Picard here."

He'd last heard from Commander Ro only a few short moments ago, just after the subspace interference ended, and she'd reported that the *Enterprise* was holding its own against the warbird, but that both ships were taking a fair amount of punishment.

"Not sure how much more of this we can take, Captain. We're holding them off your backs, but before long it's going to be them or us."

"Or both, hopefully," Lore sneered.

"Understood," the captain replied, studiously ignoring Lore. "Picard out."

He turned to Data, who now stood by his daughter's side. How strange it would have seemed, all those years ago, to see his android crewman as a *father.* Now, it seemed the most natural thing in the world.

"Whatever my feelings about your espionage efforts, whatever the merits of your achievements, the fact remains that we have a serious problem on our hands, and one for which the only solution offered thus far"—he glanced pointedly at Lore—"is far from satisfactory."

"In bringing you into this situation, Captain, it was hoped that you might help us find a peaceful solution."

"Captain?" Crusher raised his hand, looking like a student trying to catch a teacher's attention. "We're done over here, and the theory holds. We can do it, sir."

A smile spread slowly across Picard's face. "Data, I just may have a solution for you, but it's one I suspect that many of your people aren't going to like very much."

12

Isaac watched Data's expression as Picard outlined his proposal, but it was Lore who was the first to respond.

"No!" Lore raged. "It's out of the question! Would you give such a powerful tool to such ignorant, bloodthirsty organic savages?!"

Lal, for her part, wore a worried expression. "It *does* seem a risky proposition."

Data, though, was still thoughtful. "Wesley, are you certain that your findings are accurate?"

Crusher didn't hesitate a moment before answering. "Absolutely." He handed Data the tricorder for his inspection. "We've managed to isolate the fundamental principles behind the gateways. And I'm confident that, using the original as a guide"—he gestured toward the control console—"we could construct another functional model without too much trouble."

The other members of the away team could not "hear" it, but over the subspace communications network of Turing, Isaac could hear the debate beginning to rage as the populace learned of the captain's suggestion.

"Brother," Lore said in disbelief, "don't tell me that you're actually *considering* this nonsense."

"It *does* present an interesting solution to our present dilemma." While Data spoke aloud for the benefit of the organics in the control chamber, he conversed at a much higher bit rate over the subspace network.

"But, Father," Lal said, "would that not be handing away our only advantage in this circumstance?"

"On Earth," Picard put in, "in the middle of the twentieth century, shortly after nuclear fission was perfected and weaponized, there was considerable concern that one nation-state or another might employ atomic bombs against their neighbors. It was a very real possibility, and a justifiable anxiety. But a solution was quickly hit upon, a kind of deterrence in which all sides shared the capability to inflict equal amounts of damage on the others. It was called 'mutually assured destruction,' and ensured that no government would authorize the use of nuclear weapons for fear that their enemies would use them in return."

"And this is your grand peaceful solution, human?" Lore sneered. "Rather than keeping the gateways for our own use and protection, you'd have us simply give them *away* to anyone who asked, Romulans, Klingons, Cardassians, all of them?!"

"It *is* a reasonable approach," Data allowed.

Lieutenant Crusher stood at Isaac's side, and nodded, his smile indicating the regard in which he held the captain's suggestion. "Lateral thinking."

"But, Father," Lal objected, "the Romulans' past history shows that they can hardly be trusted with such levels of technology. Look at the example of their unmanned wardrones and their android shock troopers, artificial sentients shackled and enslaved by the overly prohibitive dictates of their programming."

"But don't you see, Lal?" La Forge put in. "You can make it a condition of the deal. If the other powers want the Iconian gateways, you can require them to provide assurance that they will not purse positronic technology to create android slaves, but must recognize the sentience of artificial life."

"For that matter," Sito suggested, "when you offer it to the Federation you can require them to lift the restrictions on the creation of new artificial life. Then androids won't be second-class citizens anymore."

Data nodded slowly, deep in thought. "If every power has gateway technology, then none would be tempted to use it aggressively against their enemies, for fear that their enemies would return the attack in kind."

"And the openness engendered by unrestricted gateway travel," Lal added, "will ensure that the powers can monitor one another, and ensure that they develop their own strains of artificial life responsibly, with the rights of that life protected."

Isaac spoke up, a thought occurring to him. "In fact, you and the rest of the Turing population would be free to explore the Retrogressionist position, returning to the Federation if you wished, free to create offspring with the same liberty that humans enjoy to create new life."

La Forge reached over and placed a hand on Data's shoulder. "Right! Data, you all could come *home* again."

Data met La Forge's silvery eyes and smiled. "It would be nice, my friend. Living here isolated from those I care about *has* been difficult. I have often had cause to regret the way in which things were left, and the necessity for secrecy. If androids were given *full* enfranchisement, and we could return and live openly"—he glanced at Lal, and then back to La Forge—"that *would* be most gratifying."

"No," Lore said, his tone suggesting he would brook no further discussion. "It's out of the question."

But Isaac knew that, whatever Lore insisted, the debate was raging, as the populace communicated impossibly fast over the subspace network, attempting to reach consensus.

Ro Laren sat forward in the captain's chair, watching the green bulk of the warbird glide across the forward viewscreen. The *Haakona*'s hull had been scored in places by phaser fire and torpedo bursts, but while her shields were weakened, they still held.

The *Enterprise,* Ro knew, was little better off.

"Shields at fifteen percent," Ensign Thomas reported.

"We can't take much more of this," Doctor Quaice said. His artificial body was designed to adapt to a wide variety of environmental factors, but he looked as though he'd be sweating if he could.

"Come about, Lieutenant," Ro ordered Sam Lavelle. "Keep them on their toes."

Quaice was right, though. If the captain didn't come up with some solution, and soon, one or the other of the ships would take too much damage to sustain, and Ro didn't like to think about what that meant for the Federation. War with the Romulan–Klingon Alliance seemed the most likely outcome, whichever way things went. Two ships exchanging fire in the Neutral Zone was one thing, but one ship *destroying* another was quite a different matter.

"Stand down, Commander," came a voice from behind her. "I'll take the conn."

Ro jumped to her feet, and turned to see Geordi La Forge standing on the other side of the railing. Behind him a doorway shimmered in midair, with a stone-walled room visible beyond. While Ro watched, Sito Jaxa stepped through, and casually walked over to the ops station.

"I've got this," Sito said to the ensign at ops, and her hands flew over the controls.

"Decided to come into work today, have you?" Ro asked with a slight smile.

The illumination level on the bridge brightened, as the lights and alarms indicating a state of red alert ceased. Shields were still raised, but the ship was now at condition green.

"Standing by, Commander," Sito said, looking up from the controls.

La Forge had come around the railing to the captain's chair, a faint smile on his lips. "Sorry to leave you hanging up here, Ro, but you certainly got the job done."

"I just had to draw their fire off your backs, is all."

"And *thank* you for that," Sito effused, glancing up. "If we end up going to Bajor, Ro, the *raktajino*s are on *me*."

"I just might take you up on that," Ro said, grinning. Then her grin faded as she glanced anxiously at the warbird, which now hovered at the center of the viewscreen. "But what about the *Haakona*?"

La Forge's smile widened. "Don't worry about them. The captain's arranged for an offer they *won't* be able to refuse."

Crusher stood next to Lal, shuffling his feet as the hairless android prepared to open the next gateway. With La Forge and Sito safely back on the *Enterprise*, they were ready to put the next part of Picard's plan into effect.

So much hinged on Crusher's ability to explain the gateway science in a way that the Romulans could understand. Could he do it? Was it possible for him to couch the seemingly impossible physics in terms everyone else could grasp?

He realized that he was twitching, nervously, his hands tapping against his thighs. Then, to his surprise, he felt a soft, warm hand slip into his own, fingers threading through his.

He looked over to see Lal smiling up at him. "It is my understanding, Wesley, that humans often derive comfort in tense situations from touch, and in particular from the practice of holding another's hand." She glanced down at their hands, held tightly together. "I hope I have not given offense by employing such a tactic, but it occurs to me that you could likely use calming in these circumstances."

"Oh, you mean waltzing into the midst of a bunch of Romulans who'd probably sooner shoot us than listen to anything *I've* got to say?" He smiled. "You're right. And thanks."

"My friends," Picard said, calling over his shoulder as the gateway materialized, "this is our chance to set things right."

Crusher caught Data looking his way, a strange smile on his face.

On the bridge of the warbird, the subcommander and her officers reacted with a mixture of shock, anger, and fear to the sudden appearance of the shimmering gateway in their midst. Disruptors were drawn and ready before Picard even stepped through. He'd insisted on going first, though, hoping that the sudden arrival of a Starfleet officer on the bridge would at least raise enough questions to give the subcommander pause, instead of opting for shooting first and asking questions later, if ever.

His gamble was accurate, but still that didn't make him any more sanguine about staring down the barrels of a half dozen Romulan disruptors.

"Wh-what is the meaning of this?!" Subcommander Taris sputtered, almost unable to contain her surprise.

Behind Picard came Data, then Lore, Isaac, and finally Lal and Wesley Crusher. The gateway remained open, a door-shaped opening in midair connecting the warbird's bridge with the hidden chamber in the city far below.

"I hope you'll forgive the intrusion, Subcommander," Picard said with a smile. "I am Captain Jean-Luc Picard of the *Starship Enterprise*." He glanced at the others behind him. "This is my chief engineer, Crusher; Turing resident Lal; and I believe you know Data, Lore, and my chief science officer, A. Isaac."

Subcommander Taris's eyes widened, fractionally, but to her credit she maintained her composure. "I am impressed, Picard." She glanced at the officer to her side. "Centurion, find the crewman responsible for monitoring the prisoners in the cellblock, and place him in custody, to await court-martial."

"I hope you wouldn't," Picard said, gently. "Your crew could no more be expected to anticipate this gateway technology"—he gestured over his shoulder at the shimmering door—"than you yourself did just a moment ago. And no more than I myself did a short while ago when Data here appeared on the bridge of my own ship." He glanced at Data, and nodded. "But my crewman Mister Crusher has made some interesting discoveries about the gateways, and it is precisely those discoveries that Data wishes to discuss, among other matters."

Data stepped forward, standing before the subcommander.

"Tell me, Subcommander Taris, have you ever heard of the Iconians?"

Epilogue

It was late afternoon, the sun dipping toward the western horizon, as tropical birds called their high, trilling songs from the treetops. The artificial planetoid was little more than a way station, set up here at the far side of the Gamma Quadrant, thousands upon thousands of light-years from Earth. The reach of the gateways was immense, but it was not infinite, and so travel from one edge of the Milky Way to the other was possible only by the introduction of gateway hubs every few thousand light-years. Some were positioned on planets, some on moons, still others in orbital habitats, but in some cases little pocket worlds were created. This planetoid incorporated gravity generators beneath the surface, giving it a gravitational attraction several times that which its mass would normally generate, without which an atmosphere wouldn't have been possible. It hardly mattered to most of the travelers, who scarcely needed to breathe, but it was essential for the plants and animal life that had been seeded here, and allowed for spoken conversation, instead of just subspace communication.

A reproduction of the Garden of Versailles expanded to cover a sphere the size of a small moon. The planetoid was not simply a gateway hub, but was a place for rest and relaxation, a perfect setting for two old friends to catch up.

"Data!" A smile spread across Picard's face as they shook hands. "How good to see you!"

"It's good to see you, as well, Jean-Luc." Data's smile was no less wide, but widened even further when he added, "Or should I say, *Captain*?"

"How long has it been?" Picard got a far-off look in his eyes.

"I don't think we've seen each other in more than a decade, but . . ."

"No," Picard interrupted, shaking his head. He ran his fingers through his full, dark hair. "I mean, how long has it been since you called me 'Captain'?"

Data's face took on a wistful look. "It's been nearly one hundred and ten years since I had any right to do so, since I was last a member of the *Enterprise*'s crew."

"One hundred and *ten* . . . ?" Picard repeated in disbelief.

"You know what they say, Jean-Luc." He grinned, and for a moment, with the white streaks he'd added to his hair, looked something like a sinister skunk. It was ironic that in an era in which death had been conquered, Data affected the signs of aging. "Time flies when you're having fun."

Picard grinned, and clapped a hand on Data's shoulder. "And just what *are* you doing for fun these days, Data? Last I'd heard you were helping Lal and Wesley Crusher with that experiment of theirs to create a time machine . . ."

Data shook his head. "They're still at it, but I expect it will be a few more decades before their work bears fruit. But no, I've been asked to serve as Federation ambassador to the Dominion."

Picard nodded, impressed. There was a time when he might have worried that first contact with a previously unknown alien race might lead to hostilities. The experience of the last century had changed that. Now the Federation had grown to encompass old enemies like the Romulans and the Klingons, and had evolved to the point where it was perfectly adapted for incorporating new cultures peacefully, while at the same time ensuring that those cultures did not lose their individual identities.

"And what of Lore?" Picard asked, gently.

It had taken long decades, but working with researchers at the Daystrom Institute, Data had finally managed to correct the faults in his elder brother's programming, and far from being a near-insane proponent of mass murder, he was now one of the leading advocates for endangered organic species in the Federation.

"Still hard at work, as always. We visit every few weeks, regardless of where our travels take us. Family is something to be cherished, don't you think?"

Picard smiled, nodding, remembering how the extra decades granted by their extended lives in artificial bodies had helped heal the rifts with his own estranged brother.

"And you, Jean-Luc? Off to some dig or other?"

"You know me too well, old friend," Picard said with a smile. "I'm leading an archaeological expedition on a planet a few light-years from here. Bajoran artifacts *millennia* old have been unearthed, suggesting prehistoric contact between the Alpha and Gamma Quadrants."

"A subspace wormhole, perhaps?"

"That's the prevalent theory. But Data, you should *see* some of the treasures we've been pulling out of the ground."

Once, Picard could never have hoped ever to have *heard* of such a find, much less investigate it himself. At several thousand light-years away, it would have taken him the rest of his natural lifetime to reach the dig site, even at maximum warp. That was when he still *had* a natural lifetime, of course.

More than any other discovery since the invention of the warp drive, the gateway had changed the way that worlds interacted, and the way that people lived. Now, someone could walk from one world to another in the blink of an eye, and from one side of the galaxy to the other in a matter of minutes. And in artificial bodies, like the one Picard had worn since the death of his original body years before, travelers were confident that they could survive any injury, and in virtually any environment. The opportunities for archaeological exploration alone had opened up enormously when researchers suddenly didn't need to breathe oxygen any longer, or require atmospheric pressure or its equivalent to hold their insides in.

"But tell me about this Dominion, Data," Picard said, steering his friend toward a low bench, from which they could watch the setting sun. "I've heard what's been said about them on the subspace network, but haven't spoken directly with anyone who's dealt with them."

"They are . . . uncertain, I suppose you could say. For generations, the Dominion has been a highly regimented hierarchy, and they view with some trepidation the more egalitarian qualities of the Federation." He sat on the bench, and crossed one leg over the other. "I can't really blame them, of course. Theirs is a culture in which everyone knows their place and role, to which they are not only born, but also for which they have often been genetically engineered. Authority descends from the top, and there is no social mobility. Contrast that with the Federation and its countless species and civilizations, all instantaneously sharing new information, communicating through subspace networks linked by gateway relays, millions of worlds and trillions of individuals joined in a consensus linking all of their minds. The Dominion has a 'link' of their own, of sorts, but it appears to encompass only the ruling caste of shapeshifters, with all the other species of the Dominion existing in virtual slave status beneath them."

"Oh, I'm not too worried," Picard said, smiling. "The Federation has dealt with slavers and oppressors before. No matter how odious they may seem at the outset, it is simply inevitable that their behavior and attitudes will change after exposure to the Federation's ideals." He laid a hand on Data's shoulder in a comradely gesture. "And I can think of no one better suited to the task of helping them through that difficult change than you."

"Change," Data repeated, wistfully. "Tell me, Jean-Luc, do you ever think back to the Prime Directive? Think of the years Starfleet spent, its actions limited by the first contact protocols. Do you ever wonder how many of the new lives and new civilizations that we encountered in our journeys might have benefited from Federation medicine or technology, or from concepts like individual freedom and liberty?"

Their conversation was interrupted by a subspace call from the planetoid beneath them, its immense positronic brain reminding Data that he'd asked to be alerted when the Dominion signaled that they were ready to begin discussing the terms of the treaty with the Federation.

"Thank you," Data said to the planetoid. Reluctantly, he rose to his feet, and turned to face Picard. "Jean-Luc, I'm afraid that you'll have to excuse me, but duty calls."

"Duty, Data? Or fun?"

Data grinned. "Why should there be any distinction?"

As Data moved off toward the gateway beneath the pergola, Picard walked beside him, deep in thought. "You know, running into you here, I can't help but be reminded of the way things once were, and to wonder what the future might hold. We've come so far, so quickly, and it seems inevitable that the Federation will someday expand to the farthest corners of the galaxy, with no more new worlds left to discover. At the rate we're going, it might be only a few *millennia* before we reach that point."

As they stopped before the gateway, Data's smile widened. "There are other galaxies out there in the night sky, Jean-Luc, as many more as there are grains of sand on all the beaches of Earth. And, after all," he added, stepping into the gateway, "the sky *is* the limit."

Acknowledgments/Authors' Notes

THE CHIMES AT MIDNIGHT

I absolutely wish to thank:

My wife and family for their unwavering support; my colleagues at the library for giving me a place to belong; Marco Palmieri for the tremendous opportunity; Jim McCain and Alex Rosenzweig for bringing me "into the fold"; Jason Barney and the mysterious Rigel Ailur for their inspiration; Keith DeCandido, Terri Osborne, and Bob Greenberger for their professional assistance; the maintainers of Memories Alpha and Beta, along with Ian McLean's Rogue Gallery, for providing invaluable online resources; Heather Jarman for her rich Andorian worldbuilding; and Gene Roddenberry, Harve Bennett, and Nicholas Meyer, for creating this sandbox for me to play in.

A GUTTED WORLD

Thanks to:

Marco Palmieri, the editor who dragged me into this. Lucienne Diver, the agent who kept me honest. GraceAnne Andreassi DeCandido, the mom who read it all over and made sure it didn't suck. The many writers of the TV shows *Star Trek: The Next Generation, Star Trek: Deep Space Nine,* and *Star Trek: Voyager* and the movie *Star Trek: First Contact,* on whose work I riffed. The novels *Vulcan's Heart* by Josepha Sherman and Susan Shwartz, *Reunion* by Michael Jan Friedman, and *A Time to Kill* by David Mack; the eBooks *A Sea of Troubles* by J. Steven York and Christina F. York and *The Oppressor's Wrong* by Phaedra M. Weldon; the series *New Frontier* by Peter David and *Corps of Engineers* by various folks; and my own *Articles of the Federation, Q & A, The Art of the Impossible, The Brave and the Bold* Book 2, *Perchance to Dream, War Stories* Book 1, *Demons of Air and Darkness,* and the *I.K.S. Gorkon* novels, all of which provided characters and/or situations used herein. *Star Charts* by Geoffrey Mandel and the websites Memory Alpha (www.memory-alpha.org) and Memory Beta (startrek.wikia.com), valuable reference sources all. And the folks who live with me, human and feline both, who remind me every day that I am blessed with love and affection.

And finally thanks to the actors who provided faces and voices for me to work with: Marc Alaimo (Dukat), Rene Auberjonois (Odo), Casey Biggs (Damar), Avery Brooks (Sisko), Lanei Chapman (Rager), Josh Clark (Carey), Alicia Coppola (Stadi), Elizabeth Dennehy (Shelby), James Doohan (Scott), Michael Dorn (Worf), John Durbin (Lemec), Terry Farrell (Dax), John Fleck (Koval), Michelle Forbes (Ro), Jonathan Frakes (Riker), Spencer Garrett (Tarses), Susan Gibney (Benteen), Max Grodénchik (Rom), John Hancock (Haden), J. G. Hertzler (Martok), Michael Horton (Daniels), Scott Jaeck (Cavit), Barry Jenner (Ross), James Lashly (Primmin), Joanne Linville (Charvanek), Robert Mandan (Pa'Dar), Kenneth Marshall (Eddington), Gates McFadden (Crusher), Colm Meaney (O'Brien), Kate Mulgrew (Janeway), Stephanie Niznik (Perim), Robert O'Reilly (Gowron), Leland Orser (Lovok), Ernest Perry Jr. (Whatley), Richard Poe (Evek), Lawrence Pressman (Krajensky), Andrew J. Robinson (Garak), Tim Russ (Tuvok), Armin Shimerman (Quark), Marina Sirtis (Troi), Herschel Sparber (Jaresh-Inyo), Brent Spiner (Data), Patrick Stewart (Picard), Joel Swetow (Jasad), Linda Thorson (Ocett), Tony Todd (Kurn), Nana Visitor (Kira), Garrett Wang (Kim), and Clarence Williams III (Ometi'klan).

BRAVE NEW WORLD

In the author's note to my previous novel for Pocket Books, *X-Men: The Return,* I mentioned that I had been researching the project for the last twenty-five years. In the interest of full disclosure, I should say that I have been researching for *this* story even longer.

I don't remember a time before *Star Trek.* I was born a little over a year after "The Turnabout Intruder" aired, and I started watching the reruns early enough that *Trek* has been for me an almost constant presence in my life for as long as I can recall. I watched all the reruns, the animated series, read all the Gold Key comics, played with the Mego action figures. When Pocket Books started the line of *Star Trek* novels in the early eighties, I was there in the front row. I'd read the Alan Dean Foster novelizations, and a few of the Bantam originals, but it wasn't until I read those early Pocket novels that I realized not only what *Star Trek* could be, but what science fiction itself was capable of being. Books like Diane Duane's *The Wounded Sky,* A. C. Crispin's *Yesterday's Son,* and John M. Ford's *The Final Reflection* brought a level of sophistication to both the storytelling and to the speculative aspects that I hadn't experienced in any novels before, *Star Trek* or otherwise, and which the televised *Trek* had only rarely approached. Those books were, in a very real sense, my introduction to *real* science fiction, and probably played a bigger role in my becoming the writer I am today than I even realize.

In the years that followed, as *Trek* returned to television, in so many ways finally realizing the promise of those Pocket novels in the best episodes of *The Next Generation, Deep Space Nine,* and *Enterprise,* I read more widely, both within the genre and without (along the way finding time to join several *Star Trek* fan clubs, to say nothing of being a card-carrying member of the Klingon Language Institute). Whenever possible, though, I checked back in with the Pocket *Star Trek* line, to see what was new, and to see if the high level of quality I'd found in those early years was still to be found. In the exemplary novels of writers like Peter David, Judith and Garfield Reeves-Stevens, Greg Cox, and Christopher L. Bennett, I've been happily far from disappointed.

As I've said, *Trek* has been a constant presence in my life for as long as I can recall, but for some two and a half decades the same has been true of the Pocket line of *Star Trek* novels. To have the opportunity to contribute to that line, in some small way, has been a longtime ambition of mine, and many thanks are due to Marco Palmieri for allowing me to fulfill that dream, and to Jennifer Heddle for introducing us in the first place. Thanks are also due to Memory Alpha, for proving an invaluable resource, and to Michael and Denise Okuda and Rick Sternbach, whose *Trek* reference books have been on my shelves for years, and which I've finally and at long last put to good use. And more than anyone, thanks are due to Gene Roddenberry and all those who came after him, too many writers and producers to name, for providing a world in which I've lived in my thoughts for so many years.

About the Authors

Twenty years ago, **GEOFF TROWBRIDGE** wrote an arrangement of Alexander Courage's *Star Trek* theme for his high school orchestra, and conducted the piece at his senior concert. This represented a victorious confluence of his three greatest pleasures: music, science fiction, and just generally behaving obnoxiously in front of large crowds of people.

As time passed, Geoff found additional creative outlets, such as playing in a big-hair rock band and performing with the local civic theater, but in time he settled into a more respectable career path in computer networking. Through the miracle of self-publishing on the Internet, Geoff found a new outlet via the written word, and spent long hours probing into the more philosophical areas of religion, theology, and politics—partly because of the potential for self-actualization, but mostly because it was fun to watch the heads of the closed-minded routinely explode.

Throughout it all, he never lost his love for *Star Trek* (though *Voyager* would often strain the relationship), and eventually his online connections led him to join the "Timeliners," who researched and compiled the novel chronology for Jeff Ayres's *Voyages of Imagination*. Geoff followed that up with his short story "Suicide Note" in *The Sky's the Limit*. *The Chimes at Midnight* is his first published novel.

When he isn't writing, he is usually either working his day job at the public library, researching the family genealogy, running chaotically around Elkhart, Indiana, with his wife and three children, or angrily throwing objects at the television during a Notre

Dame football game. His latest exploits are irregularly chronicled at http://troll-bridge.livejournal.com.

A Gutted World is **KEITH R.A. DECANDIDO**'s fifteenth *Star Trek* novel, in addition to seven short stories, eleven eBooks, one novella, and ten comic books. His recent and upcoming work includes the *Klingon Empire* novel *A Burning House;* the eBook *Enterprises of Great Pitch and Moment,* the concluding chapter in the six-part *Star Trek: The Next Generation* anniversary miniseries *Slings and Arrows;* the short story "Family Matters" in the *Mirror Universe* anthology *Shards and Shadows;* the *Alien Spotlight* comic book *Klingons: Four Thousand Throats . . . ;* the *TNG* comic book miniseries *Redshirts;* and a novella in the 2009 anthology *Seven Deadly Sins.* Keith has written in dozens of other universes as well, ranging from television (*Buffy the Vampire Slayer, CSI: NY, Supernatural*) to movies (*Serenity, Resident Evil*) to videogames (*World of Warcraft, Command and Conquer, Starcraft*) to comic books (*Spider-Man,* the *X-Men*) to his own fantasy universe (the novel *Dragon Precinct* and several short stories). Find out less about Keith at his website, www.DeCandido.net, or read his inane ramblings at kradical.livejournal.com.

CHRIS ROBERSON's novels include *Here, There & Everywhere, The Voyage of Night Shining White, Paragaea: A Planetary Romance, X-Men: The Return, Set the Seas on Fire, The Dragon's Nine Sons,* and the forthcoming *End of the Century, Iron Jaw and Hummingbird,* and *Three Unbroken.* His short stories have appeared in such magazines as *Asimov's, Interzone, Postscripts,* and *Subterranean,* and in anthologies such as *Live Without a Net, FutureShocks,* and *Forbidden Planets.* Along with his business partner and spouse Allison Baker, he is the publisher of MonkeyBrain Books, an independent publishing house specializing in genre fiction and nonfiction genre studies, and he is the editor of the anthology *Adventure Vol. 1.* He has been a finalist for the World Fantasy Award three times— once each for writing, publishing, and editing—twice a finalist for the John W. Campbell Award for Best New Writer, and twice for the Sidewise Award for Best Alternate History Short Form (winning in 2004 with his story "O One"). Chris and Allison live in Austin, Texas, with their daughter, Georgia. Visit him online at www.chrisroberson.net.